STORM OF PASSION

"Sweetheart . . ."

Elyse didn't even hear his endearment. All she was aware of as she looked up into his face was his gentle expression, his soft, understanding eyes, his low, comforting voice. It had been so long since a man had looked at her that way. So long since she hadn't been lonely . . .

The room brightened with a blaze of white as another streak of lightning lit the sky. Elyse jumped, her nails digging reflexively into Nathan's shoulders. He opened his eyes and gazed down at the woman lying in his arms, but before his passion-dazed mind could think of suitable words of comfort, the fear faded from her eyes, replaced by an expression of need as heated as his own. At that moment, Nathan realized he could have her. His lips hovered over hers, as his conscience battled with his desire.

It was Elyse who made his decision for him. Looping her arms around his neck, she pulled him toward her, gazing up at him with a mixture of fear and pleasure. "Please," she murmured. "Please don't go . . ."

* * *

Praise for *PASSION'S BARGAIN*

"4 ½ stars. Wonderful . . . . You'll hate coming to the end of this book."

—*Romantic Times*

"A hero to make your heart melt."

—*Affaire de Coeur*

"Sexy, passionate, and heartwarming . . . great entertainment."

—*Rendezvous*

PASSION'S GIFT
JANE KIDDER

ZEBRA BOOKS
KENSINGTON PUBLISHING CORP.

ZEBRA BOOKS are published by

Kensington Publishing Corp.
850 Third Avenue
New York, NY 10022

Second Printing: March, 1995

Printed in the United States of America

To Pat Warren
who always gives me
the greatest gift
a friend can bestow:
outright, prolonged laughter

Chapter 1

"Elyse, come quick! *Elyse!*"

Elyse Graham threw down the mixing spoon she held and rushed over to the front window of her small ranch house. Her younger brother, Tom, was just leaping off his winded horse, and Elyse knew immediately from his panicked expression that something was very wrong. "What is it, Tom?" she called, running out onto the porch. "What's wrong?"

"There's a man riding in, and I don't want him to find me here."

Elyse shook her head in confusion. "What man?"

"That one," Tom panted, pointing toward the pecan grove which fringed the perimeter of their small Texas homestead. "He's just coming through the trees over there. See? On the buckskin?"

Elyse caught sight of a horse's cream-colored coat moving through the trees, then turned back to her brother, eyeing him apprehensively. "Who is he, Tom?"

"I don't know."

"Then why don't you want to see him?"

Tom remained silent.

"You're in trouble again, aren't you?" Elyse's tremulous words were more a statement than a question.

Tom nodded, his face contorting with fear.

"Yes."

"Oh, Lord, is it serious?"

Again, Tom's eyes darted toward the grove of trees. "Yes, it's serious, but I don't have time to explain now. Just get rid of the guy as fast as you can. I think he's the law, and if he finds me, I'm as good as dead. I'm gonna hide in the barn. Come get me when he's gone."

Elyse's eyes widened with horror, but before she could question Tom further, he jumped off the porch and ran over to his horse, grabbing the reins and sprinting off across the yard.

Elyse's watched her brother disappear through the barn's wide door, then hurried back into the house and nervously began stirring the pot of stew she was making. What trouble could Tom be in this time? Lord knew, there had been scrapes with the law in the past—petty thefts from the general store and minor vandalism of other people's property, such as the time he and his friends had painted a naked man on the side of old Widow Green's house—but never had his boyish excesses been really serious. This time, obviously, whatever he had done was. And that scared Elyse to death.

"Oh, Joe," she moaned, turning to gaze at a framed picture of a young man sitting on a small table. "If only you were here. Things might be so different for Tom if he still had you to talk to."

As always, tears welled in Elyse's eyes as she thought of her dead husband, but her mournful reverie was soon interrupted by the sound of someone knocking on the front door. She slipped over to the front window and pulled aside the muslin curtain. Sure enough, the buckskin horse was outside, its reins thrown casually over the hitching rail, and the man whom Tom had seemed so afraid of was standing at her front door.

Anxiously patting a stray blond curl into place, Elyse took a deep, calming breath and opened the door.

"Good afternoon, ma'am. Is your husband at home?"

For a moment, Elyse just stared. She knew the man

had asked her a question and that she should give him an answer, but several seconds passed before she finally found her voice. "N-no," she stammered, mentally telling herself to quit gaping at the blond Adonis standing before her, "he's . . . not."

Noticing how her eyes were flicking over him, the man cleared his throat uncomfortably. "Do you expect him back soon?"

"No," she said again, shaking her head.

As the stranger continued to look at her expectantly, she added, "My husband is no longer alive, sir."

A flush of embarrassment crept across the chiseled planes of his cheeks. "I see," he stammered. "I'm sorry. I didn't . . ." His voice trailed off.

"Is there something I can do for you?"

A look of relief crossed the man's face. "Maybe," he smiled. "My name is Nathan Wellesley and I'm passing through on my way to Austin. I was planning to spend the night in Bixby, but I saw the storm building up to the north and figured I'm not going to make it. I wondered if I might bed down in your barn."

"No!"

A look of offended surprise crossed Nathan Wellesley's blue eyes. "I can't sleep in your barn?"

"I'm sorry, but it's impossible."

"All right," Nathan said slowly. "Then could you tell me if there's another farm anywhere around these parts where I *might* stay?"

Elyse bit her lip, warring with herself. In a state as large as Texas, it was a long-held tradition to offer hospitality to travelers crossing the vast, empty distances between towns, but she couldn't very well allow this stranger to sleep in her barn when Tom was out there hiding from him. "I'm sorry, but you can't stay here."

Nathan nodded, his expression becoming impatient. "You just said that. What I'm asking is if there's somewhere else I could stay. That storm is gonna break in about ten minutes and I need to find some shelter."

As if to verify his last words, an ominous rumble of thunder growled in the distance.

Elyse winced at the sound. "There isn't any other farm between here and town."

"Look, ma'am . . ."

"The name is Graham, sir. Mrs. Elyse Graham."

Nathan nodded. "Look, Mrs. Graham, I can understand you not wanting a stranger on your place, but I can assure you, you have nothing to fear from me." He reached inside his shirt pocket and lifted out a flat leather case, flipping it open and holding it up for her inspection. "I'm *Captain* Nathan Wellesley of the Texas Rangers."

Elyse's heart leaped into her throat. This situation was getting worse by the second. Undoubtedly, the last person Tom wanted to see was one of the famed troupe of Texas lawmen. Vaguely, she heard Nathan continuing to talk to her.

"So, you see, there's nothing to be afraid of. I'm not going to hurt you, I just need a place to bed down till the storm passes. I promise I'll be gone before sunup."

Elyse knew she was trapped. If she continued to refuse the man, he might get suspicious and start snooping around, guessing that she was hiding something. "You can't stay in the barn," she repeated. "It . . . leaks when it rains and you'll get soaked."

"Maybe the lean-to, then?"

"No, that won't work, either. Your horse will have to go in there and it's not big enough for both of you. I guess you'll have to stay in the house."

Nathan's eyes widened with astonishment. "In the house, ma'am? Are you sure?"

Elyse swallowed hard. "You said I have nothing to fear, didn't you?"

Nathan's features relaxed into the most dazzling smile she'd ever seen. "You don't. I promise you."

With a curt nod, Elyse took a step back and pulled the door open.

Chapter 2

"Would you like another bowl of stew, Mr. Wellesley?"

Nathan looked up at the woman nervously hovering behind his shoulder. "Don't mind if I do, Mrs. Graham," he smiled, handing her his empty bowl. "You're a wonderful cook."

Elyse forced a polite smile as she gingerly plucked the bowl from his hand. "Thank you."

Nathan looked at her curiously as she dashed back to the stove and began ladling up another portion of the fragrant stew. Why was she so nervous? She hadn't sat down once during the entire meal but had flitted around, refilling his water glass and hovering over him like a mother hen with a flock of hungry chicks. Was having a strange man at her table that disconcerting to her? Was he perhaps the first man who had joined her for dinner since her husband's death?

His musings came to an abrupt halt as he heard a startled cry of pain from behind him. Swiveling around, he looked over at Elyse, his eyes widening with alarm when he noticed hot stew running over her fingers.

"My God, Mrs. Graham!" he cried, leaping out of his chair. "Are you hurt?"

"No," she said quickly, dropping the bowl and ladle on the counter. "I'm just a little clumsy."

Without even thinking about what he was doing, Nathan grabbed her arm and pulled her over to the sink, energetically pumping water over her injured hand. "Here. This should make it feel better."

"I'm all right, really," Elyse assured him, pulling her wet hand out of his grip and clenching her scalded fingers. "I'm sorry. I . . . spilled your stew."

"There's no need to apologize. Sit down and let me take a look at that burn."

Vehemently she shook her head. "No, I'm fine. I think I have a little cherry pie in the pantry. Would you like a piece?"

For a long moment, Nathan stared at her, wondering again what was causing her strange behavior. "Would you like me to leave, Mrs. Graham?"

Yes, yes, yes!

"Of course not," she said brightly.

Get a hold of yourself or he's going to know something's wrong!

"What would make you say that?"

"You just seem so . . . uncomfortable."

"Uncomfortable?"

"Well, nervous, sort of."

"Oh," she tittered, her mind racing to come up with a plausible excuse for the discomfiture she couldn't hide. "It's just the weather. I . . . I don't like thunderstorms." Just then, an angry peal of thunder split the air, rattling the windowpanes in the small cabin and causing Elyse to visibly jump.

"Hasn't anyone ever told you that thunder won't hurt you?" Nathan asked kindly.

"Of course they have, but it doesn't help."

He took a step toward her, holding his hand out in an unconscious gesture of comfort. Just as quickly, Elyse took a step backward, her eyes widening with apprehension.

Nathan immediately dropped his hand. What was wrong with this woman? She acted as if she thought he was going to eat her.

"Why don't you make yourself comfortable while I go

make up the bed in the spare room?" Elyse suggested, trying desperately to pull her eyes away from his. She was beside herself with nerves anyway, and it didn't help that Nathan Wellesley was the most handsome man she'd ever seen. He was tall and muscular, with a chest that pressed against the front of his shirt and narrow hips that were nearly indecently defined by his tight-fitting denims. And those eyes! Bluer than even her own, with lashes thicker than any man should have. His nose was straight and his mouth was full, but with a firm set to the sculpted lips. His hair was blond, almost white in places, and much longer than was fashionable. But somehow the length suited him, giving him the careless, enticing look of a man who was not overly impressed by his spectacular physical gifts.

"Don't go to any trouble. I can just roll up in my bed-roll here on the floor."

"It's no trouble," she assured him, thankful for an excuse to leave his disconcerting presence. "It will just take me a minute."

Before Nathan could protest further, she whirled around and disappeared through one of two doors at the back of the cabin. He stared thoughtfully after her for a moment, then walked across the room and looked out the front window. His vision was blurred by the rain pelting against the glass, but, even so, as he stared off in the direction of the barn, he thought he saw a light. Squinting, he looked closer, wondering if lightning had struck and started a fire.

Hurrying over to the door through which Elyse had disappeared, he rapped sharply. "Mrs. Graham? I'm going out to check on your barn. It looks like there's a light in there and I want to make sure you haven't been struck by lightning."

On the other side of the door, Elyse's hand clutched at her throat in terror. Had Tom been foolish enough to light a lantern and, if he had, how was she ever going to explain it to the sharp-eyed Ranger?

She jerked open the door, praying her face wouldn't betray her apprehension. "There's no need, Captain Wellesley," she said breathlessly. "I . . . always leave a lantern burning in the barn during storms. I think it helps calm the animals."

Nathan shook his head. "That's not a wise thing to do. An untended lantern is a fire just waiting to happen. I'll go put it out. Your animals will be fine."

"No!" Elyse gasped. At Nathan's bewildered expression, she hurriedly added, "I do it all the time. I have the lantern in a very safe place. Really, there's no need to go out in that weather."

"Mrs. Graham . . ."

Desperately, Elyse cast around for another tack to keep the stubborn Ranger away from the barn. Forcing her lips to relax into what she hoped was a beckoning smile, she entreated, "Please, Captain, don't leave me. I'm so nervous being alone during storms. Perhaps we could go sit down on the sofa and . . . talk a bit. I've never known a Texas Ranger before, and I'd love to hear how you came to join the force. I'm sure you must have had a fascinating life."

Nathan's eyebrows shot up in astonishment at this un-expected invitation. What *was* going on here? One min-ute the woman acted like she was scared to be in the same room with him and the next, she was inviting him to sit on the sofa and share confidences with her.

"I'd be happy to tell you about the Rangers, ma'am, but for my own piece of mind, I really want to check the barn first . . ."

"Oh, pooh," she giggled, hooking her arm through his and leading him over to the sofa. "I keep telling you, it's just the lantern and there's no reason for you to get drenched going out to check it."

As they strolled toward the couch, the smell of Elyse's honey-blond hair filled Nathan's senses, causing him to inhale deeply of the sweet, fresh fragrance. Gazing down at her, he thought again, as he had at the front door, what a beautiful woman she was. Small, with delicate features, she reminded him of a Dresden doll his baby sister, Paula, had once had. Her sea-blue eyes dominated her piquant face, but her tilted nose and slightly stubborn chin bespoke a character stronger than she had thus far displayed to him.

Intrigued, Nathan allowed himself to be pulled down on the sofa, then turned toward her expectantly. "What would you like to know about the Rangers?"

Elyse turned a gorgeous smile on him, so pleased that she had finally managed to divert him from his curiosity about the light in the barn that she didn't even think about how he might be interpreting her overt flirtation. "Oh, I don't necessarily want to know about the Rangers, Captain. I'm more interested in *you*, personally."

Nathan returned her smile, flattered, despite himself, at her sudden turn of mood. "Okay, what would you like to know about *me?*"

Before she could answer, a blinding streak of lightning slashed through the window, causing Elyse to duck her head and hunch her shoulders protectively.

"You really *are* scared of storms, aren't you?" Nathan asked, his heart going out to the clearly frightened girl. Without thinking, he reached over and picked up her hand. With a small gasp, she immediately pulled it away, shaking it as if to relieve the pain the pressure of his fingers had caused.

"And that burn *is* hurting you, isn't it?" he demanded, his voice almost accusatory. Without waiting for a response, he rose and walked over to the kitchen table, picking up the butter dish. Returning to the sofa, he swept his finger across the creamy substance and gently started rubbing the balm over her fingers.

Her hands were soft and white, despite the hard work he knew frontier wives were forced to do every day. Obviously, she was a woman who, in spite of her widowed state, still took time to tend to herself. Vaguely, he wondered if she might have a beau in town. With her beautiful face and curvy little figure, he imagined that there must be any number of men who would be more than pleased to take the place of her deceased husband.

"Does that feel better?" he asked, his fingers continuing their soft stroking of her injured skin.

"Yes," she whispered. She knew she should pull away from his enticing touch, but somehow she couldn't find the will to do so. A sudden feeling of lethargy stole over her, and she felt powerless to fight it. It had been so long since a man had touched her, nearly three years since Joe had died, and although she knew it was completely inappropriate to allow a stranger to sit so close and stroke her hand, the raging storm outside, coupled with the anxiety she was feeling about Tom, made the whole situation seem unreal—almost like a dream. And everything was acceptable in a dream . . .

For his part, Nathan was feeling anything but relaxed. Rather, his every sense was heightened by the languid expression he saw gloss Elyse's eyes. A small sigh escaped her as she laid her head back on the sofa and, unbidden, he experienced a familiar and unmistakable tightening in his loins. Unconsciously, he shifted closer.

A sizzle of lightning followed by a deafening crash of thunder suddenly pierced Elyse's trancelike state, and with a startled, jerky motion, she bolted upright. "Oh, I hate this! I wish it would be over."

Nathan rose and walked over to the window, pulling aside the curtain. "It will be soon," he assured her. "It's just that the storm is on top of us now." Glancing toward the barn, he frowned. "I still don't like that lamp being on, though. I know you think it's safe, but . . ." The rest of his sentence was drowned out by another tremendous thunderclap.

Elyse gasped, and with a whimper of true terror, covered her face with her hands, visibly shaking.

Nathan immediately forgot his concerns about the lamp and hurried over to the sofa, sitting down next to the quaking woman and gathering her into his arms.

"Shh," he crooned. "Don't cry. It's all right. You're safe."

Elyse was astonished by how safe she did feel, encompassed in this big, handsome man's embrace. He was so solid, so secure, and he smelled like grass and horses and good leather. Unwittingly, she circled the huge expanse of his back with her arms and snuggled closer. "I'm so afraid of storms," she whispered.

"But why? They won't hurt you. They usually sound more dangerous than they are."

"That's not true! My husband was killed by a storm just like this one. Struck by lightning when he was bringing the horses in from the pasture. He died instantly . . ."

Nathan was stunned by her tragic revelation. No wonder she was acting so strangely. And here he was, cavalierly assuring her that she had nothing to fear.

"He was just standing under a tree," she continued, "waiting for the rain to let up a little, and . . ."

Nathan lifted her chin with his index finger, his heart wrenching when he saw the naked pain in her tear-filled blue eyes. "Shh, sweetheart," he whispered, brushing a tear from her cheek with his thumb. "Don't talk about it anymore."

Elyse didn't even hear his endearment. All she was aware of as she looked up into his face was his gentle expression, his soft, understanding eyes, his low, comforting voice. It had been so long since a man had looked at her that way. So long since she hadn't been lonely . . .

Nathan didn't realize he was going to kiss her until his lips touched hers. For a split second he almost drew away, but then he felt Elyse's mouth soften beneath his, responding to his gesture. Her lips parted and he pulled her closer, slanting his lips across hers as his warm, silky tongue accepted her intimate invitation.

The kiss deepened and he threaded his hand in the golden silk of her hair, scattering hairpins as he released the honeyed mass from the confines of her prim bun. As the thick coil cascaded down her back, Nathan drew away, burying his nose in its fragrant softness.

A bereft little sigh escaped Elyse at the loss of his lips on hers and, languidly, she turned her head toward him, enticing him to kiss her again.

Nathan shivered with desire, and this time when he claimed her lips, there was more passion than pity in his caress. His mouth covered hers, gently demanding as he coaxed her to again open to him. Elyse's response was immediate, and Nathan's breathing became harsh and rasping as wave after wave of desire crashed over him.

Shifting his hips, he pulled Elyse across his lap, cradling her pliant body as his hand lightly explored the gentle swell of her breast. To his surprise, she didn't resist but instead rubbed her uninjured hand over the heavy muscles of his shoulder, kneading away the fatigue and strain of a day spent in the saddle.

The room brightened with a blaze of white as another streak of lightning lit the sky. Elyse jumped, her nails digging reflexively into Nathan's shoulders. He opened his eyes and gazed down at the woman lying in his arms, but before his passion-dazed mind could think of suitable words of comfort, the fear faded from her eyes, replaced by an expression of need as heated as his own. At that moment, Nathan realized he could have her. He hesitated, his lips hovering over hers, as his conscience battled with his desire.

It was Elyse who made his decision for him. Looping her arms around his neck, she pulled him toward her, gazing up at him with a mixture of fear and pleasure. "Please," she murmured. "Please don't go . . ."

It was all the encouragement Nathan needed. With a soft moan, he surrendered to his desires, pulling her closer and covering her mouth with a scorching kiss as his fingers deftly released the buttons running down the front of her dress. He spread the fabric open and curved a hand around her full breast, his calloused thumb brushing sensuously across her erect nipple. "You smell so good," he murmured, his lips tracing an erotic trail across her cheek toward her ear. "So good."

At that moment, the single kerosene lamp sitting on the table guttered and went out, plunging the room into complete darkness. Elyse let out a little cry of trepidation but soon forgot her anxiety as, again, Nathan shifted beneath her, pulling her skirt up until it bunched around her waist and pressing his straining erection against her rounded bottom. Closing his eyes, he buried his face in the softness of her lush breasts, a throaty groan escaping him as he drew a dusky nipple into his mouth.

He heard Elyse's gasp of pleasure, then felt her fingers sweep lightly over the bare skin of his chest. The realization that, at some point, she must have unbuttoned his shirt flitted through his mind but quickly fled as the shimmering softness of her hair whispered against his chest and he felt the exquisite pleasure of her tongue swirling around his sensitive nipples. The combination of her provocative love play and the startling realization that she was as eager for him as he was for her intensified his excitement till he felt he might burst into flames.

Sliding down onto his back, he pulled her over on top of him until the entire length of their bodies touched. Clothes were pushed down and aside. Soft flesh pressed against hard. Hands touched. Mouths blended.

The storm without paled in comparison to the one within as the lovers eagerly explored the most intimate secrets of each other's bodies. The room was black now and silent, the only sound their ragged breathing and moans of quickly mounting passion.

Nathan felt Elyse intimately cup his buttocks, then slide her hand across his hip, subtly insinuating it between their bodies and wrapping her cool fingers around his pulsing erection. Gritting his teeth against the nearly unbearable pleasure, he rolled, taking her with him and bracing himself above her on trembling arms.

Lowering his head, he kissed her, a searing, breath-stealing melding of mouths and tongues that muffled her gasp of shocked pleasure as he slid into her warm, moist depths.

He paused a moment, allowing her a final chance to naysay him, then shivered with glad relief when, instead, he felt her relax and wind her long, satiny legs around his hips.

With movements as old as time, Nathan began love's ritual, his fervor quickly increasing as Elyse matched his ebb and flow as naturally as if they had been lovers for years. He felt her shift beneath him, taking him more fully within her, then heard her sigh of satisfaction as he filled her completely.

This final, provocative welcome sent Nathan over the crest of passion's summit, and, with a last, deep thrust, he exploded, his release made all the sweeter by Elyse's answering cry of fulfillment.

Their simultaneous climax left them both shaken and panting. Several moments passed as their breathing slowed, and the soft darkness of the rainswept night enshrouded them in its quiet, inky cocoon. Finally, Nathan eased down onto his side, gathering Elyse close and burying his face in her hair.

With a gentle, murmured endearment, he kissed the tender skin near her temple and fell into an exhausted sleep, blissfully unaware of the tears that gradually pooled in her eyes and fell, unheeded, onto his cheek.

Chapter 3

Elyse lay in bed, staring dismally out the window at the gray, watery sky. It was past eight o'clock, two hours after her normal time of rising, but this morning was anything but normal and she simply couldn't find the will to get up.

Through the thin bedroom wall, she could hear Nathan Wellesley moving around in the front room, his heavy boots clumping noisily on the wooden floor.

Why doesn't he leave? He said he'd be gone before daybreak, so why is he still here? The answer to her question was obvious, but she refused to acknowledge that he was waiting to see her. Surely he must realize that he was the last person in the world she wanted to see.

How could she have done what she did last night? *How?* Never, in all the time since Joe had died, had she so much as allowed another man to kiss her, so how could she have let this stranger have his way with her without even putting up a fight?

All night she had lain awake torturing herself with that question and, over and over, a little voice deep in her tired, overwrought mind had whispered, *"Because you wanted it, too."*

"No I didn't," she moaned aloud, grinding the heels of her hands into her tired eyes. "I didn't want it." No self-respecting woman wanted something like that to happen. That a complete stranger had looked at her . . .

had touched her so intimately . . . had made her experience an ecstasy she'd never before even known existed. No *good* woman wanted that . . .

But, in her heart of hearts, Elyse knew she had, and that was the worst of it. She had enjoyed the man's bold attentions. No, *more* than enjoyed them. She'd actually *encouraged* his lust, had reveled in it like some strumpet off the streets. She'd behaved in a manner no decent woman ever would.

"It was just a moment of madness," she told herself for the thousandth time, trying desperately to assuage the guilt and remorse she was feeling. "It was the storm. It was knowing that Tom was hiding in the barn. It was that weird darkness after the lamp went out."

Drowning in misery, she squeezed her eyes shut and tossed her head back and forth on her pillow. "It was madness. Just a moment of madness. It could have happened to anyone . . ."

But it hadn't happened to *anyone*. It had happened to *her*. And now, this morning, she had to get up and face living the rest of her life with the knowledge that she could lie in a stranger's arms and scream with pleasure at his touch.

With a moan of self-loathing, Elyse turned over in the bed she had once shared with Joe, pulling the pillow over her head and wishing she could crawl into the grave with him.

Joe. Her beloved husband, lost to her these past three years. What would he think of her if he knew what she'd done? He'd be so shocked . . . so disappointed.

Although Elyse's memories of him were beginning to dim, she could never forget his kindness, his soft voice, his gentle, undemanding touch. Never once, in the two years they'd been married, had he ever made love to her like Nathan Wellesley had last night. Their relationship had been one of a tender closeness, a rightness in being together. But, even during their most intimate moments, she had never seen Joe display the hot, pulsing need Nathan had, nor had she ever experienced the mind-shattering explosion of fulfillment he had triggered in her with his raw, unbridled passion. It was the difference between a lovely, romantic dinner and a huge, gluttonous feast . . . and Elyse had never thought of herself as a glutton. Until now.

Now she knew that if she was served the right banquet, she could gorge like a harlot, and that knowledge was the most shocking and distressing aspect of her character she had ever discovered.

The only thing to do was to try to forget it. It was over. It was a terrible mistake, but it was over, and she had to put it behind her . . . to never think about it again. After all, no one would ever know. There had been no witnesses and she'd never see Nathan Wellesley again. Everyone was entitled to a few mistakes in their life, weren't they?

Again, she heard Nathan pacing the floor outside her door. If only he would leave, it would be so much easier to begin forgetting. Since it was now nearly nine o'clock, however, she had to face the fact that he obviously wasn't going to go until he talked to her. As much as she dreaded having to face the man again, she realized that it was senseless to put off the inevitable any longer. With a heavy sigh, Elyse pushed back her blankets and rose from her bed, a wave of mortification sweeping over her as she felt an unmistakable soreness between her thighs. Even her body seemed to be conspiring to make her remember her fall from grace.

With leaden steps, she walked over to the commode and poured water into the basin sitting atop it. Gazing into the mirror, she was surprised to see that she didn't look any different than she had yesterday morning or the morning before. Tired, yes, but not really *different*. Funny how a person could experience such a soul-shattering event and still look the same . . .

"What were you expecting, a scarlet 'A'? on your forehead?" she asked her reflection. Then, shaking her head at her own foolishness, she washed and quickly dressed.

It took her several moments to comb her snarled hair, the knots and tangles serving as yet another blunt reminder of the previous night's excesses. As she pulled the brush impatiently through the unruly curls, she could again hear Nathan whispering, "Your hair is beautiful. You should always wear it down and loose." With a vengeful yank, she gathered up the heavy mass and pinned it tightly into a bun, making sure that not so much as a single tendril escaped.

Her hasty toilette completed, she took a deep breath, smoothed the skirt of her high-necked, long-sleeved gray dress and opened the bedroom door.

He was there, just as she'd known he'd be, standing by the front window and frowning impatiently out at the cloudy sky. He turned when he heard her enter the room, and for the briefest moment their eyes met.

"Good morning," Nathan said softly, the rich timbre of his voice flowing over her like sweet, dark molasses.

Not trusting herself to answer, Elyse acknowledged his greeting with a curt nod and headed over to the stove, making a great pretense of checking the fire. "I'm surprised you're not gone," she said, viciously poking at the glowing coals.

Nathan's eyebrows rose imperceptively. "I was waiting to talk to you."

Gritting her teeth in a desperate effort to keep from screaming, she whirled around. "There's nothing to talk about, Captain Wellesley. I think it would be best if you would just leave."

Nathan looked at her speculatively for a moment, then turned away to again gaze out the window. All morning long he had contemplated this encounter, wondering how Elyse would react to him this morning. Now he knew, and he chose his next words carefully. Keeping his back to her, he said quietly, "I know that what happened last night wasn't a normal thing for you, and I want you to know that it wasn't for me, either."

He turned his head just enough to see her reaction to his words. She was still standing near the stove, looking as if she was carved out of stone. "I just don't want you to think that I—"

"Would you like something to eat before you go?"

Nathan stopped short, surprised and offended by her interruption. "No," he said slowly. "I don't want anything to eat. I want to talk to you—"

"If you're not hungry, then I'd appreciate it if you'd leave. I have a lot of things to do this morning and I'm already running very late."

Again, Nathan's eyes flared angrily at her rude interruption. It was obvious she didn't want to hear what he had to say, but doggedly he tried again, determined to make her listen. "If we could just talk about this for a minute, Elyse, I think we'd both feel better." She didn't respond, and, encouraged that she'd allowed him to at least finish a sentence, he charged on. "It's important to me that you understand that I don't—"

To his utter astonishment, Elyse suddenly raced over to the front door and flung it open. "Good-bye, Captain Wellesley."

Nathan's jaw clenched in frustration, but he stood his ground. "Elyse . . ."

"I said, good-bye, sir."

For a long moment, he just stared at her. Then, with a snort of anger, he grabbed his hat and bolted out the door. "Good-bye, Mrs. Graham. Thank you for your outstanding *hospitality.*"

He immediately regretted his insulting words when he heard her quick, indrawn breath, but he was too furious to apologize. Without so much as a backward glance, he strode out to the lean-to. Heaving his saddle onto his horse's back, he jerked the cinch tight, rammed the bit into the startled animal's mouth and mounted, galloping away at breakneck speed.

"Damn her," he cursed as he thundered down the road toward Bixby. "Damn her for giving me the sweetest night of my life."

"Tom? Tom, are you in here?" Hesitantly, Elyse swung the heavy barn door open and peered into the dim interior.

"Over here, Elyse."

With a sigh of relief, Elyse walked toward the sound of her brother's voice.

"What in the hell have you been doing?" Tom demanded, suddenly appearing at her side.

Elyse felt a guilty flush creep up her neck. "What do you mean?"

"I thought that stranger was gonna move in, for God's sake. I nearly froze to death out in this leaky barn all night. Why didn't you get rid of him yesterday like I told you?"

"Tom, he was a Texas Ranger."

"What?" Tom gasped. "Sweet Jesus, if I don't have the worst luck in the world." Shaking his head, he pulled two buckets off the hook on the wall and headed for the small room where the feed was kept.

"Tom, what's going on? Who are you hiding from?"

"I'll explain that in a minute," he answered, emerging from the feed room with the buckets full of oats. "But first, tell me about this Ranger. What was he doin' here?"

Elyse took one of the heavy buckets and headed toward a stall. "Nothing. He was riding into Bixby, but when he saw the storm building, he stopped here for the night."

"And you let him stay in the house?"

"Well," Elyse bristled, "I couldn't very well put him up in the barn with you out here. What other choice did I have?"

"None, I guess," Tom muttered. "But, Christ, Elyse,

you let a strange man stay in the house with you overnight?" His eyes narrowed. "Nothing happened, did it?"

Yes, something happened! Something terrible ... something I'll have to live with for the rest of my life!

"He didn't take advantage of me, if that's what you mean," she said quietly, hoping the guilt she was suffering wasn't obvious in her voice.

"Well, I'm glad to hear that. What was his name?"

"Wellesley."

Tom blanched visibly. *"Nathan* Wellesley?"

Elyse nodded in surprise. "Yes, have you heard of him?"

"Oh, yeah. Anybody who knows anything about the Rangers has heard of him. He's one of their big guns. Used to belong to the Frontier Battalion, but he's best known for being one of the leaders of the group that caught Sam Bass."

Elyse's eyebrows rose. Isolated as she was on her small farm, she knew very little about the goings-on of the world around her, but even she had heard about the Texas Rangers' bold capture of the notorious Mr. Bass. And Nathan Wellesley had been one of their leaders.

"Elyse, did he seem to be looking for someone?"

"No, I don't think so," she answered thoughtfully, pulling a flake of hay off a bale and throwing it into a feeding trough. "I think he was just passing through. He said he was on his way to Austin."

"That makes sense. He's headquartered there. You didn't tell him anything about me bein' here, did you?"

Elyse walked out of the stall, eyeing her brother closely. "Tom, what is this all about?"

"Did you?"

"No, although I had the devil's own time keeping him from charging out here after you were stupid enough to light a lantern. He thought the barn had been struck by lightning."

For a moment, Tom looked chagrined. He'd known it was foolish to light a lamp, but he'd been so damn scared that he just couldn't endure the eerie blackness of the musty barn. "How did you keep him from comin' out here?"

Elyse swallowed hard, knowing she couldn't tell Tom the truth about the methods she'd employed to distract Captain Wellesley. "I . . . I told him I had lit the lantern to keep the animals calm."

Tom frowned. "And he believed that?"

"Why shouldn't he?" Elyse shrugged, moving on to the next stall and dumping another ration of oats into the manger.

"Because it would be a stupid thing to do. No one leaves a lantern untended unless they're tryin' to burn somethin' down."

"That's exactly what he said."

Latching the stall door, Elyse set down her empty bucket and brushed the excess grain from her hands. "Okay, Tom. Enough about Captain Wellesley. I want you to tell me why you're hiding and what kind of trouble you're in."

Tom's shoulders slumped wearily. "Everything is such a mess, I don't even know where to start."

Reaching out, Elyse took her brother's hand and led him over to where the hay was stored, sitting down on a wide bale and pulling him down next to her. "How about from the beginning?"

With a long sigh, Tom clasped his hands between his knees and stared at them thoughtfully. "The Bixby bank got robbed yesterday."

"No!" Elyse gasped. "Was anyone hurt?"

"I don't think so—not any of the townsfolk, anyway."

"Well, that's a blessing, at least. Who did it? Do they know?"

Tom hesitated a long time. Then, in a voice so soft that Elyse had to lean toward him to hear, he muttered, "It was a gang of four . . . and I was one of them."

Elyse's heart leaped into her throat and, for an instant, she thought she was going to faint. "Oh, my God,

Tom," she moaned. "Why? *Why* would you get involved with something like that? You're no criminal."

"I did it for you!"

"For me? What do I have to do with this?"

"Oh, Elyse, for God's sake, look around you. The place is falling apart. The barn leaks, half the fields are unplanted, and the house is practically falling down around us. We need money fast or we're gonna lose it. These guys offered me two hundred dollars just to hold their horses."

For a long moment, Elyse stared into space, trying to absorb what Tom was telling her. "So, you didn't actually participate in the robbery?" she asked.

"No, I just held the horses. That's all, I swear it."

"Did anyone see you?"

"I don't know. I don't think so, but everything was so crazy, I can't be sure. It all happened so fast . . ."

Taking a deep, shuddering breath, Elyse again picked up Tom's hand and looked at him, her expression brooking no prevarication. "Tell me *exactly* what happened."

"Well," he began slowly. "I was standin' outside the bank, holdin' the horses just like I was supposed to. The boys went in and a minute later, they came runnin' back out, carryin' the money. Rosas, the leader, threw me the bags and we all started to mount up, but then, all of a sudden, old Crowley, the bank manager, comes runnin' out the front door, yellin' that the bank's been robbed and shootin' his pistol off like a lunatic. Who'd think that old coot would have a gun, anyway?"

"Then what?"

"Then all hell broke loose. Men started runnin' toward the bank from everywhere. I don't know, it all got so confused. Guns were goin' off, people were yellin', the horses were goin' crazy. I just got so scared that I took off and came home."

"What about the others?"

"They took off in the other direction. I don't know

where they went, but I think one of them might have been shot."

Just thinking about the danger her brother had been in made Elyse's head reel, but she knew it was important to stay calm. Taking several deep breaths, she whispered, "What happened to the money?"

"It's hidden under that pile of straw." Tom jerked his head in the direction of a large mound in the corner of the barn.

"You mean you still have it?"

"Yeah, I still have it," he countered defensively. "What was I gonna do with it? Rosas had thrown me the bags just before the shootin' started. I couldn't very well drop them."

"Why not?" Elyse demanded. "That would have been the wisest thing you could have done."

"I guess with all those guns goin' off around me, I wasn't thinkin' about bein' wise."

Elyse sighed. "I suppose not. Well, the only thing we can do now is take the money back to the bank and you can turn yourself in. If you surrender, they might not be too hard on you."

Tom jumped up, whirling on his sister. "Are you nuts? I can't give the money back. My God, Elyse, Rosas would come after me. My life won't be worth a tinker's damn if I do that."

Elyse leaped up, too, rounding on her brother with blazing eyes. "Don't be a fool, Tom! You have no other choice. Anyway, those outlaws can't do anything to you. The law will protect you."

"Oh, sure, it will," Tom snorted sarcastically. "First of all, I'll be sent to prison. Then, in ten years or so when I finally get out, I'll be killed by either Rosas or one of his boys for betraying them."

"But, Tom . . ."

"No, Elyse, don't try to talk me into it. I'm not gonna give the money back."

"Then what are you going to do?"

"I'm gonna take the money and try to find the others. I'll hand it over, just like we planned. With any luck, they'll believe me when I tell them I wasn't tryin' to double-cross them, and I'll walk away with my life. I really don't think anyone saw me, since they were all chasin' the others in the opposite direction. If I can just get rid of the money, I think I'll be okay."

Elyse sank back down on the bale of hay. The last twenty-four hours had been a nightmare . . . almost as bad as the day Joe had died. Why, *why* did trouble seem to visit her so regularly? Why couldn't something go right for a change?

"You're not gonna turn me in, are you, Sis?"

Elyse looked up into her brother's tense face, her heart wrenching painfully at the fear she saw in his blue eyes. "No, Tom, I'm not going to turn you in. You're my little brother and I wouldn't do that. But you should turn *yourself* in. I think you're making the biggest mistake of your life if you take this money and run."

"Damn it, Elyse, you don't understand. These guys aren't nice, God-fearing folks like the people you know. They're mean desperadoes, and they'd just as soon shoot you as look at you if they thought it would net them ten cents."

"If they're so awful, how did you ever get involved with them?"

"It's a long story," Tom said wearily, "and one you really don't want to hear."

Elyse winced at the guilt and self-loathing she saw in her brother's face. He was so young, only seventeen. If only she could make him see the sense in turning himself in. "Tom, please don't do this," she pleaded. *"Please.* You're just compounding one mistake with another. Besides, if you run, what will I do here without you? I can't handle this farm all by myself. If you'd just make a clean breast of things with the law, I'm sure—"

"I don't have time to argue anymore, Elyse. I'm not

gonna turn myself in and that's that. Now, are you gonna help me, or aren't you?"

"Help you with what?"

Walking over to the large pile of straw, Tom dropped to his knees and began fishing around, finally pulling out a pair of bulging saddlebags. "I need food. At least a week's worth. I don't know where the others went after the shooting started. We were supposed to meet at Miller's Bluff, but I'm sure they never made it there. They probably headed for the border, so there's no telling how long it's gonna take me to find them."

With a weariness greater than any she'd known in her life, Elyse hefted herself off the bale of hay. "All right. I'll go fix you some food. Is there anything else you need?"

"No," he answered, leading his horse out of its stall. "That should do it."

With a resigned nod, Elyse walked back to the house and filled a large bag with bread, dried meat, cheese, and apples. She was careful to keep her mind blank as she packed up the food, knowing that if she started thinking about everything that had happened in the last day, she'd probably begin screaming and never be able to stop.

Walking back out onto the porch, she handed the food to her brother, then clasped him to her in a desperate hug. "Please be careful, and keep in touch if you can."

"I don't think I'll be able to do that," he said, shaking his head, "but I'll be back as soon as I know it's safe."

Elyse nodded, stepping back and blinking rapidly as she tried to control the tears that threatened. "I love you, Tom."

"I love you, too, Elyse. Now don't worry about me. I'll be fine."

Not trusting herself to speak, Elyse nodded and forced a weak smile.

Tom mounted, then sat atop his horse a moment, his

eyes carefully scanning the horizon for any hint of danger. Satisfied that no other riders were lurking in the trees, he clucked to his horse and, with a last wave, rode down the drive, leaving a dusty wake behind him.

Elyse watched until he was out of sight. Then, with a heavy sigh, she sank down on the front step of her small house and gave vent to the tears she had been holding back all morning.

Never had she felt so alone.

Chapter 4

June 1880

"Nathan Wellesley, it's good to see you, my boy. Good to see you."

Nathan smiled and returned his commanding officer's warm handshake. "Thank you, Major Jones. Believe me, it's good to be here. For a while there, I didn't think I was ever going to see Ranger headquarters again."

"For a while there, neither did we," Jones smiled. "Sit down and make yourself comfortable."

Major John B. Jones, although small in stature and slightly shy, was a living legend in Texas. By founding the Frontier Battalion, he had formed the finest group of fighting men the state had ever known. Renowned for his unerring good judgment and quiet, dignified leadership, he inspired respect in all who knew him. Nathan, like the other men in the famed battalion, considered it an honor to have been chosen to serve under him.

Now, as he sat down in a plush leather chair in the major's office, Nathan couldn't help but wonder why the estimable man had asked for this private meeting. It wasn't like Jones to call a single Ranger into his office, and Nathan's curiosity was rampant.

Settling himself behind his large, cluttered desk, Jones took a swallow of his ever-present cup of coffee and turned his piercing black gaze on Nathan. "First of all,

I want to thank you for your exemplary work bringing in Bob Ellis. I've read your report and both the governor and I are very proud. In fact," he leaned forward conspiratorially, "the governor is seriously considering awarding you a special citation."

Nathan smiled, pleased by the major's rare words of praise. "That's very kind of him, sir, but it isn't necessary. I was just doing my job."

Jones sat back in his chair again and nodded approvingly. "Well, Captain, citation or no citation, you did a fine piece of work and you have my sincerest gratitude."

Nathan's smile widened.

"So," the major continued, "now that we've put the Ellis matter to bed, are you ready for a new assignment? I have one that's a bit unusual and I think you're the best man for it."

Nathan straightened, intrigued by the prospect of an "unusual" assignment. "I'm more than ready, Major. What can I do for you?"

"Do you remember the Bixby bank robbery last year?"

"Sure. I could hardly forget that one since I was right outside of town when it happened."

"That's right," Jones nodded. "Didn't you spend the night out at some farm because it was raining or something?"

A wave of memories washed over Nathan. *The rain, the little cabin, the thunder and lightning, Elyse.* How many hundreds of times had he thought about that night in the past year? And how many times had he cursed his own memory for not letting him forget it?

"Yes," he acknowledged. "I never did make it into Bixby. I rode straight on to Austin the next morning and didn't hear about the robbery till I got here. Too bad, too. I might have been able to do something before the gang scattered if I'd known about it. Did anyone ever catch them?"

"No. And since it's been more than a year since the

robbery occurred, the trail's completely cold. We figured the gang took off for Mexico and that they're still down there."

"What about the money? Was it recovered?"

"Yes, and that's what I want to talk to you about. Seems there was one member of the gang who didn't actually participate in the robbery. A young kid, about seventeen or eighteen, and he just held the horses for the others. But he ended up with the money."

"Obviously, you've caught him."

"No. Actually, he turned himself in to us. All this time, he's been hiding in some little town near the border. One day last week, he just walked in the door, told us his name and said he was tired of being a fugitive. Then he handed over a sackful of money. Strangest thing I've ever seen."

"Certainly is," Nathan agreed. "What's his name?"

"Tom Carlisle. Ever heard of him?"

Nathan shook his head.

"I hadn't either, and after interrogating him, I'm convinced that he's not really a criminal. He just got mixed up with the Rosas gang and was coerced into aiding them."

Nathan's eyebrows rose. "The Rosas gang is responsible for that job?"

"Yes, and since we know this kid isn't really a member, we've decided to cut a deal with him."

"A deal?" Nathan asked, surprised. "What kind of deal?"

"Well, we figure the rest of the gang knows Carlisle still has the money. So, in return for giving him immunity from prosecution, he's going to help us set them up."

"How?"

"That's where you come in. Seems this kid has an older sister. A widow woman who lives on a ranch all by herself outside of Bixby. We're going to spread the word along the grapevine that she's holding the money. Hopefully, that will flush the gang out and we can set a trap for them when they move in to collect."

"Whew," Nathan breathed. "Sounds pretty dangerous for the sister. Has she agreed to help us?"

"Yes, but not without some prodding."

"Prodding?"

Jones nodded. "When we first approached her, she turned us down flat, but, during his confession, Carlisle let the cat out of the bag that the night of the robbery, he hid in her barn and the following morning, he said, she helped him get away."

Nathan's eyes lit with understanding. "So, you told her that if she didn't assist us, she'd be brought up on charges of harboring a fugitive?"

"Exactly."

"And she agreed?"

"Reluctantly."

Nathan sat back in his chair, pondering all that Jones had just told him. "How do I fit into this?"

"Actually, Nate, you're central to it. This is a confidence job. We need a man at the ranch to set up the trap and protect the widow. You're the obvious choice. We know you were raised on a ranch in Colorado, so we figure you know how to mend fences and bale hay, things like that. We don't know how long it will be before we can flush Rosas out, but we need a man already in place when it happens, and it's got to be someone they won't suspect."

Despite his best attempts to keep his face impassive, Nathan couldn't quite conceal his disappointment. "You mean, my cover is to work as a hand on some dirt farm?"

"Ranch," Jones corrected, his mouth quirking at Nathan's obvious disdain at posing as a hired hand. "Told you it was an unusual assignment."

"Yeah, unusual," Nathan muttered. "Sir, do you really think it's necessary to put a man on the ranch? Why don't we just move the widow somewhere and keep the place under surveillance till the gang makes their move?"

Jones shook his head. "They'd suspect something. Apparently, this sister has lived on the ranch for years. They'd never fall for it if she disappeared at the same time word leaked that's where the money's hidden."

Nathan nodded slowly, unable to argue with Jones's logic. "I suppose you're right. So, how long do you expect I'll have to be there?"

Jones breathed a secret sigh of relief, sure now that Nathan was going to agree to take the assignment. "We really don't have any way of knowing that, Nate. We have to be very careful how we leak the bogus information about the money. If Rosas is in Mexico as we suspect, there's no telling how long it will take for word to reach him. Could be a week, a month, even longer if he's dug in deep somewhere."

Nathan sighed and pulled a notebook and a pencil out of his shirt pocket. "Okay, Major, where do I find this ranch?"

"It's about five miles west of Bixby. I'm not sure of the exact location, but I figure you can stop in town and ask. Bixby is a little place and anyone there should be able to give you directions. It will also add to your credibility if, from the very beginning, the townsfolk think you're nothing more than a hired hand."

Nathan nodded.

"Incidentally," the major continued, "you're going to use a phony name, too. We know you haven't worked enough in that area for people to recognize you, but your name is too well known to take a chance of you using it."

"Who am I gonna be?"

"Nat Wells," Jones grinned. "Figured that would be close enough for you to answer to it easily, but far enough removed from your real name that it wouldn't rouse any suspicion."

"Nat Wells, huh?" Nathan chuckled, scribbling on the

paper. "Guess that'll do. And the widow's name is Carlisle?"

"No. That's the brother's name. The widow's name is, ah, let me see. I know I have it written down here someplace." Jones shuffled through the mass of papers and dispatches on his desk till he found the one he sought. Lifting it, he quickly scanned the sheet. "Here it is. Her name is Graham. Elyse Graham."

Nathan's pencil clattered to the floor.

Hurriedly, he bent over to retrieve it, hoping his face hadn't betrayed his shock. But, as he straightened, he knew that Major Jones's sharp eyes had not missed his momentary slip.

"Is something wrong, Nate?" Jones asked carefully.

"No, I just dropped my pencil."

"That's not what I mean. Your reaction when I mentioned Carlisle's sister's name. Do you know her?"

"Not really."

"Not really, but . . ."

"I've met her," Nathan admitted.

"When?"

"Last year when I was in Bixby. It was her ranch I stayed at the night of the storm."

"Really . . ." Jones mused, picking up a pen and chewing thoughtfully on its tip. "So you were actually at the ranch the day her brother assisted in the robbery."

A vision of a light glinting through a barn window flashed through Nathan's mind. "Yeah," he mumbled, trying hard to mask a sudden jolt of anger, "I guess I was."

"What was she like?"

Nathan swallowed hard as he envisioned Elyse's soft, passion-glazed eyes looking up at him in the darkness. "Pretty ordinary, really," he lied. "Kind of the sweet, innocent schoolmarm type. She was nervous about the storm and didn't talk much."

Jones's eyebrows rose. "Do you think it was really the

storm she was nervous about, or do you think she knew something?"

Hell, yes, she knew something. That's why she didn't want me to go to the barn.

"I really don't know, sir. If she did, she didn't let on."

Shrugging, Jones threw the pen down on his desk. "I suppose it doesn't matter much now. She's agreed to co-operate with us and that's all that counts."

So many emotions were surging through Nathan that he hardly heard Jones's dismissive words.

She had let him make love to her so he'd forget about the light in the barn—so he wouldn't investigate and find whoever was hiding out there. No wonder she'd been so anxious to get rid of him the next morning. Her brother was probably waiting for her. Or maybe it had been someone else she was hiding. Maybe she was involved with another member of the Rosas gang and he had been out there in that leaky barn all night, wondering why she didn't come to him.

"Nate, did you hear me?"

Nathan snapped back to the present. "I'm sorry, Major, what did you say?"

"I said, do you have a problem accepting this assignment, now that you know who you're dealing with?"

"No, sir," Nathan said quickly. "There's no problem."

What a fool he'd been, thinking about that night . . . that woman . . . all these months. Thinking that what had happened between them had been something extraordinary. No, he didn't have a problem with this assignment. In fact, he couldn't wait to have the opportunity to tell the Widow Graham exactly what he thought of her.

"Good," Jones nodded. "Then you best be on your way. I'll give you a week to get to Bixby and get set up on the ranch. Then, we'll leak the news about the money and wait for the gang to show themselves."

"And you don't think it will take more than a few weeks to ferret them out?"

"I don't think so," Jones responded, wondering again

why Nathan seemed so anxious to get this assignment over with, "but, of course, we can't be sure."

"Does the widow know I'm coming?"

"You, in particular?"

Nathan nodded.

"No. All she knows is that a Ranger is going to pose as her new hand. She doesn't know who." Jones paused, eyeing Nathan closely for his reaction to this statement. He saw nothing in Nathan's expression to alarm him, but still he couldn't quite shake a feeling of unease. "Nate, are you sure you're all right with this assignment? Like I said, I think you're the best man for it, but if you have reservations because of something that might have happened last year between you and this Graham woman—"

"Nothing happened between us," Nathan interrupted. "And I don't have any reservations."

"You're absolutely sure?"

"Yeah, absolutely. Who are my contacts?"

Again, John Jones's ebony eyes bore into Nathan. The silence between the men lengthened but, to Nathan's surprise, the major asked no further questions. Instead, he responded, "Will Johnson and Red Hilliard will be your contacts. I've already set them up in Bixby. Hilliard is working at the telegraph office and Johnson is at the livery stable."

Nathan nodded his approval. "Handy. Both of them in places where they'll hear everything."

"That's the plan," Jones smiled, relaxing somewhat now that the conversation was back on the business at hand. "I would have liked to have gotten somebody into the saloon to pick up on that gossip, but we just couldn't work it out. Guess I'll have to leave that up to you. You like a beer now and again, don't you?"

Nathan looked at his teetotalling boss and returned his smile. "Whatever it takes to get the job done, sir."

Jones rose, grinning. "Thought you'd feel that way." He stuck out his hand as Nathan also got to his feet.

"Good luck, Nate. Keep in touch through Hilliard. He'll wire me of any developments."

"I will, sir." Nathan turned and headed toward the door, but turned back when he heard the major call his name.

"Watch out for that widow," Jones advised. "Sometimes those sweet, innocent schoolmarm types can be the worst."

Nathan nodded, his mouth set in a grim line. "I understand, Major, and you don't have to worry. I'll have my eye on her every minute."

Chapter 5

Not much of a place, Nathan thought as he rode his buckskin down the main street of Bixby. With alert eyes, he surreptitiously scanned both sides of the dusty, rutted roadway. It wouldn't do to arouse suspicion among the citizens by appearing too interested in his surroundings but, still, was keenly interested in the layout of the town. To his left was a general store, the telegraph office where Red Hilliard was stationed, and an unprepossessing little building whose door proclaimed, "Ezra Banks, M.D.". Swinging his gaze to the right, he spotted a rundown boardinghouse, two saloons, and the ill-fated Bixby Bank. He didn't see any sign of the livery stable where Will Johnson was staked out, but he assumed it must be down the small town's one side street.

Pulling his horse to a stop, Nathan dismounted and clumped up the wooden steps to the general store. He opened the door, causing a little bell hanging from it to tinkle merrily, and stepped inside. As he looked around the small room, he was aware that every head in the place was turned toward him and that a quiet buzz of conversation was suddenly rippling through the crowded store as the wives of Bixby speculated as to who the stranger in their midst might be.

Pulling his hat off, Nathan walked toward the counter at the back of the store, announcing loudly, "Name's

Nat Wells. I'm looking for directions to the Graham place."

He heard the quickly squelched gasps of shock that followed his announcement but was careful not to turn around, knowing it was integral to his cover to appear nonchalant.

A small, bespectacled man standing behind the long counter darted a look at the crowd closing in behind the stranger, then said quietly, "Widow Graham lives about five miles west."

"Straight down the road out of town?" Nathan questioned.

The man nodded. For a moment he opened his mouth as if to say more, but just as quickly he closed it and turned away.

Nathan's curiosity mounted at the storekeeper's strange behavior. "I'm her new hand," he offered. "Hired on for the summer."

This information was met by another chorus of ill-concealed gasps, then he distinctly heard a woman's voice hiss, "Indeed. Another man."

Nathan felt a hand on his arm and turned to find a man in cleric's clothes standing next to him. "Are you planning to stay out at her place, stranger, or will you be needing directions to the boardinghouse, too?"

Nathan's curiosity increased. There was an obvious aura of disapproval spreading through the close confines of the store, but, for the life of him, he couldn't figure out what he might have said to bring about such an immediate air of contempt from the townsfolk. "No, thanks," he said, smiling ingratiatingly at the minister, "I don't need a room. When Mrs. Graham hired me, she told me she could put me up."

Immediately, the same woman snorted, "I'll just bet she did."

To Nathan's surprise, the minister suddenly turned away and snapped, "Lillian, please! Your comments are unnecessary."

Nathan could stand it no more and, turning, he eyed the woman at whom the minister's rebuke was directed. She was middle-aged and corpulent, with a florid face that had never been pretty, even in her youth. Her hair was skinned back in a tight bun and, at this moment, her enormous bosom was heaving with outraged offense.

"I'm sorry, Reverend," she returned, the tone of her voice making it clear that she wasn't sorry at all, "but I can't help the way I feel."

"Lillian . . ." The reverend's voice held a distinct note of warning.

With a haughty toss of her large head, the woman grabbed the arm of a young girl standing next to her. "Come along, Lucy," she said. "We needn't stand here and be publicly reprimanded for saying what we all know is true." She moved toward the door, knowing that everyone in the store was watching her exit. Then, as if determined to have the last word, she turned back, her hand on the doorknob. "She is what she is, Reverend, and everyone knows it. You'd be doing this young man a great favor if you warned him what he's getting into." She paused meaningfully. "Unless, of course, he already knows, and that's *why* he took the job."

"Mrs. Underwood!" the reverend cried. "I will not tolerate you . . ."

With a triumphant smirk, Lillian Underwood threw open the door. "Good day, everyone!" she called, effectively cutting off the minister's words. Then she slammed the door soundly behind her, leaving only the frantic tinkling of the little bell to fill the sudden silence in the store.

Nathan was completely nonplussed by the bizarre exchange he'd just witnessed, but before he could collect himself to say anything, the minister turned back to him. "Please forgive us, Mr. . . ."

"Wells. Nat Wells."

"Please forgive us, Mr. Wells. As you can see, feelings

concerning Mrs. Graham tend to run a little high among the ladies in town. I have tried my best to encourage a Christian attitude toward her, but sometimes it is difficult."

Nathan shook his head, feeling he had stepped into the middle of a blood feud. "Look, Reverend, I'm just here to help the lady on her ranch for the summer. I've never even met her."

"Oh, you'd never guess just to meet her," the storekeeper chimed in. "That's why it was such a shock to us."

"I think you're all being terribly unkind," piped up a pretty young woman standing at the rear of the store. "It's nobody's business but her own."

"I agree," chorused a large man with a fifty-pound sack of flour slung over his shoulder. "She ain't the first woman to have that happen to her and she won't be the last."

"Well, I certainly hope she's the last in Bixby!" said a skinny, pinch-faced old woman. "A few more like her and we'll have a reputation worse than Abilene's!"

"That's enough!" the minister suddenly bellowed, his booming voice immediately bringing the room to complete silence. "I don't want to hear another word from any of you." His shaming glance swept the store, causing even the formidable old crone to avert her eyes in embarrassment. "Let us all remember that ours is a forgiving God and there is not one of us in this room who hasn't something in our past to atone for. Remember, he who casts the first stone . . ."

"Humpf!"

"And that means you, too, Miss Dixon," he added, nailing the old lady with a withering glare. "Now then," he said, yanking down his vest and turning back to Nathan, "is there any more information you need, sir?"

"No," Nathan murmured, turning his shocked gaze back to the man in front of him. "I think you've all said quite enough."

"Yes, well," the minster blustered, "I can only hope you don't believe every piece of idle gossip you hear, young man."

"Of course not," Nathan answered, shaking his head. Turning, he headed for the door, his eyes roving over the set, angry faces of the assembled crowd. "Thank you very much for the directions."

"Any time, my boy," the reverend boomed, "and welcome to Bixby!"

What in hell did she do to turn the town against her like that?

Over and over, Nathan asked himself that question as he trotted down the dusty road toward Elyse's farm. *Did everyone in town know her brother had had a part in robbing the bank and that she had helped him escape? Was that why they seemed to hate her so?*

Even as that thought crossed his mind, Nathan discarded it. No one had known about Tom Carlisle's involvement in the Bixby bank robbery—not even the many law-enforcement officials investigating the case—until he had turned himself in a few days ago. Nathan knew for a fact that Major Jones hadn't leaked that information. It would totally negate their efforts to set a trap to catch the gang if it became common knowledge that Tom was now working with the law.

It must be something else. Something that Elyse herself had done that was so unacceptable that the citizens of Bixby had turned on her for it. But what?

For the life of him, Nathan couldn't imagine what it could be. For the hundredth time since leaving Austin four days before, he thought again about that night so many months ago when she had lain in his arms and made love with him. Although he now knew that her passion had been calculated to distract him from investigating the barn and finding her brother hiding there, the more he thought about it, the more he still could not believe that her perfidy that night had been typical. And even though she had displayed a carnal side to her nature that would certainly disgust a tight-lipped old harridan like Miss Dixon, that was a highly personal bit of knowledge that was strictly between him and her—certainly nothing the general populace of Bixby would be aware of. Unless, of course . . .

Nathan slowed his horse to a walk as a disturbing thought crossed his mind. Unless, of course, her provocative behavior with him was common to her—and common knowledge in town.

"I don't believe that," he said aloud, shaking his head. She had been too frightened, too nervous, too hesitant in her seduction of him to believe that it was a common occurrence. And the next morning, she wouldn't even look him in the eye! Surely these were not the actions of an accomplished courtesan, or even of a woman hoping for a generous gift or a repeat visit from a satisfied paramour.

So, what *had* Elyse done to bring about the gossip he had heard today? Was it because she lived alone? Didn't attend church regularly? Had she perhaps turned down the attentions of suitable men in town who might have tried to court her? Any of these speculations might make a single woman the object of gossip, but it just didn't seem normal that it would be as vicious as what he had heard.

"Quit worrying about it," he told himself firmly. "It's none of your business. All you're here for is to protect her when and if the gang makes a move. You're not here to get involved in anything personal with her, so just forget it. This is a job . . . just like any other."

Nathan had no intention of getting personally involved with Elyse Graham. In fact, he hoped she wouldn't even recognize him. It would make the next few weeks so much easier if they just ignored what had happened between them and treated each other in the impersonal manner this assignment demanded.

"Why not?" he muttered aloud. "It was a long time

ago, and if she does remember it, she's probably just as anxious to ignore it as I am. When I meet her again, I'll just treat her the way I would any other woman under my protection and everything will be fine."

He sighed and nudged his horse back into a trot. The words sounded good. Now, if he could just make himself believe them . . .

Chapter 6

Nathan rode up the dusty drive to the Graham ranch, his gaze sweeping over the dilapidated buildings and broken-down fences. It was obvious Elyse hadn't taken any of her brother's ill-gotten gains to fix the place up. Except for a carefully tended bed of wildflowers growing near the front door, the farm was even more dreary than he remembered.

Dismounting, he threw his horse's reins over the hitching rail, then paused a moment, eyeing the sagging front steps as if weighing whether the rotting boards would hold his weight. Finally, he shrugged and carefully climbed onto the outer edge of the first step. *How could anybody let a place get this run down?* he thought irritably. *The least she could do is hire somebody to fix the steps before she kills herself on them.*

He frowned, annoyed at his own thoughts. "It's none of your damn business what the place looks like," he told himself. "Just do your job and keep your mouth shut."

Treading warily across the creaking porch, he raised a hand and knocked on the front door, noting that the top hinge was broken.

Almost immediately, the rickety door swung open, and for the first time in fifteen months, Nathan stared into the sea-blue eyes of the woman he'd tried so hard to forget. A wave of emotions washed over him.

There was something different about her, a subtle, nearly indefinable change—a change most people wouldn't even notice, but he, who had held the image of her in his mind for so many months, was aware of it immediately. She was softer, somehow, more curved, and her lush breasts pressing against the front of her worn calico dress were even fuller than he remembered.

Elyse's reaction to him was not nearly as sentimental. "You!" she cried. "What are you doing here?"

Nathan's expression hardened. "I've been sent here by the State of Texas to protect you," he answered flatly.

"Well, you can go right back where you came from. I don't want you here!" With a quick, desperate movement, she threw her weight against the door, trying to close it on him.

"Now, just a damn minute," Nathan barked, throwing his arm out and blocking her attempt. "You knew the state was sending a Ranger here."

"Yes, I did," Elyse admitted, still pushing frantically on the door. "But I didn't know it was going to be you or I wouldn't have agreed."

Thoroughly incensed, Nathan gripped the edge of the door and gave it a hard push, causing Elyse to break her grip and take a lurching step backward.

Taking advantage of her momentary struggle for balance, Nathan stepped into the room. "You don't have any choice, lady." His eyes scanned the sparse furnishings, lighting on the small settee in the corner. Despite his anger, he couldn't help but remember what had happened between them on that settee and, unconsciously, his voice softened. "Just so you know, Mrs. Graham, I didn't ask for this assignment, but now that I'm here, we might as well try to make the best of it."

"You can go to hell!" Elyse spat. "I refuse to have you here. Get out!"

"I think not."

Nathan's cold, emotionless words caused something to

snap in Elyse and, with a small cry of fear and rage, she lunged at him, beating him on his chest with her small fists. "Oh, you vile man! I hate you! I want you out of here!"

"Stop it!" Nathan shouted, grabbing her by her wrists. "Stop this now!"

Elyse twisted out of his grasp and staggered backward, raising shaking fingers to her mouth. "Why you?" she cried, tears pouring down her face. "There must be hundreds of Rangers in the state. Why did they have to send you?"

"Damn rotten luck, I guess," Nathan muttered. Bending down, he picked up his hat, which had fallen on the floor during their skirmish. "Believe me," he continued, straightening and looking her squarely in the eye, "I don't want to be here any more than you want me to."

"Then why did you accept the assignment? Surely you could have said no and they would have sent someone else."

Nathan remained silent for a long moment. He'd asked himself the same thing a hundred times since leaving Austin and still he had no answer, either for her or himself. "Look, we both know this isn't a situation either one of us would have chosen, but I've got a job to do, so where do you want me to put my gear?"

Elyse's expression became even more mutinous. The arrogance of the man! He might think she had to accept this "situation," but he was wrong. Dead wrong. She had every intention of sending a wire to that odious Major Jones in Austin and demanding that they replace him with someone else. Anyone else. She would *not* tolerate having Nathan Wellesley living on her property.

"You can put your things in the barn for now," she said, her voice stressing the last two words.

"Did you ever fix the roof?"

Elyse's lips tightened, but she ignored the pointed reminder of his previous visit. "It almost never rains in

June and, believe me, you're not going to be here that long. I'm sure you'll be fine."

Nathan's eyes narrowed at her thinly veiled threat. "You can just forget any harebrained idea you have about getting rid of me. You might think you're important to this job, but don't let your head get too swollen. To my way of thinking, you're damned lucky you're not in jail, so don't think that just because you agreed to cooperate with us that Major Jones is going to show you any special treatment."

"Agreed?" Elyse snorted. "I didn't agree to anything, Captain. Two of your henchmen arrived at my door three weeks ago, announced that I'm a wanted criminal and demanded that I either assist your organization by allowing myself to be used as bait for your little plan or go straight to jail. I had no choice but to *agree.*"

Nathan shrugged. "That's not true. You could have gone to jail."

"What? You think I'm going to rot in some prison somewhere for a crime I didn't commit? Are you crazy?"

Nathan looked at her speculatively for a moment. "You really don't think you did anything wrong, do you?"

"I didn't," Elyse said fiercely. "I didn't even know that my brother had participated in that robbery. He arrived here that day just a few minutes before you did. When he saw you coming, he asked me not to let you know he was here and took off for the barn before I could find out why."

"And you didn't find that request a little suspicious?"

"Of course I thought it was strange," she shot back defensively, "but he's my brother. What would you have done if it was *your* brother?"

Her blunt question gave Nathan pause. What *would* he do if one of his six brothers was in trouble and asked for his help? The answer was obvious. He'd do exactly what she had done . . .

"Look, Mrs. Graham, I'm not here to debate your guilt or innocence. I'm here to protect you if and when your brother's gang comes here looking for the stolen money. That's all. Now, I'll ask you again. Does the barn still leak?"

Elyse sighed, realizing it was useless to try to make the stubborn, self-righteous lawman see her side of this mess. "Yes, the barn still leaks. That's something you can do while you're here."

"What?"

"Patch the barn roof. After all, you *are* posing as a ranch hand, aren't you?"

Nathan's eyes flared with indignation and he took an aggressive step forward, moving so close that Elyse could feel his warm breath on her face when he next spoke. "Let's get something straight right now," he growled. "You're right. I am *posing* as a ranch hand. Got it? The word is *posing*. I'm not here to mend your fences, fix your roof, or plow your fields. If I feel it's important to look busy, then I will. Otherwise, I will do exactly what I please, if I please, when I please. You will not ask me to do chores for you, nor expect me to help you in any way with your daily tasks. In fact, the less we see of each other, the better I'll like it. Do I make myself perfectly clear?"

Elyse opened her mouth to hurl another barb at the hated man, but the words never left her mouth. Instead, the room was filled with the sound of a strange, high-pitched little shriek coming from the direction of the bedroom.

"What is that?" Nathan asked, whirling in the direction of the sound.

"What?"

Nathan drew his gun and started for the bedroom. "You know very well what. Who's in the bedroom?"

"No one!" Elyse cried, "and don't you dare go in there!" Skirting the small kitchen table, she raced past

Nathan and flung herself against the bedroom door. "I will not tolerate you going into my bedroom!"

Nathan paused, unsure whether he should force his way into the room or not. It was obvious there was someone in there whom Elyse didn't want him to see but, still, he was reluctant to remove her bodily from where she stood plastered against the door. *"Who's in there?"* he demanded.

"I told you, no one. It's my ... cat. She recently had kittens. That's what you heard. They're probably hungry and calling for her."

Nathan took one more step toward her, then stopped again. She was lying and he knew it, but he also knew that whoever was in the bedroom had heard every word they'd said and was probably expecting him to burst through the door. For all he knew, it could be one of the gang members or some other equally unsavory character she'd taken up with. In that case, there was every chance that the minute he opened the door, he'd be shot dead. His innate sense of caution prevailed and, slowly, he holstered his gun. Better to wait. He'd go out to the barn for a few minutes till she lowered her guard, then return and check the room out when he had the element of surprise on his side. Drawing a deep breath, he forced a smile. "Just a litter of kittens, huh?"

"Yes," Elyse nodded, her voice breathless with relief. "Four of them. Noisy little things, too. I'll be glad when they're old enough to be outside."

"Yeah, I'll bet. Well, I guess I'll get settled in the barn. Do you have an extra stall for my horse?"

"They're almost all empty. Take your pick."

Nathan headed for the door.

"Captain Wellesley?"

"Yes?" he asked, turning.

"Supper will be ready about five."

Nathan's eyebrows rose in surprise. "Thank you. I appreciate that."

"I'll bring your plate out to the barn," she added hastily.

"The barn? You're going to make me eat in the barn?"

Elyse shrugged, barely able to contain her triumphant smile. "As you said, Captain, the less we see of each other, the better."

With a snort of disgust, Nathan clapped his hat on his head and disappeared out the door.

Nathan angrily paced the empty stall where he'd thrown his bedroll and saddlebags. "Treacherous little bitch," he muttered. "Does she really think I'm so stupid that I honestly believe all she's got in that bedroom is a litter of kittens?" For the fourth time in as many minutes, he strode over to the barn door and peered out at the house. No one had come out the door, so whoever Elyse was hiding was obviously still in there with her.

Nathan sighed and shook his head. How could he have been so taken in by her? Normally he considered himself to be an excellent judge of character. It was one of the traits that made a good lawman. But he'd been completely fooled by Elyse Graham. He could have sworn that the night they'd had together had been as unusual and unique an experience for her as it had for him. But now, after everything he'd heard earlier in town, coupled with her frantic attempt to conceal the fact that she was obviously hiding a man in her bedroom, he had to admit that he'd been wrong about her . . . completely, totally wrong.

That admission was both disturbing and infuriating. Disturbing because he now realized that a beautiful face and beckoning body could make him throw caution to the winds and give in to his basest instincts with no care for his safety. In fact, he was probably damned lucky that her brother hadn't sneaked into the house and

knifed him in the back while he'd made love to her on
the settee . . .

And infuriating when he thought of the hundreds of
lonely nights he'd lain out under the endless Texas sky
and replayed every moment of that evening over and
over in his mind, smiling at how special it had been and
wondering just what it was about this woman that made
her unique.

The Rangers were legendary characters in Texas, and
there wasn't a young girl in the whole state whose heart
hadn't been captivated by stories of their romantic esca-
pades. This reputation, along with Nathan's extraordinary good looks and easy, drawling charm had made
women a plentiful and easily obtained commodity in his
life.

He was not a man to pass up an opportunity, and
over the years, he had enjoyed more encounters than he
could even remember. But Elyse Graham had been different from all those other faceless, forgotten women.
She was the one he couldn't forget, and the night he
had spent with her in his arms had been one that would
be forever etched in his memory.

It was this very uniqueness that now made the reality
of the situation so hard to accept. The woman he had
encountered today, with her wary eyes and hateful, biting words, bore little resemblance to the sweet, smiling
girl he remembered. And for some reason, seeing the
true Elyse Graham made him feel like a child who had
just been told it's not St. Nick who brings the presents.
He couldn't remember when he'd ever felt more de-
pressed.

With a heavy sigh, Nathan glanced at his pocket
watch. Twenty minutes had passed since he'd come out
to the barn. Long enough that he was sure Elyse didn't
expect him to return.

Silently, he crept across the yard and edged his way
up onto the rickety porch. He nodded with satisfaction
when he saw the front door was still ajar, just as he'd left

it. Sliding through the narrow opening, he drew his gun, then paused, listening alertly when he heard Elyse's voice behind the closed bedroom door. As stealthily as a cat, he slipped across the room, his eyes narrowing with fury as her muffled words became clear.

"Don't you worry, my darling, I'll find some way to get rid of him. He'll never get his hands on you, I promise. Somehow, some way, I'll get him out of here."

With an enraged gasp, Nathan grabbed the doorknob and threw the portal open, hurtling himself into the room and swinging the barrel of his gun in a wide, encompassing arc. "Freeze, or I'll . . ." His words died in his throat as his gaze lit upon Elyse, sitting in a small chair in a corner of the room cuddling a blond baby.

"Don't shoot!" she screamed, jumping to her feet and hunching protectively over the startled infant. "Please don't shoot!"

"Jesus Christ!" Nathan shouted, as shocked as Elyse. Instantly, he uncocked the trigger and raised the gun barrel in the air. "What the hell . . ."

"Get out of here!" Elyse shrieked. "How dare you?" By now the baby was also screaming, incensed that its peaceful cuddle had been so rudely disturbed. Nathan had to yell to be heard over the sudden cacophony of voices.

"Where did that baby come from?"

"None of your business!" Elyse returned, trying desperately to comfort the squalling infant. "Get out of my bedroom, *now!*"

Nathan made no move to leave, but lowered the gun and stood staring at the baby as if he still didn't believe what he was seeing. "Where did that baby come from?" he asked again.

"From the normal place!" Elyse snapped indignantly, her ire now thoroughly aroused.

Despite his shock, Nathan's lips twitched at her ridiculous answer. "Is this who I heard in here before?"

"Yes, and now that you know, I want you out of this room!"

Nathan continued to stand his ground. "Whose baby is that?"

This last question caused Elyse to draw in a quick, startled breath. Determined not to let Nathan see her fear, she turned her back to him and said haughtily, "He's mine."

"Well, I *figured* that," Nathan responded, trying wildly to judge the child's age and remember exactly when he had been here the previous year. *March. It was March. Fourteen, no, fifteen months ago.*

"How old is he?"

Elyse hesitated for a split second, then turned back toward him. "Almost eight months."

Eight and nine was seventeen. She'd gotten pregnant seventeen months ago. Nathan blew out a silent, thankful breath, then took another look at the child. "I guess you must have been in the family way when your husband was killed."

For a moment, Elyse looked at Nathan in complete confusion. *Her husband?* Joe had been dead for almost four years. Why in the world would he think this baby was Joe's? Then, it suddenly occurred to her that she'd never told him when Joe had died. Seizing on this realization, she nodded her head vigorously. "Yes, yes, I was."

"What's his name?" Nathan asked, taking a step closer and holding a finger out toward the baby's waving fist.

Instinctively, Elyse drew away, wrapping her hand around the baby's fist to prevent him from reaching out toward the intriguing finger. "You don't need to know that."

Nathan's brows lowered in bewilderment. "You won't tell me his name?"

Elyse snorted in frustration. "It's Colin. *Now,* will you *please* leave? I don't know how many times I have to ask you. You found out what you came to find out and this child needs to eat and take his nap. Please, I need some privacy."

"Oh, yeah, sure." Nathan nodded, taking a hasty step backward. He was suddenly feeling very embarrassed and very foolish. "Look, Mrs. Graham, I'm really sorry for busting in here. I thought—"

"I know what you thought, Captain Wellesley. You needn't try to explain."

"I'll just go back to the barn, then."

Elyse nodded, again seating herself in the rocking chair. "Close the door when you leave, please."

With a last, chagrined smile, Nathan backed out of the door, closing it softly.

Elyse listened intently until she heard the front door close, then laid her head back and let out a long, tremulous sigh. Gazing down at her son, she shook her head in wonderment. "How could he see you and not guess?" she whispered. "You're the spitting image of him."

Chapter 7

A baby. She had a baby. No wonder she looked different!

And he'd been such an idiot, he'd thought it was a man she was hiding in her bedroom. He should have known that sound he'd heard hadn't come from any man. Even Elyse had used the excuse of kittens crying. What had ever made him think that high-pitched little wail had come from a man?

"Because you wanted to think the worst of her, that's why," he muttered to himself. Shaking his head with disgust, Nathan sank down in the straw in the stall where he'd taken up residence and leaned his back against the rough wall.

A baby. An eight-month-old baby. So, she'd been pregnant that night. Pregnant with the child of a man she'd married and lived with and loved. A man who was now lying in the small, fenced-off plot at the side of their ramshackle little house. A man who had never seen his son, never even known of his existence.

"She's gone through a lot," he mused. "A dead husband, a baby to raise alone, a brother who dragged her into the middle of a bank robbery . . ."

Unbidden, the vision of Elyse he'd held in his heart for the past year swam before his eyes. He shook his head, wanting to clear it. He wanted to dislike her, wanted to join the townsfolk in their hostile animosity toward her, wanted to believe every nasty, slanderous word he'd heard about her.

But, damn it, he just couldn't. And as much as he'd wanted not to believe her this morning when she'd angrily explained what had motivated her to get involved with her brother's nefarious activities, he was sure she'd been telling the truth.

"He's my brother. What would you do if it was your brother?" Again, her desperate words floated through his mind. Yes, she'd lied to him, deceived him, seduced him. But she'd done it to protect her brother.

"What would you do if it was your brother?"

"The same thing you did, sweetheart. Whatever it took." With a heavy sigh, Nathan flung away the piece of straw he'd been chewing on and tried to make himself comfortable on his makeshift bed. "She's right, you know, Major Jones," he mumbled, closing his eyes. "There are hundreds of Rangers in the state who could have done this job. Why did you have to pick me?"

Nathan came awake with a jerk, then looked around groggily, wondering what had disturbed him. He shivered, and pulled his coarse blanket around him more tightly. It was raining. Not a slow, gentle summer rain, but an incessant, pounding downpour—the kind of rain that was bound to last the whole night.

With a disgusted frown, he looked up at the leaking roof. "It rarely rains in June," he mimicked. "You'll be fine."

Even though he had deliberately chosen a stall under a small portion of the roof that still looked sound, the wind was blowing the rain in through the many holes around it. It was cold and damp in the drafty old building, and, for the hundredth time, Nathan cursed the day he'd accepted this assignment.

He couldn't remember when he'd been more miserable. Even when he was on a job that forced him to sleep outside, he could usually find shelter in a cave somewhere and build a fire to keep himself warm. Here, in this tumbledown old firetrap, not even that small modicum of comfort was possible.

"Enough is enough," he growled, throwing off the soggy blanket and getting to his feet. "I'm sleepin' in the house tonight whether she likes it or not."

Pulling open the heavy barn door, he stepped out into the cold, rainswept night. The shock of the water pelting his face made him gasp and, quickly, he lowered his head into the wind and raced, slipping and sliding, across the muddy yard. He leaped up onto the porch, heedless of the rotting boards, and came to a skidding halt in front of the door, shaking himself like a wet dog. To his surprise, the door opened a crack, even before he knocked.

"What do you want?" Elyse asked, peering out at him warily.

"Someplace dry to sleep."

She hesitated, as if weighing the validity of his request.

"Come on, Mrs. Graham, I'm soaked! I just want to sleep on the floor of your front room. That barn is leaking like a sieve."

Slowly, Elyse pulled the door open. "It's not much better in here."

Nathan walked into the small room and looked around in astonishment. There were literally dozens of pans and bowls scattered about, each plinking merrily as drops of water seeped through the roof and splashed into them.

"This is terrible!" he barked, rounding on her. "Why the hell don't you get your roof fixed?"

"Don't swear at me, Captain Wellesley. Not that it's any of your business, but the roof doesn't get fixed because I don't have the money to do so. All right?"

Nathan was immediately contrite. "I'm sorry. You're right, it *is* none of my business."

A tense silence ensued as they stood on opposite ends of the little room staring at each other, both of them thinking about the last time they'd been together on a rainy night.

The tension escalated as Elyse saw Nathan's eyes slide over to the settee. "I'm going to bed now," she said abruptly.

"Is it leaking in there, too?" Nathan asked her retreating back.

Without turning, she nodded mutely.

"Is your baby dry?"

Whirling around, she glared at him. "Of course my baby's dry! Do you think I'd allow water to drip on him?"

"I didn't mean that."

"What did you mean, then?"

"I mean . . . hell, I don't know what I meant. Is there anything you want me to do?"

"Absolutely not. Good night, Captain Wellesley." Again Elyse started for the bedroom and, again, Nathan's voice stopped her.

"How bad is it leaking in there?"

Elyse's hands clenched at her sides. Why did he keep asking these questions? What was he trying to do—wangle a way into her bedroom? "What different does it make?" she asked, throwing him a quelling look over her shoulder.

Nathan sighed. "There's no reason to be so hostile, Mrs. Graham." He flung an arm out, gesturing toward a chair with a quilt flung over it. "I just noticed that you seemed to be sleeping out here, and I wondered if it was because your bedroom leaked even worse than this room does."

"I *was* sleeping out here, but not because of that. I just figured that I better stay here to empty the bowls when they filled up. Is that all right with you?"

Despite his annoyance at her rudeness, Nathan's heart again went out to her. She was obviously facing a sleepless night in her efforts to keep her little house from flooding, even though she probably had a busy day ahead of her, taking care of her baby and trying to dry things out that hadn't escaped the insistent dripping through the roof.

"You go on to bed," he said quietly. "I'll empty the bowls."

"That's not necessary. You made it perfectly clear earlier that you weren't here to assist me with anything, and I wouldn't want you to put yourself out."

Nathan's lips tightened. "That's not what I said. What I said was, I'll help you if and when I feel it's necessary. I'm offering to empty the bowls. Why can't you just be gracious about accepting my offer and leave it at that?"

"Because I don't want to feel beholden to you in any way," she retorted. "Now, please, just leave the bowls. I will clean up the water in the morning."

By now, it was Nathan who was clenching his fists. "Fine! If that's the way you want it, then be my guest." Whipping the quilt off the chair, he found a reasonably dry patch on the floor and threw it down.

"Captain Wellesley, I don't want you to . . ."

"Good night, Mrs. Graham."

Without another word, Elyse turned and walked into the bedroom, closing the door much more forcefully than necessary.

Elyse was awake before first light the next morning, but when she hurried out of the bedroom, still pushing pins into her hair, Nathan was already gone.

She looked around the room, expecting the floor to be covered with puddles, but there were none. Obviously, despite her insistence that Nathan not empty the bowls and pans, he had done so anyway. "Stubborn man," she muttered, walking over and starting to gather up the empty containers. "If I'd asked him to help, he undoubtedly would have said no. Just because I told him not to, he did it." Shaking her head, she dropped the dirty bowls into the sink. As she started pumping water, a wry smile tipped the corner of her mouth. "Maybe this could work to my advantage," she mused. "Maybe if I tell him that I just love having him here, he'll leave. It would certainly be worth a try!"

She was folding a load of newly washed diapers when she first heard the banging on the roof. Scooping up the baby, she raced out the front door and hurried across the yard, skirting her flower garden to get far enough away from the house that she could see up on the roof.

To her complete astonishment, there was Nathan, straddling the peak and energetically nailing in what looked like a new shingle.

"Captain Wellesley, what are you doing?"

Nathan laid his hammer across his lap and looked down. God, but she looked beautiful. The sun was shining on her golden hair, illuminating her from the back and making her look like an angel who had just touched earth, bringing some lucky family the gift of a cherubic child who looked just like her.

"Captain!" Elyse's voice was sharper, more demanding. "I asked you what you're doing?"

"What do you think I'm doing?" Nathan called back irritably, all traces of his romantic musings evaporating. "I'm fixing your roof."

"But . . . how? I don't have any new shingles. At least, I don't think I do. Did you find those in the barn?"

"No."

Elyse continued to look up at the handsome man sitting so confidently on her roof. "Then, where . . ."

"I rode into town this morning and bought them," he muttered.

"What? I can't hear you."

"I said, *I rode into town this morning and bought them!*"

Elyse's surprise was rampant in her expression. "Where did you buy them?"

"At Richman's General Store."

If possible, her eyes widened even further. Richman's! How could he have bought anything for her at Richman's? Her credit had long since been canceled with the merchant and there was no way in the world Mr. Richman would have allowed Nathan to buy the vast quantity of shingles piled up next to the house without giving him hard cash for the purchase.

"How did you pay for them?"

Nathan pretended not to hear her question. Instead, he picked up his hammer and again began whacking at the half-attached shingle.

"Captain Wellesley!" Elyse yelled.

With a defeated sigh, Nathan put the hammer down again. "Yes, Mrs. Graham?"

"How did you pay for all these new shingles?"

Nathan hesitated a moment, then with a shrug, answered, "You're under the protection of the State of Texas."

Elyse looked at him in bafflement. What did that have to do with anything? "So?"

"So . . ." Nathan hammered in another nail, playing for time.

"So?" Elyse prodded. "What does my status with the government of Texas have to do with a new roof for my house?"

Nathan intentionally stuck the snub end of several nails between his teeth, knowing that having them there would muffle his words and, hopefully, cover the lie he was about to tell.

"So," he mumbled from between pressed lips, "the state paid for them."

"What did you say?" Elyse called in exasperation. "I can't understand a word you're saying with your mouth full of nails."

Completely at his wit's end, Nathan spit the nails into his hand. "I said," he bellowed, "the State of Texas is paying for them!"

Elyse's mouth dropped open. "It is?" she gasped. "Well, I'll be. They'd do that just because I've agreed to cooperate with their investigation?"

"Yeah." Nathan nodded, quickly turning back to his task before she saw the guilty look on his face.

"That's right nice of them."

"Right nice," Nathan muttered. *Why* didn't she go back in the house where she belonged? Any minute now, she was going to figure out how preposterous his explanation was, and he was either going to be forced to continue to lie to her or tell her the truth—that he had purchased the shingles with his own money. And that was something he *definitely* did not want her to know. "What would be right nice is if you'd go away," he mumbled. He didn't think his words had been loud enough for Elyse to hear, but when he glanced back down at her, he saw the indignation on her face and knew he'd been overheard.

"Fine," she snorted. "I'll leave you to your work." With a swish of her drab brown skirts, she headed back into the house.

Nathan's first inclination was to climb down off the roof and follow her, to tell her he hadn't meant to be rude. But how could he explain his snide remark to her when he didn't even understand it himself?

He'd been in her company for less than twenty-four hours, yet nothing he'd heard about her in town rang true. He'd been disappointed when he'd made his early morning trip to the general store and found the mercantile deserted except for the noncommittal proprietor. He'd been hoping to hear some more gossip that would explain what it was about Elyse that the townsfolk seemed to despise. Hoped to figure out why his impression of her was so different from everyone else's. Most of all, he wanted to hear something—anything—that would quell the undeniable, and unwanted, attraction he still felt for her.

"As soon as I finish with this roof, I'll go in and see

Red," he promised himself. "Maybe he knows something."

With renewed vigor, he positioned another shingle, wondering, not for the first time, why he had elected to fix Elyse's roof before seeing to his own shelter in the leaky barn.

He shook his head, dispelling the annoying thought. That was a decision he refused to allow himself to explore.

Chapter 8

Nathan walked into the tiny telegraph office and nodded impersonally at his colleague, Red Hilliard. "Need to send a wire."

"Yes, sir," Red answered, handing a receipt to an older woman standing at the counter. "That's what we're here for."

Nonchalantly, Nathan dug into his pocket and pulled out a crumpled scrap of paper. Unfolding it, he shoved it across the counter.

Red glanced down at it briefly as the little bell above the doorway tinkled, admitting another customer. *Need to talk. Is there somewhere private we can meet?*

Red looked up from the message, his expression bland. "Yes, sir. This shouldn't be any problem at all. I'll be closing down for lunch in about fifteen minutes, but I'll try to get this sent before that."

"How much do I owe you?" Nathan asked.

"Eighty-five cents."

Digging into his pocket again, Nathan pulled out the required coins, slapped them on the counter and turned to leave.

"Thank you, sir," Red called after him.

Nathan nodded blandly and exited the office. Turning onto Main Street, he idly strolled down the boardwalk, gazing into shop windows and nodding agreeably to several town matrons who passed by, wicker shopping baskets swinging from their arms.

He whiled away the next twenty minutes, getting his first good look at Bixby, then retraced his steps back to the telegraph office. The sign in the window said, "Closed For One Hour," so he proceeded around the building and knocked at the back door.

"Nate," Red grinned, pulling open the door. "Come on in."

Nathan returned his friend's greeting and stepped into the small, dingy room Red was currently calling home.

"It's good to see you," Red said, motioning Nathan to one of two chairs flanking a small table. "I've got some bad whiskey here. Want a drink?"

"No thanks," Nathan declined. "I can't stay long. I don't think anybody saw me come in here, but I don't want to arouse any suspicion."

Red nodded and sank into the other chair. "Well, I'm damn glad you finally got here. Me and Will were beginning to wonder if Major Jones was ever gonna get this operation under way."

"How long have you been here?" Nathan asked.

"Too long. A little over a month already. Will got here about three weeks ago. I tell you, Nate, I hate these undercover jobs in these stinkin' little towns. A man could go stir crazy livin' here."

"You don't like Bixby, huh?"

Red got up, walked over to a wooden shelf and picked up a bottle and two glasses. Returning to the table, he uncorked the bottle and poured a shot into each glass. "You could say that. From what I've seen, it's even more narrow-minded than Pratt, and I didn't think that was possible."

"Pratt?" Nathan questioned. "Where's that?"

"Oh, you know, that little dump that I had to hole up in last year when I was on the Pfarr case."

"Oh, yeah," Nathan chuckled. "Wasn't that the place

that was so small, it wasn't on a map and it took you two days just to find it?"

"Yeah," Red nodded. "That's the one."

Picking up the drink he'd said he didn't want, Nathan took a long swallow. "You're right, Red. This is real rotgut stuff."

Red shrugged. "Told you it was, but at least Bixby has a saloon so you can get a drink, even if it's not good. Pratt didn't even have that."

Nathan took another drink, winced, and set down his empty glass. "So, what's going on? Any word from Jones about the gang?"

Red shook his head. "Nothin' yet."

"Has Will overheard anything from the townsfolk?"

"I don't think so. You know, the robbery happened so long ago, it's old news. The only thing anybody in town talks about now is your wild widow."

Nathan's eyebrows shot up. "You mean Elyse Graham?"

Red chuckled. "As far as I know, she's the only wild widow round these parts. So, tell me, Nate, has she tangled you in her web yet?"

Nathan sloshed another portion of whiskey into his glass, annoyed at the sudden surge of anger he felt at his friend's teasing. "Hardly. She's about as prickly as they come."

"Really?" Red seemed genuinely surprised. "That sure isn't what I've heard."

Nathan glanced at Red through narrowed eyes. "Actually, Mrs. Graham's reputation as the Wild Widow of Bixby is another reason I wanted to talk to you."

"Oh?"

"Yeah. I heard the same gossip in town that I'm sure you did and, frankly, Red, I can't figure it out. What did she do to get this reputation?"

Red leaned back in his chair and looked at Nathan incredulously. "Well, I think havin' an illegitimate child is a good start."

Nathan's glass hit the table with a bang. "Illegitimate? What the hell are you talking about?"

"What do you think I'm talkin' about? That baby of hers. Seems no one in town quite knows who his daddy is."

Nathan shook his head, genuinely confused. "She told me the kid belongs to her dead husband. That she was expecting at the time he was killed."

Red let out a loud guffaw. "Then it was the longest pregnancy in history, because, according to the good wives of Bixby, *Mister* Graham has been dead goin' on four years now."

For a long moment, Nathan just stared at Red as he tried to absorb what his friend had so laughingly confided. When he finally found his voice, he croaked, "Four years?"

"Yeah, four years. I heard he was killed by a tree fallin' on him or somethin' during a thunderstorm. I'm sure that gossipy old crone, Miss Dixon, said it was four summers ago."

"Lightning," Nathan mumbled.

"What?"

"The husband was killed by lightning."

Red shrugged. "Whatever. Some freak accident, anyway. But the widow told you that the baby belonged to her husband?"

Nathan nodded dumbly.

"Why do you s'pose she lied to you?" Red asked. "Embarrassed, probably," he continued, answering his own question. Leaning over, he gave Nathan a punch on the arm. "I bet the widow took one look at that pretty face of yours and figured you were a fella of high moral fiber, so she didn't want you to think bad about her."

"I doubt that," Nathan muttered. "She barely speaks to me and I don't think she gives a damn what I think about her."

"I bet you're wrong about that," Red chuckled.

"There isn't a woman in the world, 'less she's sellin' it in some saloon, that wants a man to think she's loose."

"Mrs. Graham isn't loose," Nathan growled, surprising Red with his vehemence.

"Well, she didn't get that kid from under a cabbage leaf, Nate, and she hasn't been married for four years. In my book, that means she's had at least a lapse or two."

Nathan clamped down hard on his quickly rising temper and got to his feet. "I've gotta go. Thanks for the drink."

"What's your hurry?" Red asked. "I don't have to be back at that damn telegraph office for another twenty minutes. Sit a spell longer."

Nathan shook his head. "No. I've got things I've got to do. Tell Will to keep his ears open and I'll try to be back in touch with one or both of you in the next week."

"Okay," Red sighed. "If I hear anything important, I'll have a boy run a message out to you."

Nathan nodded and started for the door.

"Hey, Nate," Red called after him. "You watch yourself around that wild little gal now, you hear?"

"Yeah, Red," Nathan responded without smiling. "I hear."

She's nothing but a lying little whore. For the thousandth time, the insulting words pounded through Nathan's brain as he galloped down the dusty road.

You were nothing special. That night was nothing special. She obviously does it all the time—probably with any man that happens by. She undoubtedly threw you out the next morning because you didn't offer to pay her for her services.

Furious at his own disparaging thoughts, Nathan pulled back hard on his horse's reins, causing the startled animal to nearly sit down. Dismounting, he stomped over to a scraggly grove of mesquite trees and threw himself down on the ground.

She had seduced him, rejected him, then baldfaced lied to him, so why couldn't he still the niggling little voice in the back of his mind that cautioned him not to judge her too harshly? He just kept feeling that she must have had *reasons* for her actions, and if he only knew what those reasons were, he would understand what had led her to such unconscionable behavior as giving birth to an illegitimate child.

But why had she lied to him about the baby's father? It wasn't as if he wouldn't find out. Obviously, everyone in town knew the child was a bastard. What had made her think he wouldn't hear the truth?

For long moments, Nathan stared out at the endless panorama of waving grass. There had to be a reason. There *had* to be. And the only way he was going to find out was to ask her.

With renewed resolve, Nathan rose and remounted his horse, turning in the direction of Elyse's farm. "It's time to come clean, Little Miss Deceitful," he muttered, "and if I have anything to say about it, come clean you will."

Elyse wasn't there when Nathan arrived. He looked everywhere, but she wasn't there. For the briefest moment, he felt panicked. But his years of training and experience soon cooled his inflamed senses and made him analyze the situation with a professional eye. Peering closely at the ground, he searched for tracks, but there was no sign that a group of horses had been anywhere near the house.

"No one's kidnapped her," he growled, disgusted with himself for being worried. "She's just decided to take off." Shielding his eyes against the late-afternoon sun, he scanned the horizon. Nothing. Just the endless expanse of prairie.

He walked back into the house, heading for Elyse's bedroom. Everything looked to be in its place. Her hairbrush was on the bureau, her meager wardrobe still hung from its pole, even the baby's diapers were stacked neatly on a little table in the corner. *If she was gonna run off, wouldn't she take the baby's diapers with her?* Again, he felt a fleeting rush of panic that, somehow, someone had forced her to leave . . . and leave hurriedly.

He was still standing in the center of her bedroom considering what he should do when he suddenly heard the front door open. Ignoring the tremendous wave of relief that washed over him, he wheeled around and strode into the front room. "Where have you been?"

Elyse was setting Colin down on a blanket in front of the fireplace. She looked up in surprise, and seeing Nathan's furious expression, her own face hardened. "I don't see that that's any of your business."

"I don't give a damn what you do or do not see," he snarled, his face flushing with anger at her defiance, "you're going to tell me where you've been, or—"

"Or what?" Elyse interrupted. "Are you going to do something to me if I don't tell you, Captain? Hit me, perhaps?"

Nathan's face got even redder. "Hit you! Of course I'm not going to hit you!"

"Well, I'm relieved to hear that," Elyse retorted sarcastically.

"Look, just tell me where you've been."

Elyse studied him for a moment, then shrugged. "I was visiting a friend."

"Who?"

"What difference does that make? A friend."

"It makes a difference. What is this friend's name?"

Elyse knew there wasn't a reason in the world for her not to tell the Ranger that she had been visiting her neighbor, Lynn Potter. Not a reason in the world . . . except that he was demanding that she do so. She turned her back on him, making a great pretense of straighten-

ing the cups on the shelf above the sink. "It's just someone I know. The name wouldn't mean anything to you."

Nathan stared at her rigid back, then cursed himself
as his eyes strayed to her rounded little bottom. "If the
name wouldn't mean anything to me, then why won't
you say it?"

"Because it's none of your business."

"Lady, as long as you're under my protection, everything you do is my business. Now, I'm gonna ask you
one more time . . . nicely. *What is your friend's name?*"

The steely thread in his voice caused Elyse's already
strained nerves to finally snap. Rounding on him, she
spat, "I didn't ask you to come here, Captain, and I
don't want your protection. Yet you are standing in my
home, asking me personal questions like I'm some kind
of criminal. Well, I'm not a criminal and I refuse to participate in this inquisition."

Nathan waited a long moment to respond, as if
weighing his words carefully. When he finally did speak,
his voice was very low. "That's just where you're wrong,
Mrs. Graham. You *are* a criminal. You harbored a fugitive and aided in his flight, knowing that he had committed a felony. You better start rethinking your
attitude, lady, because if it wasn't for the leniency of the
Texas judicial system, your pretty little fanny would
right this minute be resting on some stinkin' cot in some
stinkin' jail. And, as far as I'm concerned, that's exactly
where you *and* your bank-robbing brother belong."

Elyse's eyes flared wide at Nathan's hurtful words.
Unconsciously, she wrapped her arms protectively
around her middle as if shielding herself from his anger.
"I want you out of here," she whispered. "I want you to
go out to the barn or wherever else it is you spend your
time and leave me alone. You have no right to be in my
house. No right at all!"

"I have every right!" Nathan thundered, losing the
battle with his tightly controlled temper. "The State of
Texas has ordered me to protect you!"

"Protect me!" Elyse shrieked, tears springing to her eyes. "You haven't done anything that even smacks of protecting me. All you've done is intimidate me and harass me and scare me."

Despite Nathan's roiling anger, her last two words sank in. Taking a step backward, he studied her closely. "Scare you? What have I done to scare you?"

"What haven't you done?" she retorted. "You yell at me, you threaten me, you browbeat me about where I've been and who I've been with. You glare at me, you criticize me, you . . . oh, never mind!" Bending down, she scooped up the baby who was by this time screaming at the top of his lungs, frightened by their loud, strident voices. "Now look what you've done," Elyse accused, tears running down her cheeks. "You've made Colin cry again!" With a desperate lunge, she pushed her way past Nathan, streaking into her bedroom and slamming the door behind her.

For a long moment, Nathan stood and stared at the ill-fitting little bedroom door, wondering how a simple question had spawned such a hullabaloo. Then, with a low, frustrated curse, he pivoted on his heel and stalked out to the soggy sanctuary of the barn.

"Now, don't you worry, little man," Elyse crooned, bending over Colin's rickety cradle and giving him a loving pat. "Mama won't let that mean man scare you anymore. You just go to sleep and everything will be fine in the morning."

She smiled down at her baby—her blond, blue-eyed baby who looked so much like his father.

Irritated that she should, as always, notice the startling resemblance between Nathan Wellesley and her son, she gave Colin a last kiss and turned away.

Blowing out the lamp on the bureau, she crawled into bed, turning on her side and staring out the window at the huge Texas moon.

"Lord but I wish he'd go away," she whispered into the darkness. Unbidden, Nathan's face rose in her mind. How could any man be so handsome and yet so unpleasant?

"If only he'd shown his real self that first night, none of this would have happened and your life wouldn't be the shambles it is now," she told herself.

But, as she thought again of that night, a sensual little shiver ran through her. His arms had been so strong, his kisses so passionate, his voice so deep and seductive . . . Could she really regret those hours when she'd languished in his embrace? And could she really regret the gift that those moments of ecstasy had given her? Regret the existence of her beautiful little boy?

"Of course I don't," she whispered, smiling over at her sleeping son. "But, despite the fact that he gave me you, I still wish he'd go away!"

Chapter 9

Elyse stood at the front door of the neat little ranch house, holding Colin. "Lynn?" she called softly. "Lynn? It's Elyse." Out of the corner of her eye, she could see the lace curtain in the front room being pulled aside. Then, a moment later, the door opened.

"Good morning, Elyse. How are you?"

"Fine, dear," Elyse answered, looking into the ravaged face of her best friend. "And you?"

"I'm all right, I guess. I'm just taking some scones out of the oven. Would you like one?"

Elyse nodded and stepped into the immaculate house. "Absolutely. I never pass up one of your scones. They're the best I've ever tasted."

Lynn smiled, a lopsided grimace that stretched her scarred lips at an odd angle. Elyse didn't even notice, so accustomed was she to the sight of her friend's disfigurement.

"Today's the day, you know," Lynn said quietly as they walked into her large, airy kitchen.

"What day is that?" Elyse asked, knowing full well what her friend meant.

"The fire. It was a year ago today. A whole year since I lost Jonathan and Isabelle." Lynn closed her eyes and, helplessly, Elyse watched tears seep through her lashes. "A whole year since . . . this." She waved her hand in front of her scarred face.

"Oh, my dearest," Elyse murmured, setting Colin down and wrapping her arms around her friend, "try not to think about it. It does no good to torture yourself. No good at all."

"I know," Lynn sobbed, "but how can I help but think about it? I lost everything that day. Everything— and all because of some spilled kerosene!"

"You didn't lose everything," Elyse comforted. "You still have your memories, and you have many, many friends who love you."

"Oh, Elyse, you know that's not true. There isn't a person in town who will look me in the face anymore."

"You don't know that, Lynn. If you would just go into town with me sometime, you'd see that people wouldn't treat you any differently than they ever did. The only one who's concerned about your appearance is you. Everyone understands what happened, and no one thinks anything about it. Your friends care about *you*, dear . . . not about your face."

"You're sweet to say that, but I know it isn't true. I've seen the horror on people's faces when they look at me. I've seen how they turn away, hoping I won't notice how repelled they are. And to think, I used to be so pretty that the young men would argue over who got to walk me home from church. Now what do I have left? My husband and daughter are dead and I look like a monster. Sometimes I wish I'd died with them."

"Stop it, Lynn!" Elyse said vehemently "I won't listen." Seeing her friend's tormented expression, her voice softened. "You have to get over this. You have to get out among the living again. You can't spend the rest of your life hiding in this house seeing only me. It's just not . . . normal."

"Normal," Lynn croaked. "I don't even know what normal is anymore."

At that moment, Colin let out a loud, demanding wail, tired of being ignored by the two women who usually fawned over him. Elyse stepped away from Lynn and handed her a handkerchief. "I'll tell you what normal is," she chuckled, determined to try to lighten her friend's bleak mood. "Normal is this baby demanding attention. If you'll pick him up, I'll pour tea and serve these scones."

Drawing a shuddering breath, Lynn nodded and plucked Colin off his blanket, holding him close. She smiled down at the baby, making a valiant effort to shake off her melancholy. "I don't think I've ever seen a prettier baby, Elyse."

Elyse turned around and gazed lovingly at her son. "I must admit, I'm a bit partial to him myself."

"He looks just like you, you know."

Elyse turned quickly back to the stove. *No, he doesn't,* she thought. *He may have my blond hair and blue eyes, but if you saw his father, you'd realize who he really looks like.* Aloud, she said, "I'll take that as a compliment."

"You should. He's beautiful. He always reminds me of a cherub in a church window."

Elyse chuckled at her friend's analogy and set two cups and a plate of warm scones on a small table. "He might look like a cherub, but he certainly doesn't act like one. He's so fussy all the time, I just don't know what to do with him."

"Maybe he's teething," Lynn suggested. "Sometimes rubbing a little brandy on the gums will help that."

"Brandy!" Elyse exclaimed. "I can't give a baby spirits!"

"Of course you can. I used to do it with Isabelle all the time . . ." Lynn's voice trailed off and a look of profound sadness crossed her face at the mention of her daughter.

Quickly, Elyse sat down and said brightly, "Tell me what you have been up to around here. I haven't seen you in almost a week."

Lynn brushed away a tear and hugged Colin closer to her. "I know, it seems like forever since you were last here. I was beginning to worry."

"I'm sorry. I certainly didn't mean to worry you. It's just that it's ... difficult to get away."

Lynn's eyebrows rose questioningly. "Difficult? Why?"

"Oh, it's that awful Ranger. He watches every move I make, and if I do manage to slip away for a few hours, he's waiting for me when I get back, demanding to know where I've been and who I've been with."

"I'm sure he's just doing his job, Elyse."

Elyse snorted contemptuously. "His job! I don't believe his job includes rummaging around in my bedroom."

"What?" Lynn gasped. "He did that?"

"Well, I don't know for sure that he was rummaging exactly. But the last time I came to see you, he was in my bedroom when I got home."

Lynn shuddered delicately. "How terrible! What do you suppose he was looking for?"

"I have no idea, and I wasn't about to ask him."

"I feel so sorry for you, dear. You've been through so much in the last few years, and now having to put up with this. It must be a terrible strain. Is this man really awful? I mean, is he coarse and crude and ugly?"

Elyse's lips twitched at her friend's assumptions. "No," she said honestly. "He's not ... ugly and he's not coarse, either. And I've never heard him be crude. As a matter of fact, he's quite polite most of the time, and I'm sure there are some women who would find him ... handsome."

Lynn raised a speculative eyebrow at her friend's faraway look and took a thoughtful sip of tea. "He sounds absolutely dreadful," she said wryly.

Elyse pinned her with an outraged look. "He *is!* He's so nosy and bossy, he just drives me crazy!"

Lynn reached over and patted Elyse's hand. "Forgive me. I didn't mean to tease you. It's just that you're talking out of both sides of your mouth about this man. In one breath, you're saying he's awful and domineering and in the next, you're saying that he's handsome and polite."

Elyse shrugged in resignation. "I guess, if the truth be known, he's a little bit of all of those things. Sometimes he's fine, but other times, he's just too overbearing to be borne."

"Where does he sleep?" Lynn asked nonchalantly.

Elyse's eyes widened at the provocative question. "In the barn, of course."

"In that leaky old place? No wonder he's ill-tempered!"

"Well, where else would I put him? He's certainly not going to sleep in Tom's room!"

"Of course not. That wouldn't be appropriate at all."

"It certainly wouldn't. Why, what would the people in town say if they heard he was staying in the house? I'm sure there's enough talk already about a single woman who lives alone hiring a hand." Despite herself, Elyse's eyes strayed over to Colin who was now drowsing in Lynn's arms. "Especially when that single woman is me . . ."

Lynn looked at her friend sympathetically, knowing that what Elyse said was true. Although she had often wondered who the father of Elyse's baby was, she had never asked, knowing that if Elyse wanted her to know, she would tell her.

And, unlike the other gossipy women in Bixby, Lynn also refused to take part in their random conjectures and sneering innuendos. Elyse was her closest friend, and Lynn felt very protective of that precious relationship.

"Anyway," Elyse continued, "he's just not the kind of man a woman would be comfortable with having in the next room."

"Really? You make him sound quite dangerous."

"He's not dangerous, I don't think. He's just too big. Too masculine. Oh, I don't know. Too *something!*"

Lynn hesitated a moment and then said, "Elyse, are you attracted to this man?"

"Attracted!" Elyse gasped. "Of course I'm not attracted to him. Why would you think that?"

"I don't know, there's just something about the way you talk about him and the look you get when you do."

"Well, I'm *not* attracted to him, I can assure you. He's not my type at all. I told you, he's nosy and overbearing and . . ."

"Big and masculine and handsome," Lynn finished.

Abruptly, Elyse rose from the table, picking up the empty teacups and returning them to the counter. "I'm *not* attracted," she insisted, furious that her hands were shaking. "I'm just trying to explain to you what he's like. I guess you'd have to meet him to fully understand."

"That's something that will never happen," Lynn said quietly.

"I wouldn't be too sure. That's another problem I'm having with him."

Lynn's looked at her apprehensively. "What do you mean?"

"He's been asking me questions about you. Last time I was here, when I got home, he demanded to know where I'd been. When I told him I'd been visiting a friend, he wanted to know your name."

"Oh, dear!" Lynn cried, clearly agitated. "I don't want him to see me!"

"Don't worry, I didn't tell him anything."

"Does he know that I know who he really is?"

Elyse shook her head and returned to the table. "No. That Major Jones made me promise I wouldn't say anything to anyone. Something about 'blowing his cover,' whatever that means. I suppose I really shouldn't have confided everything to you, but I had to talk to someone!"

"You needn't worry, Elyse. Your secret, and his, are safe with me."

"I know they are, and I appreciate that." Elyse hesitated, then added quietly, "I suppose he really isn't so bad. After all, he did fix the roof of my house when he didn't have to."

Lynn set her cup down and gaped at Elyse in astonishment. "He fixed the roof of your house?"

Elyse nodded.

"Has he fixed the barn, too?"

"No."

"So," Lynn mused, "he thought about your comfort before his own."

Elyse shifted uneasily in her chair. "Now, don't go getting any ideas about anything, Lynn. I'll admit, the man did me a good turn, fixing my roof, but that's the only nice thing he's done or said since he arrived."

"He really bothers you, doesn't he?"

Elyse nodded. "I think the thing that bothers me is that he's so . . . demanding."

"Demanding? In what way?"

"He asks so many questions. I know he doesn't trust me and I'm afraid he thinks that when I leave to visit you, I'm actually meeting some member of that gang or something. Why, I wouldn't be surprised if he followed me."

Lynn's hand circled her throat. "Do you think he followed you today?"

"No, I *know* he didn't. He went into town for some things he said he needed. He goes into town a lot, thank goodness. It's the only time I feel I can relax and be myself. In fact, I better get home before he returns and finds I've been gone. Otherwise I'll have to spend the rest of the day trying to ward off his questions."

Lynn nodded in understanding and rose from the table. "I have some sewing I'd like you to do, if you have time."

Elyse smiled gratefully. At one time, she had been the premiere seamstress in Bixby, making all types of clothes for less talented women. Since Colin's birth and her subsequent disgrace, however, her little business had fallen off until Lynn was the only woman who still used her services. Elyse knew that Lynn was perfectly capable of making and mending her own clothes, but she was terribly grateful for the coins her friend's largesse afforded her. "A new dress, Lynn? Now that your year of official mourning is over, you could start wearing something besides black."

"I don't want a new dress," Lynn said firmly. "I just have some old pants that need mending."

Elyse laughed, a melodic, rippling sound that had been heard all too seldom in the past year. "You and your pants! You really are a renegade, Lynn Potter."

"I keep telling you, you should try wearing pants," Lynn chuckled. "Chores are so much easier to do when you don't have to fight a long skirt and petticoats. Besides, who's going to see us? No one will ever know."

"I'm afraid that's not quite true for me anymore."

"I guess you're right, what with your new boarder, but as soon as all this is over and he's gone, you really should give it a try."

As the women walked toward the front door, Lynn picked up a folded pair of pants from a marble-topped table and handed them to Elyse. "You will come again soon, won't you?"

"As soon as I can. Is there anything you need from town?"

Lynn shook her head. "No, the supplies you brought me last week should last awhile longer."

They walked out into the yard, and Elyse mounted her horse, then reached down to take the sleeping baby. "Take care, dear," she said, looking down at Lynn with a smile. "And try not to be too sad."

Lynn shook her head mournfully. "I'll do my best, but telling me not to be sad is sort of like telling the wind not to blow. Anyway, you take care, too, and watch yourself with Mr. Big, Masculine, and Handsome. Better not get too close to him."

Elyse settled Colin in the crook of her arm and

clucked to the horse. "You needn't worry about that. The farther away from that man I stay, the happier I am."

Chapter 10

"Where the hell have you been?"

Elyse glared down at the man so arrogantly holding her horse's reins. "I've told you before," she retorted icily. "It's none of your business." With a quick wrench of the reins, she jerked them out of Nathan's grasp and gave her horse a hard kick, sending the unsuspecting animal leaping forward toward the barn.

"Damn you!" Nathan shouted after her, shaking his hand where the leather had burned it.

Elyse refused to look back. Instead, she trotted the horse through the barn door, ducking at the last minute so she didn't decapitate herself. *Why oh why did he have to get back before I did? Now it'll be one long interrogation all afternoon.*

She pulled the horse to a halt in front of his stall, not hearing Nathan's approach until he was beside her. "Are you absolutely nuts?" he demanded. "You should know better than to ride a horse into a barn. What if he shied or reared as you went through the door? You could kill yourself!"

Elyse remained silent. He was right, of course. No one with a lick of sense rode a horse into a barn, regardless of how docile the animal might be. She had no defense for her recklessness, except that Nathan made her so mad that she couldn't think straight.

"I don't know why you care," she muttered, hitching

up her skirt to dismount. "If I killed myself, you wouldn't have to stay around here to protect me any longer. I would think that would suit you just fine."

"Shut up and give me that baby."

Elyse looked down at him in astonishment, amazed not only by his crude command, but because he was reaching up, actually intending to take Colin out of her arms. He had never shown any interest in the baby before, and his sudden order that she hand over her son to him caused a mutinous expression to cross her face. Clutching Colin closer to her, she said simply, "No."

"What do you mean, no? Just hand me the baby while you dismount. It's hard enough trying to get off a horse when you're inside a barn, much less while you're holding a baby, too."

"I can manage just fine." Awkwardly, she attempted to swing her leg over the horse's back.

"Oh, for God's sake!" Nathan cursed, reaching up and plucking her bodily out of the saddle. "You are, without a doubt, the most stubborn, pigheaded . . ." With an arcing motion, he swung her around and set her on her feet.

Still clutching the baby tightly to her breast, Elyse threw him a furious look. "I don't know who you think you are . . ."

"Do you have any idea how dangerous it is riding all over the countryside with that baby in your arms? One tumble and . . ."

"I beg your pardon!" Elyse blazed. "I'll have you know, I'm an excellent rider and there's nowhere this child is safer than in my arms."

Nathan's eyes raked over her dubiously. "There isn't a woman in the world who can ride well enough to carry a baby with her."

"Oh? And I suppose you can."

Nathan allowed himself a smug smile. "Well, you know what they say about the Texas Rangers, don't you?"

"No, and I don't care to, either."

Nathan went on as if she hadn't spoken. "A good Ranger can 'ride like a Mexican, trail like an Indian, shoot like a Tennesseean, and fight like a devil.' "

Elyse's snort of disgust told him just what she thought of his self-serving words. "You're pretty full of yourself, aren't you, Captain?"

Nathan shrugged, still smiling. "I didn't say that *I* said that, Mrs. Graham. I said that it's said about us." Before Elyse had a chance to hurl another barb, he continued, "Why don't you make some kind of sling for the baby?"

Elyse blinked in surprise. "A sling?"

"Yeah. You know, like the Indians use. You strap the baby on your back and then you have both hands free to control your horse."

Elyse thought about that for a moment, then said, "What would you make a sling out of? It would have to be a pretty heavy material . . ."

"The Indians use hides and leather."

"Well, unfortunately, I happen to be fresh out of hides," she said sarcastically, then turned back to the horse, trying to uncinch the saddle with one hand while still holding Colin.

"Here, let me do that," Nathan instructed, stepping in front of her.

Elyse heaved a long, impatient sigh. "Captain Wellesley, I have been doing everything while holding this baby for several months now. I assure you, I'm capable of pulling a saddle off a horse's back."

Nathan slid the saddle off and swung it over the front of the stall. Despite her annoyance, Elyse found herself watching the ripple of muscles through the thin cotton of his shirt with decidedly feminine appreciation.

Nathan threw the blanket on top of the saddle and turned back toward her, brushing the dust off his hands. "Have you fed this horse this morning or did you just take off without thinking about that?"

All feelings of admiration instantly disappeared. "Of course I fed him! Long before you were even awake."

Nathan quickly looked away, not wanting her to know that he had, indeed, been awake when she'd come into the barn early that morning, clad in nothing but her wrapper and with her hair still down. He had, in fact, stayed under his blanket for several long minutes after she'd left, fighting back an infuriatingly insistent erection that the sight of her shapely little body beneath the nearly transparent robe had brought on. "Well, I'm glad to know that you were at least that responsible," he muttered. "It's the only sensible thing you've done all day."

Elyse riveted him with a hard look. "If I understood Major Jones correctly, you are not here, sir, to pass judgment on me and the way I live my life. You are here only to protect me should the need arise. Now, if you will excuse me, I am going in the house and feed my son his lunch."

Nathan swallowed hard, trying not to think about where her son's lunch was going to come from. Annoyed by his wayward thoughts, he called after her. "As soon as you're finished with . . . that, I want to talk to you about where you were this morning."

"I'm sorry, I don't have time to talk," Elyse called back. "I shall be quite busy this afternoon."

"Make time, Mrs. Graham."

Elyse's step faltered. Looking over her shoulder, she threw Nathan a look that was almost beseeching. "Please, Captain, I have things I have to do. I have a baby to take care of, a house to tend, and supper to prepare. I really don't have time for another one of your endless interrogations. I assure you, I was visiting the same friend who I visited the other day. That's all. It has nothing to do with you."

"And what is the friend's name?"

Elyse frowned, tamping down hard on her temper.

"I'll tell you once more, Captain, and this time, please try to listen. *It is none of your business!*"

Without waiting for his inevitable retort, she stomped up the porch steps, pointedly ignoring Nathan when he shouted, "Feed that baby quick, lady. I'm comin' in to talk to you within the hour."

For the next several hours, Elyse's eyes strayed constantly to the small clock which sat atop the mantel, but Nathan didn't come. As the afternoon wore on, she became more and more apprehensive, dreading the confrontation she knew was imminent, yet wishing he would get it over with.

By suppertime, she had stopped feeling apprehensive and was just plain mad. How *dare* he demand to talk to her and then not show up, she thought angrily as she stirred up a pan of biscuits. Well, two could play his little game. If he wanted her to cool her heels waiting for him, then he could do the same—without his supper.

She ate a solitary meal of biscuits and bacon, cleaned up the kitchen, put Colin to bed and sat down to mend Lynn's pants. Still, Nathan didn't show up.

Where was he? She figured he was sitting out in the barn, gleefully contemplating how she must be squirming as she waited for him, but when she went out to give the stock their evening feed, he wasn't there.

"Well, who cares, anyway?" she asked herself, stabbing her needle through the thick material of Lynn's pants. "Maybe he went back to town and got diverted by some simpering saloon girl." For some reason, that thought made her even angrier and, with a snort of disgust, she threw the half-mended pants aside.

For several long minutes, she sat and rocked, trying hard to understand her unreasonable fit of pique. "I should be relieved," she told herself firmly. But, for some reason, Nathan's failure to keep their "appointment" made her feel anything but. What if something had happened to him? What if the Rosas gang had shown up and done something to him? Why, even now, he could be lying somewhere wounded or dead—and she would be totally without protection if the outlaws decided to invade her home.

Having worked herself up into a state of near panic, Elyse rose from her rocker and started pacing the small confines of her cabin. Twice she opened the door to her bedroom, squinting into the darkness to make sure Colin was safely asleep in his cradle. It was now nearly nine o'clock—way past time that any decent man would appear at a lady's door.

Warily, Elyse peeked out the front window in the direction of the barn, hoping to see a light. Instead, she nearly leaped out of her skin when a man's form suddenly appeared on the other side of the glass.

With a small scream of terror, she jumped back, clapping her hands over her mouth. Before she could collect herself enough to bolt the cabin door, it flew open to reveal Nathan poised in the doorway, his gun in one hand, a burlap bag in the other.

"Don't shoot!" Elyse screamed. "It's just me!"

Immediately, Nathan lowered his gun. "Jesus Christ!" he bellowed. "What are you screamin' about? I thought someone was in here with you!"

It was a moment before Elyse could calm herself enough to speak. When she finally did, her voice was still shaking with fear and anger. "Why do you always find it necessary to barge into my house with your gun drawn?"

Nathan's mouth tightened angrily. "Because I'm always hearing something in here that isn't normal. Babies who I don't even know exist start crying, or you start screaming . . ." His voice trailed off abruptly as he again scanned the room. ". . . and apparently for no good reason. What the hell has you so stirred up?"

"What has me so 'stirred up,' as you call it, is you

skulking around my front door in the middle of the night!"

"It's hardly the middle of the night and I wasn't skulking!"

"Then what were you doing?"

"I was bringing you this." He held out the burlap bag.

"What's that?"

"Well, if you'll quit being so damn ornery, maybe I'll tell you."

"Oh, I don't *care* what it is," Elyse huffed, turning away and wiping off her already spotless sink.

Nathan stared at her rigid back for a minute, then said, "Why were you peeking out the window, anyway?"

"Because I was scared."

"Scared? Of what? Did you hear something?"

"No," she admitted, "I was scared because ... because you said you were coming to talk to me this afternoon and you didn't come."

Nathan looked at her as if she'd lost her mind.

"You weren't in the barn when I came out to feed the animals and I thought, well, that something had happened to you."

Nathan was surprised and more than a little annoyed by the rush of pleasure that coursed through him at her words. "Would you have cared?" he asked quietly.

"Of course I would have cared. If something happens to you after your people have set me up as a target for this gang of desperadoes, then I have no protection."

Nathan's pleasure quickly ebbed. "I see. Well, nothing has happened to me and the reason I wasn't in the barn was because I went into town to buy some suspenders."

"Suspenders? You made a special trip to town to buy suspenders? Whatever for?"

"For this." Again, he held up the burlap bag. This time, Elyse noticed a pair of suspenders dangling from it.

"What *is* that?" she asked again.

"It's for the baby."

"The baby?"

"Yeah. After seeing how careless you are in the way you travel around with him, I decided to make you a sling."

"I am not careless," Elyse gritted, infuriated that he was, as usual, passing judgment on her.

"Okay," Nathan relented, "maybe 'careless' isn't the right word. But if you insist on riding horseback with him instead of hitching up a wagon like a normal woman would, then I figured at least this should help a little." Walking toward her, he extended the strange-looking bag.

Elyse plucked it gingerly out of his hand, careful not to let their fingers touch. Carrying it over to the lamp, she examined it closely. Two holes had been cut in the bottom of the bag and the suspenders were attached at the opposite open end.

"What am I supposed to do with this? Put Colin inside it like a peck of potatoes?"

Nathan frowned at her analogy and walked over to where she stood. "Give me that and I'll show you how it works."

Obediently, Elyse handed him the bag.

"Turn around and hold your arms out to the side."

When she had done as he'd bidden, he slipped the suspenders over her arms and hiked them up to her shoulders, turning his weird little invention into a tidy knapsack. "See? It's simple. You just put the baby in the bag, slip his legs through the holes at the bottom and strap him onto your back. Or you can turn the whole thing around and strap him to your front if you prefer."

Elyse craned her head around and stared at the crude carrier hanging down her back. "It's a good idea," she admitted. "And it was kind of you to make it for me."

For the first time since his return, Nathan smiled at her, a wide, pleased grin that lit up his chiseled face and made Elyse's breath catch in her throat. She hadn't seen that smile since their long-ago night together and she'd almost forgotten how heartstoppingly handsome he was when he wasn't scowling.

Slowly, Elyse peeled the bag off and set it on the table. "Are you hungry?" she asked softly.

"As a bear."

"I have some biscuits left from supper and I could fry you up some bacon ..."

"That would be great." Unstrapping his holster, Nathan slipped it off and threw it over the back of the chair, seating himself at the table.

Elyse quickly turned away and headed for the kitchen counter. Obviously, he was planning to eat in the house tonight. She supposed she could hand him the food and show him the door, but for some reason, she didn't really want to. After all, he had spent his afternoon making Colin the carrier ...

"I thought you were going to interrogate me this afternoon," she said casually as she lifted a plate down from the shelf.

Nathan nodded at her back. "I was."

"But you didn't," Elyse continued, her back still to him.

"I know."

With a frustrated sigh, she turned and faced him. "Why not?"

A ghost of a smile twitched his lips. "Figured it wouldn't do any good. You'd just tell me you were visiting a friend, so what was the use?"

"I *was* visiting a friend."

"A friend whose name you won't tell me."

"That's right." Pointedly, she turned away again.

"Why won't you tell me this person's name?" Before the words were out of her mouth, he added, "I know, I know, it's none of my business."

"It's not."

Nathan sighed and shook his head, his eyes casually

sliding over a heap of brown material thrown on the small table near the rocking chair. "All I really want to know, Mrs. Graham, is whether this 'friend' is a man or a woman." He looked at the material again. Curious as to what it was, he reached over and picked it up.

"It's a woman," Elyse murmured, deciding that there was no harm in telling him that much.

When Nathan didn't answer, she turned to look at him. Her heart leaped into her throat as she saw him holding up Lynn's pants, his eyes cold as steel. "Really?" he snarled. "Then who, pray tell, do these belong to?"

With a furious swing of his arm, Nathan hurled the pants down onto the table. "Do you ever tell the truth, lady?" he yelled, "or do you just lie, lie, lie?" Stepping forward, he caught her by her arms, pulling her so close to him that she could feel his breath on her face. "Who are you protecting?"

"No one!" she gasped, trying to wrench out of his viselike grip. "The pants belong to my friend. She wears them around her ranch to do her chores."

"Sure she does," Nathan hissed, his teeth clamped together in rage. "And I wear my little sister's pinafores to church on Sundays."

With a sudden, jerking movement, Elyse wrenched away from him. "I don't care whether you believe me or not," she railed. "I'm telling you the truth!"

Nathan drew a deep, calming breath, suddenly realizing that it was jealousy more than fear making him act so irrationally. "Okay," he said, determined to keep his voice level, "let's suppose, just for the sake of argument, that for once, you're actually telling me the truth. What are you doing with this woman's pants?"

"I'm mending them. They're torn down the right leg."

"Oh? And is your friend incapable of mending her own pants?"

"No," Elyse admitted, "but I'm an excellent seamstress. I used to sew for a lot of ladies in Bixby to earn extra money. I don't do it much anymore, though."

Nathan knew that at least that much was true. He had met briefly with Will Johnson the previous day and had spent a goodly amount of time pelting him with questions about Elyse. Will had confided that he'd heard in town that Elyse once worked as a seamstress, but since the birth of her illegitimate son, few of the women in Bixby still patronized her. Even so, her lame story about a mysterious friend whose name she wouldn't divulge wearing men's pants to do her chores was just too outrageous to believe.

"Sorry, Mrs. Graham. I don't believe you."

"But it's the truth!" Elyse cried, lunging forward and grabbing the pants.

"Lady, you wouldn't know the truth if it came up and bit you in the ass!"

Elyse gasped in outraged offense at Nathan's crude words. "How *dare* you! How dare you stand here in my house and accuse me of being a liar?"

By now, Nathan's temper had reached the boiling point. "Because you are one!"

"I am not!"

"Okay, then," he growled, pushing his face close to hers, "tell me again who Colin's father is."

Involuntarily, Elyse's hand clutched her throat and she took a quick, reeling step backward. *He knew.* God, she should have known he'd find out . . . that one of the good women in Bixby would feel it her Christian duty to advise him of his employer's tainted past. Closing her eyes to shut out Nathan's accusing glare, she choked, "Get out. Get out of my house—right now."

For a long moment, Nathan stood and stared at her, his chest heaving with fury. "You're really something, lady, you know that? God, how I wish they'd picked somebody else for this damned assignment! I'd rather be sent in single-handed to put down a Comanche uprising than be holed up here with you!"

And grabbing his hoslter off the back of the chair, he shot out the front door, nearly sending the flimsy little portal through its frame as he slammed it behind him.

Chapter 11

The next few days passed without incident. Elyse busied herself around the house, tending Colin who was making a mighty effort to sit up, working in her small vegetable garden, and weeding the beautiful wildflowers that grew in lush profusion outside her front door.

She saw very little of Nathan, but after their late-night altercation, she was glad. She was worried sick that now that he knew Colin wasn't her husband's son, he might guess who the baby's father really was. She had finally decided that if he asked about Colin's paternity again, she would make up a story about a brief but passionate love affair.

The mere thought of telling such an atrocious lie sickened her, but she reasoned that any amount of personal humiliation would be worth it if it kept Nathan from learning the truth about Colin. Still, she actively tried to avoid him, reluctant to further sully her reputation by giving credence to the town women's malicious gossip.

Three times a day, she took a tray of food out to the barn, setting it just inside the door, then fleeing back to the sanctuary of the house. No longer did Nathan return the tray to her. Instead, he just set the empty plate back by the barn door for her to take when she brought him his next meal.

Elyse couldn't imagine what he was doing all day to keep himself busy, but she refused to investigate. Instead, she limited herself to working only in the house and front yard.

Nathan, for his part, was doing almost nothing—and by the evening of the third day, he was nearly crazy with inactivity and boredom "This is nuts," he growled to himself as he lay in his straw bed and stared at the barn's cobweb-laced ceiling. "I've got to get out of here for a while." Irritably, he turned over on his side. "Tomorrow I'll go into town ... maybe pick up another load of shingles and start on the barn roof." Squinting, he looked up at the large, gaping holes in the roof above him. "God, what a job."

With a snort of disbelief that he was even contemplating taking on the momentous task, he slammed his eyes shut. "Come on, you goddamned bandidos," he muttered into the darkness. "Make your move, so I can get the hell out of here!"

The next morning, Elyse was up before dawn. She hadn't been off the farm in four days and she was just as bored as Nathan was.

She hurried through her morning chores, determined to pack Colin into his new carrier as soon as he was awake and fed and go to Lynn's. A day spent with her reclusive friend might not be exciting, but it was a far sight better than being cooped up alone in her tiny house. Besides, she could find out what Lynn needed in the way of supplies, and the next day she'd go to town.

Usually, Elyse dreaded trips to town, knowing that women who had once been her friends now made a point of crossing the street when they saw her so as not to have to speak to her. Still, it would get her away from Nathan for the better part of a day and that thought alone made the possibility of being publicly shunned worth risking.

For the fifth time in a half hour, she walked into her

bedroom, this time smiling when she saw that Colin was lying in his cradle, looking at her.

Picking up the cooing baby, she held him close, inhaling deeply of his warm, sleepy smell. "Come on, darling. Let's have some breakfast and get you dressed. We're going visiting today."

Colin looked at her solemnly as if weighing the suggestion, then reached out and grabbed a strand of hair that had come loose from her bun.

"Ouch, you little demon," Elyse laughed, unwinding the baby's fingers from the lock of hair. Walking out to the front room, she sat down in the rocker, unbuttoning the bodice of her dress and smiling with maternal pleasure when Colin latched on to her breast greedily.

Nathan was up early also. He'd slept poorly, probably due to the fact that he'd spent most of the last three days napping, just to pass the time. After making the decision last night to fix the barn roof, he was anxious to get started. Even though he hated ranch repairs, at least it was something to do.

Quickly, he fed his horse, saddled him and led him out of the barn. He started to mount, then hesitated, realizing he should tell Elyse he was leaving, so that she didn't go to the work of fixing him breakfast when he wouldn't be there to eat it.

The sun was just coming up, and he looked at the house doubtfully, wondering if Elyse was up. The last thing he wanted to do was awaken her and have her come to the door wearing only that thin little wrapper. Seeing that sight once had been enough to give him several nights of bawdy dreams. He certainly didn't need another viewing to reinforce his already overactive imagination.

For a long moment he stood in the yard, staring at the house and running his horse's reins idly through his fingers. Then, with a shrug, he walked up the porch steps, figuring that he'd peek through the front window and if he didn't see Elyse in the kitchen, he'd leave a note.

She wasn't in the kitchen, but he *did* see her, and the sight of her sitting in the rocking chair, her breasts bared as she nursed her son was enough to make him nearly fall off the edge of the porch in his haste to get away.

My God, she's practically naked! Thank the Lord she didn't see me or the next thing I know, she'd be accusing me of being a Peeping Tom!

Drawing a shaky breath, Nathan closed his eyes and ran his hand across his face. As soon as he did, though, the vision of Elyse that he had just witnessed swam up before him.

Those breasts. Those beautiful breasts. He could remember far too well how they had felt beneath his hands, tasted beneath his lips. Like living alabaster— smooth and warm and delicate.

Hardly realizing what he was doing, Nathan stepped back up on the porch and stood at the side of the window, gazing in fascination at the half-clad woman. Elyse had finished feeding Colin and was bending over him, tickling the baby on his fat, full tummy till he laughed with satiated delight.

She still had not buttoned her bodice and Nathan stood riveted, feasting on the beauty of the lush globes so tantalizing displayed as she leaned forward.

She straightened and turned toward the window, offering him a full view of her ample, feminine charms. It took every bit of willpower Nathan could muster to step back. Swallowing hard, he jumped off the edge of the porch and hastened over to his horse, giving a disgusted pull to his suddenly too tight Levi's.

"Look at you," he admonished himself hoarsely, "horny as a bull—and from watching something as chaste as a mother feeding her child! What the hell is wrong with you?"

But he knew that his current randiness hadn't been caused by seeing Elyse nurse her baby. Rather, it had merely been the sight of her bare breasts and the memories that sight invoked. For fifteen long months, he'd thought about the beauty of Elyse Graham's body and now, seeing it again and knowing that its soft perfection had not just been the musings of a lonely man, was more than even Nathan's ironclad will could endure.

Still, he couldn't help but feel guilty. Theirs had been a momentary passion only, as the last week spent together had most certainly shown. He had no right to harbor feelings of lust and longing. Elyse could not have made her feelings of disinterest and even dislike more apparent, and Nathan knew it was pure folly to imagine that there would ever be anything more between them.

"Forget telling her about breakfast. Just get on your horse and get out of here before you make a bigger fool of yourself than you already have," he warned himself.

Again, he looked down ruefully at the telltale bulge in his denims. Riding would be no simple task, but he was determined to flee, no matter how uncomfortable he might be. Setting his jaw, he mounted, biting down hard on his lip to stifle the groan that immediately rose. After all, it was only five miles into town. Surely he could endure a little discomfort for that short space of time. And maybe if he stayed in town till after lunch, he could go to the saloon and check out the girls there. After all, what better way to erase the vision of one alluring body from his mind than to replace it with another?

He wasn't more than two miles down the road before he realized he'd forgotten his wallet. No wallet, no money. He hesitated a moment before turning back, wondering if he could convince Hiram Richman at the general store to advance him credit to buy the shingles, but he knew there was little chance of that. After all, he was a stranger in town and expected to be there only for a short time. It was highly unlikely that Richman would take a chance on him being honest enough to pay back the debt.

"Damn," he swore, turning his horse around and

heading back for the ranch, "if I could just use my real name." For the first time in his career, Nathan was being forced to use an alias, and being the unknown Nat Wells was making him realize how valuable the name "Wellesley" really was. No matter how remote the area, the Wellesley name was as well known as "Vanderbilt" and "Rockefeller," opening many social and financial doors that would otherwise remain closed. The fact that he would now have to ride clear back to the ranch to get his cash, rather than just sign his name to a bill, rankled.

Nudging his horse into a canter, he loped along, quickly eating up the ground he'd just traversed. He was nearly back to the house when he spotted Elyse riding across the near pasture, Colin strapped securely to her back in his carrier and a large sack slung over her horse's rump.

"Now where the hell is she going?" Nathan muttered in annoyance. "I swear, all I have to do is turn my back for one minute and she's off like a shot out of a gun." He reined in his horse and watched Elyse's progress across the field, trying to ascertain where she might be headed. Something about her bothered him, but it took a minute before he realized it was the large bag she was carrying. From his vantage point, he could see that it was bulky—as if it was stuffed full of something. Food, maybe? Or clothing? Or *guns?*

This last thought made his mouth tighten ominously. "One thing's for sure. She's taking supplies to somebody." Raising his hand to shield his eyes, Nathan stared hard after her. The distance between them was increasing, making it harder and harder to make out details. Realizing this was his chance to find out who she was meeting during her frequent disappearances, he turned his horse in the direction she was traveling. Glancing around, he noted that there was no place that he could take cover, making it impossible to follow too closely without being detected. "Slow down, Wellesley," he told himself. "This will be pointless if she sees you."

It was the tall Texas grass and a covey of quail that gave him away. Suddenly the bright morning sky was filled with flapping wings and outraged whistles from the small flock his horse had disturbed. One second he was silently moving through the grass and the next he had dozens of birds rising around him and a panicked horse beneath him. It happened so fast that he had no time to steady his seat, and the next thing he knew, he was on his back on the ground, batting furiously at the squawking birds.

A hundred yards ahead of him, Elyse heard the disturbance. With a startled gasp of fear, she swiveled around in her saddle, watching the birds take flight as her eyes scanned the field warily for sight of a coyote or a bobcat. What she saw, instead, was Nathan Wellesley sitting in the tall grass, cursing loudly and pulling feathers out of his hair.

"What in the . . . Blast him, he *followed* me!" Too angry to care that her bodyguard looked to be in danger of being trampled by his terrified horse, Elyse steered her mare to the left and kicked her hard, heading for the protection of a grove of pecan trees at the far end of the field. Ducking to avoid the low-hanging branches, she pulled up sharply on the reins and cast a furtive look behind her.

Nathan was by now back on his feet, grabbing for his horse's reins as he tried to subdue the prancing, snorting animal.

Out of the corner of her eye, Elyse saw something blowing gustily across the field. A smug smile tilted her lips when she realized it was Nathan's hat. "Oh, Colin, look," she said with a smirk, "Captain Wellesley seems to have lost his beloved Stetson. Should take him a while to catch up with that, the way the wind's blowing this morning." Giggling with delight at her pursuer's embarrassing plight, she nudged her horse into a trot and headed for home. When she'd put a half mile between them, she slowed to a walk and turned to look at the baby. "You know, he's not nearly as clever as he thinks he is. I'm sure the reason he wasn't in the barn this morning was because he was hiding out, just hoping I'd go somewhere so he could follow." She sighed dramatically. "Too bad he's not more accomplished at tracking."

She rode along happily until she passed through the gates leading to her house. Gazing at the lonely little cabin, her satisfied grin faded. Now she wouldn't be able to go to Lynn's, after all. Nathan would probably be back at any moment and she would once again be relegated to confining herself to the house and garden in order to avoid him.

"Damn him," she cursed, then threw Colin a shamefaced look. "Why can't he keep his nose out of my business?"

But, despite her disappointment, Elyse couldn't repress the little smile that twitched her lips. Imagine, one of the most famous of all the famous Texas Rangers being dumped on his butt by a few birds. It was almost worth giving up her visit just to have witnessed such a hilarious sight.

Elyse was still in the barn when Nathan arrived, leading his horse and limping slightly on his left leg.

"Have a nice ride, Captain?" she asked, laughter dancing in her eyes as she noticed a quail feather clinging to his hair. "I must say, that was some demonstration of 'riding like a Mexican and trailing like an Indian.' Do you shoot and fight equally well?"

Nathan threw her an incredulous look, hardly able to believe that she would have the audacity to tease him about his humiliating mishap. "Where were you going this morning?" he demanded.

"Oh, I went out for a morning jog, just like you, I

imagine. If I had known you were riding in the same direction I was, I would have warned you about those annoying birds." She clucked her tongue against her teeth in mock sympathy. "They can be such a nuisance, can't they?"

"Knock it off, lady," Nathan growled. Stepping forward, he grabbed Elyse's bag off her horse's rump. "What's in here?"

"Nothing!" she retorted, all traces of laughter disappearing. "Just something I was taking to . . . someone."

She lunged forward to grab the bag, but Nathan whipped it out of her reach and dropped to his knees, untying the cord that held it closed. Shaking the contents onto the barn floor, he rummaged through them for a moment, then threw her a bewildered glance. He'd fully expected to find guns but, instead, there were just some books, a loaf of bread, some odds and ends of cloth, and several jars filled with a thick, dark substance. Holding one of those up, he said, "What is this?"

"Blueberry preserves," Elyse retorted, planting her hands on her hips and glaring down at him. "And don't break that jar. They're hard to come by."

"Blueberry preserves! Who the hell are you taking blueberry preserves to?"

"My friend!"

Nathan picked up Lynn's mended pants. "Obviously the same friend who you say these belong to. You already told me she can't sew. Can't she cook, either?"

"Of course she can cook! The preserves are just a little gift."

"And what about this?" Nathan demanded, holding up what looked to be a small blanket. "Does she need you to keep her warm, too?" His emphasis on the words "she" and "her" made it obvious that he didn't believe for a minute they were talking about a woman.

"It's a quilt I'm making." Reaching down, Elyse grabbed it out of his hand. "Give it to me before you get it dirty."

Nathan looked up at her, his gaze icy. "You're lying again."

"Oh!" Elyse gasped, adroitly sidestepping him and tearing down the barn aisle toward the door. "You horrible, despicable, wretched . . ."

"Yeah, I like you, too," Nathan gritted, leaping to his feet and following her.

Elyse burst out of the barn door, racing across the yard toward the house as fast as her long skirts would allow. To her dismay, Nathan was only a step behind her. She shot through the front door, then turned, trying desperately to close it before he could push through. But she was no match for his superior strength, and she suddenly found herself standing in her front room, nearly nose to nose with the outraged man.

"Don't you *dare* walk away from me when I'm talking to you!" he thundered.

"Don't you dare tell me what to do!" she countered. "Get out of my house, *now!*"

"I'll get out when I'm damn good and ready."

"Don't you swear at me, you boor!" Elyse turned away, intending to close herself in the bedroom, but, once more, Nathan was too fast for her. Grabbing her arm, he whirled her around till she was again facing him. Her jerky movements caused Colin to swing back and forth precariously in his carrier. The motion, coupled with the yelling going on so close to him, made him burst into lusty howls of distress.

"I told you, I'm not done talking to you," Nathan shouted. "Now where the hell were you going—and *don't* tell me you were off to see your damned nonexistent friend. You were taking supplies to someone and *I want to know who!*"

Colin wailed louder.

"Shut up and leave me alone!" Elyse shrieked, trying again to make a break for the bedroom.

"Tell me where you were going and then I'll . . . *Jesus Christ,* that baby's got a pair of lungs! Doesn't he *ever* quit screaming?" Without even thinking about what he was doing, Nathan took a quick step behind Elyse and plucked Colin out of his carrier, swinging the baby over his mother's head and then cradling him to his shoulder. "Now, just be quiet," he muttered, looking down at the baby's downy head. "You holler altogether too much."

To the astonishment of both of them, Colin immediately stopped crying. Nathan looked down at the suddenly quiet baby in complete surprise, then up at Elyse who was staring at her son in openmouthed horror.

"What are you doing with my baby? Give him to me before you hurt him!"

"I'm not doing anything to him," Nathan answered, a pleased grin lighting his face. "And I'm not hurting him. He's perfectly all right." Jostling the baby playfully, he cupped Colin's head in his big hand and grinned down at him. "You're just fine now, aren't you, little fella?"

Colin responded to Nathan's question by reaching up and grabbing his hair, pulling at it until Nathan lowered his head to relieve the tension. "Here, don't do that," he chuckled, gently untangling the baby's hand and kissing the tiny fingers. "Just stay here like a good boy while I finish talking to your mama."

Elyse was dumbstruck . . . and horrified. She had never seen anything more natural and spontaneous than the immediate affinity between her son and this stranger. *But he's not a stranger,* a little voice deep within the recesses of her mind whispered, *he's his father. Why shouldn't there be a natural bond between them?*

"Give me my baby."

Nathan looked up in surprise, a bit disconcerted by the frantic intensity in her voice. "What's wrong with you, Mrs. Graham? Why shouldn't I hold him? I like babies . . . always have. Besides, it probably does the little guy good to be exposed to a man for a change, so he's not afraid of them."

A panic such as nothing that Elyse had ever known

welled up within her. She didn't want Nathan Wellesley holding her baby and she didn't want Colin responding to him. Colin was hers, no one else's. Drawing a deep, shuddering breath, she said again, "Give me my baby. Please."

Nathan looked at her speculatively for a moment, then, shaking his head in bewilderment, handed Colin over.

Elyse accepted the baby gratefully, holding him close and kissing his soft little cheek. "Thank you," she said quietly. "Now, I'd appreciate it if you'd leave. I have nothing more to say about where I was going this morning. I was going where I always go, and no matter how much you bully me, I'm not going to tell you where that is, so you might as well just give up."

Nathan released a frustrated sigh, then shrugged his massive shoulders and headed for the door. "This isn't over between us, Mrs. Graham. Don't think that it is."

"Good-*bye*, Captain Wellesley."

Nathan paused a moment, his hand on the door latch. "By the way, in case you haven't noticed, that baby is soaked." He made a vague gesture toward Colin, who was again starting to fuss. "If you'd put a dry pair of britches on him, maybe he'd quit squalling so much."

And with that, he disappeared out the door.

Chapter 12

"Nice day, isn't it?"

Elyse looked up from where she knelt industriously weeding her wildflowers. Getting to her feet, she brushed her dirty hands together. "Yes," she answered, her voice tentative. "Very nice."

"I'm going into town to buy a post hole digger. Do you need anything while I'm there?"

What is this all about? Elyse wondered. In all his numerous trips to town, Nathan had never asked if she needed anything before. But ever since the night he'd held Colin, he had seemed to relax his attitude toward her a bit. It was as if holding her baby for that brief moment had made him see her in a different light—perhaps as a woman instead of a criminal. He also hadn't questioned her any further about Colin's paternity, and, for that, she was exceedingly grateful.

"Thank you for asking, but I can't think of anything I need."

"How about some maple syrup? I get awful tired of eating pancakes with nothing on them except brown sugar."

Her expression became defiant. "I'm sorry if my cooking doesn't suit you, Captain. Unfortunately, maple syrup is a luxury I can't afford."

"I *can*," Nathan countered promptly, "and I didn't say

your cooking didn't suit me. I merely said that pancakes are better with maple syrup on them."

Elyse shrugged and turned back to her flowers. "Then get some if you want it."

"Do you like maple syrup, Mrs. Graham?"

Elyse sighed, wondering why he was going on and on about such an inconsequential subject. It was almost as if he was determined to carry on a conversation with her.

"Yes, I do," she admitted.

"Then I'll definitely get some. I bet Colin would like it, too." With an inclination of his head, he nodded toward the baby who was sitting on a blanket with his fist stuffed in his mouth.

"Babies his age can't eat pancakes," Elyse scoffed.

"They can't? I thought by the time they got to be eight or nine months old, babies could start eating all sorts of things."

Elyse nearly blurted out that Colin was only six months old, but she suddenly remembered who she was talking to and caught herself. "Um . . ." she stammered, "his teeth are a little slow coming in and he can't chew very well yet."

Nathan again looked over at the baby, who returned his glance with a wide, toothless smile. "Guess you're right," he chuckled. "Doesn't look like there's many teeth in there."

"No, not yet." Hurrying over to where the baby was seated, Elyse scooped him up, wishing desperately that Nathan would leave.

Suddenly, there was a loud crash from inside the house, followed by the yowl of an outraged cat. "Oh, Lord!" Elyse cried. "What was that? Myrna must have broken something." To Nathan's astonishment, she shoved the baby into his arms and rushed up the porch steps.

"Who's Myrna?" Nathan called, following her up the steps.

"My crazy old cat," she called in return. Racing through the newly repaired front door, Elyse looked around, then emitted a groan of dismay as she spotted the broken pieces of a large bowl lying on the floor next to a breakfront. "Oh, no," she moaned, stooping down and trying to fit two of the pieces together. "Not this!"

"Was that bowl a favorite of yours?" Nathan asked, looking down at her sympathetically.

She nodded. "It was a wedding present from my husband's parents. It had been in their family for years. Joe's grandmother brought it with her when she came from Europe." With a mournful shake of her head, Elyse raised tear-filled eyes to Nathan. "Now it's gone." Her misery was so intense that for a moment she didn't seem to notice that Nathan was still holding Colin. Then, suddenly, she gave out with a sharp little gasp. "What are you doing with Colin?"

Nathan's expression was incredulous. "What am I doing with him? You handed him to me outside."

"I did?"

He nodded. "When you heard the crash."

Elyse was horrified to think that the sound of glass breaking would startle her to the point that she would hurtle her baby into the enemy's arms. "I'm sorry. I can't imagine what made me do that. Here, I'll take him now." Reaching out, she pulled Colin out of Nathan's arms.

Nathan frowned as the baby was more or less wrenched out of his grasp. "Be careful of that broken glass," he warned. "Don't step on it."

Elyse nodded and turned toward the bedroom. "I'll just get Colin settled in his cradle, then I'll come out and clean it up."

"Don't worry, *I'll* clean it up."

Elyse looked back over her shoulder. To her surprise, Nathan was already squatting over the broken pieces of the bowl. "That's not necessary, Captain. I can—"

Nathan shot her an irritated glance, annoyed that she

was making such an issue over cleaning up a little broken glass. "Just go take care of your son, Mrs. Graham. I can handle this. Trust me, I've cleaned up broken glass before."

Elyse opened her mouth as if to argue further, then thought better of it and continued on into the bedroom.

Gingerly, Nathan picked up the broken pieces, examining them closely. The bowl had broken cleanly into four parts, and except for a small piece that had shattered near the rim, it looked like it could be mended. "All this needs is a little glue," he muttered. Straightening, he carefully carried the pieces out to his primitive bedroom in the barn and set them on a pile of straw.

Heading into an adjacent stall, he led his horse out and hitched him to Elyse's rickety old wagon. Climbing up onto the seat, he drove across the yard, stopping in front of the house. "Mrs. Graham!" he called. "I'm leaving now."

Elyse appeared in the front door, her eyes red and swollen from crying.

"Are you all right?" Nathan asked quietly.

"Yes." She nodded. "I'm just upset about my bowl. It was one of the last pretty things I still had."

"What do you mean by that?"

Elyse let out a tremulous sigh. "I mean, I've had to sell most of my other nice things."

"Sell them! Why?"

Her chin came up a notch, and she shot him a familiar look of defiance. "To buy food, Captain Wellesley, that's why." Before Nathan could respond, she marched back into the house.

But Nathan was not about to be gainsaid and promptly jumped down from the wagon and followed her inside. Elyse turned and looked at him expectantly. "Was there something else you wanted?"

"What did you have to sell . . . and don't tell me it's none of my business."

He was growing to know her too well, Elyse thought

wryly. That was exactly what she'd been about to tell him. Instead, she said, "Nothing very valuable. Just some little trinkets."

"What kind of trinkets?"

"Just trinkets. Little personal things. Why are you asking me all these questions?"

Nathan ignored her. "What kind of trinkets?"

"Some silver, and a little crystal bird my father gave me."

"Anything else?"

"Captain, I'd really rather not talk—"

"Anything else?"

Elyse sighed, a soft, defeated sound that made his heart wrench in his chest. "My grandmother's diamond ring."

He nodded, adding this item to the catalogue he was building in his mind. "Who did you sell the stuff to?"

"Mr. Richman."

"And what did he do with it?"

"Didn't you say you were going into town?"

"I am. What did Richman do with your things?"

"I don't know!" Elyse cried, her eyes again welling with tears as she thought of all she'd lost in the past few years. "What difference does it make? I suppose he sold everything to someone else."

Abruptly, Nathan turned toward the door. "I'm going now. Sure you don't want anything except maple syrup?"

"I didn't say I wanted maple syrup," Elyse sniffed. "You did."

"You're right. I'll see you later." He walked out the front door and climbed into the wagon, flapping the reins over the horse's back and heading off down the road.

Elyse watched him till he was out of sight, wondering what had brought on his strange behavior this morning. Finally, she shrugged and closed the door. She looked over at the bare breakfront. "One more thing gone," she murmured disconsolately. "One more thing to add to all the others."

"Morning, Mr. Wells. What can I do for you?"

Nathan smiled at Hiram Richman, surprised by the man's uncharacteristic friendliness. "Well, actually, I need a couple of things. First off, a post hole digger."

The storekeeper's eyebrows raised imperceptively and he pinned Nathan with a doubtful look. "That's a pretty expensive piece of equipment, you know."

Nathan's mouth tightened as he caught the man's drift. "I've got the money to pay for it, don't worry."

Richman had the good grace to look embarrassed at being so obvious. He nodded and walked around the end of the counter, lifting one of the heavy implements off a pile. "You still working out at the Widow Graham's place?"

"Yeah."

"Must be a whole heap of work to do out there."

"It keeps me busy."

Richman leaned the post hole digger up against the counter. "Anything else?"

"Yup. Some bacon and a good-size jug of maple syrup."

"Plannin' on a big breakfast, are ya?"

Nathan had been in the general store at least four or five times and never had Hiram Richman said so much as ten words to him. He wondered again why the man was being so congenial. Maybe it was because he'd been assured of payment. Mentally shrugging, Nathan said, "I like pancakes—breakfast, supper, anytime."

Richman hefted a jug of syrup up onto the counter. "That'll be six dollars," he announced. "Are you sure you still want all of this?"

"Yes, and I'm not done yet, either."

This time Richman's eyebrows shot clear up into his hairline. Who would have thought this drifter would ever place such a large order? He smiled broadly, his manner becoming more cordial by the minute. "Yes, sir! What else?"

Nathan struck as casual a pose as he could muster. "A ring."

Hiram Richman's mouth fell open. "A ring? What kind of ring?"

"A diamond ring, if you have one."

"A diamond ring," Richman sputtered. "I see."

"Do you have one or not?"

"Well, I just might at that. If you'll step over here to the jewelry case ..."

Nathan sauntered over to a shabby little display case at the back of the store, assuming an expression of bored nonchalance. Covertly, he scanned the meager array of jewelry, his eyes settling on the only piece of real value—a gold filigreed band inset with a sizable diamond.

"I'm afraid I don't have much of a selection in diamonds," Hiram apologized, slipping behind the case and brushing his hand across its dusty top. "In fact, the only thing I currently have in stock is this one." He pointed at the ring Nathan was staring at. "If I may be so bold, who are you buying this ring for, Mr. Wells? A sweetheart, perhaps?"

Nathan gave him a coolly assessing look, annoyed by the man's nosiness. "No, not a sweetheart."

"Not a sweetheart?"

"No. It's for ... my mother. Her birthday is coming up soon and I wanted to get her something special."

Hiram looked at him for a long moment, trying to decide whether he should take the man's money and run, or tell him how inappropriate this ring would be for his mother. After a brief mental battle, his conscience won out. "Mr. Wells, in all honesty, this is more of a wedding-type ring than a style a man would give to his mother. Perhaps this nice sapphire over here would fit your needs."

Nathan shook his head. "I want the diamond."

"But, Mr. Wells—"

Nathan raised his eyes and shot the flustered store-keeper a level look. "I want the diamond, Mr. Richman."

"Just as you say." With deft fingers, Hiram plucked the ring from its threadbare velvet nest and held it up for Nathan's inspection. "It *is* a lovely piece."

"Where did you get it?"

Hiram drew himself up indignantly. "I assure you, I came by it quite honestly."

"I'm not doubting that," Nathan responded smoothly. "I just wondered why a piece this nice isn't in a jewelry store somewhere."

Hiram expelled a pent-up breath, his good nature restored now that he realized Nathan wasn't questioning his ethics. "Actually, a lady sold it to me. She was in rather dire straights at the time and—"

"I see," Nathan interrupted. "Well, that lady's adversity is my gain, I guess. I'll take it."

Hiram looked at him with wide eyes. "Don't you even want to know the price first? It's my most valuable piece."

Nathan cursed himself for being so careless in his attitude. "Oh, yes," he said hurriedly, "I guess I should find that out."

"It's fifty dollars," Richman intoned solemnly.

Fifty dollars! Nathan knew the ring was worth ten times that much, at least. If Richman was willing to sell it for fifty dollars, what kind of a puny sum must Elyse have sacrificed it for?

"Whew!" Nathan whistled, trying hard to look shocked. "That *is* a lot of money."

Hiram sighed and closed the top of the display case. "I was afraid of that."

Nathan stood with his lips pursed as if deliberating over a momentous decision. "Mr. Richman, I just have to have it. Nothing is too good for my mother."

The astonishment on Hiram's face was so obvious that Nathan could barely control his laughter. "You're going to take it?"

"Yes."

Hiram Richman was nearly beside himself with excitement. Never in his wildest imaginings had he ever dreamed he'd actually sell the extravagant piece. He'd accepted it from Elyse only because he knew she had no other way to settle up her account with him—and because he felt having it gave his store an aura of prestige.

Richman followed Nathan back to the main counter, carefully setting the ring down. "If you'll wait just a minute, I'll total up your purchases—unless, of course, you're still not finished."

"There is one more thing," Nathan said.

For a moment he thought the storekeeper's eyes were going to pop out of his head. "Yes?"

"Some glue. I broke a bowl and I need to mend it."

Hiram's disappointment at this modest request was evident. "Certainly," he mumbled, walking over to a shelf and taking down a small bottle. "This should fix it." He added the bottle to Nathan's purchases and pulled out a scrap of paper and a stubby pencil. "Okay, that will be . . ." Nathan waited while he totaled up a column. "Fifty-six dollars and fifty cents." He held his breath, still wondering if Nathan was actually going to produce such a vast sum of money. Fifty-six dollars was more than he usually made in three days and he still could not quite believe that this drifter possessed that kind of money.

He needn't have worried. Nathan pulled his wallet out of his vest pocket, holding it down beneath the edge of the counter so Richman could not see the large number of bills inside it. Peeling off sixty dollars, he handed the money over.

Hiram smiled beatifically.

"Be sure you wrap that ring carefully," Nathan directed. "I have to travel with it."

"Don't you worry, Mr. Wells, sir. I have a pretty little box that I'll put it in."

Nathan nodded, then turned toward the shop's front door where the tinny little bell was heralding the arrival of another customer. To his dismay, Lillian Underwood steamed in like a ship entering a harbor, her shopping basket bouncing against her tightly corseted stomach. She threw Nathan a cursory glance, dismissed him, and headed over to a table of ribbons.

"Good morning, Mrs. Underwood," Hiram called, his good spirits evident in his chiming voice.

"Morning," she returned shortly. "Did my cloth come in from Dallas yet?"

"Might have. I haven't had a chance to go through yesterday's delivery."

"Well, could you do it now, please? I have a very busy day today and I don't have time to dawdle."

"Just as soon as I wrap up Mr. Wells's ring."

Mrs. Underwood's head snapped around, and she approached the counter anxiously. "Ring? What ring?" Turning an accusing stare on Nathan, she added, "You didn't buy the diamond ring, did you?"

Nathan had no chance to reply. "He certainly did," Hiram announced.

"What?" Mrs. Underwood gasped, turning to Nathan with wide eyes. "The *diamond* ring? But, how in the world . . . I mean, where would you get . . ." She broke off in midsentence, her mouth pursed indignantly. "You must be very smitten with someone, young man, to spend two months wages on such a useless gift."

"It's for his mother," Hiram advised her.

Lillian shot Richman a look that told him just what she thought of the likelihood of that, then moved off toward the display case as if to check for herself that the ring was actually gone.

"Mrs. Underwood has had her eye on that diamond ring ever since I acquired it," Hiram whispered conspiratorially.

Nathan nodded his understanding and began collecting his packages off the counter. "Thanks for your help, Mr. Richman. I'm sure my mother will be delighted."

Hiram grinned happily and sped around the end of the counter. "Anytime, Mr. Wells," he said, pulling open the front door and nearly bowing Nathan through it. "Anytime at all."

After Nathan had taken his leave, Hiram composed his features and headed back to where Lillian Underwood stood glaring at him.

"How did that man pay for the ring?" she demanded. "You weren't foolish enough to extend him credit, were you? You'll never see a dime of it if you did."

"Mrs. Underwood, please! I pride myself on being a better businessman than to take a chance like that. Mr. Wells paid cash and, I might add, he didn't bat an eye about it."

Lillian's mouth rounded into a thoughtful little moue. "Now, where would he get that kind of money, do you suppose? And who do you think he's going to give that ring to?"

Hiram shrugged. "You heard him. He said it was for his mother."

"Pshaw! What man gives his mother a diamond ring? You know what I think?"

Hiram shook his head.

"I think that ring is payment."

Hiram looked completely nonplussed. "Payment? To who? For what?"

"Who do you think?" she snorted. "Elyse Graham, of course. And I'm sure I don't have to tell you for what."

Hiram's eyes widened as the full implication of Lillian's words sank in. "That's a very serious accusation to make without having any basis for it."

"No basis? How can you say that? We all know what kind of woman she is. That young man is obviously just her latest conquest."

Hiram shook his head. "I really don't think we should be speculating . . ."

"Do you know what else I think?"

When Hiram didn't answer, she charged on. "I bet that money was stolen. No hand for hire has that kind of money unless he's gotten it by cheating at cards or stealing it. Why, for all we know, that man could be part of the gang who robbed the Bixby bank last year! In fact, that might be *our* money he's using to buy that Graham woman gifts!"

"Oh, now, Mrs. Underwood, really!" Hiram blustered. "Don't you think you're letting your imagination—"

"I have to go," Lillian announced, wheeling around and heading for the front door.

"What about your cloth?"

"I don't have time to worry about that now. I'll come back later."

"But, Mrs. Underwood!"

"Good day, Mr. Richman. Be careful you don't take any wooden nickels!"

Chapter 13

Nathan walked into the Bixby livery stable and looked around for his friend, Will Johnson. Spying him in a stall brushing a big bay gelding, he smiled and sauntered over. "Hi, Will, nice to see you."

"Mr. Wells, how are you?"

"Pretty good, and yourself?"

"Fine, just fine."

Will looked at Nathan closely as he mouthed, "Are we alone?"

Will nodded, and with a jerk of his head, directed Nathan over to the end stall where he'd set up a cot and a small table. "Welcome to my palace," he said wryly, motioning Nathan into the lone chair.

Nathan smiled and sat down. "Can you see from here if anybody comes in?"

"Yeah, but it's not likely this time of day. Everybody who wants their horse has 'em by now. The only two in here are my bay and that old nag down there who I rent out to courting couples once in a while on Sundays."

"Sounds like your life is just about as exciting as mine."

Will shrugged. "I've been in worse places. I mean, it's not like fightin' Comanches, but at least I like horses."

"So, has Red had any word from the major?"

Will shook his head. "Silent as a churchyard on Christmas Eve, I'm afraid."

"Damn," Nathan cursed, smacking his knee with his fist. "I wish something would either break on this damn case, or Jones would pull us off it."

"Sick of mendin' fences, are ya, Nate?"

Nathan's head came up. "How do you know I've been mending fences?"

"Saw the post hole digger in the back of your wagon. Can't imagine what else you'd be doin' with one of those."

"Yeah, well, I got so bored that I decided even farm chores were better than just sittin' around watchin' the prairie grass grow. And God knows, the Graham place could use some work."

"So I hear. Red tells me you don't much like the widow. I think the word he used was 'prickly.' "

"She is that," Nathan admitted. "But we're getting along a little better now. At least she doesn't scream and run every time she sees me."

Will let out a loud, braying laugh and flopped down on his cot. "Hell, Nate, you must be losin' your touch! I never knew a woman to scream and run when she seen you comin'. I thought you was usually the one doin' the runnin'."

"Not this time," Nathan grinned. "But she's not so bad, really. I think she's had a hard time. Her husband got killed, she got involved in this bank thing, she's got that baby to raise alone . . ."

"Sounds like you're beginnin' to like her."

Nathan shrugged.

"Just don't get too cozy," Will warned. "A pretty face can be mighty deceivin', and I hear she's a bad one."

"Don't believe everything you hear."

Will's eyes swept over Nathan knowingly. "Nathan, ol' boy, I do think you're sweet on the lady."

"Don't be ridiculous," Nathan bristled. "Of course

I'm not sweet on her. I just think she's been the victim of some unfair gossip."

"And what makes you think the gossip's been unfair? Has she told you who the daddy of that baby of hers is?"

"No."

"Have you asked?"

Nathan shifted uncomfortably on the hard chair. "Come on, Will. Why all the questions?"

Will chuckled with satisfaction. "You did ask her, didn't ya? And, considerin' how pruney you're lookin', she didn't tell you neither."

Nathan's lips compressed with annoyance. "I don't think Mrs. Graham's personal life is any of my business, or anybody else's, for that matter. That's what I hate about small towns. Everybody thinks they deserve an explanation for what everybody else does. The little town I grew up in in Colorado was the same way. That's one of the reasons I left."

"Yeah, and I suppose with your family bein' as rich and famous as they are, you was the target of lots of rumors."

"We had our share," Nathan admitted. "But going back to Mrs. Graham, I just think the people in this town have judged her pretty severely when they probably don't have all the facts."

Will burst into another peal of laughter. "Y'see, I'm right. You *are* sweet on her."

Nathan threw his friend a jaundiced look. "You're full of shit, Will. You always were and you always will be."

Nathan's rude remark did nothing to dampen his friend's good humor. "Say what ya will, Nate, but I know a man who's smitten when I see one."

Nathan had had enough. Standing up, he muttered, "I gotta go. I don't want to leave the widow out there on the farm alone for too long."

Will rose, too. "You goin' over to the cafe 'fore you leave?"

"No, why?"

"Well, I heard tell that little waitress, Daisy Flynn, thinks you're quite the hombre."

Nathan shook his head in disbelief. "I don't know where the hell you get this stuff, Will. I don't even know who you're talkin' about."

"Sure you do. Don't you remember? That day you and I was in there at the same time? That little red-headed gal who brought you your food. She told me later she thought you was just about the handsomest man she ever laid eyes on. Course, all the women think that about you."

"Oh, yeah," Nathan chuckled, stretching expansively. "Old 'knock 'em dead in their tracks' Wellesley. That's me, all right. They're just beatin' my door down."

"They *are!*" Will insisted. "Or at least they would be if you'd ever give any of 'em a little encouragement. And, if I was you, I'd be damn grateful for those looks of yours. Wish I had 'em."

Nathan looked at his plain friend sympathetically. "I'll tell you something, Will. Lots of times good looks are more of a hindrance than a gift."

"Sure, Nate. Sure they are."

"I mean it, Will. They are."

Will stuck his hands in his back pockets and gazed at Nathan earnestly. "How so?"

"Well, for one thing, people tend to remember you, and in our business, that's not always a good thing."

"S'pose you're right about that," Will conceded. "But I think I'd be willin' to risk bein' recognized once in a while if it also meant the ladies looked at me the way they look at you."

Nathan realized that no matter what he said, he wasn't going to convince the homely Will Johnson that a handsome face could be a liability, so he merely shrugged and headed for the stable door. "See ya, Will. You know where I am if you need me for anything."

"Sure, Nate, I'll find you. I'll just track you by the post holes you leave behind."

Nathan didn't turn around, but Will could see his shoulders shaking with laughter as he climbed up on the wagon seat.

With a sigh, Will leaned against the stable door and watched Nathan drive away. "Just one day of my life," he murmured wistfully, "I'd like to look like he does. Damn, what a day that would be!"

I do believe you're sweet on the lady.
Nathan flicked the wagon reins impatiently over his buckskin's back as Will's teasing remark drummed through his mind. His friend's words had bothered him far more than he wanted to admit, even to himself.

Until now, he had never allowed himself to analyze his feelings toward Elyse, other than to admit that he felt sorry for her and didn't believe all the vicious gossip he'd heard in town. But did his feelings run deeper than that? Deep down, Nathan knew they did, and that silent admission was damned disturbing.

"You're just horny," he growled. "You had her once, you know how good it was, and you're wishing it would happen again. That's all it is . . . just lust. If you'd go into town and find yourself a woman some night, you'd forget all about it."

That was a lie and he knew it. Despite all the other women who had drifted in and out of his life, it was Elyse's face he saw when he closed his eyes at night. Elyse's soft, stroking fingers he felt against his skin when he allowed himself to indulge in erotic fantasy. And it was Elyse's grandmother's ring that he had just spent nearly all his ready cash to buy.

Reflexively, he reached down and patted his vest pocket. The ring was still there, safe and sound. He smiled, but his satisfaction quickly faded as he thought about how difficult it might be to actually return the

ring to Elyse. After all, he could hardly just walk into
the house and hand it to her. She would never take it
from him or, if she did, she might feel that he expected
something from her in return. So what good had it done
him to buy it?

"Probably none," he grumbled aloud. "You'll most
likely carry it around in your pocket for the rest of your
life—or until some desperado steals it from you." But
despite this frustrating thought, he still didn't regret buying the ring.

Nathan shook his head and rolled his tense shoulders.
"You know, Wellesley, your brothers are right about
you. You're not nearly as tough as you think you are."

Elyse stood in the doorway of her little house and
gazed surreptitiously out at Nathan. The sun shone
down on his blond hair, and even from this distance, she
could see the sheen of sweat that glistened off his skin as
he worked bare-chested in the summer heat.

The mere sight of him made her feel hot. She had
long since admitted to herself that despite her personal
feelings toward him, Nathan Wellesley was still an ex-
traordinarily handsome man. Past that, she'd never allowed herself to think about him on any sort of personal
level. Until now. But as much as she tried to ignore it,
Elyse couldn't deny the shiver of desire that the sight of
Nathan's bronzed chest evoked. Memories she had repressed for nearly two years suddenly swamped her
mind and, unconsciously, she rubbed her fingers together, remembering the texture of Nathan's skin beneath them. Her eyes swept appreciatively over the
rock-ribbed muscles of his stomach, then settled greedily
on his upper arms, watching his biceps flex and bulge as
he worked the post hole digger.

"Stop this!" she told herself fiercely. "It's unseemly to
gawk at a man's body." She turned away, hurrying into
the kitchen and frantically wiping off the spotless

counter. Almost without realizing it, she again drifted over to the window and peeked out. He was still there. Still working. Still looking magnificently male.

"Lemonade!" Elyse said suddenly. "I'll bet he'd like some lemonade." Quickly, she headed out the back door of the cabin and down the stairs to the root cellar. Walking into the cool, dim interior of the underground chamber, she picked two lemons out of a small basket. She looked at the smooth yellow globes, then shrugged and headed back up the stairs. She refused to think about why she was willing to sacrifice the last of her precious trove of fruit to make lemonade for her nemesis. "You got them to use, so use them," she said with finality.

Ten minutes later, she walked out the front door, a pitcher of golden liquid in one hand, a glass in the other.

Nathan saw her coming across the yard and paused in his task, leaning on the post hole digger and wiping the perspiration off his forehead with the back of his arm.

"I thought you might be thirsty," Elyse said a bit shyly as she approached.

Nathan nodded. "It's getting hot."

Hoping he wouldn't notice that her hand was trembling, she poured some lemonade into the glass and held it out.

"Lemonade?" Nathan asked, throwing her a smile that made her knees feel rubbery.

"Yes. Do you like it?"

"Love it," he affirmed, swallowing the cool, sweet drink in one long gulp. "Mmm, that tastes good." Smacking his lips in appreciation, he held out the glass for a refill. Elyse lowered her eyes and silently poured.

Nathan took another swallow and looked up toward the house. "Where's Colin?"

His mention of the baby made Elyse stiffen. "Napping," she said shortly. "What are you laying in posts for?"

Nathan turned and looked at the row of neat holes he'd dug. "I thought I'd rebuild the corral."

Elyse looked at him quizzically, thinking that there were many things on the farm that needed repair more than the corral. After all, she no longer had any stock to pen, so why waste time fixing it?

Nathan caught her puzzled look. "There's a small herd of mustangs not far from here. I figured I'd catch and break a few of them. Maybe you could sell them and make a few dollars."

Elyse gaped at him in astonishment. "You'd do that for me?"

Nathan shrugged, suddenly embarrassed. "I haven't got anything better to do."

"But, still, I couldn't ask you to do something like that."

Handing her his empty glass, Nathan turned back to his post holes. "You didn't ask me," he said tersely. "I wouldn't do it if you had."

Elyse drew in an offended breath, infuriated by the unexpected insult. Pivoting on her heel, she headed back for the house. She walked into her small front room and slammed the empty pitcher down on the kitchen counter. Angrily, she stared down at her shaking hands. What was it about this man that upset her so much? Every time she thought they'd reached some sort of truce between them, he would make some crack that would totally ruin it. One minute he would seem willing to do her a kindness and the next, he would tell her he was only doing it because she hadn't asked him to. "Impossible," she gritted. "Impossible man, impossible situation. And I wish he'd quit asking about my baby. It's none of his business!"

She released a shaky little sigh, knowing that wasn't really true but hanging on tenaciously to the hope that she'd never have to admit it.

* * *

Nathan stood at the water trough, splashing his face with the cool, refreshing liquid. "You're a stupid ass," he chastised himself roughly. "The girl brings you lemonade and tries to strike up a little conversation and you respond by insulting her."

He shook his head, spraying water in a wide arc around him. Why did he always act like such a boor around Elyse? Normally, he was charming and witty, but with her, he seemed to have a compulsion to be rude and demanding. Why?

Because you're falling for her and it scares you to death.

With a sharp intake of breath, Nathan threw his head back, staring at the bright summer sky as he absorbed this unbidden thought. "You're falling for her," he said aloud. "Will's right. You *are* sweet on her."

There was no denying it, and Nathan didn't even try. For the first time in his twenty-seven years, he was falling in love. In love with a woman who mistrusted him, resented him, and had even told him she was scared of him. A woman whom he had made love to one stormy night and who had rejected him the next morning, telling him that the passion they had shared had been no more than an insane mistake and that she wanted to forget it ever happened. A woman whose greatest desire was to have him get out of her life . . . and stay out.

With a wry smile, Nathan picked up a towel and began drying his shaggy, sun-bleached hair. "Good going, Wellesley. You really know how to pick 'em."

Thoughtfully, he sauntered back to the tumbledown barn, stopping briefly in front of his buckskin's stall. "Wouldn't my brother Geoff get a kick out of this?" he asked the horse who gazed at him complacently as he munched his hay. "He always said that when I fell, it would be a sight to see. I'll bet even he didn't know how right he was."

Chapter 14

Nathan walked across the yard carrying his empty breakfast tray. Normally, he simply set the tray near the barn door before he started working on the corral, but this morning he needed to buy some wire and he'd decided to ask Elyse if she'd like to ride into town with him. He knew it was probably a mistake to invite himself to share her company, especially since coming to the realization that his feelings for her far transcended the professional, but, still, he was eagerly anticipating spending the whole morning with her.

Anticipation soon turned into annoyance, however, as he stepped through the open front door and found Elyse packing Colin into his carrier, obviously on her way out.

"Where are you going?"

Elyse let out a little gasp of surprise and whirled around. "Don't sneak up on me like that. You scared me to death!"

"Sorry," Nathan said sourly. "Where are you going?"

Elyse looked at him quizzically. He didn't sound sorry. He sounded mad. "I'm going out," she responded, turning back to the baby.

"To your friend's?"

"Yes."

"Okay."

"Okay?"

"Sure, I'll just go with you."

"No! You can't do that."

"Why not?"

"Captain Wellesley, we've been all through this before. I've explained and explained that I have to make these little visits and—"

"*Have* to?" Nathan interrupted. "You've never said that you *had* to go anywhere. Only that you *wanted* to."

Elyse bit her lip, furious with herself for the slip. "Well, I don't exactly *have* to, but I haven't been to see my friend for over a week and I don't want her to think there's something wrong."

Nathan's eyes narrowed. "Why would she think that? Have you told her about the situation here?"

"No," Elyse lied. "Of course not."

"Then why would she think something's wrong?"

Frantically, Elyse tried to devise a plausible excuse to cover her lie. "Because I always go to see her at least once a week. If I don't show up, she might worry."

"Why doesn't she ever come here?"

"She just doesn't."

"Why not?"

"Because she doesn't." Hurriedly, Elyse walked into the kitchen, trying to put a little space between them.

Nathan's eyes followed her, noting that she was wadding her skirt up in her hands. "As usual, Mrs. Graham, I think you're keeping something from me, so I guess I'll just have to follow you and find out what it is."

Elyse rounded on him, her eyes flashing. "Fine. You do that. Maybe you'll be more successful than you were last time when you ended up on your back in the weeds."

At Nathan's sudden look of embarrassment, she paused. "I'm sorry," she said contritely. "I shouldn't have said that."

"Never mind," he shrugged. "There's no shame in being dumped off a horse. Happens to the best of us, and I'm sure I *did* look pretty silly."

His self-effacing acceptance of her apology threw

Elyse off guard, and for a moment she just stared at him. Then she released a long, weary breath, knowing that she was beaten. There was no way she could prevent him from following her to Lynn's, and rather than have him continue to think she was participating in some sort of conspiracy, she decided to tell him the truth. Pulling Colin out of his carrier, she sat down at the table and plunked him in her lap. "All right, Captain, you win. I'll tell you about my friend."

Nathan's eyebrows rose despite his efforts to mask his surprise. Nodding solemnly, he seated himself across the table from her.

"Her name is Lynn Potter," Elyse said slowly. "We've known each other since we were girls in school. Lynn was married and had a daughter, but last year there was a fire at her ranch and her husband and little girl were killed."

Nathan winced, but said nothing.

"Lynn was badly burned in the fire, and although she recovered, her face was terribly scarred." Elyse hesitated a moment, swallowing hard. "Lynn was a very beautiful woman and her . . . disfigurement is almost more than she can bear."

Nathan nodded, then again waited for her to continue. When she said no more, he finally prompted, "So?"

"So . . . she has become a recluse, never leaving her ranch, almost never leaving her house. I'm her only link to the outside world. I go over to her house every few days, take her supplies and pick up lists of other things she needs in town. I'm the only person she sees."

"Why have you avoided telling me this all these weeks?"

Elyse averted her eyes and planted a distracted kiss on Colin's head. "I was afraid you might not believe me. That you might insist on seeing Lynn for yourself."

"And if I did?"

"You can't! She couldn't stand it. You can't imagine how she feels about having people see her face."

Nathan nodded his understanding. "And you said she doesn't know anything about me or why I'm here."

"Well . . ." Elyse hedged, "actually . . ."

"You told her."

"Yes."

Nathan's look of compassion quickly changed to anger. Rising, he paced the length of the room, plowing his fingers through his thick blond hair. "That wasn't smart, Elyse. You were asked to tell no one about this set-up. Even having one person know puts both you and me in a lot of danger."

"Lynn isn't going to tell anyone! Why, she doesn't even talk to anyone except me. Who do you think she'd tell?"

Nathan turned and riveted Elyse with an icy stare. "Let's just suppose for a minute that your brother's gang has had us under surveillance and that they know you go over to this woman's house every few days. Don't you suppose they might think Mrs. Potter is an easy target?"

Elyse unconsciously clutched Colin tighter. "Target? Target for what?"

"For information!" Nathan bellowed. "Suppose they want to know who I am and what I'm doing here. Who better to tell them than your girlfriend? They would naturally suspect that she knows everything since you two are together so much . . . and they'd be right, wouldn't they?"

Elyse nodded dumbly.

"So, they move in on her, threaten her, maybe even rough her up a little in order to get the information they want."

Elyse clapped a shaking hand over her mouth and stared at him in horror. "They wouldn't do that!"

"You don't think so? Come on, you're not *that* naive. These aren't nice people we're talking about, Mrs. Graham. These are hardened criminals desperate to get their hands on the big sack of money they think you have. Don't you see that by confiding in your friend, you've now brought her into this whole mess and also put her in danger?"

Elyse closed her eyes, tears seeping out from between her lashes. "I didn't think of that. I just had to talk to someone, and I knew I could trust Lynn to keep my confidence."

"You'd be surprised how fast confidences are betrayed when people are staring down the muzzle of a gun."

"Oh, God," Elyse moaned. "What have I done?"

"Hopefully, nothing, but it was damned stupid of you to gossip with your friends. This isn't a game we're playing here."

Lifting her head, she glared at him defiantly. "I know it isn't a game and I didn't gossip with my friends. I don't even have *friends* anymore, Captain. Just Lynn."

Despite his anger, Nathan's face softened a bit at this heartbreaking admission. "Then you swear to me she's the only person you've told?"

Elyse looked at him squarely. "Yes, I swear, she's the only one."

Nathan expelled a long, relieved breath. "Well, with any luck, the gang doesn't know about her. We don't think they've even heard the rumors about the money yet, so that's a good sign."

"I hope so," Elyse said, her voice breaking again. "I think I'd kill myself if anything happened to Lynn because of me!"

Nathan frowned and sat back down. "Now, don't go crazy on me, lady. I'll get some protection set up for Mrs. Potter."

Elyse shook her head. "She'll never allow it. I told you, she won't even see people anymore, much less allow a stranger to move onto her place."

"We won't have to move anybody onto her place," Nathan explained. "I'll just set up someone to ride over and check on her every day to see if she's seen or heard anything suspicious."

"She still won't allow it."

"Damn it, Elyse, she doesn't have a choice! I'm not going to have this whole case fall apart because some woman is concerned about her looks."

Now it was Elyse's turn to get angry. "What a cruel thing to say! Lynn has gone through a devastating experience. I told you, she lost her husband and her child, not to mention nearly dying herself. Why, when I think of the pain and grief she's endured. . . . How *dare* you make it sound like she's some frivolous, vain woman who's hidden herself away because she's not as pretty as she once was? She's the bravest person I know!"

Nathan held up his hands in supplication. "All right, all right, I'm sorry. I didn't mean that the way it sounded. But the fact remains, now that I'm aware she knows, we have to protect her—for her safety and for all the rest of us involved."

Elyse looked at him in surprise. "Who else is involved besides you and me?"

"I have two men posted in town," Nathan answered shortly, "but who they are doesn't concern you."

"I beg your pardon, Captain, but it most certainly does! Now I will thank you to tell me who else is involved in this little escapade of yours."

Nathan had had just about enough of Elyse's high-handedness and quickly rose from the table. Walking over to the kitchen counter, he gripped the edge of the rough-hewn plank, trying desperately to hold on to his temper. "Look," he said tightly, "the less you know, the safer you are, so quit asking me questions. I told you I'd handle this situation and I will. All I need from you is your promise that you won't tell anybody, and I mean *anybody* else about who I am and why I'm here."

Elyse could hear the barely repressed fury in his voice and prudently did not argue. "I won't tell anyone else. I promise you."

Nathan nodded, satisfied with her sincerity. "Okay. Now, I want you to go see Mrs. Potter today just like you planned. Explain that I know about her and that I'm going to have a man check on her every day. If she sees anything suspicious, anything at all, she's to tell my man immediately."

Elyse opened her mouth to protest, but Nathan cut her off. "Don't tell me she won't cooperate. It's up to you to make sure she does. You got her into this and you have to make her understand the potential danger she's in."

Elyse closed her mouth and nodded.

"I also want you to tell her that you won't be over to see her anymore unless I'm with you."

"But—"

Nathan held up a staying hand. "No but's, Elyse. We may have been lucky enough so far that the gang doesn't know about her, but you're not tempting fate any further. Until this case is over and those bandits are in jail, you will *not* see her again unless I'm there, too. Do you understand me?"

For a long moment Elyse didn't answer.

"Do you understand me?"

"Yes."

"And you won't defy me?"

"No."

"Good. Now, here's what we're going to do. First, I want you to tell me exactly where Mrs. Potter lives. Then, you ride over there for your visit. I'll take another route and keep her place under surveillance while you're there. I want you to stay as long as you normally would if you were just paying a friendly call. Tell her everything we've discussed this morning and make her understand that she *must* cooperate."

Elyse squeezed her eyes shut, trying to imagine how she could coerce Lynn into allowing a strange man onto her property every day to check on her. All she could hope for was that once Lynn understood the danger she was in, she would agree.

"Are you clear on everything?" Nathan asked.

"Yes."

"And you'll do exactly what I'm asking?"

"Yes."

He nodded again. "All right. Then, if you and the baby are ready, I'll get your horse."

Elyse rose on wobbly legs. "We're ready."

Nathan started for the door, but stopped when he heard her say his name. Turning, he looked at her expectantly.

"I'm sorry about all this," she said quietly. "I shouldn't have said anything to Lynn. I just wasn't . . . thinking."

"It's all right," he relented, smiling at her encouragingly. "Everything will work out." Picking up his gloves, he walked out of the house and headed off toward the barn, wishing he could be as sure of those words as he sounded.

Lynn Potter wrung her handkerchief between icy hands and gazed at Elyse imploringly. "I can't, dear. I just can't. It would mean that I would have to talk to this man every day. I just can't do it. I'm sorry, but I'd rather take my chances with this gang. I promise, even if they come here and threaten me, I won't say a word about anything you've told me."

"Lynn, please!" Elyse begged. "You don't know what you'd do if they were threatening you. I couldn't live with myself if something happened to you because I was foolish enough to have told you about all this."

"I'll take my chances," Lynn repeated.

Elyse could see that she was getting nowhere and quickly tried to think of some other tack to take with her stubborn friend. Glancing down at Colin who was sitting in her lap, she suddenly realized that the baby might be the answer. She hated to use Lynn's affection for him as a weapon against her, but she was desperate enough to try just about anything, no matter how underhanded.

"Please," she said quietly. "If you can't find it in your heart to cooperate for your own sake, then think of Colin. Captain Wellesley says these men are such cutthroats that they wouldn't hesitate to harm a baby. If you don't cooperate with this Ranger because you're too embarrassed to have him see your face, you could be putting Colin in jeopardy."

"Oh, Elyse!" Lynn wailed. "Don't do this to me! Can't you . . . can't you send Colin away somewhere?"

"Where would I send him?" Elyse cried, throwing her arms wide.

"I don't know. To his father for a while, perhaps? I know that you and the man, whoever he is, no longer have a relationship, but surely he'd take his son if he knew he was in danger!"

Elyse drew in a shuddering breath, knowing that she had no choice but to confess her terrible secret. Lowering her head, she murmured, "Colin's already with his father."

Lynn looked at the baby and shook her head in bafflement. "What are you talking about?"

"Captain Wellesley is Colin's father."

"Wh-what?"

"Nathan Wellesley is Colin's father."

"I don't understand," Lynn gulped. "You knew this Ranger before he came here to protect you? When? Where? Does he know Colin is his son? Why in the name of God hasn't he married you?"

Despite the anxiety she was feeling, Elyse couldn't help but smile at her friend's uncharacteristic barrage of questions. "I met Captain Wellesley about a year and a half ago when he stopped at my house seeking shelter from a thunderstorm. It was only one night. He doesn't know Colin is his son." She paused, looking up at Lynn solemnly. "And he never will. There was and is nothing between us. What happened was just a moment of sheer madness."

"Oh, my poor darling," Lynn groaned. "Why didn't you tell me?"

"I was too ashamed," Elyse admitted. "What would you have thought of me if I'd told you I'd allowed a man to—"

"*Allowed* him?" Lynn gasped. "Then he didn't force you?"

"No." Elyse shook her head. "He didn't force me. I was lonely and frightened. It was storming outside, and you know how I am about that. He began comforting me and both of us just got carried away . . ."

"Shh," Lynn soothed, getting up and walking around the table to put her arms around Elyse's shoulders. "Don't say any more. I understand."

"Do you?" Elyse asked, looking up with pleading eyes. "Do you really?"

"Yes, I do, really. Remember, Elyse, I'm a widow, too. I know what it's like to spend night after night alone, and if I had been in your position and a handsome stranger was offering me comfort on a stormy night, I might have done exactly the same thing."

"It was insane," Elyse whispered. "Even when it was happening, I couldn't believe it. After he left the next morning, all I wanted to do was forget it. But then I found myself with child and there was no way to forget."

"But you never saw him again after that?"

Elyse shook her head. "Not until last month when he appeared at my doorstep and told me he'd been assigned to protect me."

Lynn sat back down in her chair and wiped a nonexistent speck of dust off the tabletop. "Obviously, the fates brought you back together again."

Elyse threw her a jaundiced look. "The fates had

nothing to do with it. The long arm of the law brought us back together again."

"Well, something did," Lynn shrugged. "But now that he's back, don't you think you should tell him about Colin?"

"No!" Elyse said fiercely. "He must never know. If he did, he might . . . make demands. He might want to get involved with Colin's life, and I will never allow that to happen. Colin is mine. Only mine."

Lynn's expression clearly betrayed the fact that she didn't agree with Elyse's logic, but she said only, "Well, if you don't tell him, he'll never know. Colin looks so much like you that his appearance would never be a giveaway."

"That's the ironic thing," Elyse said, shaking her head. "Colin *doesn't* look like me. He looks exactly like his father."

"How can you say that?" Lynn protested. "Why, with that blond hair and those blue eyes, he's the very image of you."

"Not really. Captain Wellesley is blond and blue-eyed, too, and Colin has his mouth *and* his chin. It never ceases to amaze me that Nathan doesn't see it."

Lynn's eyebrows rose slightly at Elyse's unconscious use of Captain Wellesley's first name. "Well, you know how men are when it comes to babies. I don't think they ever truly relate them back to themselves, but I am a little surprised that Captain Wellesley never even suspected Colin might be his."

"Oh, I think he did at first," Elyse confessed. "He seemed a little shocked when he first saw Colin, and he asked me how old he was, but I lied about his age and told him Colin is two months older than he really is."

Lynn's eyes widened as she absorbed the full humiliating implications of Elyse's lie. "Then Captain Wellesley must have thought that you were . . ."

". . . already with child the night he and I were together," Elyse finished. "Yes, I'm sure he does think that. And, just like the people in town, I'm sure he thinks the worst of me. But, regardless of how tattered my reputation is, it's worth it if it prevents him from finding out the truth."

Lynn nodded, her eyes brimming with compassion.

"And the sooner he catches his band of thieves," Elyse continued, "the sooner he'll be gone from here and my secret will be safe. That's why it's so important that you help me, Lynn. I know I'm asking a lot and I'm dreadfully sorry that I've involved you in this awful situation, but I really need you to cooperate with this Ranger. *Please* say you'll help me."

Lynn released a long, shaky sigh and stared out the front window, absently toying with the scar that ran down her cheek. "All right," she murmured finally. "I'll help you. You can tell your captain that when his man comes around, I'll cooperate in any way that I can. But, please, Elyse, warn him about my face. I don't think I could stand it if this man gave me one of those horrified looks."

Elyse gazed at Lynn lovingly, knowing that her friend had just made the greatest sacrifice of her life. Tears welled in Elyse's eyes as she reached across the table and ran her hand down Lynn's ravaged face. "Thank you," she whispered. "Thank you so much. You truly are the most beautiful person I've ever known."

Chapter 15

Nathan was already waiting for her when she returned home.

"What did Mrs. Potter say?" he asked as he helped her down from the wagon.

"She said she'd allow one of your men to come on her property. She's not happy about it, but she finally agreed."

"She may not be happy now, but she'll be damn glad to have one of my men there if the Rosas gang decides to pay her a visit." Grabbing the horse's harness, Nathan started off toward the barn.

"Are you hungry?" Elyse called after him. "I have some stew . . ."

"I'm always hungry," he called back, "and I love your stew."

Smiling with pleasure at his unexpected compliment, Elyse hurried into the house.

Fifteen minutes later, she heard him clump up the front steps. She peeked out the window, smiling when she noticed that his hair was slightly damp. Immediately, she sobered, not allowing herself to consider why his washing before he came to pick up his food pleased her so much.

Nathan rapped on the door, then entered without waiting for an answer. Covertly, Elyse glanced over at him standing framed in the doorway, then she ladled up two bowls of stew and set them on the table. She didn't dare look over again to see what his reaction was to her unspoken invitation to join her for lunch. Instead, she casually seated herself, as if their eating together were the most normal thing in the world.

Nathan picked up her cue and just as nonchalantly tossed his hat on a chair and sat down across from her.

"I'm going into town after lunch," he said, accepting the plate of cornbread she handed him. "Want to ride along?"

Elyse looked at him in surprise. "Oh, I don't think so," she demurred, "but if you're going to stop at Richman's, there are a couple of things I need."

Nathan poured honey over his cornbread, then stuck the tip of his thumb into his mouth to lick off the excess. Elyse forced herself to look away.

"Come on," he wheedled. "Why don't you ride along? It's a nice day and it'll do you and Colin good to get away for a while."

"But I've already been away all morning and I really should get supper started."

"Don't worry about supper. We can just have some more stew."

Elyse toyed with her food for a moment, pondering his invitation. She really did want to go. Normally, she hated trips to town, but the thought of going with Nathan was somehow appealing. Still, arriving in town together would undoubtedly set up a firestorm of gossip. "I better not," she said with finality.

Nathan looked at her over the rim of his glass. "You're worried that people will talk, aren't you?"

Elyse looked startled for a moment, but quickly covered it. It was almost frightening how often Nathan seemed to be able to read her mind. "No, it's not that . . ."

"Sure it is. And it's a dumb thing to worry about. Everyone in Bixby knows I live here. What difference does it make if they see us together? In fact, it might even stop some of the rumors if they see that our relationship is purely one of employer and employee."

Elyse set down her spoon and leaned forward. "Rumors? What rumors?"

"Oh, hell, you know people are probably talking about us, Elyse. I mean, anytime a single man moves in with a single lady, there's bound to be talk."

"You haven't moved in with me!"

"*I* know that and *you* know that, but do you think anyone in town thinks that? All I'm saying is that if we're never seen together, people are bound to think we're hiding something, so let's just go into town this afternoon and show them there's nothing going on. You can go to Richman's and I can go over to the telegraph office and talk to my man there."

"Your man?"

Nathan cringed inwardly as he realized his slip. "I guess I might as well tell you everything," he sighed. "The new man at the telegraph office is actually a Ranger. He's been posted there to keep his ears open for any news about the Rosas gang and to give me a convenient way to send messages back to headquarters in Austin. The new guy at the livery stable, Will Johnson, is one of my men, too."

Elyse shook her head, amazed by the intricacies of the Rangers' operation. "I had no idea," she murmured.

"That's because you weren't supposed to and I shouldn't have told you. But now that I have, you must promise not to say a word to anyone. The very lives of these men may depend on your discretion."

"I promise," Elyse intoned solemnly.

"Thank you. Anyway, I need to go over and talk to Red about checking on Mrs. Potter. While I'm doing that, you can pick up any supplies you need."

"Okay," Elyse agreed. "I'll go."

"Good." Nathan smiled and rose from the table. "We better get going as soon as we can. It's already getting late." Moving toward the door, he picked up his hat.

Turning back to look at Elyse, he said softly, "Great stew, Mrs. Graham. And thanks for letting me eat with you. It gets kind of lonely out in the barn with only Buck for company."

To her mortification, Elyse felt herself blush. "Do you like pot roast?" she asked almost shyly.

"Sure."

"Then, if you'll give me fifteen minutes before we leave, I'll put one on to simmer."

"With potatoes and carrots?"

"Yes," she smiled. "With potatoes and carrots."

Nathan grinned, the dazzling smile that always made Elyse's knees go weak. "You've got it, ma'am. In fact, for pot roast with potatoes and carrots, I'll give you twenty minutes."

The trip into town was pleasant and relaxed as Nathan and Elyse chatted about inconsequential things and enjoyed the afternoon sunshine.

When they reached the main street of Bixby, however, Nathan felt Elyse stiffen beside him. He glanced over at her, noticing that her easy smile had faded. She was sitting bolt upright, her hands clenched in her lap, her eyes riveted on some indistinct point straight ahead. "Relax," he whispered. "You look like a sinner on the way to the stocks." When this comment elicited no response, he gave her a friendly nudge in the ribs. "Come on . . . everything will be okay. They're just people." To prove his point, he doffed his hat and called out greetings to everyone they passed, as if their coming into town together were an everyday occurrence.

When they finally pulled up in front of Richman's, he again glanced over at Elyse. "What are you looking so guilty about?" he chuckled. "Your face is so red, you'd think you were riding into town naked."

Elyse threw him a shocked look, but said nothing.

Gathering her faded gray skirts around her legs, she started to climb down.

"Wait a minute," Nathan ordered softly. "There's no reason for you to break your neck just because you're mad I made a joke." Jumping down, he headed around the back of the wagon. Coming up along Elyse's side, he held up his arms, gesturing impatiently when she made no move to let him assist her. "Come on," he coaxed. "I promise I won't touch anything I shouldn't."

His teasing comment made Elyse smile and immediately the tension between them evaporated.

"How long will you be?" she asked when she was safely standing on the boardwalk.

"Twenty minutes or so. Will that be enough time for you to finish your shopping?"

She nodded.

"I'll come back for you as soon as I'm done, then." Giving her one last encouraging look, he climbed back up in the wagon and headed off toward the telegraph office.

Elyse started into the store, then paused briefly and took a wary look down the street. To her profound relief, no one was paying any attention to her. Plastering on what she hoped was a breezy smile, she opened the door to Richman's and stepped inside.

"Hello, Mrs. Graham," Mr. Richman called from the back of the store.

Elyse returned the storekeeper's greeting, a little surprised that he was being so cordial. Most of the time when she came into his store, he'd eyed her as if he expected her to steal something.

"Sell those piglets of yours?"

"Yes," Elyse nodded, wondering if he was trying to ferret out whether she would be able to pay for today's purchases.

"Get a good price?"

"Reasonable."

"Good, good. Can't ask for more than that." Stepping behind the counter, Hiram spread his hands expansively and asked, "What can I get for you today?"

"I need some flour, sugar, salt . . . and a jug of maple syrup."

"More maple syrup?" Richman laughed. "You and that hand of yours sure must like that stuff. He just bought a jug when he was in here last week."

"He's partial to it," Elyse said, mortified to feel hot color creeping up her neck.

"A nice man, that Mr. Wells," Richman noted, swinging a twenty-pound sack of flour up onto the counter. "And generous, too. His mother must be very proud to have raised such a loving son."

Elyse looked at the smiling man quizzically, but didn't question him. Although she was curious as to what he might be talking about, she didn't want him to think that Nathan's relationship with his mother was of undue interest to her. Hoping to separate herself from Hiram Richman's prattle, she sauntered over to the jewelry display case. Looking down through the glass top, she drew in a sharp breath. Her grandmother's diamond ring was gone.

"Sold it," Hiram called happily. "In fact, your—"

"I'm so glad," Elyse interrupted, hurrying away from the case before Richman could finish his sentence. She didn't want to know who had bought the ring. Didn't want to know which of the pious, judgmental matrons in Bixby was sporting her grandmother's diamond. "I wouldn't want to think that you had paid me for it and not been able to get your money back."

"No worry there," Hiram grinned. "I had several people interested, but it was—"

"Is my order ready yet?" Elyse said quickly, trying desperately to prevent him from blurting out a name.

Hiram drew himself up to his full diminutive height. "Almost," he said, obviously offended by her repeated interruptions. "I didn't realize you were in such a hurry."

"I have to get the baby home for his nap," Elyse said quickly, gesturing to Colin who was drowsing in his carrier.

"Of course," Richman said, embarrassed now that he'd been so short-tempered with her. "Just a moment and I'll measure out your salt." Turning away, he plunged a scoop into a barrel and started sprinkling salt into a container sitting atop a scale. "That's quite an unusual, ah, *thing* that you have there to carry your baby in."

Elyse glanced down at the sling Nathan had built. "Yes, it is, but it's very handy."

"Where did you get it, if you don't mind my asking."

Elyse did mind, and so said vaguely, "It was a gift."

Hiram continued measuring salt. "Oh? From who?"

Elyse's expression became wary. "You know, Mr. Richman, I don't think I've ever seen you as talkative as you are today. You're usually so quiet."

Hiram looked up, his eyes sparkling like a mischievous schoolboy. "You're right, Mrs. Graham, and you're not the first person who's noticed."

"Oh?"

Richman grinned, his face splitting into a remarkably toothy smile. "It's my new wife."

"Wife!" Elyse exclaimed. "I didn't know you had married."

"Yes, I did. Marybelle Connor did me the honor of becoming my wife, oh, about three months ago now, and I must say, we are ecstatically happy together."

"Well, congratulations," Elyse smiled. In her mind, she was trying to picture the loud, domineering Marybelle Connor and the timid, retiring Hiram Richman being "ecstatically happy together." The thought was vastly amusing.

Encouraged by Elyse's sunny smile, Hiram added, "Mrs. Richman feels that in business, personality is as important as products, so she has encouraged me to be more friendly to my customers."

I'll just bet she has, Elyse thought. Bullied you into it is probably more like it. "Well, you certainly have done a good job of taking her advice to heart," she said aloud.

"Thank you. Now, back to that little carrier of yours. Who did you say gave it to you?"

"I don't think I said."

"I bet you think I'm being nosy, don't you?" Hiram chuckled. "But, actually, I'm asking for a very good reason." Leaning across the counter, he whispered conspiratorially, "Mrs. Richman has recently discovered that she is in the family way, so we will be needing something like that very soon."

Elyse's jaw dropped open before she could stop it. Marybelle Connor pregnant? Why, the woman had to be forty if she was a day, and Hiram Richman at least ten years older than that. Plus, Marybelle had to outweigh her husband by forty pounds. And this unlikely pair was going to have a baby after only three months of marriage? Obviously, they *were* "ecstatically happy."

"Well, congratulations again, Mr. Richman," Elyse tittered, unable to suppress the giggle that bubbled up.

Hiram blushed to the roots of his hair. "Thank you. Now, about that carrier?"

Elyse sighed inwardly. There was no help for it. She was going to have to tell the tenacious little man who had made the carrier. "My hired hand, Mr. Wells, made it for me," she said.

To her complete surprise, Hiram did not give her the knowing look she'd expected. Instead, he shot her another toothy grin and said, "Well, wasn't that nice of him. He's a very talented man, isn't he? And so generous, too!"

Elyse frowned. That was twice now he'd mentioned Nathan's generosity. What in the world had Nathan done that made Hiram Richman think he was so generous?

"Yes, it was very nice of him." Pointedly, Elyse turned

away and began examining some ribbons, hoping that the conversation would now end.

No such luck.

"Do you think he'd consider making one of those carriers for Mrs. Richman? Of course, I'd be happy to pay him."

"I don't know," Elyse said honestly, laying down the ribbons with a sigh. "You'd have to ask him."

"Oh, I will! I will, indeed. Mrs. Richman simply *has* to have one."

At that moment, the front door opened. Elyse breathed a huge sigh of relief as she saw Nathan stepping across the threshold.

"Mr. Wells!" Hiram sang out. "So good to see you. I've just been having a lovely conversation with Mrs. Graham, and she told me all about this clever carrier you built for her baby."

Nathan threw Elyse a perplexed look, then turned to Hiram and nodded. "Yeah, I did. What about it?"

"Do you suppose you would consider making one of those for me?" Hiram asked. "Of course, I'd be happy to pay you for your efforts."

A slight smile played around the corners of Nathan's mouth. "For you, Mr. Richman?"

"Well, of course, not for *me!*" Hiram chortled. Surreptitiously, he looked around as if checking to see if anyone had sneaked into the store to eavesdrop on their conversation. "It's a gift for my wife. She's . . . in the family way."

Elyse didn't think Nathan was going to be able to maintain his straight face, but somehow he managed. "You don't say!" he replied, his voice uncharacteristically husky. "Well, congratulations to you both. I'm sure you must be very happy."

"Oh, yes, and surprised, too!"

Nathan quickly turned away, covering his mouth with his hand and pretending to cough. "I'd be happy to make a carrier for you, Mr. Richman," he choked.

"Wonderful!" Hiram beamed. "Just name your price."

Nathan smiled and held up a hand. "Consider it a gift."

Hiram looked positively apoplectic. "Why, Mr. Wells, what a grand gesture. Thank you so very, very much!"

"You're welcome. I'll make it as soon as I have a chance."

"Oh, there's no hurry. We won't be needing it till about Christmas."

"I won't be here by then," Nathan noted, "but I'll get it to you before I move on."

"Oh, of course, I forgot, you're just here for the summer. Well, anytime that's convenient will be fine. I can't wait to tell Marybelle about this. She'll be so excited."

Now it was Elyse's turn to cough behind her hand. The thought of Marybelle Connor being excited was almost as hilarious as the vision of Marybelle being ecstatic.

"Are you ready, Mrs. Graham?" Nathan asked politely.

"Yes, all ready, Mr. Wells." Elyse gestured toward the counter, and Nathan stepped forward to gather up her purchases. "Thank you so much for your help, Mr. Richman. How much do I owe you?"

"Forget it, Mrs. Graham," Hiram said, batting a careless hand in her direction. "Since I know how much Mr. Wells enjoys pancakes and maple syrup, you just consider these supplies a trade for the carrier."

Elyse whirled around and looked at Nathan, but he merely shrugged. "Right nice of you, Mr. Richman," he said congenially. "I'll get straight to work on that carrier."

"Is there anything you need in the way of supplies to make it?"

Nathan thought a moment, then said. "A pair of suspenders."

"Of course," Hiram chuckled. "That's why you

bought those suspenders a couple of weeks ago. I couldn't understand it at the time, since the ones you were wearing looked perfectly good, but now I see." Peering closely at the baby carrier, he nodded and walked over to a rack of suspenders and belts. Riffling through them, he picked out a bright red pair. "Will these do?" he asked, holding them out to Nathan.

"Red ones, huh," Nathan laughed. "Yes, they'll do."

Hiram grinned happily and handed the suspenders to Nathan. "Always did love red. Never thought I had the personality to wear it, but maybe my son will."

"So you want a boy, do you?" Nathan asked, tucking the suspenders into Elyse's sack of supplies.

"Doesn't every man?" Hiram responded. "A fine son, just like this little boy." Reaching out, he chucked Colin under the chin. "Bet you'd like a couple of these yourself one day, wouldn't you, Mr. Wells?"

Nathan looked over at Colin and smiled. "Someday, maybe."

"We really need to go," Elyse interjected quickly, feeling very uncomfortable with the swing the conversation was taking.

Nathan looked at her in surprise, but nodded. "Yes, ma'am. On our way." Slinging the sack of flour over his shoulder, he headed for the door.

With a last fleeting smile at Hiram Richman, Elyse followed Nathan outside.

"That has to be the most incredible shopping trip I've ever had," she murmured as she settled herself in the wagon.

"How so?"

"Why, in ten years of going to Mr. Richman's store, I don't think I've ever heard him laugh. The change in the man in unbelievable. And all because of Marybelle Connor."

Nathan shrugged. "Just goes to show what the right woman will do for a man, I guess."

Elyse looked over at him, her eyes sparkling, then

gave vent to a melodic peal of giggles. "I guess," she nodded, "but, oh, Captain Wellesley, if you only knew Marybelle ..."

Chapter 16

Nathan looked up from his plate of pot roast and studied Elyse's wan face with concern. "You seem very quiet tonight, Mrs. Graham."

Elyse made a feeble attempt to smile. "I do? I'm sorry if I'm poor company."

"It's not that. There's nothing wrong with being quiet. It's just that you were so jovial while we were driving home from town. What happened between then and now to change your mood so much?"

"It's nothing. Just a personal matter."

Nathan set down his fork and crossed his hands under his chin. "Come on," he cajoled gently. "Tell me. You'll probably feel better if you talk about it. Is it something I said?"

"No, it has nothing to do with you. It's just that . . . Oh, it's not important." To Nathan's astonishment, tears welled up in her eyes, and with an embarrassed little cry, she rose from the table and rushed into the kitchen.

Nathan threw down his napkin and followed her, standing close behind her but being careful not to touch her. "What's the matter, sweetheart?" he asked softly.

Elyse's breath caught in her throat. He hadn't called her that since the night of the storm, but the low timbre of his voice was exactly as she remembered. "It's my grandmother's wedding ring."

Nathan smiled inwardly. For once, she had a problem he could easily solve. "What about it?"

She sniffed and tried valiantly to give him a smile. "It's stupid of me to be so upset. You see, I sold the ring to Mr. Richman to pay off part of the debt I owe him. For months now, the ring has been in the display case at his store. Whenever I'm in there, I always go over and look at it. Somehow, seeing it makes it seem like it's still mine. But today . . . today . . ."

A new rush of tears flooded down her cheeks. "Today when I was there, the ring was gone and Mr. Richman told me he sold it." With an agonized sob, Elyse buried her face in her hands and gave vent to all the sadness and loss she had kept pent up for so long.

Nathan hesitated a moment, his emotions fighting with his reason. It would be sheer madness to touch her, he told himself firmly. If he took her in his arms, it would change their relationship forever. That wasn't a chance he should take. Holding her would inevitably lead to kissing her, and kissing her would be a huge mistake. He'd kissed her before and it had taken him months to forget the softness of her lips, the sweet taste of her mouth. He shouldn't do it.

With a groan, he stepped forward, pulling Elyse gently into his arms and guiding her head down to his shoulder. To his surprise, she didn't pull away but instead melted into his embrace almost as if she'd been hoping he'd hold her.

"Don't cry, baby," he crooned, burying his lips in her hair.

Lifting her head, Elyse looked up into his sea-blue eyes. He was so strong, so solid, and it was wonderful to have his arms around her again. Unconsciously, her eyes drooped as she allowed herself to languish in his embrace. He smelled so good . . . felt so good.

Nathan saw her apprehension fade to surrender and knew he was lost. "Elyse," he breathed, lowering his mouth to hers. Her lips softened, then parted beneath his.

A surge of desire coursed through him, and gathering her closer, he deepened the caress, running his silky tongue along the inside of her lips. She tasted just as he remembered.

But their kiss was different than before. There was no hesitation, no shyness between them. They were no longer strangers, seeking respite from their lonely lives to share a moment of passion. This time, their kiss was the kiss of lovers who had been separated by fate's whimsy but now had found each other again.

Lovers. The word leaped into Elyse's mind, shattering the moment and causing her to step back and raise a shaking hand to her lips. The last time Nathan Wellesley had kissed her like this, they had become lovers, and no matter how much she enjoyed his seductive attentions, she would not allow that to happen again.

Damn him! she thought irrationally. Why was he so good at this? What made his kiss so different from any other man's she'd ever known?

She looked up into Nathan's tense, questioning face, her eyes accusing. "Don't ever do that again."

"Jesus Christ, Elyse," he rasped, his voice ragged and breathless. "I didn't *do* anything. I kissed you, that's all, and don't tell me you didn't want me to."

"I didn't!" She knew she was lying even as she voiced the words.

Nathan swallowed hard. "Well, if that's how you react when you don't want to be kissed, I don't think I'd live through it if you were enjoying it."

Elyse glared at him, incensed by his lusty observation and infuriated that what he said was true. She loved his kisses. Loved the shivery, shaky feeling his soft lips and questing tongue evoked within her. Loved the feeling of his hard, male body pressed intimately against her. She was mortified by what Nathan Wellesley's kisses did to

her. What *was* it about this man that made her act like
such a fool?

"I didn't want you to kiss me!" she repeated fiercely.

"Okay, then, I'm sorry," Nathan gritted, clamping his
teeth together in a desperate effort to cool the hot blood
racing through his body. "I guess it wasn't a good idea
for me to have supper in here with you, after all."

"No, I guess it wasn't," Elyse mumbled. She turned
away, not wanting him to see the guilt that she knew
must be obvious in her eyes.

*This is your fault as much as it is his. Why can't you just ad-
mit it?* But she couldn't, because admitting that would be
tantamount to violating all the values she'd held sacred
all her life.

Nathan stared at her rigid back for a long moment,
then released a weary sigh. "I have something for you,"
he said quietly.

Elyse didn't turn around. "You do?"

Wordlessly, he pulled the ring out of his shirt pocket
and set it on the table. "Good night, Mrs. Graham."

Elyse remained frozen in place until she heard the
soft click of the door latch, then she walked to the table
and leaned over it curiously. Her grandmother's diamond ring gleamed in the dim light. With a gasp of astonishment, she picked it up, staring at it in disbelief.
Her eyes filled with tears. He had gotten her ring back
for her. *He had gotten her ring back for her!*

"Nathan!" she cried, lunging for the door. "Nathan,
wait!" Racing out onto the porch, she squinted into the
darkness. She could just make out his shadow as he disappeared through the barn door. Heedlessly, she jumped
off the side of the porch and ran across the yard, clutching the ring to her bosom. "Nathan!" she panted, rushing
into the barn. "Nathan, where are you?"

He didn't answer.

She paused to listen for a moment, then experienced
an eerie sense of unease as she glanced around the dark,
cavernous building. When she next spoke again, her

voice was shrill with apprehension. "Nathan? Are you in here?"

She nearly jumped out of her skin when he suddenly stepped out of the darkness, not five feet in front of her. "What do you want?" he asked coldly.

"My ring. How did you get my ring?"

"I bought it. How do you think I got it?"

It was so dark in the barn that Elyse could not see the expression on his face, but from the tone of his voice, she knew he was still angry with her. "But why?"

Nathan stepped closer, causing her eyes to flare wide with fear as his set, angry face suddenly loomed in front of her. "Because I felt bad that you'd been forced to sell it. Because I thought you might like to have it back." His voice dropped until it was barely above a whisper. "Because I thought it would make you happy."

Elyse blinked several times, not knowing what to say. Nathan waited a moment for her to respond. When she didn't, he walked over to the stall where he slept.

"How could you afford it?" Elyse asked suddenly.

"I have plenty of money," he answered shortly.

Picking up her skirts, she hurried after him as he continued on toward the other side of the barn. "Mr. Richman was asking fifty dollars for the ring!" Coming up next to him, she reached out and touched his arm. "Surely you couldn't easily afford that much, and I don't know when I'll ever be able to pay you back."

Nathan looked at her from beneath lowered brows. "I said, I have plenty of money . . . and I don't want you to pay me back."

"But," Elyse blustered, "fifty dollars must be two months salary for you! I can't let you spend that much on me."

Nathan's expression darkened. "Stop it. I just told you, I bought the ring back for you because I wanted to. Can't you leave it at that?"

"No," Elyse said stubbornly. "It's too much— especially on a Ranger's pay."

"For God's sake, Elyse, I'm a Wellesley! Fifty dollars is less than I pay for some of my shirts."

Elyse looked at him in bafflement. "What do you mean, you're 'a Wellesley'? I know what your name is. What does that have to do with anything?"

Nathan suddenly broke into a great gust of laughter. "You've never heard of the Wellesleys?"

Elyse stared at him blankly for a moment, then clapped her hand over her mouth, her eyes widening with astonishment. "Where are you from, Captain?"

"Colorado."

"Colorado . . . That must mean that you're related to *the* Wellesleys, aren't you?"

"*The* Wellesleys?" Nathan asked, beginning to enjoy the turn their conversation was taking. "What Wellesleys are those?"

Elyse frowned in confusion. "Look, Captain, you're the one who just said you're 'a Wellesley.' Are you and I talking about the same family, or not?"

Nathan shrugged elaborately. "I don't know. What family are you talking about?"

Elyse ground her teeth in frustration. "You must know who I'm talking about. The Wellesleys! You know, that incredibly wealthy family who's always being written up in the papers. They own about half of America. I'm sure I read that they're from Colorado."

Nathan laughed out loud at Elyse's frank assessment of his illustrious family. "Oh!" he exclaimed, throwing his head back to emphasize his words. "*Now* I know who you mean. The *Durango* Wellesleys."

"I don't know exactly where they're from," Elyse retorted impatiently. "I just know there is a bunch of brothers—something like seven or eight—and one sister. They're all tremendously successful and well known."

"Ah, yes," Nathan nodded. "I have heard of them."

"Well, you must not be closely related," Elyse decided with a dismissive shrug. "I'm sure you'd know if you were. But maybe you're a distant cousin or something."

Their conversation had done wonders to improve Nathan's mood. Taking Elyse's hand, he unlatched the door to the stall where he slept and pulled her inside, gesturing toward a pile of straw in the corner. "Have a seat, Mrs. Graham, and I'll explain how I can afford to buy back your ring for you."

Elyse frowned at him in frustration, but her curiosity won out. With an irritated huff, she flounced down on the straw, settling her skirt around her.

Nathan sat down beside her, barely able to keep a straight face. "Actually, I *am* related to *the* Wellesleys, as you call them. And you're right, there *are* seven brothers."

Elyse knew she shouldn't pry, but she couldn't help herself. "Do you actually *know* them?"

"Intimately," Nathan chuckled. "I'm brother number five."

To his disappointment, Elyse threw him a look more dubious than impressed. "I don't believe you," she announced. "Why, the Wellesley brothers are famous!"

Nathan's jaw dropped. "What do you mean, you don't believe me? I wouldn't lie to you! I was born in Durango, Colorado, and I'm the fifth son of James and Mary Wellesley. As for my brothers and me being famous, all I can say is, some of us are and some of us aren't. Despite what you've heard, we're not *all* 'tremendously successful and well known,' and I'm one of the ones who isn't."

Elyse felt as if she couldn't swallow. This man belonged to one of the most influential families in America, and he was the father of *her* baby!

She knew she should quit asking questions. She didn't want him to think she was inordinately interested in his family. Unfortunately, her curiosity was stronger than her resolve and she plunged on. "If you're a member of the Wellesley family, how is it you became a Ranger? You're not even a Texan."

"Actually, there are two of us in my family who are

lawmen. I have a younger brother, Seth, who's a sheriff. I really don't remember ever wanting to be anything else. Too much time spent playing sheriff and outlaw when I was a kid, I guess."

"Wasn't one of your brothers a war hero? I remember reading something once about a man named Wellesley who was decorated for bravery during the war. I think it said that he now owns a shipping company in Boston."

"Yeah, that's Stu." Nathan paused, smiling fondly as he thought of his older brother. "And he *is* 'tremendously successful and well known.' So is Miles, my oldest brother. He owns a huge horse-breeding farm in England. He's bred the English Derby winner for the past three years. Geoffrey owns the largest timber company in Oregon, so I guess he would fit into the 'successful' category, too. But Eric is a farmer in Minnesota, and Seth and I are just common lawmen."

Elyse was counting on her fingers as Nathan reeled off these fascinating tidbits about his family. "That's six," she noted. "You're missing somebody."

For a second, Nathan looked perplexed, then he nodded and said, "Oh, yeah, Adam. He's still just a kid in school."

"Really? Where?"

"Harvard," he grinned. "So I guess he's going to be one of the 'tremendously successful,' too."

"And your sister?"

Nathan's face took on a faraway look. "Paula. She's the baby. People say she's the prettiest girl in Colorado."

"And is she?"

"I don't know about that," Nathan laughed, "but I think she's the feistiest. She got married recently to the town blacksmith. God help him."

Elyse's eyebrows rose in surprise. "The prettiest, richest girl in Colorado and she married a blacksmith?"

"Yup, and she could have had anybody she wanted. In fact, one of the Vanderbilt boys asked for her hand

and so did Marshall Grant, but Paula was having none of it. She decided Luke O'Neill was the one and that was that. What Paula wants, Paula gets, and Paula wanted Luke." Nathan shook his head. "The poor guy never had a chance."

"You love your family very much, don't you?"

"Yes," he admitted without hesitation. "I don't see them that often, but they're never far from my thoughts."

They sat for a moment in silence, each lost in their own musings.

"Captain Wellesley?"

Nathan's smile faded. "I wish you'd call me Nathan. You do it sometimes and I like it a lot better than 'Captain Wellesley.' "

Elyse averted his eyes. "Calling you by your first name seems so personal, so familiar . . ."

Nathan put a finger under her chin and raised her head until she was looking at him. "Elyse, we *are* familiar. We're as familiar as two people can be. You know it and so do I."

Before the words were even out of his mouth, he wished he could call them back. But it was too late. The easy companionship they were enjoying was instantly destroyed. With a gasp, Elyse jumped to her feet. "Don't! Don't say anything more." Whirling away, she started for the stall door.

"Elyse!" Nathan called, scrambling to his feet and catching her by the arm. "Don't go. Please."

Elyse swallowed hard and looked up into his handsome face. "I've told you before, Captain, I don't ever want to talk about that again. It was a mistake, a terrible mistake, and one that I deeply regret. I can't believe you'd be so crude as to bring it up again."

Her impassioned statement hit Nathan like a punch in the stomach. *A terrible mistake . . . one that I deeply regret.* Releasing her arm, he turned away, not wanting her to see how devastated he was by her words. "I know you don't want to hear this," he said quietly, "but I'm going to say it anyway. You may regret what happened between us that night, but I don't. It is a memory I will treasure for the rest of my life. And tonight you gave me another one, because, whether you'll admit it or not, that kiss we shared was beautiful, and you thought so, too."

"No matter what I thought about it," Elyse whispered, "you must promise me you won't do it again."

Nathan sighed, trying hard to understand why she was so opposed to his attentions. He was positive she was as attracted to him as he was to her. Why did she fight him so? "All right," he said finally. "I won't."

Elyse wasn't sure whether she was relieved or sorry at his agreement. All she knew was that she was exhausted by everything that had happened between them today and she desperately needed to get away from his overwhelming presence.

"I have to get back to the house," she said abruptly. "Colin's there alone and I've been out here far too long."

Nathan nodded, still not turning.

"Good night, Captain Wellesley."

"Good night, Mrs. Graham."

Chapter 17

As tired as she was, Elyse couldn't sleep. A full two hours after she came in from the barn, she was still tossing and turning, trying in vain to banish from her exhausted mind all the conflicting thoughts she was having about Nathan Wellesley.

Of all the disturbing revelations the night had brought, there was one that truly frightened her. Nathan was a *Wellesley*. Elyse tried to remember everything she'd ever read or heard about the famous family. She knew they were one of the five richest families in America and that James Wellesley, Nathan's father, was a man of unparalleled influence and power.

One of the five richest, most prestigious families in America. A family revered for their unlimited resources, influence, and power. And what would these titans do if they knew their fifth son had an illegitimate child living on a shabby, broken-down little ranch in Texas? The possibilities were so terrifying, she could hardly force herself to ponder them.

But she had to. Nathan was a product of privilege and power. He had laughingly mentioned that his sister, Paula, stopped at nothing to get what she wanted. Did he possess this same trait? Did he always get what he wanted, no matter what the consequences to others? From what Elyse knew of him, she suspected he did.

What if what he wanted was his son? What could she,

an impoverished widow, do to stop the all-powerful
Wellesleys if they decided they wanted to take her baby
away from her?

Determinedly, Elyse fought back a wave of panic.
"They won't get him," she whispered fiercely into the
darkness. "They won't get him, because they'll never
know."

Therein lay *her* power. No one, with the exception of
Lynn, whom she trusted implicitly, knew who Colin's father was. And no one would ever know ... especially
Nathan Wellesley. She would die before she would lay
that weapon in his hands.

Elyse didn't know how long she'd been asleep when
the sound of someone in her front room woke her. For
several heart-pounding moments, she lay rigid, hardly
daring to breathe, as she listened for any sound that
might give her a clue who was outside her door. She
knew is wasn't Nathan. She had heard his step often
enough that she could recognize it. But there was undoubtedly someone out there.

Whoever it was didn't seem to be walking around
much. Rather, it sounded as if they were looking for
something in the kitchen. Every few seconds she would
hear things being pushed around on her counter and
pans being scraped across the stove.

Finally, after several agonizing minutes, the noises
stopped. Elyse emitted a shaky breath, wondering if the
intruder had given up his search and left. She was just
throwing back the covers to go out and investigate when
she heard someone rattling the latch on her bedroom
door. With a gasp of sheer terror, she leaped across her
bed and grabbed Colin out of his cradle, pressing his
face close to her breasts to muffle his little cry of surprise.

Convinced that at any moment the bedroom door
would be flung open and she would be shot on sight, she

opened the bedroom window and crawled through. She
felt the hem of her nightgown catch on a nail and gave
it a furious tug, heedless of the long, tearing sound she
heard as she yanked it free. Running across the yard,
she burst through the barn door.

"Nathan!" she screamed, racing over to the stall
where he slept. "Nathan, wake up! There's someone in
the house!"

Nathan awoke instantly, his years of living a life of
danger allowing him to immediately shrug off all remnants of sleep. The moon was full and he could see
Elyse illuminated by the ethereal white light sifting
through the open barn door. Throwing back his blanket,
he bolted upright, lunging for his gun, then wheeled
around with his pistol drawn when he heard Elyse suddenly let out a shriek.

Training his gun at a point just above her head, he
quickly swung it back and forth, looking for whoever
was menacing her. Seeing no one, he lowered the gun
and looked at her in confusion. She was staring at him,
openmouthed, her eyes as big as saucers.

"My God, you're naked!" she cried, burying Colin's
face in her shoulder as if to shield him from the sight.

Nathan shot a distracted glance down the length of
his body. Was it possible that seeing him naked had
made her scream? "Stay here!" he barked, heading for
the door at a dead run.

"Nathan!" Elyse screamed. "You can't go in there
with no clothes on!" Grabbing his pants off the floor,
she raced out of the stall after him. "Stop! You have to
put your pants on!"

Nathan paused long enough to turn back toward her,
again presenting her with a full view of his magnificent
body. "I said, stay in the barn!" he commanded.

"But your pants!"

"Forget my pants, damn it!"

"No! You have to get dressed!" Gathering up her
nightgown, she ran out into the yard after him.

"Put these on!" she whispered loudly, racing up behind him and flinging his pants at his head.

"Damn it, Elyse! Are you nuts?"

"Put them on!"

"Oh, for Christ's sake!" Thrusting his gun into her hand, he shook out his pants and shoved one leg into them, all the while continuing to hop across the yard.

It was a big mistake. The darkness, his agitation, and the tight fit of the pants leg all conspired against him and suddenly he found himself facedown in the dirt.

"Nathan!" Elyse cried, dropping to her knees beside him. "Are you all right?"

Nathan rolled over on his back, frantically trying to kick the tangled pants off. "Hell, no, I'm *not* all right!"

"Hurry or they're going to be gone before you get in there."

"God *damn* it!" Nathan cursed, finally freeing himself from the twisted material and leaping to his feet.

"Nathan, you have to hurry! This is taking you far too long. You've got to get in there!"

Nathan threw Elyse a killing look and grabbed his gun out of her hand. "If you hadn't made me stop to put my damn pants on, I'd be in there already! Now get back to the barn and stay there till I come for you!"

Elyse had no intention of going back to the barn, but she prudently said nothing.

Nathan finally managed to get his pants on, then took off, weaving and dodging as he worked his way around the side of the house to the front door. With a hard kick, he dislodged the flimsy little portal from its frame and hurtled himself inside.

All was silent.

Elyse didn't know how long she stood in the yard, holding the now-screaming baby and staring at the front door as she waited for the sound of gunfire. The last thing she expected, was to see Nathan saunter out onto the porch—laughing.

"Come here," he called.

She didn't move.

"Come here! It's okay."

This last statement prodded her into action, and with a relieved little cry, she flew across the yard and up onto the porch. "Is he gone?"

"No," he chuckled. "He's still in there."

Elyse gaped at him as if he'd taken leave of his senses. "What? He's still in there?"

"Yup."

"You mean you overpowered him? Do you have him tied up?"

"Nope."

"No?"

"Go in and see for yourself."

"Nathan Wellesley, have you lost your mind? I'm not going in there!"

"It's okay," he grinned, reaching out and plucking the squirming Colin out of her hands. "I wouldn't let you go in there if it wasn't safe, would I?"

"Most of the time I'm not sure what you would do."

"Aw, come on. I'll go with you." Shifting the baby to his left arm, Nathan took Elyse's hand and led her through the broken doorway.

Despite his reassurances, Elyse lagged behind as they entered the house, then stood stock-still as Nathan released her hand and lit the kerosene lamp on the table.

"Come over here," he said, crooking his finger at her and walking toward the kitchen.

Reluctantly, Elyse took a step forward. To her utter astonishment, Nathan started laughing out loud and pointed to the kitchen floor. "Meet your intruder."

Warily, Elyse peeked around the corner of the counter, her brow furrowing with confusion as she spied a large gray ball on the floor. "What is it?"

"I just told you," Nathan guffawed. "It's your intruder."

Elyse threw him an enraged look. How *dare* he laugh

at her when she was so scared? "I don't think you're funny," she spat.

Nathan made a valiant attempt to sober. "I'm sorry, really I am."

"What *is* that?"

Nathan burst into another gust of laughter. "It's a possum. He must have crawled in through the window looking for food. Haven't you ever seen one before?"

"Of course I've seen a possum!" Squatting down, Elyse looked at the little creature more closely, then glared up at Nathan. "What did you do, kill the poor little thing?"

"No, I didn't kill it!" he retorted. "It's playing possum, for God's sake. They do that when they're scared. That's what 'playing possum' is. Curling up in a ball and hiding."

At that very moment, Elyse wished she could curl up in a ball and hide, not because she was scared, but because she was more embarrassed than she'd ever been in her life. She turned and watched the possum make a clumsy exit through the window. Then, without warning, she burst into tears.

Nathan's grin immediately disappeared. He took a step forward, then realized he was still holding the baby. Quickly, he walked over to the settee and put Colin down, bracing several pillows around him to make sure he didn't roll off.

Without a thought to his current state of undress, he hurried back over to where Elyse still stood and took her in his arms. "Don't cry, sweetheart," he crooned, lifting her face up to his and placing gentle little kisses on her eyes and temples. "I know you were scared and I shouldn't have laughed." He kissed her again, this time at the corner of her mouth. "Forgive me."

"I was so frightened," Elyse sobbed, clutching at his bare shoulders. "I thought the gang was here. I really did. I heard sounds and . . ."

"Shh," Nathan soothed, brushing his thumbs across

her cheeks to wipe away her tears. "It's over now. I'm here and you're safe. I won't leave you alone again." Moving his mouth a fraction of an inch, he settled his lips on hers.

"Oh, Nathan . . ." Elyse sighed when he finally lifted his head. Burying her face against the solid security of his massive chest, she circled his back with her arms and ran her hands up and down the length of him. His bare chest was warm and smooth against her forehead and the smell of his skin was intoxicating. With a little mewl of pleasure, she began kissing him, her lips blazing a passionate trail across the heavy ridges of muscle, then pausing to tease a hard, flat nipple.

Nathan groaned deep in his throat. His pants were still unbuttoned and hung loosely around his waist, exposing his abdomen all the way down to where the thick mat of hair began. He closed his eyes and threw his head back in ecstasy as Elyse's lips and tongue continued to toy erotically with his nipple.

Passions long denied quickly ignited, and with a moan, Nathan reached around and took one of Elyse's hands, guiding it downward toward his swelling arousal. "Touch me," he rasped.

Elyse didn't hesitate. With a throaty little groan of acquiescence, she lowered her hand and wrapped her fingers around his erection.

As she began to intimately stroke him, Nathan opened his eyes, wanting to see her face. What he saw instead was so startling that he immediately let out a sharp bark of fear and wrenched out of her embrace. Racing over to the settee, he grabbed Colin just as the baby began to roll off the couch.

"What's wrong?" Elyse cried, running to join him where he knelt on the floor.

For a moment, Nathan stayed in a crouched position, cradling the baby to his chest. Finally, with a relieved sigh, he straightened. "He was about to roll off the settee. I guess he kicked off the pillows I braced around him." Gesturing downward, he pointed to the three pillows that lay scattered on the floor. "It probably wouldn't have hurt him, even if he had fallen, but I didn't want to take the chance."

"Oh, my God," Elyse moaned, taking the baby and clasping him close to her. "He could have broken something!"

Nathan looked at her dubiously. "I doubt that. He was about to take a spill off a settee onto a pile of pillows, not off a cliff onto a bed of jagged rocks."

"Still," Elyse murmured, her face buried in the baby's neck, "he could have gotten hurt. Thank you for stopping him." She looked up at Nathan and, for a moment, neither of them knew what to say.

It was obvious their moment of passion was over, although Nathan's physical state certainly did not attest to that fact. Elyse's eyes flicked downward, then fled completely, as if by ignoring the manifestation of Nathan's desire for her, she could also ignore what had almost happened between them.

"Well," she said brightly, "it's late, and after the excitement tonight, I think we all need some sleep."

Nathan closed his eyes for a moment, swallowing hard. "I suppose you're right. I'm going to sleep in here, though."

"What?"

"I said, I'm going to sleep in here."

Elyse drew herself up indignantly. "Now, wait a minute! I know that I'm probably to blame for much of what . . . happened a few minutes ago, and I deeply regret if I gave you the impression—"

"God, I hate that expression!" Nathan exploded.

Elyse took a startled step backward as if to protect herself from his sudden vehemence. "What expression?"

" 'I deeply regret . . .' Why do you always say that?"

"I don't always say that."

"Yes, you do. Especially when you're talking about anything that has to do with us."

"Us? There is no 'us,' Captain."

"Oh, so now I'm 'Captain' again. You weren't calling me 'Captain' a few minutes ago when you were kissing me."

Elyse felt a guilty blush wash over her cheeks and quickly turned away. "I have to put the baby to bed now."

"No, you don't," Nathan thundered, incensed that she was obviously going to pretend their passionate encounter had never happened. "He's already sound asleep in your arms. You know how he is. If you put him in his cradle, he'll just wake up and start crying. Give him to me and I'll hold him for a while if you don't want to, but we're going to get this talked out."

"I'll hold him," Elyse whispered.

"Okay. Let's sit down."

Reluctantly, Elyse followed Nathan over to the settee. They sat down, and after she'd settled Colin comfortably across her lap, Nathan reached over and picked up one of her hands, stroking it with his thumb. "Look, Elyse," he said, his gaze direct and sincere. "I don't want to argue with you. All I'm saying is that I wish you wouldn't feel so guilty about everything. I'm a man, you're a woman. We kissed, we touched each other. That doesn't make us David and Bathsheba."

"There's more to it than that," Elyse insisted, pulling her hand away and tucking it into the voluminous folds of her nightgown. "You know we were headed for a lot more than kissing. It happened once between us and it could—"

"So," Nathan interrupted, "you're finally admitting that what happened between us that night wasn't all my fault?"

"No, it wasn't," she said quietly. "But, still, it was a terrible mistake, and one I've vowed never to repeat. I just wish you'd help me keep that vow."

Nathan shook his head wearily. "I can't promise you that. I'd like to, but I'd be lying if I did." Gently, he placed two fingers against her cheek and turned her face toward him until she was looking directly into his eyes. "Elyse, I've been attracted to you since the first moment I saw you, and, as much as I've tried to deny it, that attraction hasn't gone away. I told you the morning after the storm that what happened between us wasn't common for me, and that was the truth. I have never had an experience like you and I had together that night— not before and not since—until tonight, anyway. And, you're right, we *were* headed for a lot more than kissing and, right or wrong, I wanted it to happen. That's why I can't promise you that I'll never touch you or kiss you again. I *can* promise you that I'll never force you to do anything you don't want to do. But if the moment is right and you're willing and I'm willing, then maybe the passion we shared once will happen again. And I'm sure it will be just as wonderful as it was the first time."

He paused, searching her face for a reaction to his provocative words, but Elyse was careful to keep her expression blank. Finally, he dropped his gaze and reached back to massage the back of his neck. "Anyway, those are my feelings, and if that makes me some kind of monster in your eyes, then I'm sorry. I'm a young, healthy man and you're a very beautiful woman. Frankly, I think I'd be concerned about myself if I didn't feel a little honest lust toward you."

Throughout Nathan's lengthy speech, Elyse kept looking down at her lap. Down at her baby—*his* baby. When she finally looked up, there was a great sadness in her eyes. "There are many things about me that you don't know," she said quietly. "Many things that have made me feel the way I do. Please, Nathan, try to understand and honor my wishes."

"I'll do my best," he said earnestly, "but that's all I can promise." He stood up, running his fingers through his hair and looking out at the first gray streaks of dawn. "We really should get some sleep. It's almost morning."

"You can't sleep with me," Elyse said with finality.

Nathan turned and looked at her in astonishment. "I didn't expect to."

"But . . ." she stammered. "You said before that you were going to sleep in the house."

"I *am* going to sleep in the house," he nodded. "Tonight and every night from now on. But, you don't need to worry. I plan to sleep in your brother's room."

Elyse's expression remained wary.

"Elyse, listen to me. What happened tonight with the possum was a warning. Granted, all that was in the house was a harmless animal, but next time, we might not be so lucky. Your next late-night intruder might be one of the Rosas gang. And after the fiasco of trying to get from the barn to the house, I realized that I'm too far away out there to be of any real use. I can't hear if someone breaks in and next time, you might not be able to get away to come for me. If I sleep in here, I'll hear whatever you do and I can move a damn sight quicker to protect you . . . and him." With a nod, Nathan gestured toward Colin. "Do you understand?"

Slowly, Elyse nodded.

"Good. Then, I'm for bed." With a smiling wink, he strode off to Tom's room, closing the door firmly behind him.

Elyse wearily laid her head back on the settee. What a night! As much as she tried to ignore it, there was no denying the effect Nathan Wellesley had on her. It was absolutely sinful how she reacted to him. Even now she tingled all over, just from sitting next to him. Of course, she thought wryly, that was probably due to the fact that he never had buttoned up his pants.

A naughty little smile curved her lips. She probably should have pointed it out to him, since he didn't seem to be aware that his denims were gaping open, but, if she had, she would have deprived herself of the opportunity to covertly ogle all that beautiful golden skin.

"You're terrible!" she whispered. "You take him to task for lusting after you and just look at yourself. Why,

every time you see the man, you have wicked thoughts!"
She sighed wistfully. "How could a woman *help* but have
wicked thoughts when a man had a body like his?"

Chapter 18

Nathan poured two cups of coffee and set them on the table. "Do you have a gun, Elyse?"

Elyse was so busy trying to spoon porridge into Colin's mouth that for a moment she didn't answer. "I don't know," she said absently. "My husband had one. It must be around here someplace. You know, I wish I had one of those high chairs for the baby. Now that he's sitting up, it would make it so much easier to feed him if I didn't have to hold him at the same time."

Nathan frowned at her casual dismissal of his question. "Do you have any idea where your husband's gun is?"

Elyse looked up in surprise. "I think it's in the drawer in the breakfront. Why do you want to know?"

"Because I'm going to teach you how to shoot it this morning."

"No you're not."

Nathan threw down the spoon he was using to stir his coffee and glared at her in annoyance. "Just once, I'd like to suggest something to you and not have your first response be 'no.'"

"If you'd ever suggest something that I really wanted to do, I wouldn't always say no. Unfortunately, I do not want to learn to shoot a gun."

"Why? Do you already know how?"

"No, but I don't want to learn."

"Why not?"

"Because I don't like guns. In fact, I think most of the tragedy in the world is caused by guns."

"That's ridiculous. Guns don't cause tragedies, the people using them do."

Elyse shrugged. "That's just the answer I'd expect from a man who makes his living by one."

Nathan drew himself up in offense. "I beg your pardon, lady, but you seem to forget that my gun is used on the right side of the law, to protect innocent people like you. That is possible, you know."

"You're right," she sighed. "And I'm not trying to offend you with my opinion. But I don't like guns and I don't want to learn to use one."

"Well, you have to. It's for your own protection."

Elyse picked up a napkin and began wiping the baby's face. "I thought you just said that's what *your* gun was for."

"It is," Nathan agreed, "but I'm not always here. As you know, I do occasionally go into town and I want to go round up those mustangs now that I've got the corral mended. I'd just feel better about being away if you knew how to handle a weapon."

Elyse bit her lip. She couldn't argue with him, since what he said made complete sense. But even if she learned how to shoot a gun, would she really be able to turn one on another human being? "I couldn't shoot anybody no matter what the circumstances were," she declared.

"Yes, you could. If some desperado was threatening Colin, you'd be amazed how fast you could use one."

Elyse mulled this over for a moment, a little shiver of apprehension shaking her. "You're right," she said quietly. "I guess I could under those circumstances."

"Then you should be willing to let me teach you how to handle one properly. The most dangerous gun in the world is the one in the hands of someone who doesn't know how to use it."

"Oh, God," Elyse moaned, throwing her head back and closing her eyes. "I hate this so much!"

"I know you do," Nathan said sympathetically, "but you can see my reasoning, can't you?"

"Yes."

"Then, do whatever needs to be done with the baby and let's go have a lesson." Scraping back his chair, he rose from the table. "I'll saddle the horses."

"Where are we going?"

"Up to the ridge north of your property. There's nothing around there, so it's a safe place, in case a shot goes wild."

"What about Colin?"

"I guess we'll have to take him along. He can play on a blanket or something."

"But he's starting to crawl," Elyse protested. "I don't think he should be underfoot in a situation where there are guns being fired."

Nathan considered this for a moment, then nodded. "You're right. Could we leave with him with Mrs. Potter? Would she watch him for an hour or two?"

"I'm sure she would, but . . ."

"Don't worry. I'll stay out of sight while you take him up to her house."

Elyse nodded, her decision made. "Okay. Get the horses. I'll be ready in ten minutes."

Nathan stayed back in the trees as Elyse approached Lynn's house carrying Nathan. He watched her knock on the door, then leaned forward curiously when he saw it open.

From this distance, he couldn't see the scars on Lynn's face. Rather, he was treated to the sight of the woman who had once had every eligible young man in Bixby vying for her. She was small and slender, with dark, lustrous hair and a light, melodic voice that caused Nathan to smile when he heard it. Despite his promise to stay out of sight, he found himself edging his horse closer to get a better look. Thankfully, his surreptitious movement was undetected by Lynn, who was welcoming Elyse in the warmest of terms.

"What are you doing here, my dear? I thought you couldn't come visit anymore till all this unpleasantness is over."

"Nathan told me I could come as long as he is with me," Elyse informed her.

Lynn's smile faded, and she glanced around warily. "You mean he's here?"

"Yes, but don't worry, he can't see you. He's way back in the trees."

Nathan saw Lynn duck back into the house and knew that Elyse must have informed her of his presence. He frowned, wondering why the woman was so concerned about being seen. From the quick glance he'd had, she was lovely. Nathan was sure there must be plenty of men who would be entranced by her shining hair, trim little figure, and warm smile. In light of those attributes, any man worth his salt certainly wouldn't be put off by a few scars. He just wished there was some way he could tell Lynn that.

Less than a minute later, Elyse reappeared in the yard. She walked over to where her horse was tethered, mounted, and rode back to join him.

"I saw your friend," he commented as they headed toward the ridge.

Elyse looked at him expectantly.

"I thought she looked very pretty."

"She *is* very pretty, or at least she was. You probably couldn't see her scars from where you were."

"No, I couldn't," Nathan admitted. "But I don't think I'd feel any different even if I had."

"What do you mean?"

Nathan's eyes narrowed as he tried to put his feelings into words. "It's hard to explain. Sometimes a man sees a woman and finds her attractive, regardless of what her face looks like."

"I don't understand."

"Some women just have a way about them—a tilt of the head, or the way they gesture with their hands. Little things that might seem inconsequential to another woman, but to a man . . ."

Elyse stared at him with wonder in her eyes. Was it possible that this rugged, shaggy-haired Texas Ranger had a sensitive side to his nature? Leave it to Lynn Potter to bring out the poet in a man. She'd always had that effect. "And you think Lynn Potter is one of those women?"

"Absolutely," Nathan nodded. "And from what you've told me, she's kind and gentle, too."

"Yes, she is."

"Then, I can't think of a single man I know who wouldn't be proud to have her at his side."

"Why, Captain," Elyse giggled. "I think you're developing a crush on Lynn!"

Nathan threw her a jaundiced look. "Hardly. I'm just saying that she is worried about her face for nothing. She's a lovely woman."

Much to her surprise, Elyse felt an irrational little tug of jealousy at Nathan's effusive words. "Well," she said, her voice sharper than she intended. "I'll tell her you said so."

"Better not," Nathan advised, "I don't want to scare her, or intimidate her. But it's too bad that there isn't somebody who could make her understand that desirability has very little to do with physical appearance."

"Oh, that's easy for you to say, looking the way you do," Elyse snorted.

Nathan's eyebrows rose. "Why, Mrs. Graham, whatever are you saying?"

"Nothing!" Elyse answered quickly, cursing her wayward tongue. "What are we going to shoot at once we get up to the ridge?"

Nathan smiled at her sudden, obvious attempt to the change of subject. "Whatever we can find. Tin cans, bottles, rocks. Whatever's around."

"We should be able to find something up there. It's a popular picnic spot on Sundays."

"Have you ever picnicked there?"

"Joe and I used to go up there once in a while when we were courting."

Nathan was pensive for a moment as he wondered what Elyse must have been like when she was a young girl sparking with her first beau—before life's tragedies had put such sadness in her eyes. "You don't go up there anymore?"

Elyse shook her head. "It's not the kind of place you go . . . alone."

There was a wistfulness in her voice that made his heart wrench. "Well, maybe some Sunday, we could take Colin and the three of us could have a picnic."

"No!" Elyse blurted, then quickly turned away as she saw the look of puzzled offense that filled his eyes. "It wouldn't be proper. People would talk about us. In a town the size of Bixby, going up to the ridge for a picnic makes a statement."

"Oh? And what statement is that?"

Elyse shifted nervously in her saddle, wishing desperately they'd reach the top of the hill so this conversation would come to an end. "Most people in town, especially the ladies, look at going up to the ridge as the first step toward . . ." Her voice trailed off.

"Toward what?"

"Toward an arrangement."

Nathan looked at her innocently. "An arrangement?"

"Yes, Captain, an arrangement. A permanent arrangement."

Nathan kept his face carefully blank. "I'm afraid I don't understand."

"Oh, of course you do!" she said, exasperated. "An engagement. Most people in Bixby think that if a boy brings a girl up to the ridge to picnic, it's because he's going to ask her to marry him."

"Oh, I see."

"That's why you and I couldn't go up there with Colin. Everyone would think . . ."

". . . that I was going to ask you to marry me," Nathan finished. "Well, we certainly wouldn't want to give that impression, would we?"

"No," Elyse agreed, vehemently shaking her head. "We certainly wouldn't."

"Do you think you'll ever get married again, Mrs. Graham?"

Elyse shot him a startled look. "Really, Captain, don't you think that question is a bit personal?"

Nathan shrugged. "I suppose it is, but I'm asking it anyway."

"I don't know," Elyse said slowly. "I doubt it."

"Why not?"

The intense timbre of his voice made her look at him curiously. "I just don't think I'll ever find another man I want to be married to."

"You mean, you loved your husband so much that no other man could take his place?"

"It's not that exactly," Elyse answered honestly. "I married Joe when I was very young—and I did love him. But I have my farm and my little boy and my brother when he comes back. I don't need any more than that in my life."

"You're talking like a fool," Nathan snapped.

Elyse looked at him in astonishment. "I beg your pardon?"

"If you think all you need is your wildflowers and your milk cow and your child, then you're a fool. You're a man's woman, Elyse."

"What exactly does that mean?"

Nathan drew his horse to a halt and looked over at her almost angrily. "It means that you're the kind of

woman who gets into a man's blood like a fever. The
kind of woman who men kill each other over."

Elyse gasped in outrage. "How dare you insult me
like that?"

"Insult you! I'm saying that you're the woman every
other woman wants to be—and every man wants to
have. You think that's an insult?"

"I'll tell you what I think. I think I want this conversation to end *right now.* You brought me up here to teach
me to shoot. Well, we're here, so teach me. But please
confine your conversation to the lesson at hand, because
I don't want to hear any more of your offensive obser-
vations about my character."

Nathan shook his head, completely baffled by her reaction. "I'm sorry," he said sincerely. "I honestly meant
what I said as a compliment. I had no intention of of-
fending you."

Elyse dismounted and angrily threw her horse's reins
over the branch of a mesquite tree. "Forget it. I don't
want to talk about it anymore."

Nathan stared at her for a moment, frustrated at her
stubborn refusal to look at herself realistically. She was
a passionate, vibrant woman who had loved one man
enough to marry him and had been intimate with at
least two others that he knew of—himself and Colin's father. So, why did she always react to even the most subtle suggestion of intimacy between men and women as
if she was some shy, untouched virgin at her first ice-
cream social?

Getting down from his horse, he tied him next to
Elyse's, then retied her mare's reins so she wouldn't
wander off. "Okay," he said, determined not to let their
upsetting conversation intrude on the important task before them. "Let's get started finding some targets."

"I already have," Elyse answered, waving an empty
wine bottle over her head. "This should work."

"Once, anyway," Nathan chuckled. "Try to find
something metal that we can shoot at several times."

The next few minutes were spent gathering up various articles to use as targets and positioning them on tree stumps and fence posts.

"Stand here," Nathan directed, motioning her over to a spot about ten yards from the targets. With a nod, Elyse joined him. "Have you ever shot a gun before?"

"Once, at a fair. It was a rifle, not a six-shooter, but I doubt that makes any difference."

Nathan looked at her pityingly. "Did you hit anything?"

"Well, no."

He nodded as though he'd already known that would be her answer. "All right, then let's start from scratch. First, I'll show you how to load." Snapping open the gun's barrel, he pointed out the six chambers, then reached into his shirt pocket and pulled out four bullets, deftly inserting them. "Now, you're ready to fire the gun."

He handed the pistol to her, then looked at her quizzically as she held it in the palm of her hand and stared at it. "There's a sight that you look down," he began.

"I don't want to do this."

"Elyse . . ."

"It's too heavy and I don't feel right holding it."

"Maybe if you'd hold it by the handle, it would feel better," he chuckled wryly.

"No. I really don't want to do this." Thrusting out her hand, she tried to give the gun back to him.

"Now, wait a minute," he said, refusing to take the weapon from her. "We rode all the way up here so you could practice shooting and now you're not going to even try it?"

"Well . . ."

"Here," he said quickly. "I'll show you how. Just stand next to me and watch." Taking the gun, he cocked the trigger and trained it on the wine bottle. "See? You just look down the sight. Line up the flange in the little V and . . . fire."

The deafening explosion right next to her made Elyse scream and clap her hands over her ears. "Don't do that unless you warn me first!" she cried.

"Warn you? I did warn you."

She glared at him, then looked at the shattered remnants of the wine bottle lying on the ground. "You seem to be pretty good at this."

Nathan grinned. "It takes practice, my sweet, that's all."

Elyse ignored his endearment and reached for the gun. "All right. I'll try it . . . once."

"Good. Just do like I told you. If it feels too heavy, then hold it in both hands. That's right. Now, point it at the target you want to hit."

Elyse swung the gun vaguely back and forth between two tin cans.

"Elyse, pick one target."

The gun stopped moving, although Nathan still wasn't sure which can she was aiming at.

"Okay, do you have your eye on your target?"

She nodded.

"Hold the gun up here and look down the sight." He positioned her rigid arms so they were at the approximate height of the can. "Line up the target so it's directly behind the flange."

"Okay."

"Are you lined up?"

She nodded.

"Then, fire."

The kick of the gun caused Elyse to lurch backward, nearly knocking Nathan off his feet.

"Did I hit it?" she asked breathlessly when they'd both regained their balance. "What was that zinging sound?"

"That 'zinging' sound was your bullet ricocheting off that tree." Nathan pointed to a scrub oak off to the left of them.

Elyse looked at him in astonishment. "That's where my bullet went?"

"Yes."

"But that's impossible! I was aiming over here." She pointed straight ahead.

"I know you were, but you closed your eyes before you fired. You can't do that."

"Well, I knew it was going to make that terrible noise and I was just getting ready for it."

Nathan shrugged. "You have to get used to the noise. You also have to get used to the fact that every gun has a kick to it that you have to compensate for. Otherwise, your shots will all go wild, just like this one did."

Elyse's lips thinned with annoyance at his criticism. "Don't you yell at me, Nathan Wellesley. I told you, I didn't want to do this."

"Elyse," Nathan said patiently, "I'm not yelling and there's no reason to get mad. It was only your first shot. Let's try it again."

"No. I don't want to do it anymore."

Nathan took a deep breath, determined to hang on to his quickly fraying temper. "Come on now, you can't give up yet. Look, this time, I'll stand behind you and guide your arm so you'll get the feel of where the gun should be pointed. Okay?"

Reluctantly, she nodded.

Stepping behind her, Nathan pulled her back against his chest, then wrapped his arms around her, bracketing her arms with his own. He planted his chin on her shoulder, trying to look down the sight at the same angle she was. "The gun should be right about here. Look down the sight now. Can you see the can on the other side of the flange?"

"Not really. The flange is sort of hiding it."

"Good, that's what you want it to do. Okay, now hold the gun steady." He cupped her hands in his and steadied her aim. "See how that feels?"

"Yes," she said softly, much more aware of the arousing sensation of his hands covering hers than of how the gun felt.

"Okay, are you ready to fire?"

"I guess so."

"Good. Don't close your eyes. Now ... steady, aim, and shoot!"

The gun went off with another thunderous explosion, and to Elyse's astonishment, the tin can she was aiming at shot straight up in the air.

"I did it!" she cried, turning in Nathan's arms and hugging him around the neck. "I hit the can!" Without a thought of what she was doing, she raised up on tiptoe and planted a smacking kiss on his lips. "I did it!"

Nathan threw the gun on the ground and wrapped his arms around her waist, gazing down into her shining eyes. "Yes, you did. You hit it."

Dipping his head, he kissed her; a warm, happy caress that gradually deepened into a passionate melding of lips and tongues. He heard her breathy little sigh of pleasure and pulled her closer, bracing the back of her head with one hand while his other one cupped her round little bottom, pressing her intimately against his hips.

Neither one of them knew exactly when they sank to the ground, but, in the space of a moment, they were lying in the grass, Nathan on his back and Elyse stretched out full length on top of him. As they continued to kiss, Nathan reached up and began eagerly unbuttoning Elyse's dress. From somewhere far off, she heard the sound of his shirt buttons ripping, then suddenly her bare breasts were pressed against the hot, smooth skin of his chest.

"You feel so good," Nathan groaned, turning her over on her back and trailing hot kisses down her neck toward her breasts. "So beautiful ..."

Elyse opened languid eyes, staring up into his handsome face. His eyes were the same color as the summer sky and his thick blond hair smelled like soap and sunshine. "We shouldn't be doing this," she moaned as a niggling little voice far back in her mind pricked her conscience.

"I'm only kissing you," he rasped, nibbling her ear.

She opened her mouth to protest further, but before she could get the words out, his lips again covered hers, the passion in his caress stealing the breath from her lungs.

"You're going to make me faint," she cried, turning her head away and gulping in a great draught of air.

Nathan immediately lifted his weight off her and got to his hands and knees. "I'm too heavy for you, aren't I? You're so little . . ."

Elyse gazed up at him, her eyes filled with confusion as she warred with herself. "It's not your size that makes me feel faint," she admitted. "It's your kisses."

He smiled, pleased with her confession. "So, you like my kisses, do you?" he murmured, leaning over her again.

Elyse quickly turned her face away. "Yes, but we have to stop. We have to . . ."

Nathan again rose to his knees. For a moment he allowed his gaze to feast on her breasts, then, with a sigh, he leaned forward, pulling the bodice of her dress together. "You're beautiful," he whispered, "and I want you more than I've ever wanted anything in my life. But I won't have you crying foul after I make love to you, so I'll stop."

He got to his feet, turning away quickly so she wouldn't see how aroused he was. Holding out a hand, he helped her to her feet. "It's getting late. We better go get Colin."

"Yes," she murmured, frantically trying to button her dress. "I guess we better."

Nathan walked over to the two tin cans still sitting on fence posts, and, with a fury borne of total frustration, knocked them to the ground. For several moments he stood there, desperately trying to get his raging body back under control. When he finally felt he could draw a steady breath, he turned and walked back to where Elyse waited, already mounted on her mare. Silently, they rode down the hill.

They were nearly to Lynn's ranch when Elyse pulled her horse to a halt and turned in her saddle to face him. "Nathan?"

"Yes?"

"I want to thank you."

"For what?"

"You know, for not taking advantage. We both know you could have and I appreciate you ... helping me keep my vow."

"I told you I wouldn't force you and I won't," he said tightly.

"You wouldn't have been forcing me."

Nathan stared at her for a long moment, surprised by her candor. "It's going to happen, Elyse. You know it is and so do I."

"It can't happen. Not again."

"It will," he said positively. "And it's going to be the next time we kiss like we did today. I'm only human, and this game we're playing is driving me nuts. I can't continue to kiss you and touch you like we did just now and then casually get up and walk away. I'm giving you fair warning. If you don't want me to make love to you, then you better stay far, far away, because the next time I kiss you, it's going to be all over your body."

Elyse stared at him with wide eyes, but before she could think of a response to his astonishing ultimatum, he kicked his buckskin and galloped off down the road as if all the demons in hell were chasing him.

Chapter 19

Red Hilliard rode slowly up to Lynn Potter's house. It looked normal enough. Chickens clucking and pecking in their little pen, a milk cow contentedly chewing cud in the near pasture, a brown mongrel drowsing on the porch. Basically, the Potter ranch looked like every other homesteader's in the area, except for the charred remains of the burned-out back side of the house. Still, despite the damage to the building, no one would ever guess that an eccentric recluse lived behind those lace curtains fluttering in the front window.

Red had been furious when Nathan had told him about this new aspect to his assignment. "Just go out and check on her every day or so. She probably won't talk to you . . . maybe won't even come to the door, but just do the best you can. Leave notes if you have to, but find out if she's seen anybody strange lurking around."

Red had vehemently protested Nathan's orders, but the captain had been adamant, and since he was his superior officer, there was nothing Red could do but comply.

So, here he was, standing in this crazy woman's front yard, not knowing if she was going to fire a gun at him or offer him a cup of tea.

He'd heard all about Mrs. Potter from the women in Bixby. How she'd been the prettiest girl in town, how she'd married the handsome and popular Hank Potter and quickly produced a child as pretty and vivacious as she was. The ladies had gone into great detail to tell him how Lynn's house had tragically caught fire, resulting in her husband's and daughter's deaths. There had been much head shaking and tongue clucking as they lowered their voices and confided that in the last year since the tragedy, Lynn seemed to have lost her mind. That the disfiguring scars on her face had caused her to become strangely withdrawn, cutting herself off from society and seeing no one but the infamous Elyse Graham. And, as the vituperative Miss Dixon had remarked, "Lord above only knows why that Jezebel would be the one person Lynn Potter would still see. Why, she's not fit company for any Christian woman."

All these thoughts were tumbling around Red Hilliard's mind as he warily climbed the steps to the Potter house and knocked on the door. There was no answer.

"Mrs. Potter," he called, stepping over to the slightly open front window. "It's Red Hilliard from town. I have a wire for you." Although there was no wire, this was the phrase Nathan had told him to use to alert Mrs. Potter as to who he was. However, even this information elicited no response. "Mrs. Potter? Are you home?"

Red stood on the front porch for several moments more, idly scratching the brown dog behind his floppy ears. Finally, slapping his gloves irritably against his thigh, he walked back down the steps. He was just gathering his horse's reins when he heard a soft voice wafting out through a window. "Mr. Hilliard?"

Red immediately retied his horse and stepped back up on the porch. "Mrs. Potter?" he called softly, squinting in through the lace curtains. "Is that you?"

He watched as an invisible hand pulled the curtain back a few inches. "Could I see some identification, please?"

Red frowned, but reached into his shirt pocket and withdrew his badge. He pressed it up to the window, bending closer as he tried to make out the features of the shadowy shape on the other side of the curtain. "I just came by to make sure that everything is okay, ma'am."

"Everything is fine," came the husky voice.

Red figured that since Lynn had answered him, she must be satisfied he was who he said he was. Quickly, he shoved his badge back in his pocket. "Could I come in, please?"

"No."

"But, Mrs. Potter, I need to see you."

"No, you don't. Everything is fine. That's all you need to know."

Red straightened and took a step backward, frowning. "Did Captain Wells tell you I'd be coming here every day?"

"Mrs. Graham did," she acknowledged.

"Well, then, you know that I need to see you."

There was a long silence, then the disembodied voice said, "There is no reason for you to have to see me, sir. I assure you, everything is fine. I have seen nothing unusual."

"Mrs. Potter," Red sighed, wishing he could punch Nathan Wellesley in the nose for dumping this burden on him. "I have no way of knowing if everything is really all right unless I see you. For all I know, you could be telling me everything is all right while someone is holding you at gunpoint."

This statement was followed by another long hesitation. Finally, he heard the front door open, and looking over in surprise, he saw a petite woman wearing a heavy black mourning veil over her face standing in the doorway.

"All right, Mr. Hilliard. Here I am. As you can see, I'm safe and sound."

Red nodded and approached her cautiously. "I need to come in and look around."

"Why?"

"To make sure there's no one hiding inside," he explained patiently. As irritated as he was by this ridiculous cat-and-mouse game, he couldn't help but feel a wave of sympathy toward the woman when he saw her clench her hands in front of her.

"All right," she said reluctantly. "If you absolutely have to."

"I do," he nodded, whipping off his hat and scraping his feet on the small rug in front of the door. "It'll only take a minute."

Lynn stepped back into the house and Red followed, nodding politely as he passed her. A quick check of the front room, kitchen, and upstairs bedrooms disclosed nothing out of the ordinary. After only a couple of minutes, he walked back down the stairs. "Looks like everything is fine."

"I told you it was, Captain."

"I'm not a captain," Red corrected. "I'm just a lieutenant."

The veiled head nodded. "I'm sorry. My mistake."

"It's okay," he smiled, displaying a set of straight, white teeth. "Why don't you call me Red."

"Is that a nickname because of your hair?"

"Yeah," Red laughed, running his fingers through his fiery curls. "It's what everybody calls me."

"What's your real name?"

"William," Red answered, surprised by her curiosity. "William Henry Hilliard."

"William is a nice name."

Red shrugged. "I guess, but everyone has called me Red since I was a kid."

There seemed to be nothing else to add to this particular subject and the two of them again lapsed into silence.

Finally, Red cleared his throat and put his hat back on. "Well, I guess I better be getting back to town. I'll come again in a day or two."

"Would you like a drink of water before you leave?"

Lynn asked suddenly. Then, as if embarrassed by her offer, she stammered, "It's . . . it's rather warm today."

"If you're sure it wouldn't be too much trouble . . ."

"Not at all. I just drew a fresh pitcher. It's in the
kitchen." Turning on her heel, Lynn hurried down the
hall toward the kitchen, her mourning veil floating out
behind her. Red stood waiting for a moment, not sure
whether she expected him to follow her or wait in the
foyer. Finally, he shrugged and walked down the hall after her, pushing through the kitchen door. "This is real
nice of you, Mrs.—"

His words were cut off by Lynn's sharp scream of dismay, followed by a splintering crash as the glass she was
holding fell from her hand. "What are you doing in
here?" she shrieked. Her concealing veil was pulled
back, and as Red gaped at her in astonishment, her
hands flew to her cheeks. "Get out of here, please!"

"I . . . I'm sorry!" Red blurted, shaken not by the
sight of her scarred face but by her reaction to his being
in the kitchen. "I thought you were going to give me a
glass of water."

"I was!" Lynn's words were muffled behind her
hands. "Out in the foyer. Please, just go!"

To her further distress, Red didn't move. "What's the
matter?" he asked quietly. "There's no reason to be upset."

"No reason? You force your way into my house, then
you follow me in here . . ." Turning away, she started
clawing at her veil, trying to pull it back over her face.

"Don't do that," Red said firmly.

Lynn paused, her back still to him. "What?"

"There's no reason to hide from me. I've already seen
you, so what difference does it make?"

Stubbornly, Lynn settled her veil over her face, turning back to face him. "I'd appreciate it if you'd leave
now, Lieutenant Hilliard."

Red's next words were spoken in a voice that brooked
no interruption. "I'll leave, but not until we get a few

things straight. First of all, I did *not* force my way into your house. Second, I only followed you into the kitchen to save you having to walk back to the foyer with the water. I wasn't trying to intrude on your privacy. And third, I didn't ask for this assignment. Captain Wells ordered me to check on you, for your own safety."

"Lieutenant Hilliard . . ."

Red threw up a hand to stop the argument he knew was coming. "Just hear me out . . . please."

Lynn remained silent.

"I have to come here every day for God knows how long and I don't want to have to stand on your porch for ten minutes while you cover yourself, so let's just get this clear. I know you have scars on your face, I know you worry about people seeing you because of them, but I want you to know that your appearance doesn't make any difference to me. I'm not a potential suitor and I'm not a gossiping old biddy from town. I'm here to do my job and I don't care how you look, so quit worrying about it. Now, I've gotta go before people begin to wonder why I've been gone from the telegraph office so long."

Lynn stood absolutely still, staring at Red from behind her heavy veil. Never, since the fire, had anyone spoken to her about her disfigurement as frankly as this stranger just had. And yet, there was no appalled shock in his eyes, no horrified pity in his voice. He was merely stating his opinion and, somehow, his disinterest in her was strangely comforting.

"Let me get you another glass of water before you leave," she murmured. Turning back to the counter, she poured another glass, then walked over and held it out to him.

Red swallowed the entire contents of the glass in two large gulps. "You know," he said, handing it back to her and smiling almost shyly, "you have a mighty pretty voice."

"I do?" Lynn asked, grateful that the veil hid the embarrassed blush she could feel heating her cheeks.

"Yup. Reminds me of when I was a little kid and my ma would tell me a story when I went to bed. Her voice sounded like yours—kind of soft and whispery."

Lynn lowered her head and Red realized his flattery was making her uncomfortable, even through the veil. "I didn't mean to embarrass you," he said awkwardly.

"It's all right. It was a very nice compliment."

He shifted his weight from one foot to the other, wishing he could think of something else to say, but he couldn't. The silence stretched between them until he finally muttered, "Well, I better go."

Turning, he went out the front door and mounted his horse. Reining the animal around, he was surprised to see Lynn standing in the doorway. "I'll see you tomorrow, Lieutenant."

Red nodded, unable to explain the queer feeling of pleasure her simple words gave him. "Right, Mrs. Potter. See you tomorrow."

Chapter 20

Nathan opened bleary eyes and groped around in the darkness for a match. Lighting the lamp next to his bed, he picked up his watch. Three-ten. He shook his head, trying to clear away the last vestiges of sleep. Had Colin really been crying all night or was he just dreaming? A high-pitched wail from the next room answered his question.

Climbing out of bed, he pulled on his denims and staggered over to the door, pulling it open and squinting out into the dimly lit front room. Elyse had her back to him, pacing the length of the room as she tried in vain to comfort the squalling baby.

"Oh, dear, did Colin wake you?" she asked, turning to make another pass down the room and spotting him in the doorway. "I'm so sorry."

"It's okay," Nathan yawned. "I haven't really been asleep. What's wrong with him?"

"I wish I knew," Elyse answered. Her voice sounded as if she was close to tears.

"Is he sick?"

"I don't think so. I think that tooth he's been trying to cut is finally coming through."

"Would that make him cry like that?"

"It could. They say it really hurts when a tooth breaks through the gum."

Nathan shook his head sympathetically. "Poor little kid."

At that moment, the 'poor little kid' let out a scream that made both their ears ring.

"Colin, please!" Elyse begged, her voice betraying her nerves and exhaustion. *"Please* don't cry anymore!"

Nathan took a step forward, his concern mounting as he saw tears welling in Elyse's eyes.

"I just don't know what to do for him!" she cried. "I've changed him, I've fed him, I've walked him. Nothing seems to help."

Without a word, Nathan turned and walked back into his bedroom, lifting a half-full whiskey bottle out of his saddlebags. Returning to the front room, he went over to the breakfront and poured a liberal amount of the amber liquid into a glass. "Sit down and drink this," he ordered. "I'll walk him for a while."

"Oh, I couldn't . . ."

"Elyse, just do it!"

Elyse's mouth thinned at his abrupt command, but she settled herself on the settee and handed him the baby. "I'll just sit here for a minute," she sniffed, setting down the glass that Nathan had pushed into her hand.

"Drink that whiskey. It'll relax you."

"But I've never had spirits before."

"Well, there's no time like the present. Now, drink it. It won't hurt you."

With a tremulous nod, Elyse took a tiny sip, coughing as the fiery liquid traced a path down her throat. "It's hot!"

"So is this baby," Nathan noted, holding Colin up in front of him and shaking off the blanket he was wrapped in.

"He's hot because he's been crying."

"That may be, but it's also like an oven in here. Why didn't you open the window?"

"I always close the windows at night. Ever since the possum got in."

"I'll take my chances with a possum," Nathan commented, walking over to the window and opening it as wide as it would go.

"There, that's better, isn't it?" he asked, looking down at the baby. To Elyse's astonishment, Colin abruptly stopped crying and looked earnestly at Nathan as if pondering his question.

Shifting Colin, Nathan held him up against his shoulder, rubbing his big suntanned hand gently down the baby's back. "Look at all the stars, Colin," he murmured, turning so the baby could see out the window. "Aren't they pretty?"

Hearing his soft words, Elyse gazed over at the window. The sight of Nathan's massive frame silhouetted against the dark night sky made something deep inside her throb with a craving she tried hard to ignore. The whiskey glass slipped in her fingers, but she didn't even notice, so enraptured was she by the sight of the tiny, nearly naked baby being cuddled by the huge, nearly naked man. White skin snuggled up to bronze, softness nestled against hardness, blond hair of the exact same shade blended as Nathan lowered his head and gently kissed Colin's neck.

Elyse drew a shuddering breath, feeling that there wasn't enough air in the room to fill her lungs. Never had she seen such an arousing sight as Nathan Wellesley holding his son.

His son.

With trembling hands, she raised the glass and took a great gulp of the burning whiskey. This magnificent, handsome man was her baby's father. Colin had come from him . . . from him and her. The very thought made her shiver.

"Are you cold with the window open?" Nathan asked softly.

Elyse looked over at him, surprised that he had noticed her shudder. "No. I'm fine."

"Did you drink the whiskey?"

"A little."

"Drink all of it. You'll feel better."

"I feel fine."

"Elyse, quit arguing with me and drink it."

"But it'll make me sleepy. It already has and I've only had a couple of swallows."

"Put your head back and take a little nap. I can take care of Colin." As if to prove his point, Nathan nuzzled the baby's cheek with his nose, causing the little boy to giggle and grab a handful of his hair.

"Ow, don't do that!" Nathan exclaimed, untwining Colin's fingers. "Why do you *always* pull my hair?"

"I think he's fascinated with it because it's so thick and shiny." As soon as the words were out, Elyse could have bitten her tongue off. She hoped that Nathan had missed the obvious compliment, but the smile that lit his blue eyes told her he hadn't.

Gazing down at the baby, he said, "Is that right? Are you fascinated with my hair, little man?"

Colin gurgled a response and grabbed for his nose.

"You're not supposed to be fascinated with men's hair, Colin," Nathan admonished, his voice coming out in a nasal twang as the baby continued to pinch his nostrils. "You're supposed to be fascinated with women's hair. Like your mama's. Hers is as thick and shiny as mine . . . and a whole lot softer."

Elyse felt herself blush and hoped desperately that Nathan wouldn't notice it in the dim lamplight. Hazarding another look at him, she watched him throw his head back, effectively removing all of his facial features from Colin's reach.

Colin immediately started to fuss and Nathan shifted him to his other arm, wrapping his hand around the baby's shoulders and gently stroking the delicate white skin.

Elyse watched, mesmerized. Unbidden, the memory of Nathan's fingers caressing her own skin floated through her mind. The whiskey was beginning to have a mellowing effect on her, and she smiled dreamily as she continued to watch Nathan massage Colin's back. Funny how a hand could be so big and powerful and yet so gentle.

Her eyes drooped.

That same hand could become a murderous weapon when clenched into a fist or wrapped around the handle of a gun and yet, when Nathan had touched her that long-ago night, those rough, calloused fingers had been as soft and enticing as a whisper. Even now, she could almost feel him caressing her back, her stomach, her breasts.

With a little moan, Elyse's eyes closed, her mind swimming in a sea of sensation. She remembered how beautiful she'd thought his feet were—long and narrow with a high arch and perfectly shaped toes. Colin had those same beautiful feet.

With a supreme effort, she opened her eyes, draining the last of the whiskey from the glass and looking over at Nathan's feet. They were bare now and looked just as beautiful as she remembered. Her eyes drifted upward—sweeping over his long, lean legs and pausing to feast appreciatively on his heavily muscled chest.

Was there anything in the world more exciting than a man with his chest and his feet bare? At that moment, Elyse couldn't think of one. Smiling rapturously, she closed her eyes again.

"You smell so good," she heard Nathan whisper. She sighed, remembering another time when he'd said that to her. His next words puzzled her, though.

"Why don't you just snuggle down here against my neck and go to sleep?" *How could she snuggle up to him when he was over by the window?*

"There," he crooned. "That's a good boy."

That's a good boy. Elyse shifted restlessly on the settee, a soft mewl of disappointment escaping her. Nathan wasn't talking to her, he was talking to Colin.

She should get up and take Colin away from him. He

was quiet now and he'd probably sleep in his cradle. Nathan didn't need to hold him anymore. She would get up and go get him . . . in just a minute. With one last sigh, Elyse fell into a deep sleep.

Nathan looked over at her, his eyes clouded with longing as he drank in her beauty. He had covertly watched her fall asleep, had seen the varying play of expressions on her face as she had drifted off. He'd seen her smile, heard her sigh, watched her nestle her head into the settee pillows, almost as if nestling against a lover.

The provocative tableau had affected him physically and, with a frown, he looked down at the erection which strained against the front of his partially buttoned denims. He wanted nothing more than to put Colin in his cradle and spend the rest of the night making love to the baby's mother. His gaze swung back to the sleeping Elyse. "Fat chance of that," he muttered ruefully.

Still, as he stared over at her, he wondered if he could get away with a kiss. Just one kiss. He wanted so badly to feel her lips beneath his, her softness against him.

Padding into the bedroom, he put the sleeping baby in his cradle, covering him with a light blanket and stealing silently back out to the front room.

Elyse was just as he'd left her and, for a long moment, he stood and stared at her, a feeling of desire coursing through him that was so intense, he didn't know if he could bear it.

Just one kiss . . .

Walking slowly over to the settee, he braced his arms against its back and leaned forward, his face just inches above Elyse's. He inhaled deeply, closing his eyes as he savored her sweet, fresh scent. Slowly, gently, he lowered his lips, covering her mouth with his own.

Elyse was vaguely aware of someone kissing her. Someone who smelled good, tasted good, felt good. The kiss went on and on and she made no attempt to end it.

She loved it when he kissed her. Dreamily, she opened her eyes.

Nathan felt the startled jerk of her head as full consciousness returned. Slowly, he lifted his lips. "The baby's asleep," he whispered.

"Thank you," she whispered back, gazing at his lips as she fought the temptation to kiss him again.

For a long moment, Nathan stared at her, wanting her with the desperation of a starving man at a banquet, yet needing her to show him she wanted him, too.

He waited . . . and waited . . . and then it happened. That slight, negative shake of Elyse's head that said everything.

Clenching his teeth, Nathan straightened and turned away. "See you in the morning," he rasped, his voice hoarse with need and disappointment.

Dumbly, Elyse nodded. She heard him walk across the room, heard the soft thud of the door closing behind him. Raising her hands to her face, she covered her mouth with trembling fingers and burst into tears.

Chapter 21

The next morning, Nathan was still lying in bed at the unheard-of hour of seven-thirty. He had never gone back to sleep after returning to the bedroom. The unsatisfied desire he was suffering had caused him to toss restlessly for hours, and he was sure that if he didn't figure out some way to get his mind off Elyse, he was going to go crazy. Somehow, he had to overcome this unremitting passion he felt for her.

But what could he do? He'd gone swimming in the creek near the house about a hundred times, had mended fences, patched roofs, and built corrals until his back was nearly broken and he was so tired that he could hardly mount his horse. Still, all Elyse had to do was come into his field of vision and his manhood sprang to life, constantly reminding him that he was a young, virile male who had not experienced sexual satisfaction for over a year.

"You're gonna end up useless," he growled. "If you don't get some relief pretty soon, you're going to be useless to any woman."

Walking over to the commode, he splashed cold water on his face, then glared at himself in the mirror. "You need to find something else to occupy yourself."

With a snort of irritation, he looked out the window, his eyes lighting on a huge stack of wood sitting just outside. "There you go," he said wryly. "Nothing like chopping wood to wear a man out."

Shrugging on a light cotton shirt, he strode out into the front room, mumbling a curt hello to Elyse, who was standing at the kitchen counter mashing an apple for Colin's breakfast. Before she could reply, he was out the door.

Elyse looked after him in bewilderment, wondering what was causing his obviously sour mood and hoping it wasn't something she had done.

Nathan rounded the side of the house, wrenching the axe out of the woodpile and giving the first log a mighty whack. The wood splintered satisfyingly. "That's Major Jones's head," he muttered, "for sending me here." Chuckling at his own joke, he picked up another piece of wood, placed it on the chopping block and raised the axe above his head. *Thwack!* "That one's for Elyse's brother for taking part in the damn robbery in the first place." Another piece, another stroke of the axe. "And that one is for Rosas's damn gang for not appearing so I can get the hell out of here and get, *whack,* my sanity, *whack,* back!"

With a weary sigh, Nathan collapsed onto the chopping block, picking up a small piece of wood and staring at it thoughtfully. Maybe he should keep this little piece. He could smooth it down and whittle it into a soldier for Colin. In fact, he could work on a whole set, so when the little boy was old enough, he would have an entire army to play with.

Absently, Nathan wondered what Elyse would think if he made Colin some toys. He looked around at the other logs that still needed cutting. He could probably hone some of them down, too—maybe make that high chair that Elyse had said she'd like to have. That would probably make her happy.

With an annoyed grunt, Nathan got to his feet. It wasn't going to help to chop wood. He was hopeless. No matter what he was doing or how much he tried to distract himself, he couldn't get Elyse out of his mind. His every thought revolved around her.

"Hopeless," he muttered, getting to his feet and searching around for wood chips to add to the one in his pocket. "You're hopeless *and* useless. God, it's a good thing Seth isn't around. You'd never hear the end of it!"

Elyse stood in front of the house and looked apprehensively down the road.

"What's wrong?" Nathan asked, returning from the woodpile and stepping up on the porch next to her.

"There's someone coming."

He turned, instantly wary, and cupped his hand over his eyes. "Do you recognize him?"

"No, and I can't think of anyone who would come visiting uninvited. Maybe it's one of your men."

"No. The horse isn't familiar."

Elyse reached over and grasped Nathan's arm fearfully. "I don't like this. No one ever comes here."

Nathan nodded his agreement. "Go into my bedroom and get my gun," he said quietly. "It's in the holster, hanging on the bedpost."

Elyse immediately sped into the house while Nathan remained on the porch, his stance deceptively casual.

It took Elyse only a few seconds to locate the gun, but when she got back outside, she was astonished to find Nathan out in the front yard, his arm around the stranger's shoulder. Both men wore wide grins and were talking animatedly.

Nathan spotted her out of the corner of his eye and motioned her to join them. Elyse looked down at the six-shooter in her hand, then, with a shrug, set it on the porch railing and descended the steps. Slowly, she walked out to meet the men, her eyes sweeping over the stranger. He was tall and lean, with dark hair and warm, smiling brown eyes. A handsome man, Elyse decided, with an air about him that immediately put a person at ease.

"Mrs. Elyse Graham," Nathan announced. "This is my older brother, Eric, from Minnesota."

Elyse's eyes widened in astonishment. *His brother!* How could these two men be brothers? They couldn't be more different in physical appearance. Eric was as dark as Nathan was fair, and he was taller and more slender. Quickly, her eyes darted between the two men, but she could see no resemblance whatsoever.

"Don't look much alike, do we?" Nathan chuckled, seeing the surprise on her face. "Eric looks like our father while I favor our mother. Seems like all of us took after one or the other of them—except Geoff, of course. He doesn't look like anybody."

"I'm very pleased to meet you, Mr. Wellesley," Elyse said, stepping forward and shaking his hand.

"Likewise, Mrs. Graham."

"So," Nathan interrupted exuberantly, herding Eric toward the house. "What are you doing in Texas? And how in the world did you find me? No one is supposed to know where I am."

Eric looked at his brother, smiling at his verbosity. "I'm here in Texas buying stock. I've decided to try my hand at raising beef cattle."

"Beef cattle? In Minnesota?"

"Yes," Eric responded wryly. "We do eat meat up there, you know."

"Really?" Nathan chortled. "I thought you just ate that terrible cod stuff you forced on me last year."

"Lutefisk?" Eric grimaced. "Naw, we only eat that at Christmas. And then, only to be polite."

Both men broke out in great gusts of laughter, causing Elyse to stare at Nathan in astonishment. Never had she seen him so happy and carefree. It was a whole new side to his nature and one that she found extremely appealing.

"You should see this stuff, Elyse," Nathan said, turning his attention to her. "It's fish that's been dried and then soaked in lye."

"Lye? Are you sure?"

"He's right," Eric confirmed. "It *is* soaked in lye."

"I would think that would make it disintegrate."

"Oh, it does!" Nathan laughed. "It sort of turns it into this disgusting jellylike stuff. Then they boil it and that smells so bad, it takes weeks to air out the house afterward."

"You two are kidding me."

Nathan crossed his fingers over his heart. "No, we're not, honest! The Scandinavian folks in Minnesota consider this stuff a real delicacy. They have big parties where they all get together and eat it."

Elyse shivered. "Cod soaked in lye. Ugh!"

"I think you have to be raised on it to enjoy it," Eric chuckled.

"Well, all I can say is that I'm glad you're turning your hand to cattle, Eric. Maybe next time I visit, I'll actually be able to face coming to the table at night."

The threesome entered the house and Elyse gestured the men toward the table, walking into the kitchen to make a pot of coffee.

"How long can you stay?" Nathan asked.

"Just a couple of days. I finished my business in Dallas, but I have to wait for a northbound train that has an available cattle car. I'm taking some foundation stock back with me and I want to travel with them just to make sure they get there all right."

Nathan nodded. It was typical of Eric's cautious nature to want to personally escort a bunch of cows to Minnesota. "You never said how you found me."

"It wasn't easy, I can tell you that. I wired Ranger headquarters in Austin, asking for your whereabouts and got a very terse reply stating that you were on assignment and unavailable."

"That's standard procedure when a Ranger's on a se-

cret assignment," Nathan shrugged. "Then what did
you do?"

"I wired Father and asked him to contact the governor and see if he could get any more information. The
next day I found out you were here." Eric glanced surreptitiously over at Elyse. "What *are* you doing here?"
he whispered.

"Tell you later," Nathan murmured.

Eric nodded, then looked up and smiled as Elyse approached the table with a plate of cookies. "Are you
hungry, Mr. Wellesley? I have some fresh bread and I'd
be happy to make you a sandwich."

"Thanks for asking, but I ate in town."

Elyse nodded and headed back for the kitchen.
"You're welcome to stay here if you don't mind sleeping
in the barn. I'm afraid that's all I have to offer, though."

Eric took a huge bite of a cookie and groaned appreciatively. "That'll be fine. I like barns."

Elyse looked at him anxiously, wondering if he actually meant his strange statement or if he was being
sarcastic.

Nathan caught her look and quickly put her mind at
ease. "He really means that, Elyse. Eric's a farmer and
he loves anything that looks like dirt or smells like manure."

Eric feigned a look of offense as Elyse started to
laugh. "I beg your pardon. I do *not* love manure!"

"Oh, sure you do," Nathan quipped. "Otherwise you
would have chosen a real profession, like Seth and I
did."

"Real Cowboys and Indians, you mean."

Elyse looked back and forth between the brothers,
marveling at their easy camaraderie. She felt almost like
an eavesdropper listening to their banter, but she was
enjoying herself so much that she couldn't find the will
to leave.

"How are Kirsten and the baby?" Nathan asked.

"Babies," Eric corrected with a grin.

"Babies? You have two now?"

"Yup. Ian, who you know about, of course, and we had a daughter this spring. Sarah."

"Congratulations!" Nathan enthused, slapping his brother on the back. "You and Kirsten must be delighted."

"We are. We both want a big family and it looks like it's going to turn out that way."

"And how is Kirsten?"

Eric's face took on a faraway look. "She's fine. Just fine."

"She's one terrific lady, Eric."

"I kind of like her," Eric smiled. "Especially now that she's finally learned to cook."

Both men laughed as if at some private joke. Their merriment was suddenly interrupted, however, by a baby's cry coming from the bedroom.

Elyse quickly wiped her hands on a dish towel and hurried over to the table with two cups of coffee. "There's Colin. If you'll excuse me, I need to go tend him."

Eric smiled politely. "Colin is your son?"

"Yes," Elyse nodded, heading off toward the bedroom. "If you want cream or sugar, Mr. Wellesley, they're right there on the counter. Help yourself."

When she'd disappeared into the bedroom, Eric turned to Nathan, looking at him curiously. "Who *is* she?"

"It's a long story," Nathan sighed. "Her kid brother took part in a bank robbery last year, but he turned himself into us recently and gave back the money."

"Is he in prison?"

"No, we struck a deal with him. He isn't really a criminal, he was just desperate for money and agreed to hold the horses during the robbery. Somehow, though, he ended up with the loot."

Eric looked at Nathan dubiously.

"No, it's true," Nathan defended. "Anyway, we think

the gang he was involved with is holed up in Mexico somewhere, so we put the word out that the money is hidden here on the farm, hoping to flush them out. I was sent here to protect Mrs. Graham in case the rest of the gang should appear to collect."

"Was she involved, too?" Eric asked, jerking his head toward the bedroom door.

"Well, sort of. Indirectly, at least. Her brother came here after the robbery and she hid him until he could figure out a plan to get away."

"Get away? I don't understand. Why didn't he take off with the rest of the gang, or did they all hide here?"

"No, just him. The bank manager decided to play hero after the robbery and started shooting at the gang as they were making their getaway. There was a lot of confusion and a couple of people got hurt. The gang got separated and the brother ended up here by himself. But even after he took off again, he never got the money back to them."

"You mean a double-cross?"

"Not really. According to him, he just couldn't find them, so he hid out down on the border with the loot for almost a year. When he finally got tired of living like a fugitive, he turned himself in to us."

Eric sat back, sipping his coffee and digesting everything Nathan had just told him. "That's quite a story. A little hard to believe, I'm afraid."

"Yeah, I know. But Major Jones believed the kid was telling the truth, so I have no reason to doubt it. I just have to sit here and wait for the gang to make their move."

"Do you think they will?"

Nathan nodded. "If they hear about the money, I have no doubt they'll come after it. They think the brother is in jail and they undoubtedly know Mrs. Graham is a widow, so they'll probably figure she's here alone."

"That was going to be my next question," Eric said.

"What?"

"I wondered where *Mr.* Graham is."

"He was killed by lightning several years ago."

Eric winced. "God, what a way to go. So, what about you? Does the gang know you're here?"

"I don't think so. I've been set up as a ranch hand. Supposedly, I'm a drifter who's signed on here for the summer to help the widow with the harvest."

Eric stared out the window for a moment, then turned back to Nathan with a grin. "What harvest?"

"I know," Nathan chuckled. "It's a pretty lame excuse since Elyse doesn't have the money to put in any crops, but it was the best we could do."

Nathan's use of Mrs. Graham's first name didn't escape Eric, but, prudently, he said nothing.

"Oh, by the way," Nathan added. "I'm using the name 'Nat Wells,' so if you happen to mention me to anyone in town, that's the name you should use."

"I know. The governor told Father, and when I asked for directions at the general store, that's the name I used. By the way, I think 'Nat Wells' has a real ring to it, Nate. Very creative. You might even want to think about changing your name permanently."

Nathan reached over and punched Eric playfully in the arm. "I can do without your comments, big brother."

Eric laughed and held up his arms in surrender. "Okay, okay. There's no need to get violent. I won't say any more."

When the men had sobered, he added, "Does Mrs. Graham know who you really are?"

"Yeah."

"Can you trust her not to tell anyone?"

"Absolutely. She needs me. She's not going to blow my cover."

"It must be pretty boring for you, just sitting here. The governor told Father you've already been here for more than a month."

"Oh, it's not so bad. I've been working around the place a little bit—fixing the roof, mending some fences, that kind of stuff."

"Just the kind of chores you love," Eric said wryly.

Nathan looked a bit abashed at his brother's astute comment, but said simply, "Like I said, it's not so bad."

Eric gazed at Nathan pensively, guessing that there was more going on here than Nathan was letting on. But, as was his custom, he kept his thoughts to himself, figuring that if his brother wanted to confide in him, he would.

At that moment, Elyse walked in from the bedroom, carrying Colin. "This little boy is very hungry," she remarked, setting the baby on the floor near the table. She looked up at Nathan. "Would you mind keeping your eye on him for a minute while I finish his breakfast? I don't want him to fall over."

"Sure," Nathan responded, pleased that, for the first time, Elyse was actually seeking his assistance with the baby instead of resisting it. Leaning over, he scooped the child up, settling him in his lap. "Eric, this is Mrs. Graham's son, Colin."

Eric looked over at the baby, his eyes widening with astonishment. "Mrs. Graham's son?" he asked quietly, looking intently at his brother.

"Yes," Nathan nodded innocently. "He's nine months old."

Eric's gaze flew back to the baby, his artist's eye taking in every detail. Nathan's mouth, Nathan's chin, Nathan's forehead. There was not a shred of doubt in Eric's mind that this was his brother's son, yet Nathan didn't seem to claim him. And the governor said he'd only been here a month. Craning his head around, Eric looked over at Elyse, but she was standing with her back to him and missed his penetrating stare.

"Your baby is nine months old, Mrs. Graham?" he asked casually as she returned to the table carrying a bowl of porridge.

Elyse's heart leaped into her throat. Why was he asking her that? "Yes," she nodded as she sat down and took the baby out of Nathan's arms. "He's a little small for his age, but my husband was slight in stature."

"But . . ." Eric blurted, turning to look at Nathan curiously.

"Come on, Eric," Nathan said suddenly, scraping his chair back and leaping to his feet. "Let's get you settled in the barn."

Eric swallowed back the rest of his sentence and nodded at his brother dumbly. "Okay. Sure." Rising from the table, he smiled at Elyse, who appeared to be completely occupied with the baby. "Thank you for your hospitality, Mrs. Graham. I'm grateful."

"Certainly, Mr. Wellesley," she said softly, not looking up. "I'll see you at supper."

Eric nodded, gave the baby one last perplexed look, then turned and followed his brother out the door.

Elyse expelled a long, shuddering breath as the two men disappeared down the porch steps. Why had Eric Wellesley questioned Colin's age, she thought worriedly, and what had he been about to say after she'd mentioned Joe's small stature?

The answers were so obvious that she squeezed her eyes shut, trying to block them from her mind.

"He doesn't know," she told herself firmly, trying hard to believe her words. "He couldn't. Nathan's never noticed it in all this time. Even after last night, he still didn't see it. How could his brother catch the resemblance the first time he sets eyes on Colin? He couldn't. My imagination is just running away with me."

Casting a fervent prayer heavenward that her arguments were right and her suspicions wrong, Elyse again picked up the spoon and began feeding the baby.

"He couldn't know," she again said aloud. "He simply couldn't!"

Chapter 22

Eric settled himself comfortably in the hay in Nathan's makeshift bedroom. "So, little brother, what exactly is going on here?"

Nathan looked at him quizzically. "What do you mean? I just told you everything inside."

"No, you didn't."

"What else do you want to know?"

"Whatever you want to tell me."

"Eric . . ."

"Okay, how about, what's going on between you and Mrs. Graham, for starters."

"What do you—"

"And, don't say, 'what do you mean' again. You know very well what I mean."

Nathan silently cursed his brother's astuteness. "What makes you think there's something going on between Elyse and me?" he asked, unable to meet Eric's eyes.

Eric snorted with irritation, annoyed at Nathan's evasiveness. "What are we doing, playing Questions and Answers here, Nate? Look, if you don't want to talk about this, just tell me and I'll drop it."

"No," Nathan said, shaking his head. "I don't want you to drop it. I really need to talk. It's just that there's not much to tell."

"When did you meet her?" Eric prompted.

"I've been here about five weeks."

"That's not what I asked. Had you met her before that?"

Nathan's head jerked up and he riveted Eric with a penetrating look. "Why would you ask that?"

"Did you?"

Nathan pushed away from the rickety table he was leaning against and began pacing the straw-covered floor. "I guess I might as well tell you. I did meet her once before—about a year and a half ago."

Eric did some quick mental arithmetic. "And what was your relationship with her at that time?"

"Jesus Christ, Eric," Nathan exploded. "What's gotten into you? You sound like a lawyer in a courtroom. 'When did you meet her? What was your relationship with her at that time?' It isn't like you to play the inquisitor."

"I'm sorry," Eric said contritely. "I'm not trying to back you into a corner. I'm just upset that you seem to be denying the obvious and avoiding your obligations."

"What obligations?"

Eric frowned, completely out of sorts with his obstinate brother. "You're going to make me ask straight out, aren't you?"

"Ask what, goddamn it?" Nathan shouted.

"Is that baby in there yours?"

"What?" Nathan gasped. "You think Colin is mine?"

"Is he?"

"No."

"You know that for sure?"

Now it was Nathan's turn to get angry. Eric had always been one of his favorite brothers. Dreamy, artistic, and taciturn, Eric was the peacemaker of the Wellesley family. The voice of calm reason in a tribe of volatile, competitive boys, he could always be counted on to quietly and methodically work out everyone's problems. Never in all the years they had lived together had Nathan ever seen Eric be so accusatory, so demanding, and he didn't like it.

"Not that's it's any of your damn business," Nathan gritted, "but I know for certain that Colin isn't my son. What in hell would make you think that?"

Eric shook his head, his tense expression fading to bafflement. "Everything. First of all, he looks just like you. Secondly, Mrs. Graham was obviously lying when she told me that her husband was the baby's father, since you had said not ten minutes earlier that her husband has been dead for several years. Then you told me that Colin is nine months old, but I'd stake my life on the fact that he's no more than six or seven."

It was these last words that suddenly rang a warning bell in Nathan's mind. "You think he's only six or seven months old?"

"Absolutely. If he was nine months old, he'd probably be starting to walk, or at least pulling himself up on furniture trying to stand. Instead, he looks like he's just learned to sit up, and that usually happens several months earlier. At least it did with my kids. Then, too, I noticed when you were holding him that he's got almost no teeth. That's not normal for a nine-month-old, either."

Nathan blew out a long breath, vastly relieved that Eric's conjectures were based on nothing more concrete than teeth and posture. Surely Elyse wouldn't have lied to him about the baby's age. What reason would she have? Unless . . . Nathan gulped as his mind completed that sentence. "Maybe he's just a little slow in developing," he said lamely.

"Maybe," Eric shrugged, "but it also seemed strange to me that Mrs. Graham made such a point of telling me he was small for his age. Almost like she was trying to cover something up. And you can't deny the resemblance, Nate. The boy is the spitting image of you."

"Oh, that's just coloring," Nathan protested weakly, his head spinning with the nearly indisputable facts Eric was presenting. Could he really be so stupid as to not know that a baby he saw every day was his own son?

He couldn't be that blind. Surely, he'd know if Colin was his. Eric was just off on one of his flights of fancy. "You just think he looks like me because he's blond and blue-eyed," he argued, trying desperately to believe his own words. "But so is Elyse."

"True. But Elyse doesn't have a cleft in her chin and you do—and so does Colin."

"Coincidence," Nathan scoffed, throwing his arms wide.

Eric looked down at the floor for a moment, then picked up a blade of straw and snapped it in two. "Like you said, Nate, it's none of my business, but I'm your brother and I care about you, so I'm going to ask you one more question. If you don't want to answer, I'll understand."

Nathan nodded slowly, anticipating the question and not sure if he could face the answer he knew he would have to give.

"If, for some reason, Mrs. Graham *is* lying about Colin's age and he's really only six or seven months old like I suspect he is, is there any chance then that you could be his father?"

There was a long silence as Nathan forced himself to face Eric's blunt question. "Yes," he finally whispered. "If he's seven months old, then he could be mine."

Very slowly, Eric raised his eyes and looked at his brother compassionately. When he spoke, his voice was soft. "Have you asked Elyse?"

"Yes!" Nathan blurted. "The first time I saw Colin, I asked her who his father was. She told me he belonged to her late husband, so I assumed that when I was here the first time, Mr. Graham must have just died. Then I heard in town that he'd been dead for four years, so I knew she was lying, but I didn't question her any further."

"Why not?"

Nathan clenched his fists at his side and squeezed his eyes shut. "I don't know, damn it! I guess I just figured it wasn't any of my business. I didn't think Colin was mine, so it didn't really matter to me who his father was."

Seeing his brother's rapidly rising agitation, Eric's voice became conciliatory. "Okay, Nate, let's start from the beginning. What exactly was there between the two of you?"

"It was crazy," Nathan muttered, slowly unclenching his hands and blowing out a long breath. "I was on my way to Austin and a storm came up. I just happened to stop here, asking for shelter for the night. Elyse let me in, gave me supper, we starting talking and . . . well, you know." Purposely, Nathan left out the fact that Elyse had seduced him only to save her brother. Some things were just too painful to recount . . . even to Eric.

"I left the next morning and I didn't see or hear from her again until I was assigned to protect her."

"So you were together just one night?"

"Yes. That was the only time."

Eric shrugged, a ghost of a smile playing about his lips. "Of course, one night is all it takes."

"I know that," Nathan barked. "And, of course, when I saw the baby, the thought that he might be mine crossed my mind. But Elyse swore to me that Colin was eight months old, so I just figured that the night she and I were together, she was already a couple of months pregnant."

"She also swore to you that Colin was her husband's child. Why do you think she'd lie about that?"

"I don't know," Nathan said, plowing his fingers through his hair and pacing the length of the stall again. "I thought she was probably embarrassed that she'd had an illicit affair and gotten caught. But, Eric, if that baby is mine, I swear she'll rue the day she lied to me."

"Now, just settle down," Eric soothed, falling easily into his familiar role of diplomat. "Don't get yourself all riled up. Like you said, I may be wrong and this is all just a series of coincidences. This whole situation may be just like you thought. Elyse may have told you the baby belonged to her husband because she didn't want you to think badly of her. After all, if she admitted to you that you were the second man she'd had a liaison with in two months, you'd probably think she was loose with her favors. No woman wants a man to think they're easy—even if they are."

Nathan cocked his head, trying to remember who else had said those very words to him. Red. He had said the same thing the day they'd discussed Elyse. His tight-lipped response to Eric was the same as it had been to Red. "Elyse is *not* 'loose with her favors.' "

"I'm not saying she is," Eric placated. "I'm just trying to figure out what her motivation might be for lying to you."

"You aren't going to say anything to her about these suspicions of yours, are you?" Nathan asked.

"God, no!" Eric replied, throwing him an appalled look. "You should know me better than that. It's not my place to say anything. That's between you and her."

"But you truly think Colin might be mine?"

"Yeah, Nate, I do. And if he is, you should know it. What you do with the information if you find out it's true is entirely up to you, but I think you deserve to know, one way or the other."

Nathan sank down on the straw, chewing on his lower lip and staring absently at the wall. "I don't think Elyse would tell me, even if I asked her point blank."

"I take it there's nothing between you any longer?"

Nathan thought back on the passionate moments he and Elyse had recently shared. "Well, I can't say there's *nothing*, but I don't think it's anything other than physical attraction—at least on her part."

"And what about *your* part?"

Nathan looked at Eric and shook his head in wonder. "You're the one in the family who should have been a lawyer, you know. You have a way of getting everybody to confess everything."

Eric smiled. "Not me. I'm perfectly content to be a simple farmer. I'll leave the lawyering to Adam, if he can ever quit chasing the girls long enough to finish school."

The men shared a quiet chuckle, thinking about their youngest brother and the roguish reputation he was enjoying in Boston.

"I care about Elyse," Nathan confessed.

"Care about her? Is that all?"

"You mean, do I love her?"

Eric remained silent.

Nathan stared at the wall in front of him again. "I don't honestly know. Sometimes I think I do, but she doesn't seem to want me, so I don't let myself pursue it. I do know that in the whole, long fifteen months we didn't see each other, I never stopped thinking about her."

Eric sighed, an empathetic exhalation from one who had once been where Nathan was now. "I remember all the problems Kirsten and I had at first," he mused. "It took me a long time to realize I loved her, and by the time I finally did, she didn't seem to want me anymore."

Nathan's eyebrows rose with interest. "I didn't know you and Kirsten ever had any problems. I knew that Claire and Stuart had a rocky start and what Tory did to Miles that first year almost killed him, but I didn't know about you two. So, little Kirsten put you through some hoops, too, did she?"

"Oh, Lord, yes!" Eric chuckled in remembrance. "I was climbing in and out of bedroom windows trying to steal her money so she wouldn't have the funds to leave me and stuffing diamond rings into loaves of bread she made just to show her how much I loved her. When she finally announced she was going back to New York despite all my efforts, I begged her to pose for a portrait for me before she left. I told her I had to have the money I'd make from selling the picture or I'd lose the farm."

Nathan burst out laughing. "You made Kirsten believe you were poor?"

"I was desperate, Nate! I would have done anything to keep her from leaving."

"But didn't anybody in town tell her the truth about your wealth? Surely everybody in Rose Meadow must have known you were lying."

Eric grinned. "I took her out of town so she wouldn't have a chance to talk to anyone."

"I had no idea," Nathan murmured. "You two are happy now, aren't you?"

Eric closed his eyes, a sublime smile curving his lips. "Yes, we're happy. Very, very happy."

"So, how did you do it, Eric? How did you make her admit she loved you?"

"Well, our situation was a lot different than yours. We were already married and there was no child to complicate things."

"But, still, what did you do?"

"I took Kirsty to the Stanford Hotel outside Minneapolis and made love to her until she finally admitted she didn't want to leave me."

Nathan's jaw dropped open at his brother's scandalous confession. Never before had they ever had such a personal conversation. Eric was a very quiet, private person, and Nathan had never even suspected such a passionate being lay buried beneath his placid exterior.

"Unfortunately, I don't think making love to Elyse would solve anything between us. If your suspicions about Colin are right, making love is probably what has caused her hostility toward me."

Eric looked at him in surprise. "Is she hostile toward you? I didn't see any sign of that when the three of us were in the house together."

"Maybe hostile isn't the right word, but she's been very direct in letting me know she wants me out of her life."

"I don't understand any of this," Eric muttered.

"You're telling me that Elyse has lied to you, that she's hostile toward you, that she wants you out of her life. So, what is it about this woman that makes you think you love her?"

His question came as such a surprise that a long moment passed before Nathan was able to answer. "I don't know if I can explain it," he murmured, "but there's something about her—something brave and stoic and indestructible, yet she's also vulnerable and beautiful and passionate—"

"Okay," Eric sighed. "I'm beginning to understand."

"All I know," Nathan continued, "is that even the first time I met her, I knew she was different from any woman I'd ever known. I couldn't get her out of my mind. Then, when I heard about her brother robbing the bank and how she had helped him escape, I thought my feelings had changed. But the minute I got back here and saw her again, I realized they hadn't."

Nathan turned to face Eric, a tortured look on his face. "I think she's the one, Eric, and I don't know what to do about it."

"Unfortunately, I don't have any magic answers for you," Eric replied. "With affairs of the heart, everybody has to figure things out for themselves. But, first of all, you have to decide whether or not you're looking for a permanent relationship. Elyse may be the right girl for you, but are you ready to give up everything you've worked for in order to have her?"

"What do you mean?"

"I mean that your whole life has always been your career, and you know you'll have to give up being a Ranger if you decide to marry. Ask yourself what's most important to you—a wife and a family and this ranch, or the thrill of catching the bad guys. That's the first thing you have to figure out."

"Actually," Nathan interjected, "I don't think that would be a hard decision to make. I've been thinking a lot lately about leaving the service."

"You're kidding!" Eric exclaimed, clearly astonished.

"No, I'm not. I've been getting a hankering to settle down, raise a family, be boring like you and Miles."

Eric smiled at Nathan's little dig. "You'd be surprised how *un*boring it can be to settle down, as long as it's with the right woman. But, if you've decided Elyse is that woman, my advice is to go very slowly with her. Maybe you should try romancing her a little—see how she responds. And I don't mean throwing her down on the bed and having your way with her. From what you say, she doesn't respond to that real well."

In Nathan's mind there suddenly appeared a vision of Elyse's face as it had looked that night after they'd made love—drowsy and replete with satisfaction. "You may be right that throwing her down on the bed is not the way to romance her," he conceded, "but I've got to tell you, the night she and I had together was the best night of my life."

"And do you think she felt the same?"

Nathan smiled at Eric meaningfully. "I'd stake my life on it."

"Well, I'm happy to hear that," Eric laughed. "Maybe your battle won't be as tough as you think."

When their laughter died away, Nathan's expression again became pensive. "I've got to get this thing about Colin sorted out though," he murmured. "I just don't know what to say to Elyse to get her to tell me the truth. And I'm not sure I'd know the truth even if she told me."

"You'll figure something out," Eric said positively, getting to his feet.

Nathan looked up at him hopefully. "You think so?"

"I know so. Now, come on. Let's go sit on the porch and have a smoke. It's too nice outside to stay in here."

Nathan started to laugh. "You and your porches. I've never known anybody who likes to sit on a porch as much as you do."

"You're right," Eric grinned. "Sitting on a porch is

one of my very favorite things in life. In fact, I'd have to say that it ranks right up there with the smell of manure."

Chapter 23

Nathan never thought he'd say it, but he almost wished Eric hadn't come to visit.

"Damn him," he cursed as he tossed restlessly in bed that night. "Damn him for making me question everything, analyze everything, face everything."

Eric had always had that effect on his family. He was the one who quietly, calmly made his brothers think about things—usually things they didn't want to think about. It was no different now, even though they were grown men. Eric still made them think—and today he made Nathan think about Elyse, something he had rarely allowed himself to do.

Had she lied to him about Colin? Could it be, as Eric suspected, that Colin was his son? There had to be some way he could find out for sure, and asking Elyse was not the way to do it. But someone in this two-bit town had to know the truth. Someone who would tell him.

He had thought about confiding in Red Hilliard and then asking him to pump Lynn Potter for information. But just last week, Red had told to him that he and Mrs. Potter were developing a friendly relationship. He suspected from Red's rather embarrassed statements about his increasingly frequent visits to the reclusive widow's farm that there was more going on there than just simple friendship and he didn't want to put Red in a spot that might jeopardize that. So, Red was out.

But who else would know? Hiram Richman, perhaps? Probably, but Nathan didn't know or trust the store-keeper enough to ask such an obvious question. The women in Bixby would also undoubtedly know, but he would not add grist to the gossip mill by asking any of them, either. The less they knew about his interest in Elyse, the better.

"Unfortunately, that's everyone you know," he muttered. "There isn't anybody else. Except . . ." Suddenly, a vision of a woman's face swam up before his tired eyes.

Daisy. That was it. The waitress at the cafe who was always so friendly when he wandered in for a quick cup of coffee. She would probably know—and, if she did, she'd undoubtedly tell him. Especially if he played up to her a little bit the next time he saw her.

Nathan frowned into the darkness. Subterfuge and dishonesty were not his strong points, and he hated even considering leading the obviously smitten waitress on just to gain information about another woman. But, damn it, this was important. Perhaps the most important bit of information he'd ever tried to glean and he honestly couldn't think of anybody else who he could ask.

"Okay, Daisy, my darlin', guess you're it." Somehow, he had to think of some way to couch the conversation to get the information he wanted without giving the overly eager girl too much encouragement. After all, the last thing he needed at this point was another woman in his life!

It was Thursday morning, and much to Elyse's relief, Eric was leaving. As she stood at the sink, washing the breakfast dishes, she felt almost guilty about how happy she was to see him go. He was truly one of the kindest, most considerate men she'd ever met, yet she couldn't shake the feeling of unease that came over her every time he walked into the room. He had asked no more questions about Colin that would make her suspect he guessed the truth, but there was something about the way he looked at the baby that made her nervous.

Even now, while Nathan was in the barn saddling his horse, Eric was sitting on the floor, playing with the little boy. Despite her vow to try to act relaxed around him, Elyse found herself constantly turning around, casting covert glances at the handsome man sprawled on her front-room rug and wondering what was really going on behind those enigmatic brown eyes.

This time when she looked over her shoulder, she found Eric looking back at her. Wiping her hands nervously on the dish towel, she said, "You seem to really like children, Mr. Wellesley."

"I do," Eric smiled, picking Colin up and bouncing him on his knee. "And being around this little guy makes me realize how much I miss my own two."

Elyse tossed the dish towel down and walked over to the settee, perching on the edge as she tried desperately to make a little polite conversation. "You have a son and a daughter, don't you?"

"Yes," Eric answered slowly, "and you know, it's the strangest thing. Colin reminds me so much of my son, Ian, when he was this age that if I didn't know better, I'd swear they were related. They even look alike."

Elyse jumped to her feet, hurrying back to the sanctuary of the kitchen before Eric noticed her flaming face. "That *is* strange," she replied, cursing the tremor she heard in her voice. "It's probably just that all babies seems similar to some extent."

To her horror, Eric got to his feet also, swinging Colin up in his brawny arms and following her into the kitchen. Leaning his tall frame against the counter, he studied Colin earnestly. "Maybe, but it seems like it's more than that. Colin not only looks like Ian did, but his expressions are even similar. Although I must say, Colin reminds me more of Ian when he was about seven months old than when he was nine months. Must be because he's so small."

Elyse felt she couldn't swallow, and she couldn't trust herself to speak. The man knew. There was no doubt about it. Somehow, some way, he knew the truth and in his quiet, genteel way, he was letting her know that he was on to her.

Silently, she held her arms out and took the baby. Eric's dark gaze searched her face for a moment, making Elyse feel like he could see into her very soul. "Take good care of him, Mrs. Graham," he said quietly. "He's very special."

Mutely, Elyse nodded. Their eyes locked as a silent vow of understanding passed between them, then Eric picked up his satchel and walked over to the door.

"I hope we'll have a chance to meet again sometime," Elyse choked.

Eric smiled, that wide, heart-stopping smile that had made more than one Minnesota maiden feel like she needed to roll in the snow. "Somehow, I have a feeling we will."

His parting words lingered in Elyse's mind long after he was out the door.

"Thanks for coming, Eric. It was good to see you."

Eric swung up on his horse and smiled down at Nathan. "Good to see you, too, Nate. And how about the next time? Think you'll be married?"

Nathan shrugged. "Who knows?"

"It would sure make Mother and Father happy. Ma wants you to settle down in the worst way."

"I know," Nathan frowned. "She mentions it in every letter. I just wish she'd quit worrying about me and start concentrating on Geoff. He's the one who needs a wife."

"Oh, Geoff's a lost cause," Eric chuckled. "The only way any girl would get him to marry her is if she tied him to one of his logs and floated him down the river to the church."

Nathan burst out laughing. "You're probably right. I don't know how anybody can like trees as much as that man does."

"Guess he feels the same way about them as I do about dirt."

"Yeah," Nathan nodded. "Guess so."

Eric reached down, extending his hand. "Take care, Nate. If there's anything I can do to help, let me know."

Nathan clasped Eric's hand, pumping it affectionately. "You've already helped more than you know. Thank you."

"Anytime. Keep in touch, okay?"

"I will. I promise I will."

Eric started off down the road. Nathan watched until he was out of sight, wishing, not for the first time, that he and Eric lived closer.

"Why in hell would anybody want to be a farmer in Minnesota?" he muttered, turning back toward the house. "Fighting that weather and eating that awful fish . . . The man has to be crazy."

It was just after noon when Nathan sauntered into the "Best in Bixby Cafe" and headed for one of the back tables. Ever since Red Hilliard had pointed out to him one day that not only was the restaurant the "Best in Bixby" cafe, it was also the *"Only* in Bixby" cafe, he'd never been able to walk into the place without smiling.

Daisy Flynn chose to interpret Nathan's customary grin as a greeting to her and always made a beeline to help him before he even settled himself in his chair. Today was no exception.

"Howdy there, Mr. Wells," she sang out, leaning as close as she dared while she placed a worn menu on the table. "Haven't seen you in a long time."

Nathan looked up at the bucktoothed little waitress

with the flaming red hair and forced an interested smile. "Been awful busy, Miss Flynn, otherwise I'd come in more often."

With a delighted smile, she threw her hair back over her shoulder, preening outrageously for him. "You're just going to have to tell Mrs. Graham that you deserve a day off once in a while—a night, too, maybe. We're open for supper, you know."

"Are you?" Nathan smiled. "Well, I'll keep that in mind. So, what's good today?"

"The meatloaf. I made it myself this morning."

"With mashed potatoes and gravy?"

"Sure. Whatever you want, Nat, I'll see that you get it."

Nathan ignored Daisy's obvious innuendo and said quickly, "Then the meatloaf it is."

"Want a cup of coffee with it? I make the best coffee in Bixby. Everyone says so."

"Then I guess I'll have to have some, won't I?"

With a last flirtatious wink, Daisy whirled around and sashayed back to the kitchen, hoping desperately that Nathan was watching her.

He was, but Daisy would have been mightily disappointed if she'd known that he was thinking not about her feminine charms but, rather, about how to work his conversation with her around to Colin Graham.

His opportunity came more easily than he could have hoped when Daisy returned a moment later, carrying a steaming mug of coffee.

"So, Nat," she gushed. "How are things going with your job? Any chance that you might stay on in Bixby through the winter?"

"I don't think so," Nathan answered, blowing on the coffee and taking a swallow.

Daisy's disappointment was so obvious that he quickly added, "Boy, this coffee is great!"

"Oh, thank you!" she trilled, her good humor instantly restored. "Do you really have to leave?"

Nathan shrugged. "Mrs. Graham only needs me through harvest time, so I'll probably just be on my way after that."

"Do you think you might come back next spring?"

"Naw, I doubt it."

"Why not?"

Nathan made a great pretense of looking around the empty cafe as if checking for eavesdroppers. "Can you keep a secret?" he whispered loudly.

"Of course!" Daisy nodded, sitting down in a chair opposite him and leaning forward eagerly.

"It's that baby of hers. He drives me crazy."

Daisy's grin faded. "Don't you like children, Nat?"

"Oh, yeah, I do," Nathan amended quickly. "But that baby of Mrs. Graham's just cries and cries and cries. I thought that by the time babies got to be his age, they had stopped all that hollering."

Daisy looked at him blankly. "He's not very old."

Nathan drew in a deep breath. Here was his chance. "He isn't? I thought he was about nine, maybe ten months."

"No, you silly," Daisy laughed, waving her hand at him. "Colin Graham's only about seven months."

Nathan's heart dropped into his stomach and it was all he could do to keep from jumping out of his seat and smashing something. He waited a moment to answer, clamping down hard on his temper. Finally, in as casual a voice as he could muster, he said, "Really? Only seven months? Are you sure? I thought he was older than that."

Daisy shook her head. "I know he's only seven months because he was born on Christmas Day."

Nathan could feel himself start to shake all over.

"I remember it perfectly," Daisy continued, thrilled that she could impart such a delicious piece of gossip. "It was after church at the annual Christmas breakfast when somebody noticed that old Doc Banks wasn't there. Everybody started wondering why he would miss

the breakfast, since it's one of the biggest events of the
year in Bixby. Then somebody said that he was too tired
to come because he'd spent the night out at Mrs. Graham's delivering her baby."

She paused.

"Go on," Nathan commanded, his voice steely with
barely concealed rage.

Daisy's eyes widened in surprise at his abrupt tone,
and she giggled nervously. "Well, it was actually kind of
funny, you know. Everybody was whispering about how
Mrs. Graham was a widow and all and that she'd had
a baby on Christmas Eve night—just like when Jesus
was born—and some of the men started laughing about
how maybe since Mrs. Graham didn't have a husband,
her baby was an immaculate conception just like Jesus.
Well, then everyone started gossiping about Mrs. Graham, trying to guess who the father of her baby might
be until Reverend Jenkins got mad and started lecturing
all of us about how sacrilegious we were and how awful
it was to talk about such things on such a holy day.
But, still, everyone just kept laughing and making jokes
and . . ."

Daisy rambled on and on, but Nathan had long since
ceased to listen.

*Christmas Day. Elyse had had Colin on Christmas Day. Ex-
actly nine months after he'd been with her in March.*

An anger such as nothing he had ever known boiled
up inside him and, suddenly he could stand no more.
With a low, guttural cry, he jumped out of his chair,
nearly knocking it over in his haste.

Daisy stopped her story in midsentence, looking at
him as if he'd lost his mind. "What's wrong?" she
gasped.

"I have to go now," Nathan growled, throwing a dol-
lar bill on the table and bolting toward the front door.

"Go? But, Nat! What about your meatloaf?"

"You eat it!" he bellowed. "I have to go—right now!"

Daisy rose from the table, staring after Nathan in

openmouthed disbelief. "Wait!" she called desperately as he tore out the door. "Your food's all ready! It'll only take me a minute to dish it up."

Rushing after him, she yanked the front door open and looked wildly up and down the street. Spotting Nathan mounting his buckskin, she shouted, "Wait! Come back! I baked a fresh apple pie today, and everybody says I bake the best pies in town. Nat, come back. Nat!"

But Nathan didn't hear her. The only sound he could hear was a voice screaming at him from deep inside.

He's my son. *He's my son!*

Chapter 24

Elyse knew that something was wrong as soon as she saw Nathan ride into the yard. His buckskin, whom he usually prized so highly, was winded and sweating, and as Nathan neared the house, the look on his face was downright terrifying.

"Is something wrong?" she asked, hurrying down the steps to meet him.

"Yeah," he growled, grasping her hand and pulling her back up the steps. "You're goddamned right something's wrong."

Elyse paled, her free hand circling her throat. "It's the gang, isn't it?" she croaked. "They're back."

"No. It's not the gang. I wish to hell it was."

Elyse looked at him incredulously. "Nathan, you're scaring me. Tell me what's wrong. Is it something I've done?"

Nathan shot her a look that left little doubt that she was responsible for his anger. They entered the house and he released her hand, pointing at the settee. "Sit down."

"I don't want to," she countered stubbornly. "Not until you tell me what's wrong."

If possible, Nathan's expression became even more ominous. "I said, sit down."

Elyse sat down. "All right, I'm sitting. Please, tell me what this is all about."

"Where's my son?"

"He's sleeping in the . . ." Elyse's words died in her throat. Clapping her hand over her mouth, she looked up at Nathan with stricken eyes.

"That's right, Elyse. *My* son."

For a long moment, Elyse just stared at him in mute horror. So many times, she had mentally rehearsed how she would handle this conversation should it ever occur, but now that the moment was upon her, she could think of nothing to say.

Brazen it out, she told herself desperately. *He's just guessing. He can't know for sure.*

"I can't imagine where you came up with that ridiculous idea, but I assure you, he's not yours." She rose from the settee, praying that her legs would support her. "I have things to do, and this conversation is over."

"This conversation is far from over, lady," Nathan thundered, reaching out and grabbing her forearm to halt her headlong flight, "and the only thing you're going to do right now is explain why you lied to me . . . *lied to me* . . . about my son!"

"He's not your son!"

"HE IS MY SON!"

"He's not! He's *my* son . . . no one else's."

Her outrageous statement took Nathan completely by surprise. He'd suspected that she might deny he was Colin's father, but he'd never dreamed she'd deny the child had any father at all. "Are you saying that you conceived this child alone?" he asked sarcastically. "If you are, I can think of several newspapers that would pay you handsomely for your story."

Elyse's jaw clenched with fury. "You are despicable! I am not going to stand here and be the brunt of your crude jokes." With an abrupt jerk, she wrenched her arm out of his grip and headed for the bedroom.

But Nathan was right behind her, and the next thing she knew, his arm was around her waist and she was pressed tightly against his body. She struggled momentarily, trying to free herself from his viselike grip. "Let me go! How dare you touch me?"

She could feel his hot, rasping breath next to her ear as he answered, "That's not what you said the night we conceived him, is it, Elyse? You couldn't get enough of me touching you that night."

Elyse gasped in outrage at his reminder of her shameful behavior. "Let me go! I hate you!"

Nathan loosened his grip just enough to turn her in his arms. They were so close that his lips grazed hers as he demanded, "Is he mine?"

"You've already decided he is, haven't you?"

He gave her a little shake. "Don't play games with me. I want the truth and I want it from you. Is Colin mine? Am I his father?"

"Yes!" she cried, her voice cracking. "He's yours, but you're not his father!"

Nathan abruptly released her. "What the hell do you mean by that?"

Elyse drew herself up haughtily, giving the bodice of her worn gown a yank. "I'm saying that you might have participated in his conception, but that doesn't make you his father."

Nathan shook his head, his anger momentarily replaced by confusion.

"It takes more than a passionate moment to make a father, Nathan. Where were you when I was so sick, I couldn't get out of bed? Where were you the night he was born and I thought I'd die from the pain? Where were you those first days when he cried all the time and never slept more than an hour at a stretch? I'll tell you where you were. *Not here!*"

"I wasn't here because I didn't know!"

Elyse waved her hand dismissively. "You weren't here because you didn't care. Oh, no, the great Nathan Wellesley was too busy playing the hero and enjoying the adoration of the ladies of Austin to give a thought to the naive little farmer's widow back in Bixby. I do read the newspapers, Nathan. I know all about you and how you spend your leisure time."

"You know nothing about me," Nathan barked. "I never forgot you. Not for a single moment."

Elyse ignored his heart-wrenching admission and glared at him angrily. "Didn't it ever occur to you that I might get with child after that night? Or is it just that that's a matter of course with you? I suppose you big, virile Texas Rangers have illegitimate babies strewn all over the state. You probably brag to each other about who has the most. Tell me, Captain Wellesley, do you notch your bedpost the way I hear outlaws notch their guns?"

Nathan's eyes blazed with indignation. "You're being a bitch, Elyse, and it doesn't suit you."

"And you're a bastard, Nathan." She paused, shocked at herself for using such a vulgar word. But her anger far surpassed her sense of propriety and she plunged on recklessly. "No, let me correct that. You're not a bastard. You're the . . . how did you put it? 'The fifth son of James and Mary Wellesley.' It's my son who is a bastard."

A heavy silence stretched between them. Finally, Nathan spoke, and the steely resolve in his voice was far more intimidating than his anger. "If I had known of your condition, lady, *our* son wouldn't be a bastard. And his name would be Wellesley."

"It's a little late to try to impress me with your honor," Elyse snorted. "The truth is, I was nothing more than a night's pleasure for you."

"How the hell do you know *what* you were to me?" Nathan shouted.

"All right, if I'm so wrong about your feelings, then you tell me. What exactly *was* I to you?"

"Much more than a night's pleasure, I guarantee you that."

Elyse blinked with surprise, and much of the ire was

gone from her voice when she next spoke. "Then, why didn't you ever come back?"

"*Why?*" Nathan gritted, nailing her with an icy look. "Are you forgetting that you threw me out the next morning? Are you forgetting that I wanted to talk about what had happened—to figure out where we should go from there? It was you who said you wouldn't discuss it and that all you wanted was for me to leave and never come back."

Clenching his fists in frustration, he paced the length of the small room. "And when I did come back and I tried to talk to you about it again, you told me that what had happened between us was nothing more than a terrible mistake and one that you deeply regretted. Those were your words, Elyse. 'A terrible mistake that you deeply regretted'."

"It *was* a terrible mistake," Elyse cried. "And I *do* regret it."

Nathan rounded on her, his eyes blazing. "You regret giving birth to my son?"

Elyse opened her mouth to fling another hurtful retort at him, but the words stuck in her throat. Releasing her breath with a heavy sigh, she shook her head. This was one thing she couldn't lie about. "No, I don't regret that. I adore Colin. He's my whole life. I just regret the circumstances that begat him."

A look of pain and remorse clouded Nathan's eyes. "Elyse, there's nothing I can do about the circumstances that begat Colin, or about the fact that you had to bear him alone. You'll never know how sorry I am for the unhappiness I've caused you, but regardless of what happened in the past, I'm his father and I'm here now."

"No!" Elyse gasped, shaking her head vehemently. "Your finding out about this doesn't change anything."

"Of course it does! If you think that knowing what I know now, I'm just going to get on my horse and ride away when this is over, you're very much mistaken."

"That's exactly what I want you to do!"

"Well, it's not going to happen!"

Elyse let out a shuddering breath, trying to gird herself to ask the question that hung between them. "What do you think is going to happen here, Nathan? What do you want?"

"I want my son!"

"Why? A few weeks ago, you didn't even know he existed. Why is he suddenly so important to you?"

Nathan stared at her incredulously. "I don't believe you're asking me this. Okay, you're right. A few weeks ago, I didn't know he existed, but now I do. That changes everything."

"Why?" Elyse repeated.

"Because he's my child . . . my flesh and blood. I want to be part of his life."

"But what if that's not what I want? What if I don't want you to be part of his life?"

"It's immaterial whether you want it or not," Nathan retorted arrogantly. "Colin is a Wellesley, and you will not deny him his heritage."

Elyse felt a terror so great that she was afraid she might faint, but she refused to give in to her fear. Raising her chin, she stepped forward aggressively, looking Nathan straight in the eye. "Let's get something straight, Captain. My son's name is Colin Joseph *Graham*, do you understand me? He is mine, *mine*, and I will not let you take him away from me. I don't care who you are!"

Nathan's eyes narrowed dangerously. "I haven't said anything about taking him away from you, Elyse, but you better understand this. Whether you want to admit it or not, Colin *is* a Wellesley. He's not Joe Graham's son, he's mine, and I will not allow any child of mine to go through life carrying another man's name."

"There's nothing you can do about it, Nathan."

"Don't count on that. My family is one of the most powerful in the United States, and if you try to prevent me from claiming paternity, I will use every resource at

my command to fight you. And understand this, too,
Elyse: I will *win*."

Elyse's heart sank. She knew that Nathan meant every word he said and that he *was* powerful enough to
make good on his threats. People like the Wellesleys always got what they wanted. And what Nathan Wellesley
wanted was her son.

For the first time, Elyse realized what a formidable
enemy she was facing. She knew the odds were in his favor, but somehow, some way, she would stop him. No
matter what she had to do, no one was going to take
Colin away from her.

No one.

Chapter 25

Nathan slept in the barn that night, a decision Elyse viewed as an uncanny piece of good luck.

After he stormed angrily out of the house, she spent the next hour pacing the floor and trying to figure out what to do next. One thing was clear. She had to get away. Had to take Colin and disappear before Nathan made good on this threats and took some sort of action to take her baby away from her.

There was not a shred of doubt in her mind that he would do it, or that he would succeed. The Wellesleys could do anything. She had heard Eric tell Nathan the story of how he had found out his whereabouts by having their father contact the governor of Texas. If they were powerful enough that the governor would intervene on their behalf in a matter as inconsequential as a two-day visit, then, surely, they would have little problem inducing a judge to grant them custody of Colin—especially when any number of the hateful women in Bixby would gladly testify as to her unsuitability as a mother.

As the evening wore on and her tired mind hashed and rehashed Nathan's words, Elyse became more and more convinced that taking her baby and disappearing was her only option.

But where could she go? Pacing the room for the hundredth time, she pondered this dilemma. She couldn't seek sanctuary from Lynn. Her house was undoubtedly the first place Nathan would look. No, she had to get farther away than that. Dallas, perhaps? She had an aunt who lived there—her mother's sister—and even though they were not close, she was sure Aunt Nellie wouldn't turn her away.

Sinking down tiredly on the settee, she tried to rationally answer the next two questions that popped into her mind. When would she leave and how would she get to Dallas?

The answer to the first question came to her almost immediately. Tonight. She had to leave tonight before Nathan could stop her.

How she would get herself and Colin to Dallas would be a more difficult hurdle to overcome. She had no money, so taking the train or a stage was out. Her only other choice would be to drive her wagon, or ride.

Dropping her head into her hands, Elyse sighed wearily. The wagon was so rickety, it would never make it. She'd have to ride. But could she handle a horse and Colin, too, for six hours?

"You have to," she told herself firmly. "There's no other way." Pressing her lips together, she threw a hostile look in the direction of the barn. Damn him! Damn him for everything he had put her through.

She sat on the settee for a few minutes longer, wallowing in self-pity over all the heartache Nathan had caused her. Finally, though, she realized that if she were actually going to escape tonight, she had to get moving. Hefting herself up, she walked toward the bedroom, making a mental list of what she'd need to pack. She couldn't take much—just some food, water, and a few clothes—whatever she could fit into Joe's old saddlebags. Suddenly, she stopped short. Joe's saddlebags were in the barn. So was her horse, for that matter. And so was Nathan.

Pressing the heels of her hands against her eyes, Elyse swung her head back and forth, nearly giving in to de-

spair. How was she supposed to get her horse saddled
and out of the barn without Nathan hearing her? It was
impossible.

"Pull yourself together and *think!* There has to be
some way to do this." Again, she started her agitated
pacing. She had to get out of here tonight and she had
to get her hands on a horse to do it. Dallas was thirty
miles away. She certainly couldn't walk there, no matter
how desperate she was to escape.

"Dallas is thirty miles away," she muttered, "but
Lynn's is only one mile." She halted, snapping her fingers as an answer dawned. It was so obvious that she
was surprised she hadn't thought of it sooner. She'd just
walk to Lynn's and borrow one of her horses.

It was an inspired idea. Not only would it save her
from having to go into the barn, but it would also delay
Nathan's suspicions in the morning. If her horse was
gone, he'd know immediately upon rising that she was,
too. This way, he wouldn't suspect—at least for a while.

With a renewed sense of resolve, Elyse glanced over
at the mantel clock. Two forty-five. Lord, no wonder
she was tired! But there was no time to think about that
now. She wanted to be out of the house by four so she'd
have plenty of time to walk to Lynn's, explain the situation to her, borrow her horse, and still be on her way
by five o'clock when the sun started coming up. With
any luck, she'd be at Aunt Nellie's before lunch. She just
hoped she could find her aunt's house once she got to
Dallas. It had been years since she'd been there.

"You can't worry about that now," she told herself
firmly. "Just concentrate on getting out of here. Think
about what you need to take with you. Everything else
will work itself out."

In the end she took very little—just some clean diapers and a shirt for Colin, an extra dress for herself, and
a glass jar full of water. She considered taking some

food, but rejected the idea when she reminded herself that she'd be at Aunt Nellie's by noon.

She shoved the clothes into Joe's old rucksack, then woke Colin, strapping him into the carrier Nathan had made. Dousing the lamp so as not to rouse Nathan's suspicions when he awoke, she quietly stepped out onto the porch. She paused a moment, peering through the darkness at the barn. With a whispered prayer of thanks for the blackness and quiet of the night, she hurried across the near pasture, hardly stopping to draw a breath until she ducked under the cover of the pecan grove at the edge of her property.

Looking down at Colin, she smiled with grim satisfaction. "So far, so good, my darling. Now, be a good boy and don't make any noise. We'll be at Auntie Lynn's before you know it."

Looking back over her shoulder, she gazed longingly at her ramshackle little house. Then, with a defiant shake of her head, she turned away and strode off into the darkness.

"Probably the hardest part of this whole trip is going to be getting Lynn to answer the door," Elyse muttered, doubling up her fist and beating aggressively on the portal. "Come on! You must be able to hear me. Nathan can probably hear me!"

Stepping back, Elyse looked up at Lynn's bedroom, hoping that she might spot her friend peeking out through the window. A glimmer of light shone through the curtains. She sighed with relief, knowing that at least Lynn was awake.

"Lynn!" she called. "Lynn, it's Elyse. Let me in, *please!*"

The window opened a crack. "Elyse, is that you out there?"

"Yes. Please come down and let me in."

"Just a minute. I'll be right down."

"Thank God," Elyse murmured. Maybe she really was going to be able to pull off this mad scheme. So far, it appeared that luck was running with her, instead of against her as it had so often in the past.

The front door opened so quickly that it startled her. "What in the world are you doing here at this hour?" Lynn asked, holding up the candlestick she was carrying as if to verify that it really was Elyse standing on her porch.

"I need your help," Elyse blurted. "Please, may I come in for a moment?"

"Well, yes, of course," Lynn answered, taking a step back and ushering Elyse into her foyer. As Elyse entered the hallway, Lynn closed the door behind her, sliding the bolt securely back in place before again turning to her friend.

"Is something wrong?" she asked breathlessly. "Are you in danger? Where is Captain Wellesley? Why isn't he with you?"

"I'm running away," Elyse stated flatly, ignoring the torrent of questions.

Lynn's eyes widened incredulously. "Running away? From whom?"

"From Nathan Wellesley."

Lynn stared at Elyse in astonishment, her mind spinning with a million questions, none of which she could seem to hold on to long enough to voice.

"May I borrow one of your horses? I promise I'll—"

Lynn held up her hands to stay Elyse's words. "Just a minute. Let me get this straight. You're running away from your own home in order to get away from Captain Wellesley?"

Elyse nodded. "May I borrow a horse?" she repeated.

"Not until you come in and explain this to me."

"Lynn, I don't have much time."

Lynn shook her head obstinately. "No explanation, no horse, Elyse."

Elyse threw her a pleading look, but her friend's stubborn expression remained intact. "Oh, all right," she acquiesced. "But I have to leave as soon as possible."

"Let's go into the parlor and sit down."

Elyse nodded and followed Lynn into the spacious room. Lifting Colin out of the carrier, she perched on the edge of an overstuffed chair, unbuttoning her bodice. If she was going to have to stay here for a few minutes, she might as well nurse him. That way, she wouldn't have to stop as soon when she finally got under way.

"Now, Elyse, I want you to tell me exactly what this is all about," Lynn ordered, walking around the room with the candlestick and lighting several lamps.

Elyse offered Colin her breast, then leaned back in the soft chair. "Nathan Wellesley has found out that Colin is his son."

Lynn nodded gravely. "I suppose it was inevitable, but how did it happen?"

"It's a long story and one I don't have time to tell. Just suffice it to say that he knows and now he's making demands."

Lynn's eyebrows rose. "Demands? What kind of demands?"

"He says he's going to claim paternity over Colin."

"And you don't want that?"

"Of course not! Colin is *my* son, not *his!*"

Lynn frowned at her friend. "Elyse, you're not making any sense."

"He says he wants to be a part of Colin's life."

"That's understandable."

"My Lord, Lynn!" Elyse spat irritably. "You sound like you're on his side!"

"I'm not on anybody's side," Lynn soothed. "But I have learned a lot about Captain Wellesley from Lieutenant Hilliard."

It was now Elyse's turn to raise her brows. "Oh? I didn't realize you and the lieutenant had become that friendly."

It was difficult to tell in the dimly lit room, but Elyse could have sworn Lynn blushed. "We've been spending a lot of time together lately," she said softly. "He comes by every day to check on me."

"I know that," Lynn remarked testily. "I just didn't know you two had become confidantes."

To Elyse's surprise, her needling remark only made Lynn smile. "We . . . talk."

"About Nathan Wellesley?"

"That, and other things. But, yes, we've talked at some length about Captain Wellesley."

"I can't imagine he'd be interesting enough to talk about 'at some length.' " Elyse huffed.

"Oh, but he is! Did you know that he's one of *the* Wellesleys?"

Elyse sucked in an annoyed breath. "Yes, I did. As a matter of fact, that's one of the reasons I'm here."

Lynn's brow furrowed with confusion.

"Lynn, listen to me. Nathan Wellesley belongs to one of the most influential families in the country, right?"

"Right."

"And he has now found out that he is the father of my child, right?"

"Right."

"So, he's decided that he wants to assert his paternal rights over my child, whether I want him to or not."

"What do you mean, 'paternal rights'?"

"He wants to legally claim Colin as his son."

Lynn shrugged, failing to understand what was causing Elyse such anxiety. "That seems perfectly normal, now that he knows. And think about it, Elyse. Think of the advantages Colin would have if Captain Wellesley claimed him."

Elyse gaped at Lynn in complete shock. "I don't believe you're saying this! My God, Lynn, I hardly know this man and he wants to claim my son as his!"

"But, you told me yourself that Colin *is* his."

"No," Elyse said mulishly. "Colin isn't his. Colin is *mine*. Nathan Wellesley just contributed to his creation."

"That's an interesting way of looking at it," Lynn noted wryly.

Elyse's face darkened with anger. Colin had finished nursing and she laid him on the settee, standing up and hurriedly buttoning her bodice. "I can see that I made a mistake coming here. If I had known that you were going to take this attitude, I wouldn't have bothered you."

Lynn jumped to her feet also. "Oh, don't say that, my dear. I didn't mean to upset you. It's just that I'm having a hard time understanding why you feel you have to take Colin and leave."

"Because if I don't, Nathan Wellesley is going to have him taken away from me!"

Lynn's mouth dropped open in astonishment. "What?" she gasped. "He told you that?"

"Well, not in so many words," Elyse amended, "but he might as well have. He said that he would take whatever measures necessary to make sure that he could claim his rights over Colin, and if I tried to stop him, he'd fight me."

"My stars!" Lynn gasped, raising her fingers to her lips. "I can hardly believe he'd say something like that. Why, Lieutenant Hilliard has told me over and over that Captain Wellesley is the finest man he's ever known. Brave, honest, ethical . . ."

"Well, maybe that's how another man sees him, but with me, he's been nothing but a bully."

Lynn looked at Elyse quizzically. "Really? But I've heard that you two . . . I mean, I know you had some problems with him at first, but after Lieutenant Hilliard told me that Captain Wellesley bought your grandmother's ring back for you, I figured that you—"

"My grandmother's ring! How did Lieutenant Hilliard find out about that?"

Lynn plucked at the front of her wrapper nervously. "You don't know?"

Elyse shook her head. "No, but you're going to tell me, aren't you?"

"Oh, dear," Lynn fretted, mortified to think that she was unwittingly spreading idle gossip. "It's really nothing."

"Lynn, tell me what this is all about, please! How did Mr. Hilliard know about the ring? Did Nathan tell him?"

"Well, no."

"How, then?"

Lynn swallowed hard, knowing that there was no way out of telling Elyse the truth. "Apparently, the day that Captain Wellesley bought the ring, Lillian Underwood came into Richman's and noticed it was gone. I guess she coerced Mr. Richman into telling her who had bought it."

"Oh, God," Elyse moaned, dropping back down on the settee.

"But Captain Wellesley didn't tell Mr. Richman that it was for you," Lynn added hurriedly. "He said he was buying the ring for his mother."

Elyse's head shot up, and she looked at Lynn in confusion. "For his mother? Then, why does everyone think he bought it for me?"

"Well, you know how people talk . . ." Lynn's voice trailed off meaningfully.

"You mean Lillian Underwood just guessed that Nathan had bought the ring for me?"

"Well, she knew it was your ring and I think she just put two and two together. I mean, since Captain Wellesley has been staying at your farm all this time, she just assumed . . ."

". . . that it was payment for services rendered," Elyse finished bitterly.

"Oh, Elyse!"

"And even you believed it!" Elyse railed. "Even you, my best friend."

"That isn't true!" Lynn protested. "I just thought that you and the captain had come to some sort of understanding about things. I mean, I knew even then that he was Colin's father, so you must have had a relationship with him at one time. I just figured that maybe—"

"Well, you figured wrong!"

"You mean, he did buy the ring for his mother and not for you?"

"No," Elyse admitted. "He bought the ring for me. But I have every intention of paying him back for it!"

Lynn gazed at her friend sympathetically. "Elyse, isn't there any possibility that the two of you could work things out?"

"No," Elyse answered quickly. "None at all."

"I think you're being stubborn and foolish," Lynn said bluntly.

"Why?" Elyse cried. "Because I won't let this man steal my son?"

"No, because it's as plain as the nose on your face that you're in love with him and you're just too stubborn and proud to admit it."

"I'm not in love with him! I'm not!"

"Methinks thou dost protest too much," Lynn quoted.

Elyse threw her an anguished look. "Even if I was in love with him, it wouldn't matter. He doesn't love me."

"Horsefeathers!" Lynn snorted. "The man is crazy about you."

"How would you know?"

"For one thing, Red told me so, and he should know. He's Captain Wellesley's best friend."

"Did Nathan actually tell Lieutenant Hilliard this?"

"I don't know," Lynn admitted, "but Red said he and Will Johnson can't believe how the captain has changed. They say you're all he ever talks about."

"That's because he's been assigned to protect me," Elyse protested. "That's all it is. I'm just a job to him."

Lynn frowned, annoyed by her friend's continued refusal to admit the truth. "You can believe anything you want, Elyse, but I'm telling you, you're making a mistake running away. That man is your future. You're in love with him, he's in love with you, you have a child together. You should be sharing your lives."

Elyse stared pensively out the window at the approaching dawn. When she finally spoke again, her voice was so quiet that Lynn had to lean forward to hear her. "As usual, you're right," she murmured. "I *am* in love with Nathan. I think I have been for a long time. But he's not in love with me, regardless of what Red Hilliard and Will Johnson think. All he's really interested in is his child, and, no matter how much I may love Nathan, I'll never give Colin up."

"Give Colin up!" Lynn gasped. "Why do you think Captain Wellesley expects you to give Colin up? Can't you two share him? Even if you decide that marriage is not for you, surely something could be worked out."

Elyse shook her head vehemently. "You just don't understand, Lynn. Nathan is a Wellesley. Those people don't 'work things out.' They take what they want when they want it—but they're not going to take my baby! That's why I have to leave."

Again, she rose from the settee. "Now, since you obviously aren't going to help me, I'll be going."

"I didn't say I wouldn't help you," Lynn cried. "I just think you're underestimating Captain Wellesley. From everything Red has said, he wouldn't do the things you say he would."

Elyse did not miss Lynn's use of Lieutenant Hilliard's first name, and despite her anxiety, she couldn't help but remark upon it. "Red? So, you and the lieutenant are on a first-name basis?"

This time Lynn's blush was apparent, even in the gloom. "We've become . . . close."

Elyse smiled, a wistful little curving of her lips that was almost undetectable. "I'm happy for you, Lynn. I

hope everything turns out exactly like you hope it will."
She turned and picked up Colin. "Now, I really do have
to go."

Lynn took a quick step forward, sighing heavily as she
placed her hand on Elyse's arm. "Where are you planning to go?"

Elyse looked at her speculatively. "I'll only tell you if
you promise you won't tell Lieutenant Hilliard or Captain Wellesley. I know Nathan is going to look for me,
and I'm sure you'll be one of the first people he comes
to."

"Oh, I hope not!" Lynn exclaimed, automatically
covering her cheeks with her hands.

"He will," Elyse said positively.

Lynn drew in a long, shuddering breath. "If he does,
he does," she said stoically. "But you and I have been
friends for a long time and if you are determined to do
this crazy thing, I promise, I won't betray your secret."

"Then you'll lend me a horse?"

"I don't know, Elyse. I only have one left and it's that
old gray mare of Jonathan's. She hasn't been ridden in
so long that I'm afraid she'll be impossible to handle."

Elyse shrugged. "I'm a good rider. You know that."

"Yes, I do, but Chili is really cantankerous. I just
wouldn't want her to throw you."

"Don't worry. I'm sure I can handle her."

Lynn nodded, but her look was still doubtful. "Won't
you please tell me where you're going? I'll be worried
sick if I don't know. And besides, if you don't tell me,
how can I let you know when Captain Wellesley finally
leaves?"

Elyse thought for a moment, then said, "I'm going to
my Aunt Nellie's in Dallas."

"I've never heard you mention an aunt in Dallas."

"She's my mother's older sister. She used to come
visit once in a while when I was a child, but after Ma
died, I sort of lost track of her."

"Yet you're going to stay with her?"

"She's the only person I know in Dallas. Where else could I go? I have no money. And, after all, she *is* family. I can't imagine her turning me away."

"Oh, Elyse," Lynn wailed. *"Please* don't do this!"

"I have to," Elyse said firmly, her tone brooking no further argument.

Lynn nodded in defeat. "All right. Let's go saddle Chili."

Elyse threw her a grateful look and followed her out the back door.

"Do you have any supplies with you?"

"Just what I could fit in this sack, but I figure I'll be in Dallas by noon, so I should be fine."

The women entered the barn and Lynn pulled a bridle off a hook on the wall. With obvious trepidation, she opened a stall door and cautiously approached a gray mare. "Be nice now, Chili, and let me put this bridle on."

The mare looked at her warily, backing up a step and baring her teeth. Lynn stopped short, looking at Elyse pleadingly. "See how nasty she is?"

"Don't let her see you're scared of her," Elyse advised, "or she'll never let you saddle her."

Lynn hovered near the mare's head, making no move to put the bit in her mouth. "But I *am* scared of her!"

"Here," Elyse said, stepping into the stall and holding out the baby. "You take him and I'll do it. She and I might as well get things straight between us right from the start."

Lynn gratefully handed over the bridle and Elyse moved toward the horse. The mare's ears immediately went back and, again, she showed her teeth.

"Bite me, old lady, and you'll be sorry," Elyse warned, her voice smooth and even, but firmly confident.

The mare's ears flicked forward.

"There, that's better."

With sure movements, Elyse shoved the bit into the

horse's mouth, looping the strap over her ears and tightening the cheek straps. "Good girl," she crooned, backing up toward the stall's front wall and pulling a saddle down. "Okay, this is next."

Moving forward, she gently placed the saddle on the mare's back. The ears flattened again, but much to Elyse's surprise, she didn't buck. "I think she's going to be fine," she said, turning briefly to look at Lynn. "She just needs a firm hand."

"She's a mean old thing," Lynn said, shaking her head. "I don't know why I keep her, except that she produces such lovely foals."

"Is she bred now?"

"No, not this year. I didn't want the trouble."

Elyse nodded and slowly tightened the saddle's cinch. Chili's head swung around angrily as she felt the cinch tighten around her belly.

"Be careful, she's going to bite you!"

"She does, and she'll regret it." Elyse watched the horse out of the corner of her eye, but, as if the mare had heard the warning, she made no further attempt to bite.

Once saddled, the horse was quite docile and allowed Elyse to lead her out of the barn. "See?" Elyse said, throwing the rucksack over the saddle horn. "She just has to understand who's boss."

Hitching up her dress, she prepared to mount. Chili sidestepped, trying to prevent Elyse from putting her foot in the stirrup, but a hard jerk on the reins brought her around again. Pulling herself up in the saddle, Elyse leaned down and adjusted the stirrups, then reached for Colin.

"Thank you, Lynn," she murmured, trying hard not to react to the tears she saw welling in her friend's eyes. "I appreciate you helping me."

"You just take care of yourself," Lynn choked, forcing a wan smile.

"I will, and I'll write you as soon as I can and give you Aunt Nellie's address."

Lynn nodded, biting her lip to quell the sobs that threatened.

Reining the mare around, Elyse started off toward the road, but halted when she heard Lynn's voice calling her. Turning in the saddle, she looked around.

"Here," Lynn cried, running up next to her and holding out a large gold coin. "Take this."

Elyse stared down at the coin in surprise. "Do you always carry twenty-dollar gold pieces in your nightgown?"

"No," Lynn smiled, "but I always carry one in my shoe."

For a long moment, the women's eyes met. "You're a dear friend, Lynn," Elyse said quietly. "Thank you for understanding."

The sobs Lynn had been trying so hard to suppress finally broke through. "I love you, Elyse. Please be careful!"

Quickly, before she broke down herself, Elyse wheeled the mare around and kicked her in the flanks, heading off at a spirited trot.

She never looked back.

Chapter 26

Nathan opened his eyes, then quickly closed them again as a shaft of sunlight pierced him through the barn window. God, did he feel terrible. Not only had he not gone to sleep until well after midnight, but the huge quantity of whiskey he had consumed was definitely taking its toll.

Squinting down at the empty bottle lying next to him in the hay, he picked it up and sent it hurtling against the barn wall. "Stinkin' rotgut," he cursed. "When will I ever learn to stay away from cheap whiskey?"

With a moan, he lay back down, throwing his arm over his burning eyes. "Damn her," he mumbled. "The only thing in the world that would make me drink that much bad booze is an unreasonable woman—and she's the worst I've ever seen."

At that moment, Elyse's cow bellowed out a mournful moo. Nathan clapped his hands over his ears and threw the animal a withering look. "What the hell's the matter with you?" he growled. "Haven't you been milked yet?"

Raising himself up on one elbow, he peered more closely at the complaining bovine. "Well, I'll be damned. You *haven't* been milked. What the hell time is it, anyway?"

Rolling over, he groped around in his pocket, pulling out his watch and staring at it until his bleary eyes finally focused on the black hands. "Nine o'clock!"

He climbed unsteadily to his feet, shielding his eyes with his hands and staggering over to his boots. "What did she do? Decided not to milk you just because she's mad at me?" Leaning over, he picked up a boot, groaning out loud as the blood rushed to his pounding head. "Please, God," he muttered. "Just make this headache go away and I promise I'll never touch another drop. *Never!*"

With a supreme effort, Nathan pulled on his boots and headed out into the yard. The hot July sun beating down on his head made him feel like he was going to be sick, but he took several deep breaths and the nausea gradually subsided.

Clumping up onto the porch, he leaned against the front door, pounding on it weakly. "Elyse? Elyse, come out here and milk your cow."

He waited a moment, and when his summons received no response, he called again. "Elyse? I know you're in there. You gotta milk the cow. She's bawling like crazy."

Again he waited, and when there was still no answer, he tried the door. It wasn't locked. Opening it a crack, he peeked into the house. "Must be in the bedroom," he mumbled when he saw the front room was empty.

He took several halting steps into the room, then flopped down on the settee, putting his head between his knees and groaning loudly. "Elyse!" he bellowed. "Come out here!"

This time when she didn't answer, Nathan felt a little prickle of apprehension skitter down his spine. His headache forgotten, he bolted off the settee and hurried toward the closed bedroom door. "Elyse?" he called, his hand already on the doorknob. "Are you up?" Not waiting for a response, he opened the door.

His eyes darted from the made-up bed to the empty cradle. He swung around in a full circle, his eyes sweeping every corner of the room, but she wasn't there.

"Elyse!" he shouted, lurching back out into the front

room and yanking open the door to his bedroom. Empty.

"Elyse!"

A terrible fear gripped him, and he raced back outside, his eyes scanning the horizon in every direction for some sign of Elyse and Colin. Nothing.

"Goddamn her!" he swore, clenching his hands at his sides. "She's taken off on me again!"

Running back into the barn, he tore down the aisle to the last stall, coming to a skidding halt in front of it. To his astonishment, Elyse's horse was still there, looking up hopefully as she waited for someone to bring her her morning rations.

Nathan stared at the animal for a long moment, utterly confused by the horse's presence in the barn. Then a chilling thought gripped him, and he sucked in his breath in alarm. Maybe she hadn't left of her own volition. Maybe, while he lay in a drunken stupor in the barn, Rosas had come and spirited her away.

"You jackass!" he berated himself in a strangled voice. "You got yourself drunk and they took her!" Picking up a flake of hay, he flung it into Elyse's horse's stall, then turned and rushed back to the front of the barn. Whipping open the stall door where his buckskin resided, he grabbed his saddle and threw it over the startled horse's back. "Sorry, Buck," he apologized as he jerked the cinch into place, "but no breakfast for you this morning. We've got work to do."

Shoving the bit into the horse's mouth, he leaped into the saddle, breaking one of his ironclad tenets and riding the horse out of the barn.

The cow again bawled plaintively as he flashed by, but Nathan didn't even hear her. Driving his heels hard into his mount's sides, he took off down the road at a dead gallop.

He never slowed down until he brought Buck to a shuddering halt in front of the telegraph office. Leaping off his back, he burst through the front door, vastly relieved when he found there were no customers lined up at the counter.

"Red! *Red!* Where the hell are you?"

"Right here!" came the startled reply. Red came racing around the corner from the office, his eyes wide with trepidation as he gaped at Nathan. "What's wrong? You look like hell!"

"I *feel* like hell," Nathan panted. "But that's not important. Elyse is gone. I think Rosas took her."

For a moment, Red just stared at him, then he looked down at the telegram he held in his hand. "That can't be, Nate. I just got a wire from Major Jones saying they received word that the Rosas gang was seen yesterday outside of Laredo. They may be on their way here, but it'll take them a couple of weeks, at least."

Nathan looked at Red dumbly for a moment, then his face suffused with angry color. "Then she *has* taken off," he growled, his tone so menacing that his friend looked at him warily.

"Now, wait a minute, Nate. Just calm down and tell me what's goin' on. Maybe we can figure out where Mrs. Graham has gone."

"I *know* where she's gone."

"Where?"

"Anywhere to get away from me!"

"Nate," Red said soothingly. "You're talkin' crazy. What's happened between you two?"

Nathan opened his mouth as if to answer, then closed it again. He studied Red closely for a moment, then suddenly made up his mind. "You know Mrs. Graham's baby?"

"Yeah?"

"Well, he's also *my* baby."

Red's mouth dropped open. "How can that be?" he asked, shaking his head. "Her kid must be seven or eight months old . . ."

"I was here once before," Nathan admitted, "and Mrs. Graham and I were . . . involved briefly."

Red stared at him in utter stupefaction. "She told you this? That you're the father of her baby?"

Nathan shook his head. "No. In fact, she lied to me and told me he wasn't mine, but I finally figured it out."

"And . . ." Red prodded.

"And yesterday I told her that I knew."

"And . . ." Red repeated.

"And she didn't like it, since I also told her that I wanted to claim him as my son."

"So she took off?"

Nathan nodded. "Looks that way."

Red let out a low whistle. "Do you have any idea where she might have gone?"

"No. But I intend to find out."

"How?"

"Lynn Potter. I'm sure she knows."

Red suddenly came flying around the end of the counter, grabbing Nathan by the arm. "You can't do that, Nate. You know how Mrs. Potter is with strangers. You can't just ride up to her house and demand that she talk to you. She won't do it."

"She damn well better," Nathan snarled.

Red slapped the telegram he was still holding down on the counter and rounded on his boss. "Nate, I'm not gonna let you intimidate that woman. Now, I know you're upset and I'll do anything I can to help you find Mrs. Graham, but you're not gonna browbeat Lynn Potter."

"Since when do you give me orders, Red?" Nathan bristled.

Red looked slightly abashed by Nathan's angry retort, but he held his ground. "I have strong feelings where it concerns Mrs. Potter."

Nathan's eyes narrowed. "Is there something going on between you two?"

Red's response was unflinching. "Yes, there is."

His blunt honesty seemed to take Nathan aback for a

moment, but finally, he nodded. "Okay, then, will you go with me out to talk to her?"

Red hesitated.

"Red, listen to me. Elyse has taken off with the baby, putting her life in jeopardy as well as my child's. We've got to find her before something terrible happens. You know what the roads are like in this state. Between the Indian renegades and the Mexican bands, it'll be a miracle if no harm befalls her. Now, please, help me! If anyone knows where she's heading, it's Mrs. Potter. Elyse must have gone to her to get a horse since she didn't take her own."

"What makes you think she just didn't decide to go over to Mrs. Potter's for an early-morning visit?"

"Without feeding the stock or milking the cow? She wouldn't do that."

Red nodded reluctantly in agreement. "Okay, Nate, I'll go with you."

Nathan let out a long, relieved breath. "Thanks. I appreciate the help."

Red walked over to his desk and picked up a pen, writing the word "Closed" on a piece of paper and sticking it to the front window. "Let's go, Captain," he said, putting on his hat.

With a grim nod, Nathan followed him out the front door.

To Nathan's surprise, when they reached Lynn Potter's farm, Red rode around to the back, tying his horse to the clothesline pole and opening the back door without knocking. "Lynn, honey," he called. "It's Red."

Nathan's eyebrows shot up. *Honey?* Things must be serious between Red and Lynn Potter if Red was comfortable enough to just walk into her house and call her by such an intimate endearment. When had all this happened and how could he have been so oblivious as to not even notice?

"Oh, Red!" Lynn cried, flying around the corner into the kitchen. "I'm so glad you're—" Her words of greeting were suddenly cut off by a sharp gasp of startled dismay. "Oh! Captain Wellesley!" she cried, lifting her hands to her cheeks. "What are you doing here?"

Before Nathan could answer, Lynn whirled around and shot an accusing glare at Red. "How could you?"

"Mrs. Potter," Nathan interjected hastily. "Please don't be angry. I made Red bring me here."

Her eyes filled with distress, Lynn grabbed a tea towel off the counter and held it up in front of her face. "Please go!"

"Lynn," Red murmured, stepping up beside her and putting his arm around her shaking shoulders. "It's okay, sweetheart. Captain Wellesley has seen you before, so there's no reason for you to hide."

"Seen me before?" she squeaked.

"Yes," Nathan admitted. "I accompanied Mrs. Graham one time when she came to visit and I saw you when you answered the door."

Lynn turned beseeching eyes back to Red.

"Mrs. Potter," Nathan added, "please don't be embarrassed about your scars. I know what happened and I have nothing but the greatest sympathy for the pain and loss you've endured."

Slowly, Lynn lowered the towel. "That's very kind of you, Captain," she murmured, her eyes cast downward. "I know I'm not . . . pleasant to look at."

"Honestly, ma'am," Nathan smiled. "I think you're lovely. And I mean that from the bottom of my heart."

"You see?" Red said, squeezing Lynn tightly against him. "What have I been tellin' you? You're gorgeous."

Lynn blushed a becoming pink which heightened her color and gave both men a breathtaking glimpse of the beauty she must have once been.

Red grinned at Nathan. "I wasn't going to tell you this yet, Captain, but I guess you might as well know. When this job is over, I'm leavin' the service. I've asked

Lynn here to be my wife, and day before yesterday, she finally agreed."

"What?" Nathan gasped, his own anxiety momentarily forgotten in the face of this astonishing news. "You're getting married? Why, you old scoundrel! Congratulations!"

Red's grin became even wider. "Yup, decided it was time to give it up and settle down before one of them damn *bandidos* gets me. Just took findin' the right woman to finally make the decision."

Nathan nodded, his smile fading. "I've been thinking much the same thing myself," he admitted. "Only my road to romance hasn't been quite as smooth as yours." He looked meaningfully over at Lynn. "Mrs. Potter, I need your help."

Lynn shifted uneasily within the circle of Red's arms. "I don't know what you're talking about, Captain Wells."

"I think you do," Nathan said quietly. "Just like I think you know my name isn't really Wells and that Elyse Graham isn't just another assignment to me."

Lynn's stoic smile crumbled. "Captain Wellesley," she whispered. "Elyse Graham is my best friend. When your best friend asks you to keep a confidence, surely you feel bound to honor that request, don't you?"

"Yes," Nathan nodded. "Unless that friend has done something so foolhardy that she could be putting her life in danger."

Lynn looked down at the floor, obviously fighting a private battle within herself.

When Nathan next spoke, his voice was very soft. "Mrs. Potter, you don't have to say anything to break Elyse's confidence. Just answer a few questions, yes or no. Okay?"

Lynn didn't look up, but Nathan saw her nod in agreement.

"Good. Now, has she been here today?"

Lynn nodded.

"When?"

Lynn looked up, but she pressed her lips together and didn't answer.

"Okay, I understand. Was it early this morning? Or late last night, maybe?"

Again, she nodded.

"Did you lend her a horse?"

Another nod.

"Oh, Lynn" Red groaned. "You didn't send her off on that mean old mare, did you?"

Despite the gentleness of Red's rebuke, tears filled Lynn's eyes. Walking over to the table, she sat down, lifting the hem of her apron and dabbing at her tears. "What could I do, Red?" she entreated, breaking her self-imposed silence. "Chili is the only horse I have and Elyse couldn't very well walk!"

"What's this about a horse?" Nathan asked.

"Mean-spirited old animal," Red answered. "Terrible temperament."

Nathan threw his head back and squeezed his eyes shut. This was all he needed. Not only was Elyse gone to God knows where, but on a unpredictable and ill-tempered horse, too.

"Did she take Colin with her?" he asked.

Lynn sniffed loudly, then nodded.

Nathan's fists clenched at his sides. "Mrs. Potter, you *have* to tell me where she went."

"I can't!" she wailed. "She doesn't want you to find her!"

"I know that," Nathan said, making a supreme effort to keep his voice calm, "but that's because she'd gotten it into her head that I'm going to try to take Colin away from her, isn't it?"

Lynn gaped at him, openmouthed. "You know that?"

"Yes, and I want you to know that I have no intention of doing any such thing. Colin is my son and I want to be part of his life, that's all. To share him with her, not take him away."

Lynn's eyes darted over to Red, amazed that Captain Wellesley was being so blunt in front of his associate.

"Red knows," Nathan said, answering her unasked question.

Lynn blinked several times, trying to find the courage to ask the one question that would allow her to divulge Elyse's whereabouts. Taking a deep breath, she blurted, "Do you love Elyse, Captain?"

"She's the mother of my child," Nathan answered quickly.

"But do you love her?"

"Yes," he nodded, looking at her squarely. "I do, Mrs. Potter. We have a lot of problems, a lot of things to work out between us before I'll know if we have a future, but I do love her."

Lynn nodded solemnly. "All right. She's on her way to Dallas."

"Dallas? Where is she going in Dallas?"

"That I don't know. She told me that she has an aunt there and she is going to stay with her."

"What's her aunt's name?"

"She didn't tell me that."

Nathan blew out a long breath. "Jesus, that's not much to go on. Are you sure you don't have any idea what this aunt's name might be?"

"No. Elyse didn't say. She just said that it was her mother's sister and that her first name is Nellie."

"Her mother's sister," Red muttered. "Do you know Elyse's mother's maiden name?"

Lynn closed her eyes, chewing on her lower lip. "Just a minute, let me think. Reames. That's it. Elyse's mother's name was Lou Reames."

"Do you know if this sister is married?" Nathan questioned.

Lynn shook her head.

"And you don't have any idea where in Dallas she lives?"

"No. I'm sorry, but Elyse said almost nothing about her."

"Well," Nathan sighed. "At least it's something. Maybe I can catch up with her before she gets to Dallas. It would be a lot easier to find her on the road than it will be once she gets into the city. What time did she leave?"

"About five o'clock this morning."

Nathan glanced over at a cuckoo clock hanging on the dining-room wall. "Hell, that's almost six hours ago."

Lynn nodded. "She thought she'd reach her aunt's by lunchtime."

Nathan gritted his teeth in frustration. "I'll never catch up with her on the road with that kind of head start. I'll just have to go into the city and try to find her there."

Picking up his gloves, he started for the door. "Red, keep your eye on things at her farm, would you? Or ask Will to do it if you're too busy. I don't know how long I'll be gone, but I'll send a wire when I get to Dallas and let you know where I am. Oh, and before you go back into town, do something for me, will you?"

"Sure, Boss, what is it?"

"Go over to Elyse's place and milk her damn cow."

Red stared at his boss as if he'd taken complete leave of his senses, but before he could respond, Nathan was gone.

Chapter 27

It was hot. Miserably hot. The kind of heat that made flowers wilt, dogs pant, and babies fuss.

"Don't cry, Colin," Elyse soothed, running her hand over the baby's sweaty hair. "I know you're hot, my sweet, but just be patient. We'll stop in those trees up there and rest a minute."

Squinting up at the blazing sun, Elyse tried to gauge the time. It must be ten, maybe even eleven o'clock, judging by the angle of the fiery ball.

"It can't be much farther," she muttered. Cupping her hand over her eyes, she peered down the road, hoping to see some sign of a farm or a small settlement that would indicate they were getting close to Dallas. Unfortunately, she saw nothing but shimmering heat waves and dust devils whirling up from the deserted road.

The trip had seemed endless, with more stops than Elyse could even count. So far, to her extreme relief, they had met with very few other travelers, but, even so, every time she heard the creak of a wagon wheel or the nicker of another horse, she guided Chili off the road and hid behind whatever cover she could find. The newspapers constantly warned of the hazards of the road and, despite the bright daylight, she was taking no chances.

The ill-tempered horse had been a trial throughout the journey, shying at the slightest stirring of leaves or an attempt to calm himself, but, still, when he turned and saw her naked in the bed, it almost brought him to his knees.

Elyse was lying on her stomach, her arms held close against her sides to conceal her breasts. She had the sheet pulled up past her waist, but, still, the entire alabaster slope of her back was exposed to Nathan's hungry gaze.

Like a man in a dream, he walked forward, staring at the perfection of her body. Unable to take his eyes off her for even a moment, he felt around like a blind man for the jar of cream. When he finally located it, he again dipped his fingers in the silky substance, then sank down on the bed and began massaging her back in wide, sweeping circles. Despite the cool cream, Nathan felt as if his fingers were on fire. His breathing became harsh and ragged, and beads of perspiration broke out on his forehead.

Elyse lay very still. She could hear Nathan's rasping breath, could feel the tension in his fingertips, but she didn't know what to do about it.

Deep inside, she could feel the coils of her own desire unfurl and the center of her womanhood become hot and tingly. Every female instinct within her cried out for her to turn over and join herself to this man, but she knew if she did, she was sealing her fate. She had made love with him once before and then he had ridden away, leaving her only with the gift of a golden child who looked just like him and the memory of a night of passion she would treasure for the rest of her life. But that was all. If she allowed herself to make love with him again, the very same thing could happen, only now, knowing him and loving him as she did, she didn't think she could bear to have him ride away again.

She knew that all she had to do was say the word and Nathan would marry her, but she wouldn't bind him to her with obligation. The only way she would share her future with Nathan Wellesley was if he loved her—and, despite many opportunities, he had never told her he did.

In a desperate attempt to cool the passion burning inside her, she clenched her teeth and willed her hips to remain still, but it was impossible. Despite her resolve, as Nathan's fingers continued to work their magic on her back, she found herself squirming against the mattress, trying desperately to find a position that would ease the exquisite agony she was suffering.

Suddenly, the erotic massage stopped and Nathan lifted his hands from her back. For a brief moment, Elyse felt bereft, but then she exhaled a long, silent sigh of relief. It was over and she had not succumbed.

Her self-congratulations were short-lived, however, for instead of feeling Nathan's weight ease from the bed as she expected, she felt his lips graze the nape of her neck, nibbling and kissing the delicate skin near her ear. She squeezed her eyes shut, frozen with indecision. She didn't want him to stop, but she was also terrified to let him continue.

His lips moved downward, trailing a passionate path down her spine, then sliding to the right across her uninjured shoulder blade. Elyse felt him nuzzle provocatively at the point where her arm hugged her side and knew that the moment of decision was at hand.

Slowly, she raised her arm.

It was the sign Nathan had been waiting for. With a groan, he lowered his head, kissing the sensitive side of her breast and burying his nose against the soft fullness as he inhaled her sweet scent. Elyse didn't move, didn't stop him, but something deep inside Nathan made him hesitate. He wanted to continue their lovemaking with every fiber of his being, but he needed her to tell him that she wanted him, too. Then he heard her breathy little sigh of surrender and he knew he had her answer. Quickly accepting her subtle invitation, he rose from the bed and shed his clothes.

Elyse heard his pants hit the floor and turned her

head to gaze at him in the candlelight. He was magnificent in his nakedness, reminding her of some ancient, golden god. The tight muscles of his chest rose and fell with his labored breathing and his impassioned manhood stood out proudly from his body, throbbing with excitement and promise.

"You're beautiful," she breathed, her eyes perusing every tawny inch of him.

"Turn over so I can see you," he murmured.

The sound of his husky, passion-laced voice was Elyse's final undoing. With a seductive smile that nearly set him on fire, she threw back the light sheet and turned onto her back.

"My God," Nathan moaned, his eyes raking the lush beauty of her naked body. "I'd forgotten."

He returned to the bed, kneeling above her and staring down in awe. "You're even more perfect than I remember."

Elyse blushed, then reached up to run her hand lightly down his chest. "The other time it was so dark, you couldn't see me."

"I know," he nodded, running a finger across a breast, then tracing a circle around her nipple. "This is much better."

Elyse's lips parted in reaction to his sensual touch and, unconsciously, she arched her back.

Nathan leaned forward, running his tongue down the cords of her neck, then continued his erotic quest until his mouth closed around her nipple. He toyed with her provocatively, his silky tongue swirling round and round her hardened nipple until she squirmed against him, pleading for relief. Finally, he moved down her body, his tongue leaving a molten track across her stomach and abdomen. Reaching the juncture of her thighs, he paused again, lifting his head to look at her. A tremor of desire shuddered through him when he saw that she was staring back at him, her eyes hot with passion as they drank in the sight of him crouched above her.

She reached for him, pulling him down on top of her and parting her lips for his kiss. Nathan covered her mouth with his own, his silky tongue plunging into the warm, welcoming cavern.

Elyse could feel his pulsing erection pressing heatedly against her thigh and, instinctively, she shifted her position, bringing his hot, stiff shaft closer to the center of her. "Let me touch you," she murmured, her lips still fused with his as she reached down with one hand and wrapped her fingers around him.

Nathan knew that he'd never experienced anything in his life as exciting as Elyse's fingers sensuously stroking his turgid length. Breaking their kiss, he reared back on his haunches, throwing his head back and emitting a low groan of ecstasy.

Elyse felt something deep inside turn to liquid as her body answered Nathan's primitive call. Reaching up with one hand, she pulled him down again, opening her mouth to his plundering tongue as she continued to intimately caress him. Subtly, she spread her thighs until he lay cradled between them, his manhood nestled at the very threshold of her body. "Make love to me," she murmured, moving her hand around his hips and pulling him more firmly against her.

"Your shoulder?" he whispered huskily.

"I'll be fine." She wiggled her hips, moving down slightly in the bed so that the tip of his manhood penetrated her.

Nathan stared down at her for a moment, astonished by her sensuality. Then, drawing his knees up, he lifted her off her injured shoulder and smoothly entered her.

He winced as he felt her gasp, thinking that his long-denied passions had made him too large for her. "Am I hurting you?" he asked softly.

"It's just been a very long time."

"I know," he smiled. "It's been just as long for me."

Elyse's body stilled and she looked at him in astonishment. "Really?"

"Really."

She smiled, thinking that was the sweetest bit of news anyone had ever told her.

Despite the fevered state of his desire, Nathan set a gentle rhythm, wanting to give Elyse time to adjust to him. But, before long, their starved senses demanded release and Nathan soon increased his pace, his thrusts becoming deep and rapid.

Elyse wondered briefly if she would find the same fulfillment that he had shown her once before, and when the pressure started to build within her, she gasped with anticipation, knowing that this time was going to be as incredible as the last.

Nathan felt her climax approaching, and with great effort, held himself in check until he felt the pulsing contractions begin. Only then did he finally give rein to his own passion, exploding within her as they found their private heaven.

When the waves of ecstasy finally subsided, he carefully lowered her back into the pillows and together they languished in love's afterglow, still intimately joined. Finally, he rolled over on his side, taking Elyse with him and nestling her close against his chest. "Please don't tell me this was a mistake," he whispered. "Please don't say you regret it."

"It wasn't a mistake," she breathed, her voice drowsy with contentment. "And I don't regret it."

Nathan sighed with relief, his happiness nearly complete. Only one more barrier stood between them, and even though he didn't expect it, his next words brought that crashing down, too. "Elyse?" he said softly.

"Yes?"

"Say you'll marry me. I love you so much, I don't think I can stand it if you send me away again."

Elyse's eyes filled with incredulous joy. For a long moment she lay very still, letting herself absorb the words he'd just uttered, then she tipped her head back and stared at him in wonder. "Did you say you love me?"

"More than anything in the world," he murmured, kissing her lightly at the corner of her mouth.

She pulled away, needing to talk and knowing that if he started kissing her again, they wouldn't. "Nathan, do you truly mean this? You're not just saying it because of what we just did?"

"What we just did is only one of about ten million reasons why I love you," he answered honestly.

"My Lord," Elyse sighed. "I can hardly believe it."

"Sweetheart, I've been in love with you since that first night. You were so frightened and so brave and I thought you were the most entrancing woman I'd ever met. All the time we were apart, I wanted to come back. I can't even tell you how badly I wanted to come back."

"But you never did, and I thought—"

Nathan brushed her lips with his, halting her words. "I know what you thought, but I'm telling you the truth. I didn't come back because I didn't think you'd want me if I did, and I didn't think I could stand it if you turned me out again."

"Oh, Nathan," Elyse sighed, raising up on her elbow and gazing at him rapturously. "I've been such a fool."

He smiled, knowing that at long last, his battle was finally won. "So you believe me?"

"Yes," she nodded, "and I'm so sorry that I—"

"Shh," he whispered, placing one finger over her mouth and following it with a gentle kiss. "It's behind us now. Just tell me you love me and promise you'll marry me."

Elyse looked up at him, her eyes alight with joy and love. "I do love you, Captain Wellesley, with all my heart. And I'd be honored to be your wife."

"Thank God," he sighed. "Now I can quit worrying."

"Worrying? What were you worried about?"

"That you'd get pregnant again before you agreed to marry me," he said, trying hard to sound serious. "I just didn't know how we'd ever explain it to Mrs. Underwood."

Elyse stared at him in disbelief, stunned that he was thinking about Lillian Underwood at a time like this. Then she saw the laughter in his eyes and she started to giggle. "I don't think we would have had to worry about explaining anything to old Lillian."

"Oh? And why is that?"

"Because if I showed up in town with another father-less baby, she'd drop dead from a heart attack!"

Nathan gave vent to his amusement, then reached for Elyse, pulling her over on top of him. They laughed to-gether for a moment, then sobered as they stared into each other's eyes. "I love you," Nathan murmured.

"And I love you," she whispered back.

Pulling her head down, they kissed again, long and passionately. The flames of desire quickly reignited and it was another two hours before they finally went to sleep.

Nathan's last thought before he drifted off was of Eric. Thinking of his older brother's advice, he grinned into the darkness. "Sorry, old boy. I tried it without pas sion, I really did, but it just didn't work."

Glancing over at Elyse cuddled up next to him, he re-alized that he'd never been happier in his life to see a plan fail.

Chapter 30

"Wake up, sleepyhead, my son is starving."

Elyse opened her eyes, surprised to see that the sun was already high in the sky. "What time is it?" she asked sleepily, pushing her hair out of her eyes.

"Past eight," Nathan said. "I think you have the potential to be a real slugabed if I let you."

Elyse yawned, sitting up and plumping the pillows behind her. "Guess that's what happens when you only get twenty minutes of sleep the whole night." Settling back comfortably in the pillows, she took her first real look at Nathan sitting on the bed next to her, wearing only a pair of light linen underwear. "My word, Nathan, you're practically naked!"

Nathan looked down at himself and shrugged. "Colin doesn't care, do you, little boy?" Holding the baby upright, he buried his face in his neck, then blew. The rush of air against Colin's skin sounded like a foghorn, making the baby squeal with delight. Raising his head, Nathan leered at Elyse, his eyes roving over her appreciatively. "If I remember correctly, madam, you spent a great deal of last night naked yourself."

Elyse blushed, pulling the silk wrapper she'd hastily donned more tightly around her. "I know. It felt so decadent, sleeping with no clothes on. I've never done that before in my life."

Nathan grinned and handed her the baby. "You *are*

decadent. I've never had a woman give me such a
workout in one night in my whole life."

"Nathan!" she gasped. "You're embarrassing me."

Nathan's grin widened, and he leaned forward, giving
her a smacking kiss. Then, with a ripple of muscles, he
bounded off the bed, yanking on his denims.

"Where are you going?"

He looked at her in surprise, his heart in his throat.
"I figured you'd want me to leave while you feed
Colin."

"Don't go," she said softly, her eyes fluttering downward. "Stay here and talk to me."

With a smile like a cat who'd just gotten into the
cream, Nathan quickly divested himself of his Levi's and
crawled back into bed.

"I didn't mean that you had to get undressed again,"
Elyse giggled.

"If you expect me to stay in those tight pants while
you sit here half dressed and looking gorgeous, you're
crazy, lady." Leaning forward, he nibbled on her
earlobe suggestively.

"Nathan, behave yourself! I have to feed this child."

"I know," he smiled, his expression softening as Elyse
loosened her robe and guided the hungry baby to her
breast, "and I've waited a long, long time to be a part
of this." His voice trailed off and a quiet moment passed
as they shared the simple joy of watching their son
nurse.

"What does Colin do after he finishes eating?" Nathan asked.

"He usually takes his morning nap."

"That's what I thought." His eyes darkened with anticipation.

"Stop looking at me like that," Elyse ordered. "I can't
spend the whole day in bed with you. I have chores to
do."

"No you don't, because the chores are all done. I got
up about five and did them. Besides, your ankle isn't

strong enough for you to be up and around, so you might as well stay in bed." Stretching his arms over his head, he yawned expansively. "Guess I will, too."

Elyse threw him a shaming look. "Aren't you ever satisfied? I mean, what was it, three times?"

"Yeah," Nathan grinned. "Three times." Reaching out, he traced a finger provocatively across her lips. "Come on, lady, tell the truth. Wouldn't you like to make it four?"

Pointedly ignoring his suggestive invitation, Elyse held the sleeping baby out to him. "Would you please put him back in his cradle?"

Nathan nodded and carried Colin over to his little bed, tucking him beneath the soft blanket. He lingered a moment, smiling down lovingly at his son, then he turned back to Elyse. "Now, back to what we were discussing. He usually sleeps about an hour, doesn't he?"

Noticing the burgeoning lust in Nathan's eyes, Elyse yanked the sheet up almost to her neck. "Yes, but, in case you didn't notice, *we* weren't discussing this, *you* were. And I still want you to behave yourself."

"Too late," Nathan chuckled, looking down meaningfully at his stirring manhood.

Elyse's eyes followed the path his had taken, feasting for a moment on his rapidly swelling erection. Then, with more reluctance than she ever would have admitted, she forced her eyes back up to his face. "Nathan, now stop this. We can't make love in the middle of the morning with the baby sleeping not five feet away."

"You're absolutely right," Nathan agreed. "We can't."

"Well, I'm glad to see we're agreed on something," she said primly, trying hard to remain stern as she climbed out of bed and walked over to the bureau. "After all, there's a time and a place for everything, and we can't spend *all* our time in bed."

She picked up her hairbrush, then glanced in the mirror, her arm stilling in midair. Whirling around, she gaped at Nathan who was walking toward the door, carrying Colin, cradle and all. "What in the world are you doing?"

"Just giving Colin what every boy wants."

Elyse threw the hairbrush down and planted her hands on her hips. "And what, pray tell, is that?"

Nathan winked lecherously. "A room of his own."

And before she could utter another word, he disappeared out the door.

Elyse opened her mouth to call him back, but suddenly a vision of how he'd looked a few minutes before floated up in her mind. She closed her eyes, seeing again his tousled hair, muscular chest, and hot, lusting eyes. With a shiver of desire, she untied the belt of her robe and let it fall to the floor. Hearing the door to the other bedroom softly close, she jumped back into bed and pulled the sheet up to her neck.

Nathan walked through the door, surprised to find her in bed again. Then he saw her bare shoulders gleaming above the closely held sheet.

Climbing onto the end of the bed, he tugged gently at the sheet, gathering the material in his fingers as he inexorably pulled it down Elyse's body.

"Tell me, Mr. Wellesley," she asked coyly. "Do you intend to make up for the entire fifteen months we were apart in one day?"

"No," Nathan murmured, bending over her and placing a scorching kiss on the breast he'd just bared, "I intend to make up for it for the next fifty years."

Lowering his body to cover hers, he began rotating his hips, insinuating his erection between her slender thighs as he continued to kiss and caress her. His lips and his hands seemed to be everywhere, touching her, fondling her, arousing her till she didn't think she could bear the pleasure.

So overwhelming had his passion been for her the previous night that Elyse thought they must have tried everything it was possible for a man and woman to do together. Little did she know as she lay here now, sighing with pleasure beneath Nathan's experienced hands and lips, that he had planned yet a new temptation for her this morning.

Slowly, sensuously, he moved down her body, his lips kissing and nibbling as he slid ever closer to the center of her. When his mouth reached the soft curls at the juncture of her thighs, he paused, waiting to see if she would stop him.

Instead, Elyse let out a little moan, her entire body beginning to tremble in reaction to his warm breath fanning the sensitive skin.

Nathan heard her whisper his name, and encouraged by her soft call, he dipped his head lower, stroking her intimately with his tongue.

Elyse let out a sharp little scream of surprise, then clapped a hand over her mouth, scandalized by her own reaction to Nathan's provocative ministrations. Tossing her head back and forth on the pillow, she moaned his name over and over, her seductive call exciting him beyond anything he'd ever known.

Nathan was sure that his attentions were swiftly bringing Elyse to completion, and as soon as he felt her body begin to pulse with the first throes of ecstasy, he sat up, pulling her up, too, until she was seated facing him, their legs wrapped around each other's hips. Leaning back slightly, he entered her with one smooth lunge.

Elyse's lips parted, and Nathan placed his hands on either side of her face, kissing her passionately. The room became still for a moment, but the silence reigned only briefly, for in two hard thrusts, Nathan's climax was upon him. He tore his lips away from Elyse's, throwing his head back and joining her cry of delight with his own shout of lusty, masculine triumph.

The crashing waves of ecstasy finally ebbed and, together, they collapsed on the bed, panting and sweating from the exertions of their fevered coupling. Untangling their legs, they indulged in one last torrid kiss, then snuggled down in the pillows together.

"You really are a wicked man," Elyse giggled, nestling her head under Nathan's chin. "I used to always get up before the birds, work all day, and be asleep by sundown. Just look what you've done to me."

Smiling with repletion, Nathan put a finger under her chin and lifted her eyes to his. "What have I done to you, pretty lady?"

"All sorts of things," she sighed happily. "You keep me awake way after sundown making love, you talk me into sleeping without a nightgown so you can make love to me again in the middle of the night, you seduce me into making love again in the morning . . ."

"Sounds to me like the only thing I've done is show you how much fun it is to make love," Nathan murmured.

"No, that's not the only thing you've shown me."

"What else, then?"

Reaching up, Elyse threaded her fingers through Nathan's soft, thick hair and smiled at him lovingly. "You've shown me what it's like to be happy again. And for that, I'll be grateful for the rest of my life."

Their lips met one last time in a gentle lovers' kiss. Then they slept.

It was late in the afternoon. Nathan had spent the afternoon working with the horses, while Elyse tidied up the house. A full week of Nathan's housekeeping had left the tiny abode in desperate need of cleaning, and, even though her injured ankle forced her to sit down every few minutes, she was pleased with the progress she'd made.

A pot of stew was simmering on the stove and the table was set for two when Nathan came into the house, his hair still damp from washing at the pump. "Looks like we're going to have company," he announced.

Elyse felt a familiar fear grip her. "Company? Do you know who it is?"

"Yeah," he smiled. "And you might want to put a couple more plates on the table. It's Red Hilliard and Mrs. Potter."

"No!" Elyse gasped. "Lynn Potter is coming over *here?*"

Nathan nodded. "She sure is, and she's not wearing that veil, either."

Elyse pulled herself out of her chair and limped over to the window. "I can't believe it," she murmured, turning to Nathan with a happy smile. "That man has worked a miracle."

Nathan placed a soft kiss on the nape of her neck. "I think *this* man has worked a miracle, too. I've never seen you smile as much as you have today."

Elyse blushed to the roots of her hair. "You're terrible!"

"You certainly didn't think so last night and again this morning. I recall you using words like wonderful, incredible, amazing . . ."

". . . and a shameless liar." Elyse finished, laughing.

The couple walked outside, hand in hand, and waved at the approaching wagon. Red and Lynn smiled as widely as their hosts as they climbed down and hurried forward to greet them.

"How are you?" Lynn asked, hugging Elyse and then stepping back to carefully look her over.

"I'm fine, really. My foot and my back are still a little sore, but other than that, I'm none the worse for wear."

"That awful mare," Lynn clucked as she gazed sympathetically down at Elyse's bandaged ankle. "I don't know why I keep her."

"You were right about only using her as a brood mare," Elyse chuckled. "She's really not much as a riding horse."

The foursome laughed at Elyse's quip, then walked into the house together. Elyse headed directly for the kitchen with Lynn just a step behind. "I can't believe you're here," Elyse whispered, pumping water into the kettle for coffee. "It's been so long since you've been in my house."

"I know," Lynn nodded. "Too long. Red has finally made me realize that."

"Well, I think it's wonderful. I could kiss him for what he's done for you."

"I heard that," Red called, "and I'm ready anytime you are, Mrs. Graham."

Elyse walked back into the room and planted a loud kiss on Red's forehead. Then she stood back and grinned at him, knowing that he never expected her to actually follow through with her glib comment.

"Hey, what's this?" Nathan laughed. "You're kissing Red instead of me now?" Turning to Red, he whispered loudly, "And just last night, she told me she'd marry me. How's that for fickle?"

Nathan's announcement was met by a shout of congratulations from Red and a squeal of delight from Lynn, who came rushing out of the kitchen and threw her arms around Elyse. "I can't believe it!" she trilled. "Both of us getting married again."

Elyse nodded and returned her friend's hug. "Nathan told me about your plans. I'm so happy for you, dear."

"This is just too wonderful," Lynn continued, walking over and perching on the arm of Red's chair. "We'll all be neighbors, and won't it be nice for the men to have someone nearby who they already know?"

Elyse looked quickly over at Nathan. They hadn't talked about where they were going to live and she wasn't sure how he felt about staying in Bixby. For the first time, she considered that he might want to move somewhere else. The disturbing thought made her smile fade. But, Nathan's next words put her fears quickly to rest.

"It'll be nice, all right. Now I'll have somebody to borrow stuff from, so I won't be having to run into town all the time."

"Oh, speaking of town," Red interjected, "that's one

of the reasons we came over today. We wondered if you two wanted to go to the Founder's Day picnic with us on Sunday."

Elyse looked over at Lynn, her eyes wide with surprise. "You're going to the Founder's Day picnic?"

"We plan to," Lynn answered, her voice a bit tentative.

"And she won't be wearing that black veil, either, I'm happy to say," Red added.

Lynn threw him a slightly accusing look. "I couldn't, even if I wanted to, since you threw it away."

Elyse's eyes widened even further. "You threw her veil away?"

"Yeah," Red beamed. "Put it in the trash barrel and burned it."

"Good for you," Nathan approved. "Now we'll all get to see Mrs. Potter's beautiful eyes when she talks to us."

"And my beautiful mouth, too," Lynn muttered.

"*I* think your mouth is beautiful," Red said, pinning Lynn with a look that dared her to disagree. "In fact, why don't you give me a kiss with that beautiful mouth of yours right now."

Lynn blushed becomingly and leaned over to swat Red on the arm. "The things you say," she admonished. "And in public, too!"

"We're not 'public,' " Nathan corrected. "And as far as I'm concerned, you two can kiss all you want to while you're here. In fact, I haven't had a kiss from you, Elyse, in at least ten minutes. Don't you think you're overdue?"

"What I think is that you two men are pretty sassy this afternoon," Elyse laughed. "Come on, Lynn, let's stir up some biscuits to go with the stew. Maybe if these two have something to eat, it'll take their minds off kissing for a while."

"Don't count on it," Nathan laughed. Getting up, he grabbed Elyse around the waist, bending her back over his arm and kissing her soundly. When he finally lifted his lips, he pressed them against her ear and murmured, "I'm mighty hungry, sweetheart, and stew and biscuits ain't gonna do a thing to appease me."

Elyse answered his lecherous words with a shaming look. Sternly, she untwined his arms from around her waist and took a step back. Nathan looked at her woefully and she tempered her prim actions by whispering, "I'll see what I can do to solve that problem later, Captain."

"I was hoping you'd say that," he whispered back.

Red, whose relationship with Lynn was not yet as intimate as Nathan and Elyse's, watched the passionate look that passed between the couple. Shifting in his chair, he cast a covert glance over at Lynn, wondering if she had also noticed that their hosts looked as if they might start making love right there on the floor in front of them. Lynn was red as a beet.

Hoping to save his fiancée from an attack of apoplexy, Red cleared his throat loudly. "Hey, Nate, how about if we go outside and you show me those mustangs you caught. I noticed when we rode in that one of them has a halter on. Have you started breaking them?"

Nathan reluctantly drew his eyes away from Elyse, looking over at Red absently. "What? Oh, yeah, I have. The one with the halter is almost ready to sell."

"That's great," Red enthused, slapping his palms on his knees and jumping out of his chair. "Let's go take a look."

"Okay," Nathan said, casting one last longing glance at Elyse. "Let me get my hat and I'll be right with you."

Lynn's eyebrows nearly disappeared into her hair as she watched Nathan walk into Elyse's bedroom. Careful to keep her eyes averted from Red, she got up from the settee and walked into the kitchen.

Nathan reappeared from the bedroom, his hat in his hand. "We'll only be outside for a few minutes, Elyse."

"Take your time," she smiled. "Lynn and I have a lot of catching up to do."

Nathan joined Red at the corral, looking at his friend curiously when he saw his huge grin. "What is it? What are you grinning about?"

Red reached over and clapped Nathan on the back. "My God, Nate, have you got it bad for that woman, or what? For a minute there, I thought you two were gonna fall on the floor and do it right in front of us."

Nathan had the good grace to look embarrassed. "It's that obvious, huh?"

"Obvious!" Red guffawed. "Why, I was expectin' you to start snortin' and pawin' the ground next."

"Oh, cut it out!" Nathan laughed. "I wasn't that bad."

Red chuckled and shook his head. "I've just got one piece of advice for you, friend."

"Yeah? What's that?"

"You better marry that little gal quick 'cause if what I saw in there is any indication of how you two are spendin' your time, she's gonna be havin' another one of your babies before Easter. It might be nice if this one's name is Wellesley."

Nathan nodded. "That's something you don't have to worry about. The next one, whenever it comes, will damn well be named Wellesley. In fact, the one we've got now is going to be carrying his rightful name, too—and long before Easter."

"Really? How are you gonna do that?"

"I'm going to adopt him. That reminds me, I need to send a wire to Austin. I know a lawyer there—a Mr. Hanford. He's an old friend of my father's and I'm sure he'd be willing to handle the legalities."

"No problem," Red assured him. "Just write out the message before we leave and I'll send it as soon as I get back to town. Oh, and speaking of town, you never did say if you and Elyse wanted to go to the picnic."

Nathan shrugged. "I'd like to, but I don't know how she'll feel about it."

"Well, if she doesn't want to spend the whole day, the

two of you could at least come to the dance Sunday night."

"Yeah, that's an idea. I'll talk to her about it and let you know."

The two men spent the next few minutes looking over the horses Nathan had caught. It was when they were starting back for the house that Red suddenly remembered the main reason why he'd needed to see Nathan. "Oh, by the way," he said, slowing his pace, "I got another wire from Major Jones today."

Nathan stopped dead in his tracks. "Oh?"

"Yeah. The gang's been sighted again."

"Where were they this time?"

"Just south of San Antonio. Appears they're heading this way, but they sure are taking their sweet time about it."

Nathan grimaced with frustration. "I wish to hell they'd make their damn move so we could get this over with."

"Yeah, you and me both," Red agreed. "I've already wired the major to let him know that as soon as this assignment is over, I'm resigning. Now that I've made the decision, I just want to get it behind me."

Nathan nodded and stared at the ground pensively.

"What about you, Nate? When are you gonna tell Jones?"

"I don't know," Nathan said, tracing a half-moon pattern in the dust with the toe of his boot. "I haven't decided whether I'm gonna tell him before or after we're finished with this case. I'd kind of like to talk to him in person, and since I'll have to report back to headquarters once this is over, I'm thinking that I might just wait till then."

Red looked at him closely for a moment. "Are you sure gettin' married is what you want, Nate? Bein' a Ranger has always been so important to you."

"I know," Nathan sighed. "But I can't be a Ranger and have Elyse, too. I have to choose one or the other and, in my mind, there's no choice to be made. She's it."

"You love her that much?"

Nathan looked at his friend, his grim expression giving way to a contented smile. "Oh, yeah. That much and more."

"It's funny, ain't it, how we both came here figurin' it was just another job, and look what's happened to us. Guess there's just somethin' about these Bixby women."

"Yeah," Nathan sighed. "They are one enticing bunch. What do you suppose it is about them that makes them so irresistible?"

"I don't know. Maybe it's something in the water."

Red's ridiculous comment made both of them laugh uproariously. "Whatever it is," Red added when he finally caught his breath, "I wish old Will would catch a case of it."

"Ah, yes, Will," Nathan mused, realizing he hadn't thought about the other Ranger for several days. "How's everything down at the livery stable?"

"Fine, I guess," Red shrugged. "I know he's bored as hell, so everything must be fine."

"Have you told him about all our personal stuff?"

"Naw, I figured it would just put a burr under his saddle if I told him we were both quittin'. Thought I'd let you do that."

"Oh, thanks a lot!" Nathan laughed. "Now, I'll have to sit and listen to him whine about how there's no justice in the world for a homely man."

"You're right," Red guffawed. "But better you than me. Now, come on, let's go in and get somethin' to eat—that is, if you can keep your hands off that little blonde long enough to eat."

"It'll be tough," Nathan sighed dramatically, "but with the night we have planned, I better eat or I might not make it through. It takes a whole lot of energy to keep up with that little girl."

The two men were laughing when they came back

into the house, and their laughter continued all the way through supper as Nathan put away the biggest meal Red had ever seen him consume.

be had—" he cigarette —

Chapter 31

It was very late when Nathan and Elyse finally got to
bed that night. Red and Lynn lingered at the table long
after the stew was gone, drinking coffee and chatting.
When they finally got up and Nathan was sure they'd
leave, Red suggested a game of cards. Knowing his
friend as well as he did, Nathan was convinced Red had
purposely drawn the evening out just to annoy him.

It was after ten when they finally drove away. Elyse
immediately excused herself and hurried into Colin's
new bedroom to check on him, leaving Nathan to lock
up. He made a quick tour of the barn and corral to
make sure the animals were settled for the night, then
sat on the porch for a few minutes, smoking a cigarette
and thinking about how satisfying simple tasks could be.

He was surprised at how much he'd changed in the
last few months. Now, instead of dreading the thought
of spending day after day involved with tedious, repeti-
tious chores, his mind wandered to the improvements
he wanted to make to the ranch, to the possibility of
breeding a new strain of cattle more adapted to the rig-
ors of the Texas range, and to Elyse.

Elyse. Just the thought of her made him smile. Never,
until he met her, had he even considered marrying and
settling down, but now he couldn't imagine life without
her. He should have listened to his heart all those
months ago. Should have come back here at his first op-

portunity instead of spending all those lonely months brooding about her. If only he'd returned when he'd first thought about it, it would have saved both of them so much pain, so much heartache.

"Don't think about that," he muttered out loud, grinding the butt of his cigarette out with the heel of his boot. "You're together now, and you have the rest of your lives to be happy."

Clinging to that very pleasant thought, he walked back into the house, locking the door behind him and heading for the bedroom.

Elyse was already undressed when he came through the door, and the sight of her standing in front of the bureau clad in nothing but her camisole was so arresting that Nathan felt his entire body begin to tremble.

"I think you're the most beautiful woman God ever created," he whispered, coming up behind her and burying his face in her long, shining hair. He nuzzled her neck, kissing her hungrily as he wrapped his arms around her and seductively fondled her breasts.

"You know," Elyse murmured, goose bumps rising all over her body, "it's funny you should say that."

"Oh? Why's that?"

"Because I was just thinking the very same thing about you."

"What, that *I'm* the most beautiful woman God ever created?"

"No, silly," she giggled, turning in his arms and brushing his lips with hers. "That you're the most beautiful *man.*"

Nathan ran his tongue along the seam of her lips. "You wouldn't say that if you'd ever met my brother, Seth."

"You mean he's even more beautiful than you are?"

"So they say." His lips trailed across her cheek until they settled on the sensitive skin just beneath her ear. "He looks like me, only better."

Privately, Elyse didn't think that was possible, but out

loud she teased, "Maybe I better think about this, then. Is Seth married?"

"Yup. You're a couple of years too late."

"Oh, drats, just my luck. Well, since he's not available, I guess I'll just have to settle for you, plain as you are."

Nathan tipped his head back to look at her, and Elyse was surprised to see that his eyes were suddenly dark and serious. "Are you sure about that, sweetheart? Are you absolutely sure I'm what you want?"

"Oh, Nathan," she sighed, her heart in her eyes, "I'm only teasing you. I've never wanted anything in my whole life as much as I want you."

"God, am I glad to hear you say that," he sighed. His tense expression relaxed, and with deft fingers, he unfastened the two tiny buttons on her camisole, spreading it wide and exposing her breasts to his fiery gaze.

Elyse put her hands over his, moving them so they covered her nipples, then she arched her back and pressed the excited little nubs into his palms. "Got any plans tonight, cowboy?" she whispered, rubbing her breasts sensuously against his tingling palms.

Nathan's jaw dropped. "Where did you learn to do this, you little vixen?"

"I read a scandalous dime novel once," she answered throatily.

Dropping her hands from his, she began unbuttoning his denims, rubbing the backs of her knuckles seductively against him as she worked each button out of its hole.

Nathan threw his head back, continuing to massage her breasts as he reveled in the erotic little game she was playing with him. "Did you learn this in your dime novel, too?" he asked hoarsely.

"No," she purred, hooking her thumbs inside his waistband and shimmying his pants down his lean legs. "I thought this up all by myself."

Dropping to her knees, she pulled off each of his

boots in turn, then lifted a foot so he could step out of
his clothes. "You have beautiful feet," she murmured,
running her fingers slowly along his instep. She trailed
her hand over his calf, past his knee and up his thigh,
her eyes following the route her fingertips was taking
until she reached his throbbing erection. For a long moment, she stared at it in rapt feminine appreciation, then
she reached out and stroked him. "In fact, Captain
Wellesley, you have beautiful everything."

Nathan closed his eyes, emitting a low groan.

Cupping him in her hand, Elyse leaned forward and
kissed him along his long, hard length, her lips caressing
him provocatively as she worked her way down to the
hot, moist tip.

Gently, she closed her mouth over him, swirling her
tongue around and around until Nathan thought he
would explode from the sheer eroticism of her touch.
Barely a moment passed before he felt himself reaching
the brink of his control, and in a hoarse, impassioned
voice, he called her name, begging her to come to him.

Elyse broke their intimate contact, but she continued
to kiss and caress him until Nathan reached down and
drew her into his arms. "I can't take any more," he
panted, falling backward onto the mattress and pulling
her down on top of him.

"You can't?" she asked innocently. "No more?"

"You never cease to amaze me," he rasped, drawing
her legs apart until she was straddling him.

Elyse wiggled her hips suggestively. "Why's that?"

"Because proper little Texas widows just don't *do* that
sort of thing."

"Proper little Texas widows don't make love with
strange men on stormy nights, either—but I did," she
reminded him. "Guess I'm just not quite as proper as
Texas widows are supposed to be."

"Thank God for that," Nathan sighed.

They kissed, long and slow and sensuously, until Elyse

finally lifted her head and whispered, "I bet there's something else proper little Texas widows don't do."

"What?"

"This." And raising herself above him, she sat down, impaling herself on his stiff shaft.

Nathan let out a cry of pleasure that Elyse was sure could be heard all the way over at Lynn's. She watched his eyes grow dark with need, then arched her back, propelling herself up and down as she reveled in her newly discovered sexual power.

Never had Nathan known a woman to make love with such passion. Grasping her hips, he guided her frenzied movements, teaching her the nuances of this new and exciting position until they exploded together, their shouts of satisfaction reverberating off the bedroom walls.

Elyse collapsed on his chest, their labored breathing the only sound in the tiny room. Several minutes passed before enough strength returned to Nathan's limbs that he could lift Elyse off his body and ease her down on the mattress beside him.

They rested in satiated silence for such a long time that Elyse was nearly asleep when she again heard Nathan's soft voice. "Elyse, my sweet, will you tell me something?"

"Of course," she mumbled, trying hard to open her eyes.

"Was it like this with Joe?"

Her eyes flew open. Never had Nathan so much as mentioned her relationship with Joe, much less ask such a personal question. As shocked as she was, though, she never considered telling him anything but the truth. "No," she answered, looking directly into his blue eyes. "Joe and I loved each other and we had a . . . nice relationship, but it was never like this. This is incredible. What we have is more than just loving, Nathan. This is *being* in love, and I've never known that with anyone but you."

Elyse's simple, honest words were the sweetest Nathan had ever heard. He wanted to say something. Wanted to tell her what her declaration meant to him, but he was beyond words. Instead, he pulled her into his arms and held her close to his heart, falling into a sublimely peaceful sleep.

"What do you think about going to the Founder's Day picnic?" he asked the next morning.

"Oh, I don't think so," Elyse demurred. "What fun would it be? You know how those women in town feel about me."

Nathan looked up from his eggs and frowned. "That'll change. Just wait till those old biddies find out you're marrying one of the Wellesleys. Believe me, you'll soon be the most popular matron in town."

It was Elyse's turn to frown. "That may be, but 'those old biddies,' as you call them, don't know who you are yet, and they won't by next Sunday, either. Besides, I don't want 'friends' like that—women who shun me when I have a fatherless child but then are happy to forgive my sins and accept me when I marry into an influential family."

"I understand what you're saying, sweetheart, but if we're going to stay in Bixby, we have to make an attempt to become part of the community, regardless of the past. We can't live out here on this ranch by ourselves for the rest of our lives with only Red and Lynn for company."

Elyse gazed at him thoughtfully for a moment. "Maybe things would be easier if we moved away after we're married. We could go somewhere where no one knows me. That way we could make a new start and you wouldn't have to bear the stigma of people knowing you married a fallen woman."

Nathan threw down his napkin and rose from his

chair, walking around the table and tipping Elyse's chin up until their eyes met.

"Have you forgotten who's responsible for you taking that fall?" he asked quietly. "Besides, you make it sound like we're criminals. Why should we have to 'make a new start'? We haven't broken any laws. Granted, we made a mistake and had a baby before we were married, but it's not like we're the first couple that's ever happened to. What's important is that we're correcting that mistake. We're getting married and I'm adopting Colin. To my way of thinking, we have nothing to be embarrassed about—except, maybe, that we gave in to our passions a little earlier than most people would consider appropriate."

Elyse shot him a wry little smile. "I'm afraid we gave in a *lot* earlier than most people would consider appropriate."

"That's beside the point. The real question here is, do you *want* to move away?"

"Not really," she admitted. "This is my home. But I also understand that you're probably used to living on a much grander scale than in a rundown little house on a ranch in the middle of nowhere."

"Sweetheart, I haven't lived in *any* kind of house, grand or otherwise, since I left home ten years ago. I've only lived in rented rooms or on the back of a horse, so if you're worried about that, don't be. However . . ." He paused, leering at her shamelessly. "I do have plans to outgrow this house very quickly, so it might be a good idea to think about building a bigger one."

Elyse gasped, her eyes lighting with excitement. "A brand-new house?"

"Sure." Nathan smiled. "A brand-new house with a stove that doesn't smoke, a roof that doesn't leak, and lots and lots of bedrooms. We could even hire a decorator from Chicago to help you with rugs and curtains and furniture."

"A decorator!" Elyse exclaimed. "Why, I wouldn't

know what to do with a decorator. Besides," she added shyly, "I think I'd rather choose my own things."

"Okay, then we'll go to Chicago ourselves and get whatever you want. Or, if you prefer, we could go to San Francisco, or New York, or even Paris, for that matter."

"Oh, Nathan, what a thought! Imagine me having furniture that came all the way from Paris."

With a wide grin, Nathan pulled her out of her chair and hugged her close. "If furniture from Paris is what you want, then furniture from Paris is what you'll have. I told you before, nothing is too good for you."

Elyse looked up at him with shining eyes. "I don't need furniture from Paris, Nathan—or draperies from London or rugs from Timbuktu. All I need is you."

Nathan felt as if his heart might burst with the love he felt at that moment. "I feel the same way," he chuckled, "but when the spring rains start next year, a house with a solid roof might come in very handy."

"I guess it might, at that," she replied.

"So, it's settled, then. We're going to stay in Bixby, we're going to build a new house—and we're going to go to the picnic Sunday and have a good time. Agreed?"

Elyse's sunny smile faded. "I'm still not sure about the picnic. I just know that if I show up there with you and Colin, there's going to be talk."

Nathan shrugged. "Let them talk. You're not alone in this anymore, Elyse. We're both responsible for Colin's rather untimely appearance, and, from now on, if anybody says anything about him—or you—I'll handle it."

Elyse sighed happily. It had been so long since she'd had someone to rely on, so long since she hadn't been alone with her problems. It was wonderful to know that she now had Nathan beside her. "Thank you," she murmured. "Thank you for being the man you are."

Nathan smiled and kissed her gently. "Come on now, say you'll go Sunday."

"All right," she nodded. "I'll go. But promise me one thing."

"Anything."

"Don't leave me alone with Lillian Underwood!"

Chapter 32

They couldn't have asked for more perfect weather for a picnic. Sunday dawned bright, sunny, and warm, with a gentle breeze that caressed their faces and blew wispy tendrils of hair into Elyse's eyes as they rode into town.

She was quiet during the brief journey, sitting rigidly on the hard wagon seat and holding Colin tightly against her.

Finally, just as they reached the outskirts of Bixby, Nathan pulled the wagon off the road. "Elyse, we don't have to go today if you really don't want to."

She looked over at him, her eyes wide and overly bright. "Of course we'll go. You want to, so we will. Besides, we promised Red and Lynn we'd be there."

"But, sweetheart—"

"No, Nathan, I'm fine. I know I have to do this sometime, and there's no time like the present. I guess if Lynn can find the courage to face the townspeople, I can, too."

Nathan nodded approvingly. "That's my girl." Clucking to the horses, he guided them back onto the road and they continued on their way.

They heard the sounds of revelry even before they reached the field where the picnic was taking place. Long tables had been set up for the food each family had donated and a flat section of land had been cordoned off for children's games. Everyone in town seemed to be in attendance, and as Nathan helped Elyse down from the wagon, she looked around nervously at the many clusters of chattering women.

"I don't think I can do this," she whispered. "I haven't been to an event like this since before Joe died."

"You'll be fine," Nathan assured her. "Just remember that you have nothing to answer to anyone for. Hold your head up and relax. We're going to have fun today."

Elyse glanced at him doubtfully, but she picked up Colin and, together, they joined the revelers.

Just as she'd expected, she heard several gasps, followed by loud whispering as they threaded their way through the crowd, but she was careful to keep her eyes averted. They reached the table where the food was laid out and Nathan set down the casserole they'd brought. "Quit acting so damn guilty," he hissed. "It's no wonder the old crows talk about you. You bring it on yourself."

His blunt words had exactly the effect he'd hoped for. Elyse raised her eyes, glaring at him, then glanced around at the other picnickers, smiling a bit defiantly.

"Lord but this food sure looks good," Nathan said loudly, adopting the thick cowboy drawl he always assumed when dealing with the townsfolk. Out of the corner of his eye, he saw Marvel Dixon, the prudish old maid he'd met his first day in town, set a large layer cake down on the far end of the table.

"Woowee! Just look at that cake! Did you bake that, Miss Dixon?"

Marvel stopped fussing with the doily under the cake and looked over at the handsome man in pleased surprise. "Yes I did, Mr. Wells. I always make chocolate cakes. They're my specialty."

"Well, ma'am," Nathan beamed, his drawl so thick you could cut it, "it certainly does look delicious. In fact, I can't wait to eat, just so I can have a piece of that cake afterward. Mrs. Graham, come over here and take a look at Miss Dixon's beautiful chocolate cake."

Marvel Dixon was the very last person Elyse wished to converse with, but since Nathan was making such a fool of himself over her cake, she had no choice but to join him. She threw him a killing glance, then turned to face Marvel, smiling sweetly. "Miss Dixon is famous in Bixby for her chocolate cakes, Mr. Wells," she informed him. "In fact, when I was a little girl, I took piano lessons from her, and if I did a very, very good job on my scales, she would sometimes give me a piece afterward. Isn't that so, Miss Dixon?"

"That's true," Marvel admitted, her mouth pinched so tight that she looked like she'd been sucking lemons. "But, if memory serves me, you didn't get very many pieces."

"She's right," Elyse sighed dramatically. "I was hopelessly untalented when it came to the piano."

"Nonsense," Miss Dixon snorted. "If you had been untalented, I wouldn't have wasted my time with you. Your only problem, missy, was that you didn't practice. You were always too busy playing to pay attention to your lessons." Pointedly, her gaze settled on Colin. "There's nothing that will get a girl into trouble faster than too much time spent on leisure and not enough on work."

Elyse's eyes flared wide at the old crone's blunt remark, but Nathan quickly intervened. "Well, I'm certainly glad I don't have to play the piano to get a piece of your cake today, Miss Dixon," he chuckled. "I'm sure I wouldn't meet your standards and I would hate to miss out on such a treat."

With his blond good looks and drawling charm, Nathan had never had any problem charming women—and Marvel Dixon was no exception. "I will personally save you a piece, Mr. Wells," she gushed, "if you promise to tell me how you like it after you've finished."

"I'd be proud to, ma'am," he answered, promptly

melting the old spinster's heart with his seductive smile. "Now, if you'll excuse us, there's someone over here I have to speak to." Taking Elyse's arm, he adroitly steered them away from the table.

"You're shameless, Nathan Wellesley," Elyse chastised as they sauntered over toward a group of young matrons seated beneath an oak tree. "Playing up to that dried-up old prune like that."

"Whatever it takes, my sweet," he answered pleasantly, nodding and smiling to everyone they passed.

As they approached the group under the tree, a pretty young woman holding a child about the same age as Colin jumped up and hurried over to them. "Elyse, how wonderful to see you!" she greeted. "And look at Colin. My word, he's getting big."

Elyse smiled, relaxing for the first time since they'd arrived. "Mr. Wells, this is my old school friend, Stella Pence—and this is her daughter, Lara."

"Mrs. Pence," Nathan nodded, whipping off his hat. "It's a pleasure. I've met your husband many times."

Stella looked a bit discomfited. Bill Pence owned Hanover Hall, Bixby's premier saloon, and Stella doubted that Elyse had any idea how much time her hired hand had spent there, charming the saloon girls right out of their garters the first few weeks he'd been in town. Bill had told her that Nat Wells hadn't been in for a long time, but the saloon girls still rhapsodized about him. Now that Stella had a chance to see him firsthand, she wasn't surprised.

"So, Elyse," she smiled, extending a hand, "come over and talk to me. I haven't seen you in ages."

The women drifted off to sit in the shade with the babies and Nathan turned away, scanning the crowd to see if he could spot either Red or Will. He thought he saw Will standing near the area where the foot races were to be held and started off in that direction. He'd taken no more than a few steps, though, before Daisy Flynn si-

dled up next to him and placed a proprietary hand on
his arm.

"Why, Nat Wells, you handsome thing! Where have
you been? I was beginnin' to think you'd moved on, it's
been so long since I've seen you."

Nathan watched Will join a group of men pitching
horseshoes and, with a frustrated sigh, turned his attention to the woman latched on his arm. "Howdy, Daisy,"
he smiled. "You look right pretty today."

"Why, thank you!" she gushed. "Do you like my new
dress?" Removing her clinging hand, she spread her
skirts and pivoted in a circle. "I made it myself."

"Did you now?" Nathan responded absently, trying to
keep his eye on Will without Daisy noticing.

"Oh, yes," she trilled. "And everyone says that I
make the prettiest dresses in Bixby."

Nathan's gaze swept over the garish, orange-and-
black plaid frock. "Well, it's very nice—and colorful,
too. Now, if you'll excuse . . ."

Daisy's eyes widened with dismay as she realized he
was about to abandon her. Grabbing his arm again, she
pulled him up against her side. "Y'know, Nat, I still
haven't forgiven you for runnin' out on me that day at
the cafe."

"Sorry," Nathan muttered. "I'd remembered something important I had to do."

"It must have been *real* important the way you shot
out of there."

Nathan glanced down at her, surprised and a bit annoyed by the sarcastic tone in her voice.

"But now that we're together again, I'm willin' to put
that in the past," she quickly added.

"Well, thank you for that," he murmured, his eyes
sliding over to where Elyse was sitting. The group of
women under the tree had grown, and although Elyse
seemed to be involved in animated conversation, Nathan couldn't help but notice that the other matrons
were keeping a watchful eye on him and Daisy. Frown-

ing, he again uncurled Daisy's fingers from around his arm. "I'm sorry, Miss Daisy, but I really have to go. There's a man over by the horseshoe pit who I need to talk to."

Daisy's mouth pursed into a hurt little pout. "Well, okay," she sighed, running her hand longingly up his sleeve. "If you have to."

"I do," Nathan nodded, taking a quick step backward.

"You're gonna be at the dance tonight, though, aren't you?"

Nathan shook his head. "I don't think so. I have chores I've gotta do out at Mrs. Graham's place. You know, animals to take care of, that kind of thing . . ."

"Oh," Daisy huffed, stamping her foot in frustration, "I think it's just terrible the way that woman never gives you any time off!"

Nathan took another couple of steps backward. "Yeah, well, that's what you get when you're a hired hand, I guess. Work, work, work."

Daisy nodded dismally. "Next week when you're in town, why don't you come in and have some pie? It's rhubarb season, you know, and I make the best rhubarb pie in town. Everyone says so."

"I'll do that," Nathan promised, walking backward as fast as he dared. "I know how famous your pies are . . . and your coffee . . . and your meatloaf. I'll make a point to come in when I'm real hungry so I can try them all. Bye now!"

Without giving the smitten waitress time to say anything more, Nathan turned on his heel and fled across the field, looking around for Will. As if on cue, the little man suddenly came up behind him. "Hi, Nate . . . ah, *Nat,*" he quickly corrected.

Nathan breathed a huge sigh of relief, so glad to see his friend that he didn't even take him to task over his slip. Will never had been any good at subterfuge. "Hi, Will."

"Saw ya over there with Miss Daisy," Will teased. "I told ya she was sweet on ya."

Nathan shook his head and rolled his eyes. "I never thought I was gonna get away from her. She's one determined little lady."

Will sighed dramatically. "Women are always determined when it comes to you, Nat."

"Yeah, well, some of them are a lot more determined than I'd like them to be."

Will laughed, a loud braying sound that made Nathan wince. "Oh, to have your problems!"

Nathan cupped his hand over his eyes and scanned the milling crowd. "Have you seen Red and Mrs. Potter?"

"No," Will replied. "They're not here yet, I don't think. Y'know, I'd lay a wager there's somethin' serious goin' on between them two."

Nathan looked at the homely little man affectionately, knowing the time had come to break the news to him. "Come on over here and let's sit down, Will. I want to talk to you."

The two men grabbed tumblers of lemonade off the end of a nearby table and sat down on a bale of hay. "What's up, Nate?" Will said, again forgetting to use Nathan's alias.

"Well, quite a bit, actually," Nathan smiled.

"You've heard that the gang is closin' in, haven't ya?"

Nathan nodded. "Yeah. My guess is they'll be here in about a week. In fact, I want to meet with you and Red tomorrow to discuss strategy, now that we know for sure they're headed this way."

"Have you told Mrs. Graham they're comin'?" Will asked, taking a long swallow of the tart drink.

"No, and I'm not going to for another few days. There's no sense worrying her until it's absolutely necessary."

"S'pose you're right," Will agreed. "But I, for one, am mighty thankful that somethin's finally happenin'.

The sooner that damn gang makes their move, the sooner we can all hightail it back to Austin."

Nathan shifted on the hay. "That's what I want to talk to you about, Will. Red and I aren't going back to Austin, at least not permanently."

Will lowered his glass of lemonade, staring at Nathan in bewilderment. "What the hell you talkin' about?"

"Red and Mrs. Potter have decided to get married."

"I knew it! I just knew it. I always can tell when a man's gettin' serious about a woman. They get a look in their eye ever' time her name is mentioned and, boy oh boy, does Red ever have that look."

"Does he?" Nathan smiled.

"Yes, sirree, he sure does."

"Tell me, Will, do I have that look, too?"

Will's grin faded. "You, Nate? Why would *you* have that look?"

Nathan remained silent.

"Oh, no," Will moaned, the light suddenly dawning. "You're joshin' me, right?" He paused, looking at Nathan hopefully.

"No, Will, I'm not joshing you. As soon as this assignment is over, Mrs. Graham and I are getting married, too."

The look on Will's homely face was so crestfallen that Nathan felt like he'd just told him he was dying of a dread disease rather than sharing happy news.

"This is my fault," Will muttered. "All my fault."

"What are you talking about?"

"You and the widow. It's my fault you've decided to get married."

"How so?"

"That day," Will explained. "That day you came to see me at the livery when I said you acted like you was sweet on her. That put it in your mind, didn't it?"

Nathan looked at Will in surprise, remembering that the man's teasing comments that morning *had* been instrumental in making him start to analyze his feelings for Elyse. But, knowing how Will felt about his getting married, it was the last thing in the world he was going to admit. "No, Will, that didn't have anything to do with it. My relationship with Mrs. Graham goes back much farther than you know."

"What do you mean, 'farther'?"

Nathan looked around to make sure their conversation couldn't be overheard by any of the strolling picnickers, then leaned close and whispered, "Remember when you said that everyone in town wondered who her baby's daddy was?"

Will nodded.

"Well, it's me."

"No!" Will cried, leaning back and staring at Nathan in stunned disbelief. "But that's impossible! That baby's way too old to be yours."

Nathan frowned as Will's outburst made several people turn and look at them curiously. "It's not impossible, Will. I've known Mrs. Graham much longer than just the few months we've been here."

Will's ugly little face scrunched up in consternation. "Somehow, this whole thing ain't settin' right with me, Nate. I've known you for a lot of years and it just wouldn't be like you to get some little gal in the family way and then abandon her."

"I didn't abandon her," Nathan said a bit defensively. "I didn't know about the baby. In fact, she swore to me that the baby belonged to her dead husband, but that morning, after you told me he'd been dead for several years, I got suspicious and started investigating. That's when I found out the truth."

"Whew," Will whistled, shaking his head. "That's some story. I guess you decided you had to do the right thing by her and that's why you're marryin' her now."

"No, it's more than that," Nathan corrected. "I love her, Will. I want to marry her, baby or no baby."

Will sighed disconsolately. "This is a sad day, Nate.

Imagine, the great Nathan Wellesley quittin' the Rangers. Who'd have ever thought it?"

"Bound to happen sooner or later," Nathan shrugged. "Besides, I've been thinking about it for a long time, you know that."

"Yeah, but we *all* think about it, Nate. I never took you serious and I bet Major Jones didn't, either. By the way, have ya told him yet?"

Nathan shook his head. "No. I plan to when I go in to make my report on this job."

Will nodded slowly. "I don't know what to say. If this is what ya want, I guess I'm happy for ya, but, hell, it sure ain't gonna be the same without ya." He sighed wistfully. "Guess this'll teach Jones a lesson."

"A lesson?"

Will chuckled. "Yeah. It'll probably be a good long time 'fore he assigns another handsome devil like you to protect a pretty young widow."

Nathan started to laugh and good-naturedly clapped Will on the back. "I'm gonna miss you, you ugly little weasel."

"Yeah," Will nodded, trying hard to keep his quickly rising emotions in check. "I'm gonna miss you, too, Nate. After all, you was the best lure in the whole damn force to get saloon girls to hang around a table. Now who are we gonna use as bait for us ugly guys?"

Much to her surprise, Elyse was enjoying herself immensely. She had been at the picnic for more than an hour and so far no one had said a single unkind word to her, except for Miss Dixon, of course.

As she and Stella Pence sat beneath the oak tree, several other young mothers joined them to swap recipes and compare child-rearing techniques. The easy conversation and amusing anecdotes reminded Elyse of the long-ago days when they'd all been schoolgirls together and had spent many a lazy afternoon gossiping about boys and dreaming of romantic futures.

So involved was she in jotting down Mary Beth Miller's pie crust recipe that she didn't notice how Stella's eyes kept drifting between Colin and Nathan as she silently compared the man's handsome features with the child's.

Nathan, however, was very aware of Stella's perusal. As he talked to Will, he sensed someone looking at him and several times he glanced over toward the oak tree and caught Stella studying him closely. At first, he thought it was just the usual feminine interest women always showed in him. Hundreds of times, he'd witnessed strange women staring at him across hotel lobbies, train depots, and restaurants. He had, over the years, become very astute in interpreting the looks women threw him and, more than once, he had accepted their silent invitations, a practice that had resulted in many brief but pleasant encounters.

But something about the speculative look in Elyse's friend's eyes made him realize that it wasn't the possibility of a passionate night spent in his arms that she was thinking about. Rather, he noticed that every time she pulled her eyes away from him, they immediately settled on Colin. The realization that she was comparing his son's features to his own was disconcerting, since he didn't know enough about Stella to know whether she was friend or foe.

As the minutes passed and Stella's unwavering gaze continued to bore into him, he ended his conversation with Will and wandered over to where she sat with the rest of the women.

"Good morning, ladies," he drawled. Covertly, he watched Stella's eyes again dart between him and Colin. "Would anyone like some lemonade? I'll be happy to get y'all a glass." Purposely, he let his smile roam over each upturned face.

His offer was followed by much tittering among the

women as one by one they succumbed to his charm. They *all* wanted lemonade, which was exactly what he'd hoped for. Looking around at them as if perplexed by the mechanics of serving so many people, he said, "I wonder if one of you might be willing to come with me and help me carry the glasses. I don't think I can handle six at once."

Several of the smitten matrons opened their mouths to offer their services, but Nathan had anticipated this and immediately added, "Mrs. Pence? Could I perhaps, impose on you, since your baby is asleep?"

Stella looked up at him in surprise, but nodded agreeably and handed Lara to Elyse. Rising to her feet, she lifted her skirts and followed Nathan over to the refreshment table—much to the disappointment of several of the other women.

When they reached the table, Nathan took a quick, cursory glance around. Noting that they were reasonably isolated, he said without preamble, "You're right, Mrs. Pence. He's my son."

Stella drew in a sharp, embarrassed gasp and looked at Nathan warily. She didn't know what she expected his expression to be, but his proud smile was definitely a surprise.

"Elyse and I are getting married in a few weeks," he continued, his voice low. "I wish the wedding had happened much sooner, but it's taken me this long to talk her into it."

Stella stared at him in astonishment, and Nathan could hardly contain his relief. She was obviously interpreting his words exactly as he'd hoped she would. If she was prone to gossip, it would only be a matter of time before every woman in Bixby thought that Colin was the result of a long-term love affair and not the product of a promiscuous woman's one-night fling. Under the circumstances, it was the best he could do to salvage Elyse's reputation.

"Well," Stella murmured. "I guess congratulations are in order. When are you announcing the nuptials?"

"I don't think we'll actually announce them," Nathan answered. "We'll probably just have a quiet ceremony with a couple of witnesses."

"Oh." There was a distinct note of disappointment in her voice which Nathan found oddly touching.

"Mrs. Pence?"

"Yes?"

"Would you like me to let you know when we set a firm date?"

"Oh, yes," she smiled, her face lighting with pleasure. "I certainly would."

"All right. I'll make sure you know."

Stella nodded happily and picked up three glasses of lemonade, holding them in a triangle between her fingers. Nathan watched her balancing act closely, then did the same. Together, they headed back toward the tree.

"Mr. Wells?"

"Yes?"

"Thank you for telling me ... everything."

Nathan smiled, convinced he'd done the right thing. "You're welcome, Mrs. Pence. Thank you for helping me with the drinks."

Stella's wry smile told him that she saw right through his little charade, but Nathan was so relieved to have an ally among the town's women that he didn't even care.

Everyone at the picnic enjoyed a huge meal, then settled down to listen to the mayor give a longwinded speech about the founding of Bixby. They had all heard the speech before, since the mayor gave it every year, but, still, the majority of the participants were polite enough to sit through the boring recitation again.

Colin soon became restless from being restrained in his mother's lap and began fussing so loudly that Elyse finally got up and began walking him. It was while she was strolling by the now-empty refreshment table that Will Johnson approached her.

"Afternoon, Mrs. Graham."

Elyse looked at the bandy-legged little man and smiled. "Afternoon, Mr. Johnson. Are you enjoying the picnic?"

"Well, not as much as I thought I would," Will admitted.

"Oh? I'm sorry to hear that."

"It's nothin' to do with the festivities or nothin,'" he said quickly. "It's just that Nate told me your news this mornin'."

Elyse's eyes widened with surprise. "He did?"

"Yeah." Will hung his head despondently. "I just want to say congratulations."

"Mr. Johnson, you look so sad! Are you upset that Mr. Wellesley and I are getting married?"

"No, not really," Will shrugged, lifting his head and squinting at her. "I'm just sure gonna miss havin' Nate on the force. He was the best Ranger we ever had in the Frontier Battalion. I never expected him to leave. Some of the others, sure, but not Nate. Why, bein' a top Ranger was his whole life."

Elyse smiled stiffly, not knowing what to say.

"You must be some lady, Mrs. Graham, for him to give up somethin' he loved as much as he loved bein' a Ranger to marry you."

"Mr. Johnson . . ."

"Please don't get me wrong, ma'am. I ain't sayin' nothin' against you. I guess I'm still just a little bit shocked. I mean, in fifteen years on the force, I never saw a man more born to the law than Nate Wellesley. It's just kinda hard picturin' him bein' a rancher. He always said he left his daddy's ranch in Colorado 'cause he hated that kinda work."

Will's thoughtless words trailed off as he noticed the concern mounting in Elyse's eyes. He hadn't meant to upset the pretty lady and now he felt terrible that he ob-

viously had. "Guess he musta decided he liked ranchin'
after all," he added quickly. "Men do that sometimes."

"Do they?" Elyse asked dully.

"Sure they do. All the time." His words trailed off
again and the awkward silence between them became so
strained that he wished the earth would open up and
swallow him whole.

"Well," he finally stammered, "I guess I better be
gettin' back to the stable. People'll be startin' to come
for their rigs pretty soon. Congratulations again, ma'am.
You got yourself a mighty fine man."

"Thank you," Elyse answered, her voice sounding
thick and strangled. "I appreciate your good wishes."

Quickly, she turned away, not wanting the little man
to see how close to tears she was. Clutching Colin
tightly, she hurried away from the crowd, not stopping
until she reached the relative seclusion of a cluster of
trees at the edge of the field. There, shielded from pry-
ing eyes, she gave vent to her misery.

*You must be some lady for Nate to give up something he loved
as much as he loved being a Ranger. . . . The Rangers were his
whole life. . . . It's hard to picture Nate being a rancher.*

Elyse squeezed her eyes shut, trying to block out
Will's words, but they continued to drum through her
mind like a litany. *The Rangers were his whole life. His whole
life!* How could she expect Nathan to give up a career he
loved that much just to do the right thing by her?

*It's hard to picture Nate being a rancher . . . he always said he
hated that kind of work.* She knew that was true. Nathan
had even told her that when he'd first arrived.

Everything was suddenly very clear. Nathan was such
an honorable man that he was willing to give up everything he cared about in order to marry her and give
their child a name.

She couldn't let him do it. She loved him too much
to condemn him to a life of misery—and after her conversation with Will, she knew that was exactly what
marriage to her would be for him.

Somehow, she had to think of a way to set him free—without his ever knowing that was what she was doing.

But how? After all they'd shared in the last few weeks, would he believe her if she told him she didn't want to marry him? She knew he loved her, or at least he thought he did, and if she rejected him again, it would undoubtedly be a devastating blow to his ego. Could she live with herself, knowing that she was responsible for breaking his heart?

Broken hearts eventually mend, a little voice in the back of her mind whispered. Better to break his heart temporarily than make him miserable for the rest of his life.

But what about *her* heart? she thought plaintively. Nathan's heart might mend, but would hers?

"That doesn't matter," she told herself fiercely. "Right now, you have to think about him. Only him."

Blinking hard to hold back the tears that threatened, Elyse nodded decisively. She'd do it. She'd tell him she'd changed her mind about marrying him. It would undoubtedly be the hardest thing she'd ever done, but Nathan's happiness was worth any sacrifice.

Drawing a deep, steadying breath, she stepped out from behind the trees and walked purposely toward the crowd.

Her decision was made.

Chapter 33

"You're awfully quiet tonight, sweetheart. Did the picnic wear you out?"

Elyse looked up from her untouched supper and forced a stiff smile. "I guess it did." Rising, she picked up her dishes and carried them out to the kitchen. "In fact, I think I'll go to bed as soon as I get the kitchen cleaned up."

Nathan stacked his cup and bowl on top of his plate and followed her. "Tell you what. You wash and I'll dry. Then we can both turn in early."

"That's not necessary," Elyse responded hurriedly, her voice sharper than she'd intended.

Nathan set down his plate and looked at her curiously. "What isn't? That I help you with the dishes or that we go to bed together?"

The glass Elyse was holding slipped through her trembling fingers and broke against the side of the sink. With a startled, little cry, she jumped back, clutching her wet hands together to still their shaking. "We have to talk, Nathan," she blurted.

A terrible sense of foreboding gripped Nathan. "What's wrong?" he asked quietly.

Elyse skirted around him and headed for the settee. She sat down for a split second, then immediately rose again and began to pace.

"Elyse, what's wrong?"

"Nothing's wrong, really. It's just that I've had time to think about a lot of things and I've decided that . . ." Her voice trailed off with a choking sound.

"Decided what?" Nathan demanded, rounding the corner of the counter and striding toward her.

Elyse backed up until her legs hit the breakfront. "I've decided not to marry you." The words came out in a strangled whisper, but their portent stopped Nathan dead in his tracks.

"Why?" he asked, his voice soft and frighteningly calm. "Do you think we're moving too fast? If that's it, we don't have to get married this summer. We can wait until—"

"It's not that," Elyse interrupted, the finality in her voice making Nathan feel as if he'd just been punched. "I've decided not to marry you at all. Not this summer, not ever."

There was a moment of terrible silence as Nathan digested her cruel edict. When he finally spoke again, his voice was filled with such anger and pain that his next word boomed through the room like a clap of thunder. *"Why?"*

Elyse turned her head away, unable to meet his furious gaze. "Because I don't think it would work."

He moved so close to her that she could feel the heat emanating from him. "What in the hell are you talking about?" he raged. "What wouldn't work? My God, Elyse, it's already working. We're living together, sleeping together, raising our son together. What else is there?"

"That's different," Elyse defended shakily. "That's just for now. What I'm saying is that I don't think it would work out between us in the long term."

"Why?"

"Quit asking why, Nathan! There are a million reasons why."

"Fine," he snarled. "Give me about a hundred thousand of them and maybe I'll believe you."

Desperately, Elyse tried to think of something plausible. "We want different things from life," she finally said. "It's as simple as that."

Nathan stared at her for a long moment, his angry expression giving way to one of tortured confusion. "I don't understand. What do you want that I don't? Two days ago, we were talking about building a new house. Now you announce that you've decided you don't want to marry me. What happened between then and now?"

"Nothing," Elyse lied. "Nothing happened. I've just had time to really think about this, and the more I do, the more I'm convinced it won't work."

"This is nuts!" Nathan shouted, raking his fingers through his hair. "No one can change their mind that fast." He leaned forward, his eyes blazing and his mouth so close that Elyse could feel the hot rush of his breath against her cheek. "You're going to have to do better than that, Elyse. Something has happened to make you change your mind about me, and I damn well want to know what it is!"

"I told you, it's nothing!"

"That's a lie and you know it. Now tell me, damn it! Did you meet some old suitor at the picnic today? Is that it?"

"No! It's nothing like that."

"Then, what?"

Bracing her arms against his chest, Elyse pushed him away and bolted for the other side of the room. "I keep telling you, it just won't work between us."

Nathan drew a long, shuddering breath, willing himself to stay calm. "Are you saying you don't love me?" Something deep inside Elyse felt like it was dying. How could she say she didn't love him? She couldn't lie to him about that. It was because she loved him that she was giving him up. "I'm not saying I don't love you," she whispered. "I'm just saying I can't marry you."

Nathan closed his eyes, his anger and bewilderment

so acute that his head was reeling and a cold sweat had broken out all over his body. Blowing out a long breath, he tried once more to make her see reason. "Elyse, don't do this to us," he beseeched softly. "I don't know what's wrong, but whatever it is, we can work it out. If you'd just tell me——"

"There's nothing to tell," she cried, her heart breaking as she gazed into his tortured face. She had to end this. If she stood there any longer, she was going to break down, and she couldn't allow herself to do that. "Can't you understand, Nathan? I don't know how to make it any clearer. I'm not going to marry you. It's over."

"Hell if it's over," Nathan bellowed, racing across the room and grasping both her arms until she was forced to look at him. "We have a son! What about him?"

"He'll be fine. I'll take care of him."

"I don't want you to 'take care of him'! He's my son, too, goddamn it! Have you forgotten that?"

"No, of course not. I'll . . . we'll figure something out about him."

Knowing she could no longer hold back the threatening tears, Elyse wrenched away from him and fled to the sanctuary of her bedroom.

For a long time, Nathan continued to stand in the front room, staring at the closed bedroom door. There was a reason for this. There *had* to be and, by God, he would have it. If Elyse thought she was going to send him packing again without any explanation, she was wrong. She'd done it once, but not this time. This time, he would have some answers.

Clenching his hands into fists, Nathan slammed out the front door and headed for the barn, wishing that the gang would ride up the drive this very minute. The way he felt right now, he could kill the whole bunch of them with his bare hands.

* * *

The next morning found Nathan, Red, and Will huddled around the table in Red's room, nursing cups of coffee and planning strategy.

"What's our guess?" Red questioned. "Three days before the gang gets here?"

"Three days sounds about right," Will agreed. "What do you think, Nate?"

"What?" Nathan turned to look at Will, staring at him as if he'd never seen him before.

"What the hell is wrong with you this morning, Boss? You're the one who called this meeting, but ya haven't said five words since ya got here. Somethin' wrong?"

"Yeah," Nathan admitted, "but it doesn't have anything to do with this. Now, what did you say?"

Will frowned and shot a quick glance over at Red, but his only response was a perplexed shrug. "I said, do you agree with me and Red that the gang'll probably get to Bixby in about three days?"

Nathan nodded. "Sounds about right. We know they left San Antonio last week and at the rate they've been traveling, my guess is Thursday or Friday."

"Unless they start ridin' like hell," Red interjected, "then it could be sooner."

Nathan shrugged. "There's no reason to think they're gonna change their pace."

"What about your fiancée?" Red asked, stretching the last word out teasingly. "Does she know they're comin'?"

"No," Nathan answered shortly. "I didn't want to worry her, so I decided not to tell her till the last minute. I'll do it tomorrow. By the way, she's no longer my fiancée, so cut the jokes, okay?"

Both Red and Will's jaws unhinged at Nathan's astonishing announcement. "What're ya talkin' about?" Will demanded. "Everything was fine yesterday."

"Yeah, well, that was yesterday," Nathan growled. "Today is today—and things aren't fine anymore."

"What happened, Nate?" Red asked quietly.

"Nothing much. Last night, after we got home from the picnic, the lady simply told me that she'd changed her mind and decided not to marry me."

Red shook his head. "That's crazy. Did she tell you why?"

"Oh, yeah," Nathan replied grimly. "She said she didn't think it would work out between us long term."

"That's it?"

"That's it."

Will squirmed uncomfortably in his chair. "Shit, I hope it wasn't nothin' I said made her decide that."

Nathan's head snapped around, his eyes boring into Will's. "What do you mean, 'nothing you said'? What the hell did you say?"

Will's expression became wary. "Nothin', really. I was just tryin' to give Mrs. Graham a compliment and, instead, I think I upset her. You know how I am with women, Nate. I always say the wrong thing."

Nathan rose to his feet, looming over Will like some large, predatory bird. *"What did you say to her?"*

Desperately, Will glanced over at Red as if seeking protection, but Red's face was set and angry also. Looking back up at Nathan, he mumbled, "I just told her that she must be some kinda lady to get the famous Nathan Wellesley to quit the Rangers to marry her. I was just pumpin' you up a little, Nate. I told her how you was the best Ranger on the force and how you always took it more serious than the rest of us and that I just couldn't picture you bein' a rancher. That's all."

Nathan's enraged expression faded to bewilderment. "That's all?"

"Yes," Will nodded vehemently. "I swear, that's all I said."

Nathan sank back into his chair. "I don't understand. Why would that have upset her?"

"I think I understand," Red said quietly. "Will tells Elyse that you're the best, most committed Ranger in the whole state of Texas and that he can't imagine what magic she performed to make you to give it all up to marry her. Now, how do you think that's gonna make Elyse feel?"

"I didn't say it like that," Will protested. "I didn't say nothin' about magic."

"Maybe not," Red shrugged, "but I bet that's how she took it—like you thought she was some witch who'd put a spell on the captain."

"It wasn't nothin' like that!" Will argued. "But, since you suddenly seem to have all the answers, Red, how do you think what I said made her feel?"

Red snorted with annoyance. "It made her feel guilty, you jerk. You made it sound like Nate is giving up everything he cares about for her. She probably already thinks at least part of the reason he's marrying her is because of Colin and now you tell her that you can't imagine Nate bein' anything but a Ranger because he loves it so much. Of course she's gonna feel guilty. Shit, Will, after you laid all that on her, she probably thinks she's doin' Nate a favor."

Red looked over at Nathan who was staring at him in amazement. "What's wrong with you? Don't you agree with me?"

Nathan nodded. "I completely agree with you. I'm just wondering when you got so damn smart."

"I always have been," Red chuckled. "You've just been too busy catchin' the bad guys and charmin' the ladies to notice."

"That's a mistake I won't make again." Scraping his chair back from the table, he rose. "I've gotta go. Mrs. Graham and I have some talking to do."

Red reached out and grabbed Nathan's arm, pulling him back down in his chair. "Hold on a minute there. I know you're in a hurry, but we've got to get things settled here before you leave. What do you want us to do to help you nail Rosas and his gang?"

Nathan slapped his gloves down on the table, annoyed that his departure was going to be delayed, but knowing that Red was right. They did need to get their strategy figured out and this morning might be their last chance. "Okay. Here's how I think we should handle this. Starting Thursday morning, you two take turns hanging out on Main Street. The gang is coming from the south and the only way they can get to the ranch is to ride through town, so I want one of you on the lookout at all times. When you see them coming, both of you get out to the ranch as fast as you can. You should be able to beat them out there with no problem. And, since there's only three of them, we shouldn't have any trouble taking them." He paused, looking back and forth between the two men. "Any questions?"

"Yeah, I've got one," Will remarked. "Just in case things don't go like we plan and we don't get to the ranch before the gang does, can Mrs. Graham use a gun? I'd hate to think of you tryin' to handle this all alone."

Nathan shook his head. "I can't count on her. I've taken her up to the ridge a dozen times to practice shooting, but, I swear, the girl can't hit the broad side of a barn."

"Let's not worry about that," Red said. "We'll be there in plenty of time. The gang is sure to travel down the main road out of town, and if we skirt through the woods past Lynn's place, we can cut off fifteen minutes at least. We're bound to get there before they do."

Nathan nodded, relieved that Red seemed so confident of success. "By the way, Mrs. Potter is another thing we have to think about."

"I already have," Red said. "I'm gonna bring her into town with me. She can spend the time visiting her friends. After all, none of them have seen her for over a year, so they should have enough gossip to catch up on to keep them busy for as long as needs be."

"Sounds like a good plan," Nathan nodded. Again, he stood and picked up his gloves. "*Now*, is everybody clear on everything?"

Will and Red both nodded and Nathan moved toward the door, pausing when Will caught him by the arm.

"I'm sorry, Nate, about what I said to Mrs. Graham. I didn't mean to cause trouble between ya."

"I know you didn't, Will. Don't worry about it. I think I know how to convince her how I feel."

"Yeah?" Will smiled, raising his eyebrows suggestively.

"Not that," Nate snorted. "I've got a letter I think will do it."

Will looked so disappointed that Nathan reached out and punched him in the arm. "Hopefully, if the letter works, that'll come later."

"Thank God," Will guffawed. "I thought there for a minute that you was losin' your touch."

"Not on your life," Nathan chuckled. "I'm planning on Colin having a little sister by next year at this time."

With a last grin, he hurried out the door. Mounting his horse, he tore off down Main Street at a dead gallop, anxious to show Elyse the letter he'd mentioned. Please God that it would be enough.

"Elyse! How wonderful to see you. Come in."

"I can only stay a minute," Elyse said, walking into Lynn's foyer and shrugging off her shawl. "I was worried about you and thought I'd come over and make sure everything is all right."

Lynn looked at her friend closely, noting her pale cheeks and the dark smudges of fatigue beneath her eyes. Something was obviously very wrong, but she could tell by Elyse's bright smile that she was trying to hide it.

"Everything is just fine," Lynn assured her as they walked into the kitchen. "Does Nathan know you're here?"

Elyse shook her head. "He's in town meeting with Red."

"That's right," Lynn nodded. "Red told me they had a meeting this morning. Wouldn't Nathan be upset if he knew you were here alone?"

"Probably, but I figured I could get back before he found out, and I really was concerned about you. Why weren't you at the picnic yesterday?"

"Oh, that." Lynn waved her hand dismissively. "I had one of those terrible headaches I get sometimes and I just wasn't up to going. I told Red he should go without me, but he wouldn't hear of it, so we spent a quiet day at home. I'm sorry if you were worried."

Elyse looked at her speculatively. "Are you sure it was a headache, Lynn?"

"Why would you ask that?"

"I know it was the first time you planned to go out in public since the fire, and I just wondered if maybe, at the last minute, you found that you weren't ready to face it."

Lynn's face crumbled. "If only Red hadn't thrown away all my veils. I wanted to go to the picnic, Elyse. I really did. But after I got dressed and looked in the mirror, I just couldn't go through with it. All those people . . . staring."

"I understand," Elyse said softly. "Don't worry, Lynn. It'll all come in time."

Lynn sighed wistfully. "I hope you're right. I just worry that Red will give up on me."

"He's not going to give up on you," Elyse said positively. "He loves you."

Lynn poured two glasses of lemonade and set them on the table. "Let's talk about something more pleasant. How was Founder's Day? Tell me all about it."

Now it was Elyse's turn to look stricken. "It was one of the worst days of my life," she choked. "I think there must be some kind of black cloud over me, Lynn. Ever since Joe died, I seem doomed to never be happy again."

"My word, Elyse!" Lynn exclaimed. "What happened? Does it have anything to do with that Daisy Flynn and Nathan?"

Elyse was so surprised by this unexpected question that she stopped crying and gaped at Lynn in bafflement. "Daisy Flynn? You mean the waitress at the Best in Bixby? Why would you think this has anything to do with her?"

Lynn winced, cursing herself for mentioning the gossip she'd heard. "Oh, no reason," she said nonchalantly, sitting down again.

"What do you mean, 'no reason'?" Elyse gasped. "Is there something going on between Daisy and Nathan that I don't know about?"

"Of course not. It's just that Susie Martin stopped over earlier this morning to chat. That's all." Lynn shrugged and took a leisurely sip of her lemonade, silently letting Elyse know that that was all she planned to say on the subject.

But Elyse was not about to let her off the hook. "And . . ."

Lynn sighed and set her glass down, disappointed that her ploy hadn't worked. "And, apparently, some of the women at the picnic yesterday noticed that Nathan was talking to Daisy, so they're naturally assuming that there's something going on between them. I knew it wasn't true, of course, but since you and Nathan haven't publicly announced that you're getting married, I didn't dare say anything."

Elyse stared absently out the window for a moment, wondering how she could have missed seeing Nathan and Daisy together. Obviously, from what Lynn had just said, she was the only one who had. She supposed she shouldn't even care *who* Nathan flirted with, but, still, it rankled that he even knew the frowsy redhead. "He was probably just being polite," she said, turning back to Lynn.

"Of course he was. You don't have anything to worry about. Why, I've never seen a man more in love with a woman than Nathan is with you."

Her words brought another rush of tears to Elyse's eyes.

"Elyse, *please* tell me what's wrong!"

Elyse took a handkerchief out of her reticule and dabbed at her eyes. "I've decided not to marry Nathan."

This announcement was met by complete silence.

"Lynn, did you hear me?"

"Yes," Lynn choked. "I heard you. I'm just speechless at your decision. Don't you love him?"

"Love him?" Elyse asked, her eyes filled with anguished regret. "Yes, I love him. I didn't know it was possible to love a man the way I love him."

"Then, why?"

"Because of something Will Johnson told me."

"Will Johnson? You mean the man at the livery stable?"

"Yes. Did you know that he's a Ranger, too? He was posted at the livery stable just like Red was at the telegraph office."

Lynn shook her head. "I didn't know that. But, still, what does Mr. Johnson have to do with anything?"

"Well, he and I got to chatting at the picnic yesterday and he told me that he could hardly believe Nathan and I were getting married since it would mean that Nathan would have to leave the Rangers. He said he'd never known any man who was more committed to his work than Nathan was."

Lynn looked at her blankly. "So?"

"Lynn, don't you see? Nathan is giving up everything he cares about to marry me because he thinks it's the right thing to do."

"Hogwash," Lynn snorted. "Nathan is marrying you because he loves you."

Elyse sighed heavily. "I wish I could believe that, but I think it's more a matter of honor with him. Nathan is a very honorable man."

"I know he is, but I also know he's stubborn and strong-willed and he wouldn't marry anyone unless he wanted to."

"You forget, Lynn, a child is involved."

"I haven't forgotten that, and I have no doubt that Nathan would provide for any child of his, regardless of how he felt about its mother. But I also have no doubt that knowing he was providing for a child would satisfy his honor. Everything else is based on love. It's like what you told me about Red. He puts up with my problems because he loves me. Well, Nathan loves you, and that's why he wants to marry you. No other reason."

Elyse shook her head miserably. "Even if that's true, I can't let him do it. He doesn't want to be a rancher. I know he doesn't. He told me when he first came here that he hated mending fences and patching roofs and planting crops. He's a lawman. That's what he wants and that's what he should be. How can I marry him, knowing that I'm taking him away from that? I'm afraid he'd eventually come to hate me for it, and I couldn't bear that. I'd rather not marry him at all than have him be miserable."

"I think you're wrong," Lynn said stubbornly. "I think you're making the biggest mistake of your life if you refuse Nathan, but you're a grown woman and you have to make your own decisions." Getting to her feet, Lynn came around the table and hugged her friend. "Whatever you decide, my dear, you know I will support you. But, please, *please*, think very hard before you send that man away. This time, he might not come back."

"I know that," Elyse said, rising also and walking toward the front door, "but my mind is made up."

"The problem with you, Elyse Graham, is that you're as stubborn and strong-willed as he is."

Elyse smiled wanly. "Take care of yourself, dear, and thanks for listening." Mounting her horse, she turned and started off down the path.

Lynn stood on the porch and watched her go. "I'll give them a few days to work this out," she muttered, "and if she doesn't come to her senses by then, I'll go talk to the captain myself. This is one marriage that *will* take place, even if I have to drag that girl down the aisle myself."

Chapter 34

Elyse was weeding her wildflowers when Nathan arrived home. She looked up at him, disappointed and a little offended when he didn't stop but merely nodded and rode on, heading for the barn. With a sigh, she returned to her weeding. *You should be glad he's ignoring you. How else are you going to stand it until he leaves?* Lost in her own dismal thoughts, she didn't even notice him approaching until he was right next to her.

"Come here, you," he said, reaching down and pulling her to her feet. "There's something I want to show you." He held up an envelope, waving it tantalizingly in front of her face.

Elyse opened her mouth to protest, but closed it again, her curiosity about the letter overcoming her desire to refuse him. Nathan led her into the house and walked over to the settee, sitting down and patting the spot next to him. "Sit down a minute."

Elyse frowned. "I have to finish my weeding, Nathan, before it gets too hot."

"This will only take a minute," he muttered, pulling several sheets of stiff vellum stationery out of the envelope.

With a resigned sigh, Elyse sat down. "What is that?"

Nathan didn't answer but concentrated instead on scanning the letter's first page. Not finding what he was looking for, he moved on to page two, his finger moving quickly down the bold script.

"Ah, here it is," he announced, thrusting the paper in front of her. "Read this—from here to here." Again, his finger stabbed at the stationery.

Elyse glared at him, annoyed by his highhanded attitude, but she took the paper and began reading.

I was surprised and, I must admit, delighted when you mentioned in your last letter that you're thinking of retiring from the Rangers. I know how much your work with them has meant to you and that the contribution you've made has been invaluable, but I truly think you are making the right decision. From what you've told me, that life doesn't sound like one that anybody could handle forever and I think it's very prudent of you to recognize when it's time to move on.

Now you need to decide what you want to do for the next forty years. I imagine you're thinking about becoming a town sheriff like Seth, and I'm sure you'd be very good at it, but if you ever consider something besides the law, please remember that my offer to come here and become my partner in the shipping business still stands.

By the way, Claire wanted me to be sure to tell you that our daughter, Savannah, has been accepted at Miss Porter's School and will be attending . . .

The letter continued on with other family news. Elyse stopped reading and set the pages on her lap, looking over at Nathan. "Who is this from?" she asked quietly.

"My brother, Stuart, in Boston." Reaching over, he picked up the letter and shuffled the sheets until the first page was again on top. "Now look at this," he directed, pointing at the very top.

"What, the date?"

He nodded.

"November 30, 1879."

"Yeah, November 30, 1879. Nine months ago, Elyse. Nearly seven months before I came back here."

Elyse lowered her eyes, hope welling in her heart. "Why are you showing me this?"

"Because Will Johnson told me about the conversation you two had yesterday." Reaching out, Nathan placed his index finger beneath Elyse's chin and gently raised her head till their eyes met. "Did you tell me you wouldn't marry me because you didn't want me to have to give up being a Ranger?"

Very slowly, Elyse nodded.

"Is that the only reason you changed your mind?"

Again, she nodded, her lips trembling and her eyes filling with tears.

"Now that you've seen this letter and you know that I've been thinking about resigning long before I came back here, will that change your mind again?"

"Oh, Nathan!" she cried, launching herself into his arms and covering his face with teary kisses.

"Wait a minute, wait a minute!" he laughed, pushing her gently away. "You haven't answered my question." His smile faded and he picked up one of her hands, gazing at her seriously. "Will you marry me, Elyse?"

"Oh, yes, Nathan, I will!"

His face lit up with a blinding grin. "Okay, *now* you can kiss me some more."

With a joyous little cry, Elyse wrapped her arms around his neck and kissed him. The caress deepened and became more passionate until Nathan finally pulled her across his lap, cradling her like a baby. "Where's Colin?" he rasped, his fingers flying down the buttons of her dress.

"Taking his nap," Elyse returned breathlessly, arching

her back as she felt his palm sweep over her uncovered breasts.

"In his room, or ours?"

"His."

Nathan closed his eyes, uttering a silent thank-you to whatever benevolent god was responsible for Elyse making *that* decision.

Rising, he carried her into the bedroom and set her on her feet, then turned to the task of removing his shirt.

"Hurry!" Elyse pleaded, shimmying out of her dress and petticoats. She kicked the discarded clothing aside, then brushed Nathan's hands away, not satisfied with the progress he was making. Grasping the top of his shirt, she ripped it open from top to bottom, spraying buttons in every direction.

Nathan stared down at his ruined shirt in slack-jawed astonishment. "I don't believe you did that!" he exclaimed. "That was a brand-new shirt!"

"I don't care," Elyse panted, running her lips across his bare chest. "I just had to touch you."

Nathan's eyes widened as he felt her hand slide inside his pants. They had made love so often in the past month that he thought he had discovered every aspect of Elyse's passionate nature, but she was certainly putting the lie to that belief this morning. She was like an aroused tigress, demanding to be satisfied, and her uninhibited sensuality made his entire body catch fire.

"I thought you had to weed your flowers," he growled, cupping her thrusting breasts in his hands.

Elyse dropped to her knees, yanking off his denims. "They can wait."

"I think they're gonna have to." Nathan's amused chuckle trailed off to a low moan as she began running her fingers up and down his jutting erection. "God, lady," he groaned, "you are making me crazy. I think I'll propose to you every morning if this is how you react."

Elyse's only response was a felinelike purr as she began kissing his hard length.

Nathan withstood the erotic torture till he was ready to burst, then he reached down and pulled her to her feet, giving her a searing kiss. "You know, sometimes you're almost more than I can handle."

"Really?" Elyse drawled, reaching down and intimately fondling him. "Would you prefer that I was more demure?"

"God, no!" Picking her up by her narrow waist, he tossed her down on the bed. "I don't ever want you to be any different than you are right now."

He knelt above her, pausing in his playful lovemaking to gaze down at her pale beauty. As always, the sheer perfection of her took his breath away. "I've never seen anyone like you," he breathed, running his hands up the inside of her thighs until his thumbs met at her very core.

He massaged her sensitive little bud till she cried out in delight, then he paused, arching an eyebrow at her questioningly. "Do you like that?"

Elyse closed her eyes and emitted a low, seductive moan, answering his question more succinctly than words ever could. Her muted groans soon gave way to shrieks of pleasure, however, as she suddenly felt his finger delve deep inside her. "Nathan," she gasped, squirming beneath his seductive touch. "Please, I can't stand any more."

Nathan immediately withdrew and sat back on his heels. "You want me to stop?"

"No!" she gasped, looking down hungrily at his throbbing arousal. "I don't want you to stop. I want you to . . ."

Nathan lowered his head, feathering kisses down her abdomen. "What do you want me to do?"

"I can't say it," she cried, her hips bucking off the mattress at the first intimate touch of his lips.

Nathan flicked his tongue against her sensitive flesh,

teasing her mercilessly. "Sure, you can." He sat up again, waiting.

"Nathan, I can't!"

"Well, then," he sighed, "I'm afraid I'll just have to guess." Thrusting his hips forward, he positioned himself so just the tip of his hot, wet manhood penetrated her. "Is this what you want?"

"Yes!"

Instantly, he pulled back. "Then ask me for it."

"Oh," Elyse groaned. "You're a terrible, cruel man."

Nathan smiled. "And wicked, too, I know. You've said all that before. Ask me, Elyse."

Elyse opened her eyes and gazed longingly down at his erection. "Nathan?"

"Yes?" He drew the word out sibilantly.

"Will you make love to me now?"

"Is that what you want?"

"Yes." She drew the word out just as he had, then added, "Please?"

"Ah," Nathan sighed. "Weak man that I am, I never could resist a pretty request." And lowering himself above her, he pressed into her soft, enveloping warmth.

So much touching and playing had aroused both of them to the point that it was over almost before it began. After just a few lusty strokes, Nathan let himself go, releasing his essence with passionate fervor. His rapid finish was exactly what Elyse wanted and his groans of ecstasy were immediately joined by her own.

Finally, the climactic moment waned and they lay wrapped in each other's arms, replete in the knowledge that ten thousand more of these passionate encounters lay before them if they so desired.

Elyse closed her eyes, exhausted from a night spent without sleep and a morning spent in her lover's arms. She was just dozing off when a loud wail from the next room brought her quickly back to reality. "Oh, Lord," she groaned sleepily. "It's the baby."

Nathan braced himself on his elbow, tracing lazy little

circles around her nipple. "Don't complain too much, sweetheart," he whispered. "Just remember, it's doing this that makes that happen."

"I know," she nodded, slipping out from beneath him and pulling on her wrapper. "And if we don't stop doing this so much, another one of those is going to happen sooner than we expect."

Nathan smiled and and bounded off the bed. Grabbing Elyse around the waist, he held her close for a moment, burying his lips in her tousled hair. "Didn't you know? That's my fondest wish."

Elyse wriggled out of his grasp and threw him an arch look. "Ah *ha*. Then that explains why you work so hard at it."

Nathan's laughter followed her all the way into Colin's room.

"Seriously, Nathan," she called as she put the last pin in Colin's clean diaper, "we really should be more careful. It would be nice to have the new house finished before we actually do have another baby." She walked out of Colin's bedroom, looking around in surprise when she saw the front room was empty. "Nathan?"

No answer.

Her brow furrowing with bewilderment, she peeked back into her bedroom, but it was empty also. "Nathan?" she called louder. "Nathan, where are you?"

"Right here," he answered, clambering up the porch steps. "Open the door. I've got a present for you."

Elyse set the baby down and hurried over to the door, her eyes widening with delight when she saw his gift. "How wonderful!" she exclaimed. "It's one of those high chairs for babies. Nathan, I could just kiss you! Wherever did you get it?"

"Forget about where I got it," he laughed. "Just give me the kiss."

Standing on tiptoe, Elyse kissed him lustily. "Now," she said, stepping back. "Where did you get it?"

"I made it."

"Really?" She looked closely at the carved spool legs and hand-rubbed finish. "I didn't know you knew how to build things. This is beautiful work."

"There's lots of things I do beautifully that you don't know about," he teased.

"And a few that I do," she countered.

Nathan grinned, well pleased with her saucy response. "I whittled Colin a set of soldiers, too." Reaching into his pocket, he withdrew several little carved men. *"And* I remembered to make them big enough that he couldn't put them in his mouth."

Elyse smiled happily, her heart in her eyes as she gazed at the man she loved. "You know, Captain Wellesley, you're a wonderful father." She stepped closer, running a nail up his bare chest. *"And* a wonderful lover."

"I plan to be a wonderful husband, too," he promised softly.

Her nail trailed slowly back down his chest. "I have no doubt."

With a shaming look, Nathan closed his hand around her fingers and lifted them away from his chest. "Stop that," he admonished, "or my son is never going to get his lunch."

"You're right," Elyse sighed. "Lunch." She walked back into the kitchen, throwing one last greedy look at Nathan over her shoulder. "You know, it would certainly help me to get my mind off you and on to lunch if you'd put your shirt back on."

"Oh? And what shirt is that? The one with no buttons?"

Elyse had the good grace to blush. "I'm sorry about that. I got . . . carried away."

Nathan walked into the kitchen and pulled her against his bare chest. "Don't you dare say you're sorry. I can find a thousand more shirts like that one, but I'll never find another woman like you."

They kissed, long and lovingly, breaking apart only

when Colin crawled over and pulled himself up on Nathan's boot.

"Well, look at this," Nathan grinned, bending down and scooping the baby up in his arms. "He's trying to stand up."

"Lord help me," Elyse laughed. "I don't know if I'll be able to stand two Wellesley men strutting around here."

Nathan drew her close again, wrapping his arm around her so the three of them were locked in a gentle embrace. It was a moment Elyse would remember for the rest of her life. Years later, she would tell her grandchildren about the beautiful summer day when she and Nathan and Colin had first discovered the unique joy of being a family.

Chapter 35

It was early Wednesday morning when Nathan realized he was low on ammunition. "Damn," he cursed, looking through his saddlebags one more time. Half a box for his Colt and a handful of bullets for the rifle. Why hadn't he remembered this when he was in town on Monday? *Because you were so upset about Elyse that you weren't thinking about anything else.*

Frowning in irritation, he headed back to the house. He'd just have to go into town this morning and buy some more ammunition. At least he'd noticed it today, rather than tomorrow or Friday. Better to realize it now than when he actually needed it.

He walked into the house and smiled thoughtfully at Elyse. He was planning to tell her tonight about the gang's imminent arrival. Briefly, he flirted with the idea of telling her before he left for town, but he knew she would spend the rest of the day worrying, so he decided against it. After all, he wouldn't be gone more than an hour or so, and the gang wouldn't reach Bixby until at least tomorrow.

"I have to go into town this morning," he said. "Want to come along?"

Elyse shook her head. "No, thanks. I picked a whole bucket of blueberries yesterday and I'm going to stir up some jam this morning."

Nathan nodded. "Okay, I won't be gone long."

Elyse watched him head out the door, wondering if she'd have time for a quick trip to Lynn's before he got back. She knew that Nathan would be furious if he knew she was making these clandestine visits without him, but she was aching to tell Lynn that everything was all right between them again and she couldn't very well have that conversation if he was sitting right there with them. If she only stayed twenty minutes or so, she'd surely have enough time to get there and back without his ever knowing. Making her decision, she picked up Colin and hurried into the bedroom.

She watched through the curtains until she saw Nathan trot down the drive, then raced out to the barn with Colin already in his carrier strapped to her back. She quickly saddled her mare and mounted, glancing over once toward the road. She much preferred to ride on the road, but she knew she'd make better time if she cut across the fields between the two ranches. With a wistful shrug, she nudged her mare's sides and headed off across the pasture.

Several times as Nathan cantered toward town, he pulled Buck to a halt, looking back over his shoulder as he tried to rid himself of a niggling sense of uncase. He was a great believer in instinct, since it had saved him from disaster on more than one occasion, and, right now, the old familiar knots were tightening deep inside him, telling him that he shouldn't be making this trip.

Sitting on his horse in the middle of the road, he battled with himself, knowing he needed ammunition badly, but unable to shake the feeling that something was wrong. Finally, with a growl of frustration, he wheeled Buck around, heading back for the ranch. Jam or nor jam, he was going to make Elyse go with him to town, and if it took telling her about the gang to convince her, then so be it.

* * *

Elyse was halfway across the pasture when they burst out of the trees. There were three of them—dark, ugly men with unshaven faces and filthy hair—and they were headed straight for her. A jolt of fear coursed through her and she kicked her mare hard. The startled horse leaped forward so quickly that Elyse nearly lost her seat, but somehow she managed to hold on as they streaked across the pasture toward Lynn's.

But the little mare was no match for the bandits' stronger, heavier horses, and they soon overtook her. Elyse heard them coming up behind her and, with a terrified scream, she tried to veer off in another direction. It was no use. Instead of freeing her, her evasive maneuver sent her right into the path of one of the pursuing men and, the next thing she knew, he had her mare by the bridle and was hauling her to a stop. Elyse screamed again, her strident, terrified shriek piercing through the quiet morning air.

"Shut up!" the bandit hissed, pulling her down from her horse and clapping a dirty hand over her mouth. Elyse fought like a wildcat against the suffocating, stinking hand, but her struggles only made the man hold her tighter.

"Get the baby," he directed, nodding at one of his henchman. Elyse felt Colin being yanked off her back. She bit down hard on the side of her captor's hand, causing him to briefly release her as he yelped with pain. She opened her mouth again to scream, but before she could get the sound out, his hand crashed against the side of her face. Her head exploded with pain and she spun away from him, falling to her knees.

"What do you want?" she whimpered, looking up at him through bleary eyes. "Give me my baby!"

"You give us the money, we give you the baby."

"I don't know what you're talking about." Her denial netted her a booted kick in the leg and, this time, she let out a scream of pain that could be heard halfway to

Bixby. Staggering to her feet, she lunged at the man holding Colin. "Give me my baby, you monster!"

"Get rid of the kid," the first man directed.

The man holding Colin immediately turned toward his horse.

"No!" Elyse screamed, throwing herself at him as she tried to claw Colin out of his arms. "Give him to me!"

"For God's sake, shut her up!" the head bandit bellowed. The third man in the group was holding the horses, but at this new directive, he dropped the reins and whipped off his neckerchief, covering Elyse's mouth with the foul rag and tying it securely behind her head. Elyse felt the sour taste of bile rise in her throat and swallowed hard, trying to keep from vomiting, since she knew she might choke to death if she did.

"Take the kid to the woods," the leader ordered.

The man holding Colin grimaced. "What am I supposed to do with him, Rosas? I don't know nothin' about kids."

Elyse's head snapped around when she heard the man call the leader by his name, Rosas. So, it *was* the gang! Dear God, why had Nathan gone to town? She'd be dead by the time he got back.

"I don't care what you do with him," Rosas snarled. "Knock him out if ya have to, but keep him quiet."

Elyse let out another scream at Rosas's callous words, but the gag effectively muffled the sound so it was barely audible.

"Get on your horse, woman," Rosas ordered, shoving her into her mare's side. "We're goin' back to your ranch, and you're gonna show me where your two-timin' brother hid my money."

Elyse shook her head vehemently, trying again to reach the man holding Colin.

"Stop it!" Rosas snarled, lifting her onto her horse's back and grabbing the reins. "You do what I say or you'll never see your kid alive again."

This terrifying threat brought Elyse's struggles to an

instant halt. She nodded slowly, her mind teeming with disjointed thoughts of how she could escape. If she could just stall them until Nathan came home, maybe there would be a chance that they all might come out of this alive. But how? They would only have to dig for a few minutes to realize there was no money.

Her eyes blazing with a combination of fear and fury, she watched the man with Colin head off in the direction of the woods surrounding Lynn's ranch. *Maybe Lynn will see him,* she thought desperately. *Maybe she'll see him and go for help. Surely, if she looks out her front window, she'll see the bandit hiding in the woods with the baby and try to get word to Red. Please,* Elyse pleaded silently. *Please, Lynn, please help me!*

Her thoughts were abruptly cut off as Rosas yanked on her mare's reins and they lurched off toward the ranch. Elyse grabbed the saddle horn, then turned to look toward the road, hoping to see Nathan. To her despair, the thoroughfare was empty. Nathan was nowhere to be seen.

Pounding down the road at breakneck speed, Nathan thought he heard a scream. Instantly, he jerked back on the reins, bringing Buck to such an abrupt halt that he nearly sailed over his head.

"Quiet!" he ordered as the horse snorted his displeasure. Nathan listened intently, trying to figure out if the noise he'd heard had actually been a woman's cry or just an irate bird screeching at a predator.

Then he heard it again—louder this time. "That's no bird!" he snarled, a blast of rage exploding within him. The noise sounded as if it had come from the near pasture, and it was in that direction he wheeled the big buckskin, digging his heels unmercifully into his sides. Enraged, the horse let out a shrill cry, then took off at a frenzied gallop, his huge strides eating up the ground between the road and the pasture. Nathan raced up to the top of a steep knoll, sawing back on the reins as he quickly scanned the horizon.

To his horror, he spotted two mounted men leading Elyse toward the house while, in the other direction, another rider was racing pell mell toward the woods at the edge of Lynn's land. This man was farther away, and Nathan squinted against the bright morning sun, trying to get a closer look at him. What he saw made him bellow with rage. The bastard had Colin.

Kicking the nervous, dancing horse again, Nathan tore down the hill, drawing his gun as he galloped across the pasture after the fleeing bandit. He quickly caught up to the slower moving man, but, in his fury, he gave no thought to subterfuge or safety. The bandit heard him coming and drew his weapon also.

Nathan leveled his gun as the man turned in his saddle, but he hesitated, trying to get off a clear shot without taking a chance of harming Colin.

This infinitesimal delay was all his adversary needed. Nathan trained his gun at the bandit's head and squeezed the trigger, but in the split second before the outlaw fell, Nathan felt something slam into his shoulder, then a searing pain spread through his body, nearly toppling him off his horse. Looking down through suddenly cloudy eyes, he watched blood spurt through his shirt, the crimson stain rapidly spreading across his chest and down his stomach.

He shook his head, fighting to stay conscious, then leaped off his horse and ran toward the prostrate man and screaming baby. Careful to keep his gun trained on the outlaw, he leaned down and scooped Colin into his arms. Nudging the man's body with his boot, he turned it over and looked down into the glazed eyes. He was dead.

Nathan gulped in great draughts of air as he staggered back to his horse. Mounting awkwardly, he headed toward Lynn's house. He had to get Colin to safety before he went back for Elyse and, at that moment, Lynn's was the only place he could think of. Please God that she would be home.

Lynn was out in the yard when she heard the shots. "Good God in heaven!" she shrieked. "They're coming!" For a moment, she stood as if paralyzed, having no idea what she should do or where she could hide.

Suddenly, she thought of Red. She had to get Red. Running into the barn, she threw open Chili's stall door and hefted a saddle over the cantankerous mare's back.

"Don't you even think about it," she warned as the mare pinned her ears back. Lynn tightened the cinch and forced the bit through the horse's teeth in record time, then raced out of the barn, pulling the angry, snorting animal behind her.

"Please be good," she entreated, patting Chili's neck encouragingly. Holding her breath, she put her foot in the stirrup, but promptly stepped down again when she spotted Nathan galloping into the yard.

Her face betrayed a momentary rush of relief, but her expression quickly changed to horrified disbelief as she saw his blood-soaked shirt. Running over to him, she instinctively held her arms up for the baby. "Captain Wellesley," she cried. "You're hurt!"

Nathan gratefully handed Colin down to her. "I know," he gasped. "The gang's back and one of them shot me. The others have Elyse. Go into town and get Red and Will. Tell them to come quick."

Lynn stared up at the pale, shaking man, then down at the baby she held. "How can I ride into town with Colin?"

"I don't know. Just do it!" Not giving her a chance to protest further, he wheeled Buck around and took off down the drive.

"Oh, God," Lynn wailed, looking down at the squirming baby. "I'll never make it!"

Running into the house, she looked around frantically

for something to carry Colin in. She couldn't just hold
him in her arms as she'd seen Elyse do, since she knew
she wasn't a good enough rider to carry the heavy baby
and control the fractious mare at the same time.

What she needed was some kind of carrier like Elyse
used. Turning around in distraught circles, she searched
for anything that might suffice. Her eyes lit on her
heavy wool shawl, thrown carelessly over the back of a
chair. Maybe if she wrapped Colin in that and tied it
around herself, she could hold him that way—like Indian women did.

Racing over to the chair, she spread the shawl out
and laid the baby on it. "Okay, my little papoose," she
giggled, fear making her giddy. "Let's see if I can do
this." Picking the baby up, she held him against her
stomach, tying the shawl tightly around her. Then she
slid him around to the back and retied the shawl, making the knots even tighter so there would be no chance
of him slipping out.

"I did it!" she cried proudly, looking over her shoulder at the baby pressed against her back. "Come on,
Colin, let's go get Red and Will."

Racing back out to the yard, she leaped onto Chili's
back and kicked her hard, sending the surprised animal
thundering down the drive. For the first time in over a
year, Lynn Potter was on her way to town.

Stall them, stall them, stall them! The words pounded
through Elyse's head over and over as she and the two
outlaws galloped back toward her house. Somehow, she
had to make the men believe she knew where the
money was hidden long enough for Nathan to return.
Otherwise, they'd kill Colin for sure.

Arriving in the yard, the men dismounted. Rosas
walked over to Elyse and dragged her unceremoniously
off her horse. "I'm gonna take the gag off," he growled,
"but if you scream again, I'll kill you."

Elyse nodded, her eyes wide with fear.

Reaching behind her head, Rosas untied the knots and removed the filthy neckerchief. Elyse promptly gagged, vomiting her breakfast all over his boots.

"You bitch!" he cried, raising his hand to strike her again.

"Aw, come on, Rosas," his partner protested, grabbing his arm in midair. "She's sick, for God's sake. Besides, if you hit her again, you might knock her out, and how will we find the loot if she can't talk?"

Rosas glared at Elyse menacingly, but lowered his arm. "Where's the money?"

"It's buried behind the barn," Elyse choked, wiping her mouth with the back of her hand.

"Where?"

"Right next to the manure pile. The side closest to the barn door." Despite her terror, Elyse felt a tiny sense of satisfaction, knowing that she was making Rosas dig in the most unpleasant spot on the whole ranch.

Rosas made a face, then turned to his accomplice. "You stay here with her and keep watch. I'll start digging." Walking up to Elyse, he pressed his face close to hers, his foul breath making her feel like she might be sick again. "You better not be lyin', or I'll go get your kid and kill him right in front of you."

Elyse swallowed hard. "I'm not lying," she whispered. "The money is out there, but it's buried real deep. It's going to take you a while to get to it."

Rosas studied her closely as if trying to assess the truth in her words, then he turned on his heel and strode off toward the barn.

For several moments, Elyse and the other man stood in the yard as, desperately, she tried to formulate some plan to get his gun away from him. Finally, she turned to him, adopting a pleading look. "Do you suppose I could go in the house and get a drink of water? It's awfully hot out here. Maybe you'd like one, too. I could get some for both of us."

"No," he answered flatly, tightening his grip on her upper arm. "You ain't goin' nowhere, and neither am I. Now, just shut up and stand here."

Undaunted, Elyse tried again. "Well, then, could I at least sit down? I'm feeling a little shaky. Maybe we could wait for your friend on the porch swing."

"No," he said again. "And I told you to shut up."

Elyse sighed with disappointment. So much for appealing to his sensibilities . . .

Her captor saw Nathan before she did. Feeling the man suddenly stiffen beside her, Elyse looked over at him curiously. He was staring intently at something down the road, and as Elyse turned to follow his line of sight, she noticed a small cloud of dust.

"Hey, Boss," the outlaw called. "Better come. We got company."

By the time Rosas appeared in the barn door, Elyse had recognized Nathan's buckskin. For a brief moment, she felt a tremendous wave of relief, but her reprieve was short-lived as she noticed that Nathan was slumped in the saddle at a strange, listing angle, almost as if he was about to fall. Both bandits drew their guns.

Buck galloped into the yard, then came to a shuddering halt ten feet away from them. The outlaws raised their guns directly at Nathan, but before either of them spoke or fired, he fell off the horse, almost at their feet.

"Nathan!" Elyse shrieked, horrified to see that his shirtfront was soaked with blood. With a strength borne of pure terror, she wrenched away from Rosas's man and raced over to Nathan, dropping to her knees at his side.

Nathan was white as a ghost from loss of blood and his eyes were glazed with pain, but he used his last ounce of strength to push his gun into Elyse's hand. "Shoot 'em," he breathed.

If Elyse had stopped to think, she never could have done it. But there was no time for thought. She heard the crunch of gravel as the bandits walked toward her, then the next thing she knew the gun in her hand was firing.

She plugged all five remaining bullets into the two men, then stared in astonishment as they both fell to the ground, neither of them having had time to fire a single retaliatory shot.

For a long moment, Elyse didn't move. She just continued to kneel beside Nathan, staring dispassionately at the two men she'd just killed.

Nathan struggled up on one elbow, gazing over at the dead outlaws and then up at Elyse's pale face. "Well, I'll be," he murmured. "You *can* hit something." Then he fell back and passed out cold.

"Nathan," she screamed, frantically ripping at his bloody shirt. "Please don't die. I love you so much. Please, don't die!"

She had no idea how long she remained bending over Nathan's still form, but the next thing she knew, a large hand was clamping down on her shoulder. Unconsciously grabbing for the gun, she jumped to her feet and swung around, ready to do battle again.

Suddenly, she found herself being slammed against a man's chest and a calm, soothing voice said, "Elyse, it's me, Red. It's all right, honey. It's over."

Elyse pushed away from him. "Red? Is it really you?"

"Yes," he nodded, his eyes quickly assessing the bloody scene surrounding them. "It's okay. Will and I are here now. Give me the gun. You're safe."

"Oh, Red!" she cried, throwing herself back into his arms. "They're dead! I killed them and they're all dead. Nathan's dead, too!"

"No he's not," Will said quickly, pressing his ear to Nathan's chest. "But he's losin' a lot of blood and he needs a doctor quick."

"The others?" Red asked tersely, still holding Elyse tightly against him.

Will simply shook his head.

"Go back into town and get Doc Banks out here quick," Red directed. "I'll move Nate into the house."

"Colin!" Elyse gasped. "Oh, Red, there's another man and he's got Colin! We have to . . ." With a quick, twisting movement, she again tried to push away from Red's wide chest.

"Elyse!" Red interrupted, shaking her to prevent her from becoming hysterical. "It's all right! Colin is fine. He's with Lynn. Nathan got the man who took him. Lynn said that's how he got shot."

"Colin's all right? Are you sure?"

Red nodded firmly.

"Oh, thank God," Elyse moaned, sagging against him. "But, Nathan . . ." Again, she turned her attention to him.

"Mrs. Graham?" Will said, mounting his horse.

Elyse looked at him vacantly. "Yes?"

"Did you really shoot both them outlaws?"

She nodded.

"Well, I'll be damned," he muttered, shaking his head in wonder. "Now, don't you worry about a thing, ma'am. Nate's gonna be okay. It's just a shoulder wound. He's strong as a bull and I've seen him pull through much worse. He'll be right as rain in a couple of weeks." Before Elyse could reply, he dug his spurs into his horse's sides and galloped off down the drive.

Red gently released her and knelt down beside Nathan, closely examining his wound. "It looks like the bullet went clean through and came out the back," he muttered. "That's a good sign."

"Let's get him into the house," Elyse said, suddenly galvanized into action as the shock of the last few minutes finally receded. "You put him on the bed and I'll rip up some linen for bandages. There's a bottle of whiskey in his saddlebags. Get that, too. Maybe we can get the bleeding stopped before the doctor gets here."

Red nodded, amazed by Elyse's sudden command of

the situation. Hefting Nathan up on his shoulder, he followed her into the house.

"Put him in the second bedroom," she directed, already pumping water into a basin.

Red angled himself through the narrow bedroom door, carrying Nathan to the bed and returning to the front room. He paused by the window, looking out at the two dead outlaws lying in the yard. Then, with an incredulous shake of his head, he gazed again at Elyse, watching her deftly rip up a white petticoat. Who would have ever guessed that beneath that delicate blond exterior pounded the heart of a tigress? Nathan was a lucky man. Almost as lucky as he was.

For a moment, his mind wandered back to Lynn's unbelievable arrival in Bixby that morning, her insecurities about her scarred face forgotten as she flew hell bent for leather down Main Street with Elyse's baby strapped to her back. Even that cantankerous old mare had behaved. It had been some sight to see, and one that Red would never forget. What a lady. What a triumph!

He walked back toward the bedroom. "Tell me when you're ready and I'll help you with the bandages."

Elyse nodded, but didn't look up from her task.

Red reentered the bedroom and sat down on the bed next to Nathan. "You're gonna be fine, Boss," he murmured. "In fact, with these women lookin' out for you, you don't have any other choice. It's like I told ya before. There's somethin' real special about these Bixby women."

Chapter 36

"Nathan, are you absolutely sure you feel well enough to get married today?"

Nathan frowned into the tiny mirror above the breakfront, realizing it was impossible to tie a tie with one hand. "Of course I'm sure," he called, glancing toward the bedroom. "After all, it's been four weeks. But I'm afraid you're gonna have to help me with this damn tie."

"I'll be out in just a minute," Elyse answered.

Nathan stared down at the sling that encased his left arm and flexed his fingers experimentally. Doc Banks had said his shoulder had to rest for six weeks, and never had Nathan known a period of time to pass more slowly. The inactivity was driving him crazy.

"Here I am," Elyse said from behind him.

Nathan turned, his jaw dropping in awe as he drank in the sight of his bride. She was exquisite. Her long blond hair was piled on her head in a myriad of curls and ringlets, and she'd woven late-summer flowers into the artfully tousled mass.

"It was worth the wait," he breathed, his eyes sweeping the length of her petal-pink gown.

Elyse had spent nearly every evening of the last few weeks cloistered in their bedroom as she worked on her wedding dress. It had irritated Nathan no end to be forced to spend his evenings alone in the front room while she created her masterpiece, but seeing her now, dressed in yard upon yard of shimmering pink silk, more than made up for the temporary lack of her company. "I see how you could have made a living being a seamstress," he murmured. "That dress is incredible. Turn around so I can see the back."

Elyse pirouetted gracefully, the dress's wide skirt belling out around her slender legs. "Actually, I feel sort of silly," she confessed. "This gown is more suited to a formal ball than to a simple wedding with only five people in attendance."

"Nonsense. Every bride should wear a beautiful dress on her wedding day and that, my dear, is one beautiful dress."

"Thank you, sir," she blushed, delighted by his enthusiastic approval of her efforts. "Now, come over here in the light and I'll see what I can do about that tie."

"I'll be so damn glad to get this sling off," Nathan groused, following her over to the window. "I can't remember when anything has annoyed me so much."

"I know," Elyse said wryly. "You've done nothing but complain about it for the last three weeks. I think you convalesce better when you're unconscious."

"Oh, thanks a lot!" Nathan retorted, trying hard to look offended. "I would think you'd be glad to see this thing come off, too. You must admit, it's put something of a damper on our love life."

Elyse glanced up from the tie, throwing Nathan a shaming look. "You seem to have managed all right, despite it."

Nathan leaned down and kissed her on the end of her upturned nose. "You've just forgotten what it's like when I have both arms free," he leered.

Elyse gave his tie one final yank and turned away before he could see her smile. "Behave yourself, Nathan," she admonished primly. "Brides aren't even supposed to know about lovemaking, much less have as much experience with it as I do."

Nathan grabbed her around the waist and hauled her back against his chest, ignoring her shrieked protests that he was going to ruin her hair. "I, for one, like your experience," he growled, burying his face in her neck and kissing her.

"And well you should," she giggled, "since you taught me nearly everything I know."

His hand dropped from her waist to gently caress her abdomen. "Anything going on down there yet?" he asked hopefully.

"No, thank goodness! The last thing I want is to give the old biddies in Bixby a reason to count on their fingers even after we're married." Sternly, she removed his hand. "Now, stop it. You're going to wrinkle me." Noting his disappointed expression, she tempered her words with a quick kiss. "Come on, Captain Wellesley, we better go or we're going to be late for our own wedding."

Nathan picked up his hat and gloves. "I sure wish we could take our honeymoon right away. Somehow, it doesn't seem right to get married and then just come home like nothing special happened."

"*We'll* know something special happened," Elyse murmured, running her fingers lovingly down his cheek. "And we're going to take a trip in October, don't forget that."

"Oh, I haven't forgotten, believe me. I can't wait to show you San Francisco. You're going to love it."

"I'd love anywhere as long as you were there," Elyse said honestly.

Nathan lifted her hand and gently kissed her fingertips, knowing he'd never loved her more than he did at this moment. "Come along, madam," he said, taking her hand and leading her toward the door, "your bridal carriage awaits."

"Or, bridal wagon, as the case may be," Elyse laughed. They stepped out onto the porch, and the rippling sound of her laughter abruptly halted as she beheld a magnificent, polished mahogany phaeton parked in the yard. Two perfectly matched grays were harnessed to the luxurious vehicle, stamping their feet impatiently as they awaited their driver.

"Nathan," Elyse breathed. "Where ... how ... Is that ours?"

"Yup," Nathan grinned. "It's a wedding present from Stuart and Miles. Miles sent the horses over from his farm in England, and Stuart had the carriage sent piece by piece from Boston. Will has spent the past two weeks putting it together."

Elyse clapped her hands to her cheeks in delighted disbelief. "I can't believe it! I've never ridden in anything so grand in my life."

"Get used to it, sweetheart," Nathan smiled. "After all, you're about to marry one of—"

"I know, I know," Elyse interrupted. "One of those 'tremendously successful and well-known' Wellesleys. How could I forget?"

"You better not," Nathan growled playfully.

Elyse didn't think anything could surprise her more than the carriage until she caught her first sight of Will Johnson, looking hot and uncomfortable in an ill-fitting suit, standing near the horses' heads.

"Our driver, milady," Nathan whispered, his eyes dancing with amusement at the sight of Will in his tight, starched collar.

"Right this way," Will announced, flinging open the carriage door. "And may I say, Mrs. Graham, that you look real beautiful today."

"Put your eyes back in your head, Will," Nathan muttered as he helped Elyse into the carriage. "And after this afternoon, I want you to start remembering to call her Mrs. *Wellesley.*"

Will grinned good-naturedly and slammed the door behind Nathan. "Just sit back and relax," he invited. "We'll be at the church in no time. By the way, where's the baby?"

"Mary Ellen Jenkins came and got him early this

morning," Nathan informed him. "He'll be at the church when we get there."

Will nodded. "You got the ring, Nate?"

Nathan threw him a jaundiced look. "Yes, Will, I've got the ring. Now, just get up on the damn seat and drive, okay? Everything is taken care of."

"Just wanted to make sure." Saluting Nathan jauntily, he disappeared.

Elyse looked at Nathan in surprise. "When in the world did you have time to get a ring?"

"I didn't," he admitted. "I had to borrow one, but I didn't think you'd mind wearing this for a while till I can buy you your own in San Francisco." Reaching into his pocket, he withdrew the diamond ring that he had reclaimed for her from Hiram Richman. "Will this suffice in the meantime?"

"Oh, Nathan, I can't think of any ring in the world I'd rather wear than that one!"

"I thought so." Nathan pushed the ring back into his pocket. "Nevertheless, I *will* buy you your own."

Elyse nodded happily. She would be perfectly content to wear her grandmother's ring forever, but she sensed it was important to Nathan that she wear a ring he had picked out and purchased.

The ride into town passed so quickly that it seemed like no time at all before she heard Will call "whoa" to the horses and pull back on the reins. As the carriage stopped in front of the church, Elyse peeked out the window, then gasped and ducked back into the seat cushions, looking at Nathan with wide eyes.

"What's the matter?"

"Half the town is out there!"

"They are?" he exclaimed, feigning innocence. He leaned forward to look out the window, then sat back and nodded. "I'd say more than half."

"What are they doing here?"

"I don't know. Maybe they're here to attend a wedding."

"Nathan . . ."

"Okay," he relented. "Stella Pence asked me if she could invite a few of your old friends to the wedding and I told her to go ahead. Truthfully, though, I didn't expect a crowd this large."

"I wasn't aware that I had any 'old friends,' " Elyse said, her voice betraying a hint of sarcasm.

"Oh, don't get testy. It's time to make a new start, my sweet. We're getting married today. Let's just enjoy the town's well wishes and let bygones be bygones."

Elyse frowned mutinously for a moment, then her expression softened. "You're right. It *is* time to make a new start."

Nathan smiled with relief. "Good. Now, let's go get hitched."

The couple alighted from the magnificent carriage amidst many cries of welcome and much oohing and aahing over Elyse's dress.

"Oh, my dear, isn't this exciting?" Lynn gushed, suddenly appearing at Elyse's side.

Elyse looked over at her radiant friend. "Did you know about all this?"

Lynn nodded. "I did hear some talk about it last week at my wedding." She paused, glancing over adoringly at Red, then turned back to Elyse. "You're not angry, are you? Please don't be. Nathan was so excited, and I honestly think people wanted to come today as a way of apologizing to you and making amends."

Elyse smiled and hugged Lynn affectionately. "Perhaps you're right. Anyway, I'm so happy that nothing could upset me today."

Nathan walked up just as she said that, and leaning close to her ear, murmured, "I'm glad to hear you say that because both Lillian Underwood and Marvel Dixon are here."

"Oh, no," Elyse moaned, looking at him anxiously.

"Don't worry," he smiled. "They aren't going to say a word. I guarantee it."

Elyse looked at him doubtfully, but before she could protest further, he took her arm. "Come with me a minute before we go in. There's someone here who's come a long way to see you."

They threaded their way through the crowd, nodding and smiling as well wishes were called to them. Nathan guided Elyse over to the side lawn of the church where a man stood alone, his back to them. It wasn't until they had nearly reached him that Elyse realized who it was. With a joyful, disbelieving cry, she launched herself against the man's broad back.

"Tom!"

Her brother spun around, his eyes widening as he beheld his beloved sister in her wedding finery. "Elyse!" he cried, wrapping her in his arms and holding her tightly against him. "I can't believe it's really you. I never thought I'd see you again."

Elyse kissed and hugged him until both their faces were wet with tears, then she turned in his arms and gazed at Nathan. "You did this for me, didn't you? You made sure he was here."

"He sure did," Tom answered, grinning at Nathan. "He expedited my release and even sent me the money for the train fare to get here."

"Oh, Nathan," Elyse sighed, stepping forward to give him a grateful kiss. "I don't know what to say."

"You don't have to say anything," Nathan murmured, brushing her tears away with his thumb. "But I *would* appreciate it if you'd get in that church and marry me before I'm too old to enjoy my wedding night."

At that moment, Reverend Jenkins appeared at the top of the church steps, his prayer book in hand. "Come along, everyone," he called. "It's time to take your seats." The boisterous crowd immediately quieted and filed into the building.

"Will you give me away, Tom?" Elyse asked softly. "It would mean a lot to me if you would."

Tom nodded happily and held out his arm. As they

started back toward the church, Elyse looked around curiously. "Where did Nathan go?"

"He's already in the church," Tom laughed. "When Reverend Jenkins called everyone in, he was the first one up the steps. I think you've got yourself one eager bridegroom there, Leesie."

Elyse looked up at her brother and smiled. "I think I do, too," she murmured. "And I also think I'm the luckiest woman in the world."

The ceremony was lovely. Stella, Lynn, and several other young women from town had made huge bouquets of bluebonnets. They hung on the ends of the pews, while day lilies sat in large urns on the altar.

As Elyse stood next to Nathan, listening to the ancient words of the marriage ceremony, she could hardly believe that with all that had happened between them, they had actually come to this moment. How could anything that had started off so badly turn out so well? She knew she would thank God every day of her life for sending Nathan Wellesley to her doorstep that rainy night.

Suddenly, Reverend Jenkins's voice interrupted her romantic reverie. "Do you, Elyse Athena, take this man to be your lawfully wedded husband?"

Elyse looked up at Nathan, astonished to see him smiling during this portentous moment. Then she saw him mouth, "Athena?", and it was all she could do to say, "I do" without laughing.

"And do you, Nathan Buffington, take this woman to be your lawfully wedded wife?"

Now it was Elyse's turn. Reaching over and squeezing Nathan's hand to get his attention, she mouthed, "Buffington?"

Nathan shrugged and mouthed back, "Family name."

Reverend Jenkins cleared his throat loudly. "I said, do you, Nathan—"

"I do!" Nathan interrupted loudly, causing a wave of titters to ripple through the congregation.

Reverend Jenkins threw them a frown of disapproval. "I want to speak to you both later about the seriousness of marriage," he muttered.

Nathan and Elyse exchanged suitably contrite glances, then turned their attention back to the minister. They exchanged their vows without further incident, and Nathan slipped Elyse's grandmother's ring on her finger. "For now," he murmured.

"By the power vested in me, I now pronounce you man and wife. You may kiss the bride."

Nathan drew Elyse close and kissed her for so long that the reverend again cleared his throat. Breaking away from each other guiltily, they bowed their heads for his blessing.

But, to Elyse's surprise, Reverend Jenkins did not immediately give them the final blessing. Instead, he took both of them by the shoulders and turned them toward the congregation. "I would like to be the first to introduce you to Mr. and Mrs. Nathan Wellesley."

There was a moment of complete silence among those assembled, then Marvel Dixon's voice piped up. "That's wrong, Reverend. His last name is 'Wells.' "

"No, I'm afraid you're wrong, Miss Dixon," Reverend Jenkins answered gleefully. "His last name is 'Wellesley.' "

"Nathan Wellesley of the Texas Rangers?" Hiram Richman gasped.

"Nathan Wellesley of *the* Wellesleys?" Lillian Underwood chorused.

Nathan suddenly let go of Elyse's arm and moved up a step to stand next to Reverend Jenkins. "You're both right," he smiled, "and I think it's time that I explain a few things. I was sent to Bixby under the auspices of the Texas Rangers to protect Elyse from the Rosas gang. Some of you might be aware that Elyse's brother, Tom, was involved in a robbery here a couple of years ago. I want you to know that he has been completely exonerated of all charges against him and that he was principally responsible for myself and my fellow Rangers, Red Hilliard and Will Johnson, as well as my bride . . ." He paused, winking at Elyse, "to successfully do away with these criminals. Incidentally, Elyse cooperated with our efforts at much risk to her own safety. I believe that much of her decision to do so was based on a previous friendship that she and I shared." He looked briefly over at Elyse to see her reaction to his words, but she simply stared back at him trustingly.

Nathan turned back to the stunned crowd. "Now you know the truth. There is, however, one other thing I want to say. Next Sunday, all of you are invited to attend the baptism of Elyse's and my son, Colin Joseph Graham Wellesley. I hope you'll all be able to share this important event with our family."

Every head in the church swiveled around to stare at Mary Ellen Jenkins who was standing at the back of the church holding Colin. She smiled and whispered to the baby to wave—which, to everyone's amusement, he promptly did.

Red leaned over to Will and muttered, "That little announcement should leave them wonderin' for a good long time."

Will looked back at his friend, his homely face splitting into a wide grin. "Leave it to Nate. I bet it'll be standin' room only at that baptism next week."

Nathan stepped down just as the out-of-tune organ blasted the first notes of the wedding march recessional. Holding his arm out to his wife, he said, "After saying all that, are you still speaking to me, Mrs. Wellesley?"

Elyse didn't hesitate a moment. Looping her hand firmly through the crook in his arm, she answered, "Absolutely, Mr. Wellesley."

Nathan smiled, relief evident on his handsome face. "And, after saying all that, do you also still love me, Mrs. Wellesley?"

Elyse gazed up at her husband, her eyes luminous. "More than I ever thought possible."

Together, they walked out of the church and into the sunshine.

Epilogue

"Elyse!" Nathan called, struggling through the front door with a huge, flat package. "Come quick. We got another wedding present."

"Another one?" Elyse asked, hurrying out of the bedroom. "Who is this one from?"

"Eric," Nathan beamed, setting the package down on the table and racing into the kitchen. He grabbed a sharp knife off the counter and returned to the table, carefully slicing through the string tied around the package. "I hope this is what I think it is."

Standing the package on end, he ripped the paper, then stared at the contents, a slow smile spreading across his face. "Oh, Elyse, look at this." Removing the rest of the paper, he held up an oil painting. It was a portrait depicting a beautiful young woman seated on an ornate chair with a golden-haired baby on her lap and a tall, handsome man standing proudly behind them.

"Oh, Nathan," Elyse gasped, stepping up to take a better look. "It's us."

Nathan nodded, his eyes feasting on the baby at the center of the picture.

"It's the most beautiful thing I've ever seen," Elyse breathed, bending down to examine the intricate detail of the woman's dress. "I know you said Eric was an artist, but I had no idea he had this kind of talent."

Nathan shook his head, as awed as she.

"How can we ever thank him? Oh, Nathan, let's go visit next spring. I'd love to meet Kirsten and—"

"Next spring!" Nathan interrupted. "I can't go gallivanting off to Minnesota next spring. I've got a sorghum crop to put in."

Elyse started to laugh, astonished, as always, by the change that land ownership had made in him. "Well, then, Farmer Wellesley," she teased, "how about if we go visit this winter?"

Nathan grimaced. "I suppose we could, but do you really want to go to Minnesota in the winter?"

Elyse shivered, just thinking about it. "Maybe we better just invite Eric and Kirsten to come here."

Again, she gazed at the portrait, noticing for the first time that there was a small brass plate nailed to the bottom of the frame. "Look," she pointed. "I think Eric gave the picture a name."

Nathan leaned closer to read the tiny print engraved on the plaque, then straightened and gazed at Elyse lovingly. "He did   and it's perfect, too."

"Well, what is it?" Elyse demanded, standing on tiptoe to try to peek around his broad shoulder.

Nathan pulled her into his embrace and kissed her. "He called it 'Passion's Gift.' "